ERIN HART

Haunted Ground

NEW ENGLISH LIBRARY
Hodder & Stoughton

First published in Great Britain in 2003 by Hodder and Stoughton
A division of Hodder Headline
First published in paperback in Great Britain in 2004
by Hodder and Stoughton
A New English Library paperback

5 7 9 10 8 6 4

A CIP catalogue record for this title is available from the British Library

ISBN 0 340 82760 2

Typeset in Plantin Light by Palimpsest Book Production Limited, Polmont, Stirlingshire

Printed and bound by
Clays Ltd, St Ives plc

Hodder and Stoughton
A division of Hodder Headline
338 Euston Road
London NW1 3BH

To Paddy
mo ghrá geal

One crow, sorrow.
Two crows, mirth.
Three crows, a wedding.
Four crows, birth.
Five crows, wealth.
Six crows, strife.
Seven crows, travel.
Eight, a troubled life.

Traditional counting rhyme

Contents

ACKNOWLEDGEMENTS

I thank the many people who contributed to the writing of this book: my friend Dáithí Sproule, for a long-ago invitation to visit his family in Donegal, and for his indispensable and ongoing assistance with questions about Irish language and literature; Eilis Sproule, who first sparked my imagination with the tale of a nameless, beheaded red-haired girl; Dr Barry Raftery, of the Department of Archaeology at University College Dublin, who generously shared his firsthand experience with the real-life *cailín rua*, and who, in addition to providing invaluable advice and information on archaeological matters, was kind enough to offer introductions to many of his colleagues; Dr Máire Delaney, of Trinity College Medical School, for sharing her expertise and experience with rare bog remains; Garda Síochána officers Patrick J. Cleary and the late Vincent Tobin of the Collator's Office in Cork City, and Detectives Frank Manion of Tralee, County Kerry and Michael Ryan of Loughrea, County Galway, for essential background and assistance on police procedure; Dr Raghnall Ó Floinn, of the Irish Antiquities Division at the National Museum of Ireland, for help with museum information and procedure; Rolly Read, Keeper of Conservation at the National Museum of Ireland, for allowing me access to the conservation lab at Collins Barracks; archaeologist Malachy Conway, who generously offered a guided tour of his excavation work at a medieval ecclesiastical site; Terry Melton of Mitotyping Technologies, for information on mitochondrial DNA; Angela Bourke, Ann Kenne, Thomas O'Grady, Peter Costello, and Donna Wong, for much-needed assistance with Sean O'Driscoll, James Kelly, John and Mary Kelly, Susan McKeown, Niamh Parsons, Dolores Keane, and the many other wonderful traditional players and singers who inspired the music in this book. The help of these persons undoubtedly prevented many factual errors; any that remain are solely my responsibility.

I also owe a debt of gratitude to Susan Burmeister-Brown and Linda Davies of *Glimmer Train*, for publishing my first short story, thereby setting this book in motion; to Vickie Benson of the Jerome Foundation, and to the Dayton Hudson, General Mills, and Jerome Foundations, for their generous support of the research for this book; to Paulette Bates Alden, for her kind and thoughtful critique; to Susanne Kirk at Scribner, for expert and judicious editing; and to my agent, Sally Wofford-Girand, for making a leap of faith and for her collossal patience through many rough drafts. To the many friends and colleagues who cheered me on, most especially Susan Hamre, Lynda McDonnell, Cheryll Ostrom, Claudia Poser, Liz Weir, Eileen McIsaac, Bonnie Schueler, Pat McMorrow, Jane Fallander, and Jo Coffman, I offer sincere thanks. Finally, for their unflagging support and encouragement, I am most deeply indebted to my remarkable family (especially my mother, for her insightful plot and character analysis) and to my beloved husband, Paddy O'Brien, whose fiercely creative spirit infuses my life with joy and inspiration. Of all those whose contributions I may have neglected, through failure of memory or character, I most humbly beg forgiveness.

This story makes mention of many real institutions and localities in Ireland. And although Drumcleggan Bog, Drumcleggan Priory, Bracklyn House, and the villages of Kilgarvan, County Clare, and Dunbeg, County Galway are based in part on real locations, and may in fact share the names of places that can be found on a map, they exist nowhere but in my own imagination.

BOOK ONE

A Fateful Wound

Créacht do dháil mé im árthach galair.

A fateful wound hath made me a hulk of sadness.

– Irish poet Dáibhí Ó Bruadair, 1652

Chapter 1

With a sodden rasp, Brendan McGann's turf spade sliced into the bank of earth below his feet. Had he known all that he'd turn up with the winter's fuel, perhaps he would have stopped that moment, climbed up onto the bank, and filled his shed with the uniform sods of extruded turf that a person could order nowadays by the lorry-load.

But Brendan continued, loosening each sopping black brick with the square-bladed turf spade, tossing it over the bank, where it landed with a plump slap. He performed his task with a grace and facility that comes from repeating the same motion times without number. Though his father and grandfather and generations before had taken their turf from this same patch of bog, Brendan never thought of himself as carrying on an age-old tradition, any more than he considered the life cycles of all the ancient, primitive plants whose resting place he now disturbed. This annual chore was the only way he'd ever known to stave off the bitter cold that crept under his door each November.

Chilblains were the farthest thing from Brendan's mind this unusually sun-drenched late-April morning. A steady westerly breeze swept over the bog, chasing high clouds across the watery blue of the sky, and teasing the moisture from the turf. *Good drying today*, his father would have said. Brendan worked in his shirtsleeves; his wool jacket, elbows permanently jointed from constant wearing, lay on the bank above his head. He paused, balancing his left arm on the handle of the upright *sleán*, and, with one rolled-up sleeve, mopped the sweat from his forehead, pushing away the damp, dark hair that stuck there. The skin on his face and forearms was beginning to feel the first pleasant tightness of a sunburn. Hunger was strong upon him at the moment, but just beyond it was an equally hollow feeling of anxiety. This might be the last year he could cut turf on his own land without interference. The thought of it burned in the pit of his stomach. As he clambered up the bank to fetch the handkerchief from his coat pocket, he searched the horizon for a bicycle.

Forty yards away, his younger brother Fintan made a comic figure as he struggled against the weight of a turf-laden wheelbarrow. Fintan dumped his two dozen wet sods at the end of a long row, one of many that lent the surface of the bog the temporary texture of corduroy. For a good square mile around them, little huts of footed turf covered the landscape. Here and there on the neighbours' allotments, large white plastic bags bulged with sods dried as hard as dung.

'Any sign of her yet?' Brendan shouted to his brother, who raised his shoulders in a shrug and kept at his work. The two men had been hard at it since nine, with only a short tea break mid-morning. Their sister Una was to bring them sandwiches and tea, and pitch in with footing the turf. It was cumbersome, backbreaking work, turning the sods by hand so that they dried in the sun. It would be another month before this lot could be drawn home.

Tucking his handkerchief in his back pocket, Brendan descended once more into his gravelike void, noting with a small grimace of satisfaction the angled pattern his *sleán* had made down the wall of the bank. He was reaching the good black turf now, more appreciated in these parts for its long-burning density than for the fact that it had remained in this place, undisturbed and undecayed, for perhaps eight thousand years.

He set to work again, trying to drown out the rumbling in his belly by concentrating on the sound and the rhythm of cutting. He was used to hard physical labour, but there was no doubt about it, something in the bog air put a fierce hunger on a man. What might the day's lunch be? Chicken sandwiches, or egg, or perhaps a bit of salty red bacon on a slab of brown bread. Each stroke became a wolfish bite, a slug of hot sweet tea to wash it down. One more row, he thought, heaving each successive sod with more violence, just one more row – and then his blade stopped dead.

'Shite!'

Fintan's head poked into view at the edge of the cutaway. 'What's the matter? Strike a bit of Noah's ark down there?'

'Ah, no,' Brendan said. 'Only a bit of horsehair.'

There were four things, their father always said, that could stop a man cutting turf. Brendan could hear the old man's voice: *Wig, water, blocks, and horsehair.* Then he'd hold up four fingers in front of their faces. *Meet any of them, boys, and it's your Waterloo.*

'Hand us down the spade, will yeh?'

Fintan obliged, then leaned on the handle of his fork to watch. Though these things typically turned out to be tree trunks and roots, other wonders turned up in bogs occasionally – rough beams of oak, ancient oxcarts, wheels of cheese or wooden tubs of butter. Stores buried for keeping in cool wetness and long since forgotten –

objects caught and suspended outside of time by the watery, airless, preserving power of the bog.

Working deliberately, Brendan dug around the perimeter of the fibrous mat, probing for its edges, and scraping away loose bits of peat. He knelt on the spongy bank and pulled at the strands that began to emerge from the soaking turf. This wasn't horsehair; it was tangled and matted, all right, but it was too long, and far too fine to be the rooty material his father called horsehair. Brendan worked his broad fingers into the dense black peat he'd pried loose with the spade. Without warning, a block in his left hand gave way and he cast it aside.

'Holy Christ,' Fintan whispered, and Brendan looked down. Almost touching his knee were the unmistakable delicate curves of a human ear. It was stained a dark tobacco brown, and though the face was not visible, something in the line of the jaw, and the dripping tangle of fine hair above it, told him at once that this ear belonged to a woman. Brendan struggled to his feet, only dimly aware of the cold water seeping through the knees of his trousers and down into his wellingtons.

'Sorry, lads. You must be perished with the hunger.' Una's breathless apology carried towards them on a bit of breeze. 'But you should have seen me. I was literally up to my elbows . . .' Her voice trailed off when she saw the faces her brothers turned toward her. Brendan watched her stained fingers tighten their grip on the flask, and on the sandwiches she'd wrapped hastily in paper, as Una stepped to the edge of the bank beside Fintan and looked down at their awful discovery.

'Ah, Jaysus, poor creature,' was all that she could say.

Chapter 2

Cormac Maguire was in the shower when the call came. He let it ring, as he customarily did, until the answerphone came on. But hearing the excitement in Peadar Wynne's voice, he hastily wrapped himself in a towel and sprinted down the stairs, hoping to catch Peadar before he rang off. Cormac stood just over six feet and, though he'd begun to feel a few creaks during the passage of his thirty-ninth year, still possessed a rower's lean, muscular frame. His dark brown hair was cut short; intense dark eyes, a long, straight nose, and a square jaw defined his angular face. His pale olive complexion would soak up sun as he spent time in the field during the summer months. He had neglected to shave for the past couple of days, and now water dripped at irregular intervals from his chin to his bare chest.

Peadar – a technician in the archaeology department at University College Dublin, where Cormac was on the faculty – was a normally languid young man, whose concave frame and large hands invariably put Cormac in mind of a stick figure from an ancient cave painting. The cause of Peadar's agitation was soon clear: some farmers cutting turf had discovered a body yesterday in a raised bog near Lough Derg in the southeast corner of County Galway, about two and a half hours west of Dublin.

Although hundreds of bog bodies had turned up in central Europe, mostly in Germany and Denmark, they were somewhat of a rarity in Ireland. Fewer than fifty such discoveries had ever been made in Irish bogs, and they offered an unparalleled opportunity to gaze directly into the past. Peat bogs not only preserved skin, hair, and vital organs, but even subtle facial expressions, and often revealed what a person who drew his dying breath twenty centuries ago had taken for his last meal on earth. Modern turf-cutting methods often damaged bog bodies. If this was a complete specimen, it would be the first in nearly twenty-five years, since the ancient remains of a woman had been discovered at Meenybraddan in Donegal. This body today had been found by a man cutting turf by hand, so there was a good chance that it was intact.

With Peadar's voice seeping into his ear, Cormac crossed to the desk to put on his glasses and culled from the flow of words the few that were pertinent to the matter at hand. 'Has Drummond been there?' he asked. Malachy Drummond, the chief state pathologist, visited the scene of any suspicious death, to decide whether it should be classified as a police matter. Drummond had been to the site this morning, Peadar said, and upon examination of the remains had declared it a case for the archaeologists rather than the police. The National Museum had jurisdiction over all such bog remains, but as it happened, Peadar explained, their entire conservation staff had just left for a conference in Belgium and would be away for the next four days, so the museum's keeper of conservation had phoned from Brussels to see whether Cormac would be available to do the excavation.

'He said he realized you were on leave, but that he'd consider it a personal favour.'

'Phone back, would you, Peadar, and tell him I'm on my way.'

Cormac paused to clear his throat before he broached the next subject. 'I presume somebody's informed Dr Gavin.' Nora Gavin was a lecturer in anatomy at Trinity College Medical School, an American with a particular interest in bog bodies – and as it turned out, the one person Cormac felt disinclined to have working beside him, though he didn't see how it could be avoided. It would be easier if he didn't have to phone her himself.

'She's already been notified. Says she'll meet you there,' Peadar said.

Twenty minutes later, Cormac was on the road. What would they find at the bog? Given the natural preservatives in peat, it was difficult to tell at first how long someone had been buried in it. He remembered an account of English workmen uncovering the remains of a middle-aged female in a fen during the 1950s, spurring a tearful confession from a local man who told police he'd killed his wife and dumped her body in the marsh. Later – shortly after the remorseful husband hanged himself in his prison cell – the corpse in question turned out to be a woman who died sometime in the late Iron Age. The remains of the missing wife never turned up.

Cormac felt a growing excitement as he considered the possible significance of this new find. It had been ten years or so since he himself had been involved in an excavation of bog remains; he and a colleague had uncovered a fully articulated hand and arm at a bog road site in Offaly. He remembered studying the grooved and brown-stained fingernails, in particular. It was curious how arbitrary preservation in bog environments could be; sometimes bones were completely decalcified, but the skin, hair, and internal organs were intact. A well-preserved ancient body could often be found alongside completely skeletized remains in what one would quite naturally presume were the same conditions.

Cormac was dressed for the field, in jeans, a dark cotton pullover, and a bright blue anorak; he had tossed his waterproofs and wellingtons in the back of the jeep. As he drove through the confusion of suburban developments that had begun sprouting along the major roads out of the city, past the point where the built-up areas began to give way to the expansive pastures of prosperous farms and the tree-lined edges of stone-walled estates, he looked forward to escaping the din of Dublin. This journey would take him west across the great shallow basin of low bogland and pasture that formed the Midlands, and to the lip of the Shannon estuary, the place he always considered the most significant border on this little island. The larger world invariably imagined Ireland divided into north and south, but for him a greater division had always existed between east and west, especially between the lush, fertile planters' dominion around Dublin that early English settlers had dubbed 'the Pale' and the stony, wind-beaten west, where the last vestiges of Gaelic Ireland had long since been quite literally banished. You could still hear the echo of an ancient culture in the traditional music, of course, but it was also in the way people spoke, in their manner, in the very pace of their lives, which seemed to slow perceptibly the farther west he travelled. This drive always seemed to take him backwards in time.

The trip would take at least two and a half hours, so Cormac fished with one hand in the glove box and brought out a tape of Jack Dolan, a flute player of the old puff-and-blow Leitrim style. Beside him on the passenger seat was his wooden flute case – East Galway was an area fairly saturated with flute players, and you never knew when a bit of music might turn up. Alongside the instrument case was Cormac's site kit, which he carried in his father's old medical bag. The small gilt 'J.M.' on its worn leather surface reminded him that he was also heading back into his own past, to a place only an hour's drive from where he had grown up, on the west coast of Clare. He should, he knew, make a trip to the church in Kilgarvan where his mother was buried. He berated himself for harbouring such ambivalence about her. There was nothing to be done now, except to try to understand her better in death than he had in life. He'd visit her grave – if he had a chance.

Cormac disliked driving the motorways. When he wasn't in a hurry, he savoured crawling along the secondary routes. Today there was a reason for haste: once removed from its sterile environment, a bog body was susceptible to dehydration and rapid decomposition. The usual procedure was to excavate around and then cut away the entire section of turf containing the body, continuing to use the peat in its preservative capacity even after the remains reached the lab at Collins Barracks in Dublin. Conservation methods used on bog bodies so far – tanning, freeze-drying – had yet to prove successful over the long term. Bacteria and mould still set in too easily. The current approach was to pack remains in wet peat, then in several layers of black plastic sheeting, and keep them refrigerated indefinitely at four degrees Celsius. The National Museum recently had a room-sized unit built specially for the purpose. Not ideal, certainly, but the best current option.

Cormac's mind began sorting out the details of the excavation. If one cubic metre of waterlogged peat weighed a ton, what type of a crate would have to be built to contain two cubic metres? And how long would it take to excavate the whole area by hand? But beneath the ticking metronome of these conscious thoughts was a hidden melody, aroused by a chance connection to a human being whose life and death were about to intersect with his own. He wondered for the first time whether this new bog body was man or woman. It mattered little to his work whether the person was male or female, ancient or modern, but each individual found in the bog – and indeed any human remains – had a unique story to tell. The question was always how well you could decipher the story from what was left behind.

It's easy to get caught up in the methodology, in all the highly technical aspects of what we do, his colleague and mentor Gabriel McCrossan had once told him. *But that's just our way of seeking knowledge, it's not the essence of what we're about. Keep in mind that our main concern is people – we learn about ourselves by studying those who have come before.*

This would be his first trip into the field without Gabriel. Only three weeks ago, he had dropped by the office and found the old man dead at his desk. The fountain pen had tumbled from his right hand, and a large blot of ink had formed where it had last made contact with the paper. Cormac knew the old man would have shared his excitement about this new find.

Gabriel had always maintained that all scientific inquiry, whether it was undertaken through the lens of a microscope or the lens of a telescope, consisted of peering at the vast universe through one tiny peephole. He had often spoken of their archaeological work as seeing through a glass darkly, trying to reconstruct the past with sparse and imperfect evidence. Gabriel had relished the moments when something turned up. *Another piece of the puzzle, my boy,* he'd say, rubbing his hands together in anticipation. *Another little piece of the puzzle.*

Cormac had just crossed over the Roscommon border at Athlone, noting the gradually shrinking proportions of the fields, the increasing narrowness of the roads, the first signs that he was well and truly in the West, when he remembered the potentially awkward situation that awaited him at the site. Gabriel had first introduced him to Nora Gavin. Although Nora was American, her parents were from Ireland, and she and the old man had some sort of prior connection; he'd been at university with her father or something. It was hard to tell how old she was; probably somewhere in her late thirties. From the way Gabriel had kept mentioning Nora, and insisting that Cormac must meet her, he also guessed that she was unattached. She seemed intelligent, and pleasant enough on the few occasions when they'd met, but nothing had come of Gabriel's prodding. Then one evening about six months ago, he and Nora had both been among a small group of people invited to supper at Gabriel's house, and the old man had pressed him into giving her a lift home. Cormac remembered how annoyed he'd felt, letting himself be manoeuvred into a corner. Nora lived in one of those modern blocks of flats along the Grand Canal, not far from his own place. He'd hardly spoken a word to her on the drive, and hadn't even waited to see whether she got inside safely. As he pulled away, he glanced into the rearview mirror to find her at the kerbside looking after him. He hadn't seen her since. Surely she'd been at Gabriel's memorial, but his memory of that day was too clouded by grief to be trusted.

At Ballinasloe he turned off the main road and headed south toward Portumna, the town at the head of Lough Derg. To the west, the ground sloped gradually upward to the feathery pine forests that covered the Slieve Aughty Mountains; to the east lay what remained of the ancient body of water that once covered the whole centre of Ireland. Farther down the lakeshore were the holiday resort towns of Mountshannon and Scarriff, but in this remote corner of Galway, there was only farmland and mountain overlooking small, hidden lakes and treeless stretches of bog. As he approached the lakeshore, he began to see homemade signs posted along the road. At first he thought they were To Let notices or adverts of some kind, but as he drew near the first one he read, 'No Bog Licence'; a bit farther on was one that said, 'No Bog Evictions', and finally:

Year 1798
REBELLION

Year 1999
TURF-CUTTING PROHIBITED

Year 200?
???

He wasn't surprised to see such sentiments expressed along the roadside. There had long been controversy about Ireland's use of peat, since it was an unrenewable resource. Irish bogs also provided a wildlife habitat unique in all of Europe, and there was increasing pressure from the EU to consider the environmental consequences of turf-cutting.

Cormac arrived at the site at a quarter past two. The sun was still fairly high overhead, barely veiled by a few wispy clouds. Here and there the bog's heathery surface was scarred with deep black gashes. There were no ditches here, no fencing, no visible evidence of property boundaries on this raised blanket of turf. And yet he'd wager each of the locals knew precisely where his own turf allotment ended and his neighbour's began. A random scattering of spiky, pale green furze bushes, not yet covered in bright saffron blossoms, stood close to the road. Beyond them, a patch of bog cotton shivered in the breeze. And beyond that, about fifty yards away, Cormac could see a small group of people, including Nora Gavin and a uniformed Garda officer. He felt something like dread as he stepped into his waterproof trousers, then carefully removed his shoes and plunged each stockinged foot into a sturdy wellington. He stood for a moment at the roadside, squinting as he surveyed the horizon for some fixed point, a church steeple or radio tower, anything that would help him map out exactly where the body had been discovered; nothing appeared. A short distance down the road, the door of an ancient-looking Toyota opened, and a squarish man in a brown leather jacket emerged. A slight protrusion of the man's midsection suggested a fondness for porter, and the sunlight glinted off his silvery-white hair. He seemed to have been waiting. Cormac lifted his jacket and site kit out of the passenger seat and extended his hand as the man drew near.

'Cormac Maguire. The National Museum asked me to oversee the excavation.'

'Ah, the archaeologist,' said the man, taking the hand Cormac proffered and giving it a firm squeeze. Now that Cormac was closer, he could see the man's fresh pink countenance belied his hoary head; he was probably no more than forty-five.

'Detective Garrett Devaney,' the man said. 'Dr Gavin will be glad to see you. Said she had to wait for you to begin.' Devaney spoke out of the corner of his mouth, as if every word were an aside, and his pale blue eyes darted slantwise under their lids, giving him a perpetual look of wry amusement. Then the policeman tipped his head across the bog, and they turned to make their way to the gathering, treading carefully over the soggy ground, with Devaney leading the way and talking backward at Cormac. 'You probably know most of it, local farmer cutting turf. According to him, nobody's so much as opened a drain on that section for a hundred years or more. Malachy Drummond – you know Drummond, the pathologist? – apparently agreed. He was in and out of it in about ten minutes this morning.'

'If you don't mind me asking, what's a detective still doing here, all the way from . . .'

'Loughrea.'

'. . . from Loughrea, if this isn't reckoned to be one of your unsolved murders?'

'Ah well, we didn't know that for certain, now did we? There was some notion it might be a woman gone missing from nearby. I'm just here to clear up any questions on that score. And I live just down the road.'

'Is there much disturbance around the body?'

'It's fairly clean,' Devaney said. 'Once he realized what he was onto, the lad with the spade set it down in a bit of a hurry.'

Nora Gavin approached as they drew nearer the cutaway. She was taller than Cormac remembered, and dressed as he was, in jeans and wellingtons, but no waterproofs. Her large blue eyes, dark hair, and milk-white skin exemplified the paradoxical features so common in Ireland. Occasionally some word or inflection would hint at her Irish origins, but for the most part, Nora's accent betrayed the years she'd spent in the broad middle of America. Her hair was different, perhaps shorter than the last time they'd met, and drew Cormac's attention to the graceful line of her neck, something he'd not noticed before. In his recent fit of self-recrimination for the way he'd behaved toward her, Cormac had quite forgotten how thoroughly attractive she was, and felt vast relief that the excitement of the occasion seemed to have removed any awkwardness about their last encounter.

'Cormac, it's good to see you,' she said, reaching out to take his hand. 'I'm realizing I must have driven the whole way like an absolute maniac, and I'm sorry to say I've been pestering these poor people with questions.'

'I apologize for keeping you waiting,' Cormac said. 'Good to see you as well.' He turned to Devaney. 'The man who found the body – is he here?'

'Brendan McGann,' Devaney said, indicating the stocky man of about thirty who stood a few feet from him, leaning on the handle of a two-grain fork. The shaggy curls that framed McGann's face cast it into shadow. Apart from the reticent farmer, the mood of the group was expectant as Devaney introduced them. Declan Mullins, the young Garda officer, obviously fresh out of the academy at Templemore, had a slender neck and prominent ears, which lent him the air of an overgrown altar boy. The fair-haired woman in the denim jacket and Indian skirt, whom he guessed to be in her mid-twenties, was McGann's sister Una. Cormac was struck by her large dark eyes, and the way her broad mouth turned up slightly at the corners. But most unusual were her hands and fingernails, which were stained as though they'd been steeped in blackberry juice.

'All right if I have a look?' Cormac asked Brendan McGann, who said nothing, but put his lips together and tipped his head to signal assent. Cormac climbed carefully into the hole with his site bag, feeling the soggy turf spring like rubber under his weight. The cutaway was a space a couple of metres in length, but narrower than a man's arm span – large enough for one person to work comfortably enough, but extremely close quarters for two. One wall rose higher than the other, and its surface, which graduated from sepia to coal-black, bore the oblique impressions of a foot *sleán*. The floor was uneven, and Cormac turned his attention to the area of loose peat where Brendan McGann had apparently been stopped in his work. He knelt and used his bare hands to scrape away the damp peat that had been replaced over the body. It was too risky to use a trowel in a bog excavation: a sharp metal edge could too easily damage waterlogged objects. His breath came faster as he caught the first glimpse of finely preserved hair and skin, but he was unprepared for the wave of pity that struck him at the sight of an ear, as small and fragile as that of a child. He looked up to see Nora Gavin crouched at the very edge of the cutaway, captivated by the grisly image that had just emerged from the peat.

'Are you ready?' Cormac asked. She nodded wordlessly, then climbed down into the cutaway beside him.

'First we have to determine the way the body is situated before we begin the complete excavation,' Cormac said. 'The head appears to be turned at roughly a forty-five-degree angle to the cutaway floor here, which means the body could be articulated in any number of different ways.' He was aware that this was probably Nora's first experience of a bog body *in situ*, so after carefully covering the head once more with wet peat, Cormac pulled paper and pencil from his bag and hastily drew a sketch to show her what they were about to do.

'So, here's the head – right? The body could be fully extended or flexed, and it could also be angled downward, if it's intact. We'll mark out as much of a circle as we can, then dig small test pits, like this,' he said, making small circles on the diagram, 'starting from the outside of the circle and moving inward. That way we can establish how large a block of peat will have to be removed. The pits should be about fifty centimetres apart, and twenty to thirty centimetres deep. We'll have to dig with our bare hands; that way we can't do any damage, and it's important for sensing the texture of the surrounding material.' He unstrapped his wristwatch, glancing at it briefly before putting it into his pocket. 'If only it weren't so late in the day. We'll have to work quickly.' He handed her his waterproof jacket. 'You can kneel on this if you like. Any last thoughts before we get stuck in?'

'I don't think so,' she said. Her eyes rested for an instant on his stubbly chin, and as she turned away, Cormac felt a faint flush of embarrassment; in the rush to get out here he hadn't taken the time to shave. He lifted his sweater over his head and rolled up his sleeves. As he worked, plunging his bare arm into the dense, waterlogged peat, he considered that there was nothing in the world quite like the consistency of turf. If a bog wasn't exactly liquid, it wasn't quite solid either, but a curious mixture somewhere between the two. It was also extremely cold; with their sleeves and shirt fronts completely soaked through, both he and Nora had to stop every few minutes to warm their hands. After nearly twenty minutes thoroughly probing almost the entire arc of their circle, they had turned up nothing at all.

'Is it just me,' she asked, leaning back and rubbing off the tiny flecks of wet peat that stuck to her arms, 'or is something missing here – like any sign of a body?'

'Let's have another look at her,' Cormac said. With Nora watching over his shoulder, he removed a larger portion of the protective peat, to find the woman's features obscured by her long red hair, which clung like seaweed on a victim of drowning. Bog tannins gave hair of every hue – even black – a reddish tinge, but it was still possible to tell the original colour. Cormac carefully lifted the damp strands and laid them aside, then froze when he saw what lay beneath. The girl's mouth was clamped tightly shut, her top teeth deeply embedded in the flesh of her lower lip. One eye stared wildly; the other was half closed. Her face seemed distorted with fear, a far cry from the images he'd seen of Iron Age bog men, whose unblemished bodies and tranquil expressions led to theories that they were either drugged, or willing victims of sacrifice. In its brief exposure to the air, the girl's hair had already begun to dry, and a few strands began to play in the breeze that scooped down into the trench. Something about this tiny movement made it seem, for one surreal instant, that she was alive. Cormac felt Nora Gavin's involuntary start beside him. 'Shall I go on?' he asked. Nora's head slowly turned until her eyes met his, and she nodded.

Cormac continued scraping away the soft black turf with his fingers, until what he had half suspected was confirmed. The girl's neck ended abruptly, he estimated, between the third and fourth vertebrae. He sat back on his heels.

'My God,' Nora said. 'She's been decapitated.'

The girl was young, perhaps no more than twenty, and, if you removed the ghastly expression, had probably been quite beautiful, with a gracefully arched brow, high cheekbones, and a delicate chin. Beside his knee, Cormac could make out a ragged fringe of rough fabric, like torn burlap. Who was this girl, that she had come to such a harsh and desolate end? When he rose slowly to his feet again, he found the McGanns and the young policeman gazing at her solemnly, as he and Nora had, in silence.

The sound of voices came from the road. Detective Devaney was having words with a newcomer – a tall, fair-haired man dressed in jeans and heavy work boots. The man broke away from Devaney, and began to cross in long strides to the digging site. Devaney followed after, leaping sideways through the heather like a terrier. They could hear the policeman's words: '. . . completely unrelated . . . Haven't we promised to notify you if there's any news at all?' The tall man ignored Devaney, and marched stone-faced through the scrub. When he reached the cutaway, the man was breathing heavily, though he still said nothing. His eyes met Cormac's for an instant, but his gaze was distracted until it at last seized upon the terrible, upturned face of the red-haired girl. And at that moment, all purpose seemed to drain out of him. He fell to his knees and clapped a hand over his eyes, as if suddenly overcome by extreme exhaustion or relief. After a moment or two, Una McGann stepped to the man's side and helped him to his feet.

'Hugh,' she said, looking into his face intently, 'you know it isn't Mina.' He nodded mutely, then straightened and let her walk with him away from the trench. Devaney's eyes had never left the tall man's face. Now the policeman raised a hand to the back of his neck and sighed. Cormac caught another slight movement with the corner of his eye, and glanced up to see Brendan McGann twisting the two-grain fork in his hands, his eyes trained on his sister's back.

In the course of his work, Cormac had often felt like a detective, sorting through evidence and piecing together clues to unlock the secrets and the lives of those long dead. Here were two mysteries dropped in tandem right into his lap. What – if anything – had they to do with one another? He wished he could keep digging until he had discovered what word or thought or deed had brought the red-haired girl to this place. But archaeology was not that kind of science. Whatever small knowledge he could gain came in shards, in fragments, in frustrating, piecemeal fashion. Would they ever find out who she was, or why she died? He looked down into the dead girl's once-beautiful face, and pledged that he would try.

Chapter 3

Nora Gavin found it strange that no one had said a word when Una McGann and the tall fellow walked away from the site, but she had followed Cormac's lead and fallen to work again. The initial shock of seeing the dead girl's hair, so like Tríona's, had been unsettling enough. Nora knew she must not think about her sister, at least not while there was still work to be done. She forced herself to focus instead on Cormac's instructions, and on what she must do once she got back to Dublin. She'd call and arrange for a technician to meet her at Collins Barracks tonight, so that this curious relic might be deposited in the refrigeration unit as soon as possible. Tomorrow she'd take the hair and tissue samples they needed for carbon dating and further chemical testing. She'd schedule a CT scan at one of the local hospitals immediately after the preliminary exam, if they could fit her in. Much of what they knew about bog specimens today was based on past blunders. The primary mistake had usually been in waiting too long before beginning examination and conservation, and the result was that the specimens had begun to decay. This girl might not be as important a find as the Meenybraddan woman back in 1978, but Nora wanted to make sure that they found out as much as they possibly could from her.

The crowd at the cutaway had thinned considerably

by the time they finished the excavation: the farmer, Brendan McGann, had cleared off shortly after his sister left the scene, and the young Garda officer had eventually drifted back to his station in Dunbeg. Only Detective Devaney remained, standing by with arms crossed, looking down at his feet and occasionally toeing the earth like a hopeful suitor. The block of peat that she and Cormac removed, though not large, was extremely heavy. Cormac had rigged a sort of makeshift stretcher but it took two of them to lift the thing and convey it across the bog to the road, where they set it gently in the trunk of her car. As she arranged the items in the trunk to keep the plastic-wrapped bundle from sliding in transit, Nora wondered why the policeman had bothered hanging around so long. There was something tentative in his manner, as if he felt he really ought to return to work but couldn't let go of some idea that was rattling around in his brain. Maybe he was waiting until the three of them were alone to tell them what was going on here. And if he didn't bring it up, then she bloody well would.

'I'll stay on and clear up around the site,' Cormac said to her. 'You'd better be heading back.'

'So that's it – you're finished here?' Devaney asked.

'Well, we've searched the immediate area pretty thoroughly,' Cormac said, wiping his hands. 'We can't just go tearing up turf at random. Things shift around in bogs, Detective. It's almost like an underground lake. Even if the girl's body had been nearby at one time, there's no telling where it's got to by now.'

Devaney's tone was studiously nonchalant. 'I don't suppose ground-probing radar would be any use?'

'No use at all on a bog,' Cormac said. 'All the organic material is waterlogged. Doesn't matter what it is – turf, tree stump, body – it all reads exactly the same. That's what makes a bog the ideal place to hide a corpse. But I'm sure you know that, Detective.' Devaney frowned and rubbed his chin.

Did Cormac know something that she didn't? 'Would you mind filling us in?' she asked the policeman. 'Who was that guy? And who's Mina? It seems like I'm the only one here who doesn't have the full story.'

Devaney considered them both for a moment before speaking. 'His name is Osborne. Local gentry, I suppose you'd call him – lives at the big house on the lake beyond. His wife disappeared just over two years ago. Maybe he thought we'd found her.' Nora felt as though she'd been punched.

'The whole area was searched at the time of the disappearance – civil defence, underwater units, the lot – and none of the search teams came up with anything. Last year all the bog holes in East Galway got another going-over. We've put out numerous appeals, and there's been a generous reward all along, but nobody's come forward. Nobody knows a thing. It's as if the ground just opened and swallowed her up.'

'Don't you have any suspects?'

'We've no proof a crime was even committed,' Devaney said, the dismay audible in his voice.

'What about that guy, Osborne?'

'He was interviewed several times. No solid alibi for the time of the disappearance, but nobody could manage to find any material evidence that would crack his story. And without a body . . . Now the higher-ups want to lump his case in with a whole string of women gone missing over the last five years – in spite of the fact that it doesn't fit.'

'Why not?' Cormac asked.

'Well, for one thing, none of the others involved a child. Osborne's young son is missing as well.'

'Could Mina have had some reason to leave, Detective?' Nora heard herself asking. 'People sometimes disappear on purpose.'

'If you're running away, usually someone's got a clue. Nobody's seen Mina Osborne. And I mean no one. Not her family, not her closest friends. And we couldn't find a reason that she might have left. According to all the world, the Osbornes had the perfect marriage. No one says a word to the contrary.'

'How do people know what really goes on?' Nora murmured. That's what people had said about Peter and Tríona as well, but they couldn't have been more wrong. She felt queasy. First the red hair and now this; the coincidences were beginning to unnerve her.

'So what do you think happened to them, Detective?' Cormac asked.

'At this point I don't think anything at all.'

'It seems to me if you're hanging around asking questions about ground-probing radar, you might have some theories,' Cormac said.

'Oh, I have a few. But the trouble with theories is they don't prove a fucking thing' – he cast an apologetic look at Nora – 'if you'll pardon the expression. And evidence-wise, everything has come up blank.' He paused. 'But I know two things: as far as we know, Mina Osborne hasn't made contact with anyone since her disappearance. And her husband's been pushing to get turf-cutting in the area banned altogether. I have to ask myself why.'

'The man was devastated,' Cormac said. 'We all saw him.'

'So we did,' came Devaney's terse reply.

Nora felt her throat constrict as she tried to understand

what the policeman was saying: that Osborne's show of grief could have been exactly that – a show. Her face felt frozen; she hoped it could mask her feelings. She felt a hand on her elbow.

'Nora – are you all right?' Cormac asked. His dark eyes scanned her face. 'You look a bit pale.'

'I'm fine,' she said, pulling away. 'I just need a drink; I'm a bit parched.' She went around to the driver's side of the car to fetch her water bottle, and lifted it to take a long swallow, hoping that her hand wasn't visibly shaking.

'I shouldn't really be talking about any of this,' Devaney finally said. 'It's an ongoing investigation.'

'Thanks for explaining, Detective,' Cormac said. Nora could still feel his eyes on her. 'We'd like to help, of course, but I'm not sure there's anything we can do. Dr Gavin's got to be leaving straightaway for Dublin. I'll stay and finish up here in the morning, but—'

'You're doing what you have to do,' Devaney said, looking away. 'So are we all.'

As she indicated her turn and pulled cautiously out onto the main road to Portumna, Nora allowed her thoughts to settle on the strange cargo she carried. It was difficult not to think of it; at every rough patch in the road, she could feel the weight of the waterlogged block of peat in the boot of the car. Remembering the expression she had seen stamped on the young woman's features, Nora felt a shiver. She told herself it was the damp. She hadn't bothered to change before leaving the site, and now her jeans felt clammy against her skin, and the small bits of peat that still stuck to her arms were beginning to itch beneath her thick sweater. She reached forward to turn on the car's heater.

If only there were some clue, some lead that would help them find out more about this red-haired girl.

Unfortunately they had found no clothing of any kind, which was often useful in dating bog bodies. Nothing but that piece of burlap. Perhaps the absence of the body was a clue in itself. Was the girl's head intended as a trophy of some kind, an offering to some terrible deity? She'd often read that the ancient Celts revered the head as the seat of the soul, and had decorated their shrines and holy places with the skulls and desiccated heads of their enemies. Several of the most well-preserved bog bodies in Europe were thought to be human sacrifices, because they'd undergone what Celtic scholars called a 'triple death' – ritual garrotting, slitting of the throat, and finally drowning, their bodies weighted down with stones or branches – perhaps to appease a bloodthirsty pagan trinity. Was this red-haired girl among those chosen for such a role, in which the last stage of her triple death was beheading? Had she committed some unpardonable sin in Christian times – adultery, perhaps, or murder – for which her community had wreaked its punishment and cast her into the bog? Or was she simply the victim of murder, carved up and disposed of in such a gruesome way?

Nora was not unaware of the reputation that she was beginning to earn for what some considered, even in the medical community, a rather macabre and sensational preoccupation. In addition to her duties as a part-time anatomy lecturer at Trinity, she was pursuing graduate level work of her own: a major research project studying the physical and chemical effects of bog burial. The irony was that this was her first experience of an actual bog body; all her research thus far had been carried out on mummified museum specimens, or on 'paper bodies' – written records of remains that had been destroyed or reburied soon after their discovery.

Why should this unfortunate creature be any different from the dozens of other nameless souls who lost their way or were left purposely in such dangerous, deserted places? She remembered poring for hours over the gazetteer of Irish bog bodies that Gabriel McCrossan had been helping her to update, and being moved by its bare descriptions – devoid of identity, but imbued with unforgettable detail: a young child of indeterminate gender dressed in a pinafore, with boxwood comb, leather purse, and ball of thread still in its pocket; a man's left foot with stocking and leather shoe intact; the partially preserved body of a young woman, and, nearby, the skeletal remains of an infant with a small buckled leather strap around its neck. Each of these had a story as well, but they were all lost now, and would never be discovered. The red-haired girl would no doubt end up as just another anonymous entry, the minutiae of her life erased by time. And yet Nora found herself unable to abandon the idea that even a single clue might point the way towards the red-haired girl's identity. She tried to remember whether the girl had any kind of distinctive hairstyle – any kind of plait or knot that would help suggest a date. All at once her memory was overtaken by a sensation, the feeling of the wiry strands against her fingertips as she pulled the hairbrush through her younger sister's luxuriant mane with quick, sure strokes, parting and twisting three strands into a single thick braid – *Ouch, Nora, you're pulling too hard*, Tríona's plaintive cry echoed in her head, along with her own peevish reply: *I am* not *pulling. If you'd ever stop squirming—*

The edges of the road swam as tears welled up in her eyes, and Nora felt as if she would choke, but she pulled off the road and fought against the memory. The events of this day opened a fissure in the wall she had tried to build around her heart, and now she felt it crumble and give way, engulfing her once more in a fierce, pulverizing flood of grief.

She had told no one in Ireland about her sister's brutal murder. Gabriel had come to know a few of the facts, but he didn't know that the strongest suspect was Tríona's own husband, Peter Hallett. And Nora was certain that no one had told Gabriel how the desire to see her sister's killer brought to justice had taken over and consumed her. That single, desperate need had pushed aside everything else: her job, her relationships, her whole life. She should have stayed and kept fighting, for Elizabeth's sake; the child was only six when Tríona died. A few months after the murder, when Peter found out Nora was helping the police to find evidence against him, he had abruptly cut her off from any contact with her niece. After three years of bitter frustration, Nora's endurance had nearly been exhausted. She told herself she had not given up – that would never happen – but she had come to Ireland eighteen months ago to think and recover her strength.

But to come all this way and be faced with another red-haired victim, a missing wife, a husband who might have killed her – Nora knew that if she were in a slightly more paranoid frame of mind, she could believe that someone, something, was deliberately mocking her sorrow.

Chapter 4

Nuala Devaney was standing in the doorway to the kitchen, fiddling with the clasp on her necklace when her husband stepped forward to help.

'I might be late,' she said to him over her shoulder. 'It's a couple over from Belgium, so I told them we might go out for a drink after they look at the house, you know, showing off the local.' Devaney settled the tiny clasp, then stepped back to gaze at his wife, admiring the way she looked in that particular pale green suit. He often felt that while approaching middle age had diminished him in many ways, it had only improved Nuala.

'Thanks, love. The kettle's just boiled, and your supper's in the cooker. Would you believe they're looking at a place up in Tullymore? A ruin. None of them are the least bit interested in a new house; they all want the old falling-down cottages. Preferably thatched, if you don't mind.' She paused and looked straight at him, as if trying to gauge whether he'd heard a word she'd said. 'Are you all right, Gar?'

'Grand,' he said. 'I've some paperwork to do.' He gestured toward the briefcase sitting at the other end of the kitchen table. 'And then I'm headed down to the session.'

'Right,' she said with a wry half-smile, but evidently relieved that his plans were at least settled. 'I'm off, then.' He watched out the kitchen window as she backed her sleek new silver sedan out of the narrow drive.

As he took the hot plate of food from the oven, Devaney told himself once again how glad he was that Nuala enjoyed her work. They were certainly better off financially since she had begun working, and he was proud that she was the best auctioneer in this part of the county. But it also pained him that she had no time for the music; he winced at her insistence that the children pursue things that would be – in her words – 'more useful.' For all her acuteness in reading people on the verge of buying property, he sometimes felt that she could no longer read him – or maybe she didn't want to. Music was all he had to pass on. He'd nothing at all of any value, except for the tunes and stories he'd collected in hours spent drinking cups of tea and pints of porter with thick-fingered old men in baggy-kneed trousers who never washed but once a week, if that. He thought of the hollow ruin of a thatched house Nuala was showing tonight, and the sheer quantity of culture that was wiped out whenever any one of the old players was laid to rest. How often had he travelled up the road when he was younger to have a few tunes with Christy Mahon, God rest him, a grizzled old fiddler who had the time – and above all the patience – to sit and go over the tricky part of a tune with him, making sure he got the notes and the ornamentation just right. Their musical companionship had to do with something neither of them could begin to put into words, and thankfully, they didn't have to; the music did it for them. A wild, lonely melody could carry him back to a place beyond his own lifetime, when music and poetry had been kept alive in secret, carried on in defiance of death and despair. Through him, this music was his children's connection to the joy and pain of a past all too easily forgotten or denied.

Devaney thought of his children. His firstborn, Orla,

whose name meant 'golden', was fair-haired like her mother, poised and intelligent. At seventeen, Orla was already a champion debater; she'd make a fine president, he thought, then revised himself. Why settle for a figurehead job like president? Give her another few years and she'd make a better prime minister than some of the fucking magpies they had running the country today.

Pádraig, whose dark looks reminded him of himself as a boy, was fifteen this year. He had only recently been transformed from a bright and talkative boy into a hollow-chested, silent teenager, whose entire life seemed to revolve around acquiring the latest computer game or piece of athletic gear. Devaney had felt himself diminish in his son's eyes these last two years. It was inevitable, he supposed, remembering how his own father had suffered a similar reduction in stature. Pádraig had once shown a bit of interest in the fiddle when he was younger, but he didn't have the *grá* for it, the hunger and thirst for music that would have kept him going.

His younger daughter, Róisín, who had just turned eleven, was still a riddle. Dark-haired, thin of face, and serious beyond her years, Róisín still called him Daddy, as she had when she was small, and was the only one of the three who seemed to value his company at all any more. Perhaps because she was the youngest, he felt his age most at her growing up.

Pádraig was at football practice this evening, and Orla and Róisín were in their rooms doing schoolwork. Devaney found himself alone in the kitchen as the evening light waned, sipping on a lukewarm mug of tea. He'd always been restless, but the feeling had increased since he'd given up smoking eighteen months ago. *This is a lovely new house*, Nuala had said, *please let's not have it reeking of cigarettes.* He'd complied, partly because he knew he ought to give them up anyway, and partly to keep the peace. But it was devilishly hard to quit, and he wished right now for the familiar sight of a fag in an ashtray beside him, and the feeling of smoke filling his lungs. He took another drink of tea instead, looking out his back window, imagining Dunbeg just a few miles down the lakeshore. Strange to think how much he knew about all the people in the town. Even though he worked out of the detective unit fifteen miles away in Loughrea, being any sort of a policeman in a small town was a bit like being a priest: receiving and keeping private confidences was part of the job, whether you invited them or not. It went both ways, of course. They all knew about him as well, or thought they did. They knew he'd seen his share of city policing, perhaps more than his share, in seven years on the murder squad in Cork. Many of them knew the recent transfer to Loughrea had not been his own idea.

But none of them would ever fully grasp the twist of fate that had brought him to this place. Devaney himself, despite all the thousands of times he'd relived every second of that pursuit gone fatally wrong, could never put his finger on it. Had it been a conscious decision or pure instinct that made him ultimately responsible for the deaths of two people? One was a suspect he'd been after for months, a twisted piece of work named Johnny Comerford, who had terrorized and battered to death an elderly couple in their own home. The other was a seven-year-old child named Julia Mangan, the daughter of Comerford's sometime girlfriend. On his way home from the Anglesea station one evening, he'd seen Comerford leaving a pub along the quays, so he'd followed, not expecting the bastard to take off. The girl was so small he hadn't even seen her in the car. Once outside of town, Comerford missed a turn at a T-junction and ploughed head-on into a stone wall.

Although Devaney himself hadn't been injured, he'd been placed on mandatory medical leave for the duration of the inquiry into the crash. He wasn't charged, but when his medical leave was up he was told his choices were Loughrea or leaving the Guards altogether. He had taken the transfer – which was in essence a demotion – because he had not known what else to do. And in the weeks he'd spent on leave, the music had been his only solace, the only thing that could replace the memory that kept replaying in his head, of approaching Comerford's silent, demolished car, and the sinking horror of finding that child's shattered body in the passenger seat. Perhaps that's why Nuala disliked hearing him play, he thought, if it brought back to her that terrible time, without knowing that in playing the same tunes, the same sequence of notes again and again, he found a kind of release, and that release – not his family and not his work – was the one thing that kept him from being slowly crushed to death by the weight of remorse.

As he drained the last of the tea from his mug and got up to set his dinner plate in the sink, Devaney realized that he'd been plagued the past couple of days by the turn of a reel that had been travelling through his head. He crossed and took out his fiddle from behind the pine dresser. It was in an old-fashioned case, not the new moulded-plastic variety, but a wooden box, wide at one end and narrow at the other, the precise shape and size of a miniature coffin. He always thought of the instrument as Christy's fiddle. The old man had handed it on when the arthritis had got into his fingers and he could no longer play. After applying rosin up and down the length of the bow, Devaney took up the fiddle and played easily through the first part of the troublesome tune, feeling his way around the contours of the notes, knowing that as he played each one, his fingers would remember their places the next time it came to him. He attacked the irksome phrase again and again, until he finally made it through the turn, the music spilling forth from his bow, flowing like the water of a stream that has finally found its way through a rocky crevice.

That was the way he had always worked through stubborn cases as well; it was always a matter of approach, of taking a run at the thing from various angles. There had to be some crack in the Osborne case, he was sure of it. And his conviction had been further cemented by the odd conversation he'd had with the superintendent this evening, just before leaving the office.

'You wanted to see me, sir?' Devaney had only stuck his head in at Superintendent Boylan's door after putting his jacket on; Boylan took a particular exception to detectives coming into his office in shirtsleeves. Despite the fact that he'd never had an original thought in his life, Brian Boylan possessed a rare instinct for the kind of political manoeuvring that had got him where he was today. His office had been done up far beyond the basic standard issue for a superintendent of detectives. And with his smartly tailored suits and manicured nails, Boylan had always stood out among his colleagues; the man had the look of an actor, someone who took on whatever role others expected him to play. Devaney himself had seen too many shrewd, capable detectives passed over for promotion because they didn't look the part the higher-ups had in mind for their modern police force, and some bollocks like Boylan did. Like it was some fucking film they were casting. Boylan had been handling

Devaney cautiously to this point, no doubt worried that he might crack under pressure, so he'd been given only the most elementary cases, the most plodding detective work – essentially to keep him occupied, and everyone in the Loughrea station knew it.

'Ah yes, come in, please,' Boylan said, making no effort to rise or offer a chair, which felt like a transparent attempt to underscore their difference in rank. The superintendent made a show of marking his place in the massive interdepartmental report he was reading, then finally looked up and addressed Devaney with an air of preoccupation. 'I wanted to let you know that you may have to make do without a partner for the time being. It's in process, however, and I'll let you know as soon as the paperwork is complete.' Devaney's most recent partner had celebrated his retirement a fortnight ago. 'Remind me again what you're working on at the moment?'

'A break-in at Tynagh, and the rash of fires around Killimor.'

'Good, good,' Boylan said, nodding.

Devaney felt like a right eejit standing on the carpet. He thought: *You should know, you're the one making bloody sure I get all the scut work around here.*

'I heard Hugh Osborne turned up at that business out at Drumcleggan today,' Boylan said. 'I think you know that case has gone to the task force in Dublin.'

Devaney kept his face impassive. 'Yes, sir, I had heard that.'

'They've got the resources, let them have a go. It's out of our hands now.' Devaney remained silent. 'How would it look if one of my officers seems to be questioning the decision to make that referral?' Here was the real sore point.

'It doesn't fit the profile,' Devaney said. He recognized

immediately that he'd made a mistake, but it was too late. 'There's the child, for a start—'

Boylan cut him off. 'You'll leave it alone.' The superintendent's voice was even, but the colour had drained from his face. 'Do you understand?' His eyes locked on to Devaney's, daring him to say something, anything, in defiance of a direct order.

'I understand,' Devaney said. He found it curious that Boylan's eyes dropped first. 'If that's all, sir.'

'Yes, that was all.' Boylan turned his chair away, turned to his place in the thick report once more.

Fuck Boylan anyway, Devaney had thought as he trudged back down the corridor. When he returned to the detective division office he saw the Osborne file at the corner of his desk. Someone might have seen the thing and mentioned it to the superintendent. He'd cast a glance around, and, on finding he was alone in the office, casually slid the bulky file into his bag.

Devaney stopped playing abruptly and set the fiddle back in its case. He remembered as he reached for the file his initial curiosity about the Osborne case when he'd first come to Dunbeg. One particularly slow afternoon, he'd gone through the drawer full of unsolved cases, and had been intrigued by this one. The file was nearly three inches thick, crammed with written reports, witness statements, photographs, and news clippings. It was exactly the kind of case that he knew from experience would get under his skin, gnawing at his conscience every day that it went unsolved.

The case had gone to Operation Trace because of growing speculation that a series of disappearances over the past five years might be related. There was talk of a serial killer. But a blind man could see that Mina Osborne stood out from the other victims. Every one of the women had disappeared while walking along quiet country roads. But all the rest were younger, between the ages of seventeen and twenty-two; Mina Osborne was twenty-nine years old. And all of the younger women went missing within a forty-kilometre radius of Portlaoise. Mina Osborne was the only one well outside that circle. And finally, there was the little boy. None of the others had a child in tow. One of the younger girls had a baby, right enough, but the child was spending the night with the girl's parents when she disappeared.

Devaney remembered the sudden urge he'd had that afternoon to drive a bulldozer into Drumcleggan Bog and dig up the whole fucking thing. If Osborne was responsible, his performance as the grieving husband out on the bog could have been deliberately staged to throw them off the scent. Devaney knew he'd have to work through this, step by step. If Mina Osborne and her child were already dead, there was no use rushing if he couldn't build a case against the person – or persons – responsible. There had been a thorough investigation, but something was still missing, some element they hadn't yet considered. The trouble was, you couldn't tell which piece was missing until the thing was nearly put together.

He turned to the original missing person report. Here was something he had never noticed before. The signature at the bottom of the form was 'Detective Sgt BF Boylan'. So Boylan had headed up this case. No wonder he wanted to get it off his desk and into the hands of the national task force. Beneath the first report was a photograph of Hugh, Mina, and Christopher Osborne – at some holiday or other, it looked like. Mina was sitting in a chair with the child on her lap; Osborne knelt by her side, holding one of his son's hands in his own, his free hand gesturing toward the photographer. The little boy looked curious and excited, his face upturned toward his mother's. Mina Osborne was a beautiful woman, Devaney thought. Her straight teeth seemed very white in contrast to her dusky skin, and she wore a colourful sari, dark crimson cloth woven at the edge with gold. Her look was one of contented amusement. He wondered who took the picture. The back of the photo was blank.

He turned back to the missing person report on Mina Osborne and read through the full description: height, weight, build, and smaller particulars like teeth, voice, accent, gait, and distinguishing marks; haunts and habits. There was a sketch of a distinctive hair clip that several people reported seeing her wearing just before the disappearance – a pair of metal filigree elephants.

What did they have? A disappearance. Murder, suicide, accident, kidnapping, flight – there was not enough to prove or disprove any one of several possibilities. But there were small things, not even clues, really, that pointed toward some possibilities and away from others; perhaps that was the place to begin.

There had evidently been some brief discussion of kidnapping, but there had never been a demand for ransom. Could Mina Osborne have fled, as Dr Gavin had suggested, skipped the country without leaving a trail? If she had, the question was not only how, but why. Devaney made a note to check through the file for medical records on Mina and Christopher Osborne, to see if there was ever any suggestion of physical abuse. Provided all the family and friends they'd contacted were telling the truth, no one had heard from Mina Osborne since she went missing.

In the case of accident or suicide, you'd expect to find bodies. Certainly there were cases of people disappearing down bog holes. Mina Osborne hadn't lived in the area long enough to know the safe shortcuts through the bog like the locals did. But hardly anyone travelled on foot through bogland any more, not like in the old days, and nothing in the circumstances immediately suggested that possibility. Besides, Drumcleggan Bog was on the other side of her home from the village; there was no reason to be crossing it at all. No, if Mina Osborne was in the bog, it wasn't her own doing. Murder was the likeliest scenario, and Hugh Osborne remained the likeliest suspect.

Osborne had phoned the Dunbeg Garda station at 10 p.m. one night in early October, just over two and a half years ago. His story was that he'd been away for three days, attending an academic conference at Oxford. He'd taken an early afternoon flight from Heathrow and driven up from Shannon Airport. When he got home around six that evening, he found his wife's car in the old stable that served as their garage, but she and their son were nowhere to be found. According to another occupant of the house, a Lucy Osborne, Mina had left for Dunbeg with her son around one o'clock that afternoon. Apparently it wasn't unusual for her to travel the short distance to the village on foot, with Christopher in a collapsible pushchair, so the car in the garage suggested nothing out of order. When there was still no sign of them at half-seven, Osborne reported that he'd begun searching the house and grounds, and that just after ten he had phoned the Gardaí. But because Mina Osborne was a responsible adult, and because there was no evidence of foul play, the police could do nothing further until seventy-two hours had elapsed from the time she was last seen.

When the next day and the next passed without word, extra Guards were brought in to help mount a search. They began scouring the fields and roadsides between the house and the village, and combing the grounds at Bracklyn House on foot. Photos of the missing mother and child were dispatched to seaports, train stations, and air terminals all over the country. The police also began questioning people in town. Mina Osborne had first gone to the local AIB bank branch, where she had withdrawn two hundred pounds. Then she'd taken her son into Pilkington's and bought him a new pair of red boots, which he had worn out of the shop. She was last seen leaving the village on the Drumcleggan road, presumably on her way home. Those who had seen her in the village described Mina's mood as quieter than usual, even downcast. No one had ever found the pushchair. Heavy rain in the days following the disappearance had washed away any evidence of tracks. When the ground search turned up nothing by the fourth day, they searched the lakebed around the house and the village. The divers had come up empty-handed.

It was only then that the police had begun questioning Hugh Osborne more closely concerning his whereabouts on the actual day of the disappearance. He had indeed been travelling home from a conference, but his return flight from London had landed in Shannon at noon, a full six hours before he'd arrived home at Bracklyn. The drive from the airport couldn't have taken more than two hours. The only explanation Osborne offered was that he'd been up late the night before, that he'd felt tired and pulled over along the road above Mountshannon and fallen asleep in the car. They'd found no one to confirm or refute his story. He'd been the primary suspect from that point on. If he were just making it up, surely he could do better than that. They had only the word of two other inhabitants of Bracklyn House, Lucy and Jeremy Osborne, to confirm that Hugh had indeed arrived home from Shannon at six. Now there was a strange setup, Devaney thought: Lucy Osborne was only the widow of some distant cousin, and yet she and her son had been living at Bracklyn for the past eight years. It was possible these two were lying, of course; why should they want to jeopardize their position by grassing up the person who fed them and put a roof over their heads?

Osborne apparently had no major assets other than the house and a few small parcels of land, and in fact was rather strapped for money at the time of his wife's disappearance. Devaney paged through the file until he found the document he was looking for. According to a statement from Kevin Reidy, a representative from Hanover Life Assurance, from the time of his marriage Hugh Osborne had a substantial life insurance policy on his wife – 750,000 euros – and the same amount on himself, each with the surviving spouse listed as beneficiary. Maybe that wasn't an unusually large amount for someone like Osborne, though by anyone's standards, it provided motive enough for murder. But what was the use of killing your wife for the insurance money if you couldn't produce a body? No damning evidence of foul play that way, Devaney supposed, but no claim could be made either, until she was legally dead – seven years in the case of a disappearance.

All right, say you wanted to get rid of a body – or bodies, in this case – so that they'd never be found . . . Devaney's thoughts ticked through the various methods of disposal. Whichever you selected, it was a challenge, and the choice often depended on whether the murder was a crime of passion or carefully planned. Burning and burial both took time. The search had concentrated on the outdoors, looking within a radius of ten to fifteen kilometres from Dunbeg, and mainly for any areas of disturbed earth that might indicate a shallow grave. The police had also searched open wells and bog holes. But what about the inside of Bracklyn House? When the focus narrowed in on Osborne, the place was gone over, but old fortresses like that were usually rotten with secret rooms and passages. Nuala had pressed him into a family trip to Portumna Castle last summer, and he remembered the tour guides showing off a hollow built into one of its walls where the family had hidden priests during penal times, when Catholicism was outlawed. Devaney made a note to check on any architectural drawings of Bracklyn House, past or present.

Maybe trying to come up with bodies wasn't the best approach. In every murder investigation, you tried to get to know the victim. The more you knew, the easier it became to imagine why anyone would want her dead. Mina Osborne was an artist – a painter, he seemed to recall. It might be useful to take a look at her work.

Those years in Cork had taught him that there were plenty of incentives for killing – greed, jealousy, revenge, even love that had turned to bitter hatred. Maybe the investigation had failed to go deep enough into that shadowy realm of impulse and instinct. He remembered, as a young policeman, attending the postmortem of a young woman, an apparent suicide by poisoning. The pathologist had explained what he was about to do: *We'll go for the poison, and we'll go for the womb, and I'll wager we find our answer in the latter.* And so they had: the girl was several months pregnant – by her married lover, as it eventually turned out.

Hugh Osborne had indeed appeared devastated out

on the bog. Did that mean he couldn't possibly be responsible for killing his wife? Nothing could be taken for granted, not even a father's love for his own child. Devaney closed the file with a sigh, and remembered the expression on Hugh Osborne's face when he saw that the person in the soaking turf was not his wife – a complicated mixture of dread, disappointment, and relief. But was the relief from realizing that the woman he loved might still be alive, or simply that her body had not been found? Whoever she was, that red-haired creature in the bog had managed to set something loose, like the genie from a bottle, and he was going to make fucking sure it didn't get back in again.

Chapter 5

Just past seven o'clock, Cormac was splashing at the tiny sink in his room above Lynch's pub in Dunbeg. Devaney had helped him sort out lodging. The accommodation was basic: a single bed and no shower, but at a tenner a night, it would certainly do.

Cormac's chin was now covered in white lather; as he removed it with short, deft strokes of the razor, he pictured the red-haired girl's distorted countenance, and tried pressing his own teeth into the pliable flesh of his lower lip. His nostrils recalled the pleasantly rusty tang of the bog air, occasionally layered with the clean, soapy scent of Nora Gavin working closely beside him.

They'd arranged to meet at Collins Barracks in Dublin tomorrow afternoon, and Cormac felt himself looking forward to the prospect. But for that one slight flinch down in the cutaway, Nora had remained perfectly composed throughout the excavation – he reminded himself that this was a woman used to working on cadavers, after all – but unless he was mistaken, she'd suddenly gone rigid when Devaney started telling them about the disappearance of Mina Osborne. Of all the things they had seen and heard today, why should that be so upsetting to Nora? Osborne's anguish had seemed perfectly convincing, but he didn't envy Devaney the task of sorting truth-tellers from dissemblers. How could you not become jaded, dealing with utterly convincing liars every day?

Cormac rubbed the last bits of lather from his ears and was absently checking his clean-shaven face in the mirror when he heard the sound of a creaking footfall in the hallway outside his door, then silence. A vague disquiet passed through him, then was gone. He swung the door open to find Una McGann with her hand raised, ready to knock.

'Oh, Jaysus Christ, you gave me a fright,' she said.

'Sorry, I thought you were Devaney again,' Cormac replied, crossing to the chair where he'd hung his fresh shirt, feeling suddenly naked and self-conscious at close quarters.

Una remained at the doorway, apparently not wanting to intrude into the small space, but also slightly wary of him, Cormac thought. She crossed her arms and looked at her feet. 'I can imagine what he's been telling you. But I really came to ask if you'd want to join us for supper. There's nothing open here in the village this time of day, and I thought you could use a decent meal after all your work.'

'You're very kind; that sounds great,' Cormac said, sitting on the edge of the bed to put on his shoes. 'I won't be a minute. Devaney mentioned there's a good traditional session here on a Tuesday night.'

'It's brilliant. My brother Fintan always goes along for it. Do you play, yourself?'

'Flute.' He indicated the instrument case that lay beside him on the bed. 'What's Fintan at?'

'The pipes. Ah, sure, Fintan's pure stone mad for the music – always was.'

'I was hoping for another chance to speak to Brendan, too,' Cormac said, pulling his last shoelace tight. McGann had disappeared from the bog so quickly this afternoon that he hadn't had a proper chance to bring up the subject of financial compensation. Artefacts found on Bord na Móna lands paid a fairly decent finder's fee – mainly to keep the turf board workers honest – but there was no regular system of payment for objects that turned up on private property. Most people didn't expect anything for discovery of human remains. But part of his job here was to find out whether that would be a problem – without actually asking the question, of course.

'He can be a bit rough, I know, but Brendan is really the decentest man you could meet,' Una said. 'He's just out of sorts because it's another setback. It's already the end of April, and he figures we should have finished footing the turf a fortnight ago.'

As they drove out of the village, Cormac began to feel he was getting his bearings about the place. Dunbeg was in the centre of a small peninsula that jutted out into Lough Derg. He knew that around the curve of the small inlet north of the town was Bracklyn House, and beyond that another quarter mile down the shore lay the brown expanse of Drumcleggan Bog. The day's fair weather had lasted into evening, and now there was a high, milky cast to the sunlight that played on the waves of Lough Derg, visible now and again through the overgrown hedgerows as they made their way up the high road out of the village.

Una was quiet for a moment, then asked: 'You got the *cailín rua* safely off to Dublin, then?' The *cailín rua*, Cormac thought. It was a fitting name for her: the red girl. 'Nobody said what's going to happen to her.'

'Well, Dr Gavin and the museum staff will see if they can estimate her age, and try to figure out how she died, I suppose. There'd be more to go on, obviously, if the body were also intact, but they can still gather quite a lot of information.' Una was silent, and he could feel her discomfort in the face of his enthusiasm.

'That's not what you wanted to know, is it?'

'Actually, what I meant was what will happen to her in the end, after all that?'

'Well, at the moment the National Museum is keeping all its bog specimens in a special fridge,' Cormac answered, feeling as he said the words how callous it sounded.

'But what's it in aid of? Maybe the poor girl deserves some peace.'

'If we can preserve bog remains, then we have a chance to answer questions in future that we haven't even conceived of yet. The examinations are carried out with the greatest respect.' Una didn't seem satisfied by his answers, but said no more.

As they rounded a bend in the road, a forbidding tower house hove into view among the trees. The imposing stonework looked mostly intact, but its roof gaped open towards the sky and tufts of grass and wild phlox grew out of the chimney stones. Narrow windows were slashed into the sides of its grey stone bulk, which was half enshrouded in ivy. Though he'd been down this road earlier, Cormac had not seen it before.

'That's O'Flaherty's Tower,' Una said. 'They were the big family around here once. It belongs to Bracklyn House now – to Hugh Osborne.'

As Cormac slowed the jeep to study the tower more closely, a large crow appeared out of one of the upper windows, spread its wings, and began to wheel around the ruin. A second bird joined it, then another, and another, in rapid succession until the topmost part was enveloped in a whirling mass of dark wings and a cacophony of croaking calls. The sight touched that place inside him, unrevealed to anyone, where he tucked away such otherworldly images and impressions, things connected somehow to myth and memory, to times and places that modern humankind could not completely understand.

Then, as unexpectedly as they had appeared, the noisy crowd of birds vanished, leaving a single dark shape dipping and soaring around the castle walls, the evening light glinting off its jet-black wings. A voice broke through beside him: 'Are you all right?' Una asked. Cormac looked down and saw his hands on the steering wheel, feeling as if he'd just awakened from a dream. The jeep wasn't moving. He'd come to a full stop in the middle of the road.

'People say the place is haunted,' Una continued, 'and looking at you just now, I'm half tempted to believe it.'

'Sorry,' he said, pressing on the accelerator once more. Around a curve in the road, the dense forest around the tower gradually gave way to light undergrowth, and finally to the stone-walled grounds of the Osborne estate.

'This is where Hugh Osborne lives?'

Una nodded. Through the imposing stone and wrought-iron gates Cormac could see a lawn and formal gardens, and Bracklyn House itself, a sturdy manor house of dark grey stone, its steep slate roof rimmed around with stepped gables and crenellations. It was modest, as Irish country houses went, and retained the rough-hewn look of the century in which it was built.

'Fine old place,' he said. A harmless remark, but one glance at Una told him that it had tipped the scale.

Her words came in a torrent: 'I suppose Devaney explained to you how the police have tried over and over again to pin the blame on Hugh for what happened? Of course there's no proof, because he didn't do anything.

Just a lot of malicious talk from spiteful people with nothing better to occupy their minds. Whatever happened to Mina and the child, I'm certain Hugh had nothing to do with it. Anyone could see how he adored his family. The last two years have been awful, on top of everything else to have the police sniffing around asking questions, and the whole town watching, and waiting—' She stopped and took a breath, but seemed determined not to shed any tears. 'Sometimes I really hate this feckin' place.'

Why did he imagine that Una McGann had more than once been in the position of defending Hugh Osborne? 'I suppose you've known him a long time?' He watched her face and posture soften.

'Not long, actually. He's quite a bit older, and he was always away at school when we were growing up. But I got to know him when I was taking some classes at the university in Galway – he teaches geography there. I'd be hitching up to school the odd time and he'd give me a lift.'

'What were you studying?'

'Studio arts,' Una said. 'I never finished.' Her tone suggested there might be more to the story, but he gathered it was not something she felt comfortable talking about. 'You're very good, listening to me go on,' she said.

'Did you know his wife?'

'Not really. Just to say hello. We used to pass along the road. I don't know how Hugh has kept going at all.'

Cormac hadn't reached a point where he'd begun to think of himself as a confirmed bachelor, but he had never been married, never been a father. He searched the windows of Bracklyn House for signs of life as he tried to put himself in Hugh Osborne's place. Una followed his gaze, then looked down at her hands, doubled into fists in her lap.

He wanted to ask Una what she thought might have happened to Mina Osborne, but thought better of it. As they pulled away from the gate, Cormac wondered whether Una's ministrations to Osborne out on the bog were anything more than neighbourly concern. He remembered the fork twisting uneasily in her brother's hands as well.

They had driven less than a quarter mile when Una spoke up: 'You can turn in at the next gate on your left.' Cormac did as she instructed, and the jeep thundered over a cattle grid and up a steep drive. The McGann house was all but invisible from the road, tucked up against the side of the hill, and surrounded on three sides by pale green fir trees that brushed against its eaves. Like many old farmhouses, it was broad-shouldered and compact, close to the ground, with small-paned windows. The exterior had been freshly whitewashed, and the front door and window frames recently painted with glossy black enamel. An old-fashioned dog rose grew to one side of the door, and every flowerbed looked lovingly tended. An ancient black car was parked on one side of the tin-covered shed in the yard. Everything about this place suggested a family farm of thirty, perhaps even forty years ago.

'Brendan's the man with the spade and the paintbrush here,' Una said. 'He loves this place as if it were his child. He was *that* upset when my father replaced the old thatched roof – he slept out in the shed for three days. When they wanted to build a new house, he was like a briar. Wouldn't hear of it.'

Cormac understood. A man who still insisted on cutting his own turf by hand wouldn't exactly be a man who thrived on change. Una pushed open the shiny black front door. The house was divided in two equal halves, with the main hallway down the centre. She led him into the kitchen, clearly the heart of the house. A heavy pine table stood in the middle of the room, its oilcloth heaped with onion skins and carrot peelings, and a dresser full of blue willow delft china stood beside the sink. The old stone fireplace still dominated the room, but it was cold at the moment. What heat there was apparently came from the enormous cooker that stood to one side of the fireplace, and the smell wafting from the cast iron pot that sat on top of it reminded Cormac that he was ravenous.

'You'll have tea? Of course you will,' Una answered for him. 'Fintan must have finished up the stew before he went out. The lads pretend to be useless, but they're well able to fend for themselves.' She checked the kettle, and began to fill it at the sink, giving Cormac a chance to look around the space.

A narrow stairway led up to a closed loft that hung over the far side of the room. Cormac wondered if the bedrooms here were like those in his grandmother's house: he pictured the horrid flowered wallpaper in musty rooms of his childhood, furnished with swaybacked metal beds and pictures of the Sacred Heart. Beneath the loft stood a second cooker, this one covered with white enamel buckets. In shelving all around it were large glass cannisters, all labelled in the same neat hand. They contained mysterious organic substances that looked like bark, roots, and other dried plant material. He recognized pale green lichens, coppery onion skins, and the fibrous rhizomes of wildflowers, but others were strange in name and appearance: 'Madder root', 'Cochineal', and 'Hypernic'. Hanks of yarn, some dyed, some natural, bawn-coloured wool, were stacked in binlike baskets in another set of shelves. The low ceiling, coupled with the strange-looking contents, gave this place the atmosphere of a medieval alchemist's lair. In the back corner of the kitchen, beneath the stairs, stood a large loom, its complicated system of warp and weft temporarily at rest. Hanging on the wall beside it was a length of cloth, a textured landscape in earthy tones reminiscent of lichens and sphagnum moss, with flecks of purple foxglove and butterwort. Cormac's eye was drawn to the subtle variations in colour; he could make out the incomplete arcs of two circles, almost like the long-buried footprints of a pair of ringforts.

'This your work?'

'Yes, such as it is,' Una said, sounding somewhat preoccupied. She swept around him, scooping up a pile of papers, a jumper, and a newspaper from the well-worn sofa whose back rested against the front window. 'Please, do sit down, and forgive the mess. I've become a bit blind to it, I'm afraid.' What she called mess was the comfortable, familiar flotsam of everyday life, and it gave the room a sense of warmth and animation he suddenly felt his own orderly house in Ranelagh sorely lacked.

'What is all that?' he asked, gesturing toward the area under the loft.

'I suppose you could call it my studio. It used to be all very tidy when I was just doing the weaving. But since I've begun making my own dyes, it's taken over the whole bloody kitchen. I'm hoping to get a bigger space soon.'

Cormac heard a commotion at the back door, and a small girl about five years old burst through the door, her round face circled by a corona of fair ringlets. She wore denim overalls, yellow wellingtons, and a tweedy green jacket with large red buttons. The child's bright eyes travelled to Una, then to Cormac, and she darted out the back door again as quickly as she'd come in.

'Fintan, will you come *on*?' they could hear her plead in an exasperated tone, as though he'd been holding her up all day. 'We've got company for tea.'

A clean-shaven young man in a baggy sweater smiled and nodded as he stuck his head in through the door, and set down a basket that seemed to be laden with moss and mushrooms, then turned to pull off his boots outside. 'Stew should be nearly ready,' he said to Una through the open door.

'Cormac Maguire, this is my brother, Fintan, and this,' Una said, as the child scurried around to her side, 'is my daughter, Aoife.'

Conversation at the McGanns' supper table reminded Cormac of the few times he'd gone home for a weekend with a classmate from school. At home there was only himself and his mother, and they never wanted for conversation, but in the circle of a larger family than his own, there was a kind of uncontrolled energy he found irresistible. The subject matter around this kitchen table was nothing lofty, and yet Cormac watched with fascination as words and laughter leapt and slid across the table. There was only one party noticeably silent: Brendan had barely acknowledged Cormac's presence when he came in, and after answering a few questions, sat apart from the rest of them at the end of the long table. He chewed noisily, mopping the meaty juice of the stew with rough pieces torn from a heel of brown bread, and spoke not a word to anyone. Soon he pushed away from the table and retreated to the chair beside the fireplace, grinding tobacco between his rough palms and filling his pipe in a way that suggested years of habit. Indeed, everyone behaved as if this were a perfectly normal occurrence, and perhaps it was.

No one had mentioned Aoife's father. Perhaps he was absent, as Cormac's own father had been. After the meal, the little girl set out the spoils she'd collected – a broad white toadstool, acorns and chestnuts, soft patches of pale green moss, and, finally, a small sprig of white hawthorn flowers. Brendan's face darkened.

'Aoife, take those outside. Right now – do you hear me? It's bad luck bringing them into a house. And you,' he said, jabbing a finger at Fintan, 'ought to know better.'

'Ah, Brendan, they're lovely,' Aoife protested, as she playfully thrust the pale flowers into his face. He recoiled and stood, towering awkwardly over the little girl.

'Why must you always argue? Jaysus, you're just like Una,' he said, the pitch of his voice rising. 'Can you not just do as you're told?' He wrenched the flowers from the child's grasp and marched to the back door to fling them out into the darkness. Cormac remembered his grandmother's horror when he'd brought a similar bouquet home as a small boy. His mother had tried to explain that it was just superstition. It was only years later he'd read that hawthorn was considered unlucky because its sweet, stale fragrance suggested the smell of death. What would a child know of that?

'Maybe I'd better be getting back,' Cormac said, remembering the music session in Dunbeg. He turned to Fintan. 'I can give you a lift in, if you like.'

The pub was already fairly crowded when they arrived, and a handful of musicians had gathered just inside the door near the stone fireplace. A half dozen pints of porter, creamy tops measuring their levels, stood waiting on the short tables at the centre of the group, while the air above their heads coursed with the swirling rhythm of a reel that Cormac recognized immediately as a splendid setting of 'Rakish Paddy'. As Fintan stepped to the bar to order drinks, one of the fiddle players turned to look at them – it was Garrett Devaney. The policeman raised his eyebrows by way of greeting, all the while keeping his bow in motion and his chin lovingly pressed to the body of his fiddle.

When Fintan handed him his pint, Cormac sat down and began putting together his ebony flute, carefully wedging together the silver-rimmed seals of waxed string, lining up the finger holes, testing the sound and the feel of it against his lower lip. As he did so, he watched Fintan's elaborate process of assembling and strapping on his uilleann pipes, one narrow leather belt buckled around his waist, the other around his right arm to work the small bellows. It had always seemed to Cormac a ritual akin to strapping on the phylacteries of some ancient religion.

As the pulsating rhythm of the tune ended, an old man with a bald head burst out laughing as he set down his flute and reached for his full pint. 'Be the holy, that was a good one,' he said to the fellow beside him. 'A real scorcher.' Fintan quickly introduced Cormac around the circle. The stocky man beside the chortling flute player sat leaning forward, listening intently. At first Cormac wondered what set this man apart from the others. No instrument, for a start, but as the fellow reached out and touched the table for his drink, Cormac realized that he was blind, though he moved like a person who hadn't always been so.

'That's Ned Raftery, my old schoolteacher,' said Fintan. '*Great* fuckin' singer.'

Devaney broke in beside them with a sideways glance. 'Glad you could join us.'

Cormac didn't quite know what to make of the policeman. The wry look didn't disguise the fact that Devaney's eyes were everywhere, even here, among his friends and neighbours, sizing things up, cannily recording and filing everything away.

The pub door swung open, and Hugh Osborne entered. Conversation suspended for the briefest instant as his presence registered around the bar, then resumed at normal volume, but Osborne seemed completely unaware of the momentary stir he caused. As he surveyed the room, his gaze alighted on Cormac, hesitating slightly, as though he only half recognized the face. He moved to the bar, where he ordered a drink and stood alongside a young man whose dark, cropped head seemed barely suspended between the peaks of his shoulders. Osborne spoke a few words to the boy, who jerked his arm away awkwardly, though Cormac would almost swear he hadn't been touched.

In contrast to the work clothes he'd been wearing at the site this afternoon, Osborne was dressed expensively, even elegantly now, in a black silk jacket and camel-coloured slacks. But it wasn't just the clothing; the man had a natural physical grace that was all the more noticeable because of his height. Fintan followed Cormac's gaze.

'You get the story on him?' he asked confidentially. Cormac nodded, and Fintan continued: 'I don't know if he's as guilty as everybody around here likes to make out. A lot of 'em are just fuckin' delighted seeing the big man down in the mud. I think that's a load of bollocks. But I wish Una would wise up all the same.'

'Maybe they're just friends,' Cormac said.

Fintan looked at him. 'Right,' he said, 'maybe they are.'

A while later, on his way back from the gents, Cormac passed by the end of the bar, near the young man to whom Osborne had spoken. The crowd hushed as one of the fiddles began to play 'The Dear Irish Boy,' an old air whose haunting melody never failed to raise the hairs on the back of Cormac's neck. He stopped for a moment to listen, feeling his chest and throat tighten at the desolation in the pleading notes. The boy at his side drew back and stared hollowly at Cormac for a long moment, then turned unsteadily, lifted a glass to his lips, and drank greedily, as if by draining the glass he could dive headfirst into oblivion. And so he could, Cormac thought. The young man rapped his glass once on the bar and Cormac heard the publican whisper furiously: 'You've had enough, now. Clear off.' There was no response but another rap of the glass. 'Go home, will yeh? Before you get us both in a rake of trouble.' The boy peered blackly at the barman, then lurched away and stumbled in slow motion through the crowd and out into the night. Hugh Osborne followed the boy, ducking his head as he pushed his way out the door. Cormac saw that he wasn't the only one watching: Devaney was taking it all in as well.

Chapter 6

It was morning. Cormac could hear the pub coming to life downstairs, the unloading of aluminium casks of beer, the clink and rattle of bottles in wooden crates, the puttering diesel roar of a lorry as it pulled away to the next delivery. He'd slept wretchedly, his rest disturbed by fearful, brackish dreams of being pursued by a shadowy assailant through a dark wood.

He turned over to try to sleep again, but a knock sounded at the door. 'Mr Maguire?' a raspy, adolescent voice inquired. 'It's nine o'clock. You asked to be called.'

'Bollocks,' Cormac muttered under his breath. Aloud he said: 'Yes, all right. Thanks very much. Any chance of a cup of tea?' There was no reply except the sound of a large pair of trainers bounding down the narrow carpeted stairs. He'd better make a move if he was going to meet Nora in the lab at two.

There was tea – a full breakfast, in fact, waiting for him in the bar below. He'd just tucked into a mighty-looking fry of eggs, sausages, rashers, and tomatoes when the pub door opened. Una McGann entered, followed by Hugh Osborne, who appeared reluctant to be disturbing anyone's breakfast.

'Please forgive the interruption,' Una said. 'I've just had a brainwave.' The two men shook hands, then stood for a moment awkwardly.

'Won't you join me?' Cormac asked. Behind the bar,

he could hear Dermot Lynch, the publican, clattering together spoons and crockery.

Settling his large frame onto one of the small upholstered stools that stood like dwarves about his knees, Hugh Osborne first cast a glance at Una, then addressed Cormac: 'I'm developing a parcel of land for a workshop that will demonstrate and sell traditional crafts.' Cormac realized at that moment that he'd never heard the man's voice. It had a deep bass timbre, and an accent that was neither Irish nor wholly English, but somewhere between the two. Osborne leaned forward, and the dark circles under his eyes suggested that he'd not slept well the previous night either.

'We've enlisted a couple of other weavers, a metalsmith, and several potters,' he continued. 'And of course, Una's dyeworks is a central part of the plan.' Listening to him, Cormac got the sense that Hugh Osborne was a naturally diffident person. He remembered what it was like to live an eventful life in a small town, and felt a surge of compassion for the lanky figure who faced him across the table.

'It's an ideal setting, really, given the history of the place . . .' Osborne's voice trailed off.

'Sounds promising,' Cormac said, 'although I'm not quite clear how it involves me.'

'Sorry, sorry, I should have explained that at the outset,' Osborne said, colouring slightly. 'We're due to be putting in electrical and gas lines in a few weeks' time. And I'm sure you know that in order to get planning permission, we first have to make an archaeological survey of the site. We were all set to begin, and the consulting firm I originally hired to do the work pulled out. Conflict with another project that's taking longer than anticipated. And every other licensed archaeologist

I've contacted is fully booked. I realize you probably don't normally do this sort of thing, but we're behind schedule as it is. I'd pay the usual fees, of course. It might take a week or two. Rather a busman's holiday, I suppose – but you could stay at the house while you work. Of course, I don't know what your schedule looks like.'

'I'm actually on sabbatical this term,' Cormac said. 'The thing is, I'm supposed to be finishing a book; the publishers are breathing down my neck.'

'I understand completely,' said Osborne.

'And I told Dr Gavin I'd be back in Dublin this afternoon for the exam on that girl from the bog.' Cormac realized that he had been vaguely unsettled by Devaney's suspicions. He looked across the table, where Una and Hugh studied his face in anticipation. 'I don't know what to say. Can I let you know?'

'By all means. Think it over.'

'I'm sorry I can't be more definite just now.'

Osborne rose. 'Quite all right. I do understand.' He offered no handshake this time. One flicker of the deep-set eyes was enough to let Cormac know he wasn't the first to baulk.

'Good-bye then,' Osborne said as he moved toward the door of the pub. 'I'm sorry if we disturbed your breakfast.' Una McGann gave Cormac a bewildered look, and pressed a slip of paper in his hand. 'Here's the telephone number.'

'Tell him I'll ring this afternoon,' Cormac said. The words sounded unconvincing even to himself.

At one o'clock in the afternoon, the head of the nameless red-haired girl lay, still embedded in peat, on an examining table in the conservation lab at Collins Barracks in Dublin. Perched on a stool at one end of the table,

Cormac studied the strange bundle as he waited for Nora Gavin. The scent of wet turf filled the room, and diffused daylight streamed in from a single unshaded casement window that looked out onto the expansive stone-paved courtyard. Just over a century ago, when this building was still the largest army barracks in the British empire, Queen Victoria had made a visit here to inspect her troops. Something of the spartan, military ambience of those days remained in these chambers, despite the fact that two wings of the quad were now occupied by the National Museum.

Cormac could hear Nora speaking on the phone in the adjacent office. 'That would be great. Okay, see you soon. Thank you so much.' She pushed open the door to the lab. 'That was radiology up at Beaumont Hospital,' she said. 'They can fit us in for a CT scan at six, so we'll have to get a move on here.'

Nora reached into a drawer beneath the table for a pair of surgical gloves, pulling them on over the cuffs of her lab coat. As she performed this ordinary task, her professional demeanour seemed to snap into place as well, fitting her as smoothly as the thin layer of latex against her skin. She gingerly removed the black plastic, then began to remove the larger piece of sopping turf, and to arrange the matted strands of reddish hair. As the young woman's features emerged in the merciless fluorescent glare of the lab, her expression was even more ghastly than it had seemed out against the earthy blackness of the bog, but Nora's hands were steady, and as gentle as if her patient lived. Whatever had so visibly affected her yesterday seemed to have loosened its hold. Cormac wondered what sort of a life Nora Gavin had left behind her in the States, and in particular why she had pulled up stakes mid-career and moved to Dublin.

He had a suspicion that Gabriel McCrossan had known more about her circumstances than he'd been willing to share.

'We'll have to wait for Drummond to do the official postmortem, of course. He said he might be available tomorrow, provided things remain quiet.'

As she spoke, Nora was carefully removing bits of peat from the red-haired girl's face, and applying a mist of deionized water from a spray bottle. Cormac suddenly realized that if he apologized for the way he'd behaved the night of Gabriel's dinner party, she would have absolutely no idea what he was talking about. There was something about that realization, and about sitting here watching Nora Gavin at her work, that he found enormously enjoyable. As he drew closer to observe, Cormac saw that the red-haired girl's skin, now washed clean of its protective peat, was soft and brown as tanned leather. He studied the lifelike curve of her upper lip, the faint covering of down on her cheek, and had to resist an urge to smooth her furrowed brow.

'Is she the first you've ever seen up close?' she asked. He nodded. 'Me too. You can help if you like,' she said. 'But you'll have to wear these.' She handed him a pair of gloves from a drawer. 'We have to keep her as clean as possible.' She crossed to the door and called into the next office, 'I'm ready for a hand, Ray, whenever you are.' Raymond Flynn, the conservation technician, joined them. Cormac watched and occasionally lent a hand as Nora and Flynn measured the circumference of the girl's cranium and the length of her damp red hair, taking photographs and carefully noting their measurements as they went along, pausing frequently for the spray bottle. When they were finished with that phase of the exam, Nora carried the girl's head at arm's length to the adjacent X-ray room, positioned it on a negative plate, then retreated outside and closed the chamber door while Flynn activated the machine.

'We might be able to hazard a few guesses about how old she is,' Nora said when they'd returned to the examining table. 'It's tough to determine age with any accuracy unless we can get a closer look at her molars. The jaw looks pretty pliable, but we'll have to be extremely careful.' She used surgical tweezers and a pair of scissors to extract a small piece of skin and a lock of hair for chemical analysis, then a tiny sample of muscle tissue from the girl's severed neck. She saw Cormac watching closely as she carefully removed a small section of an artery.

'Turns out cholesterol is the most reliable stuff for carbon-dating bog bodies; it's insoluble in water, less likely to be contaminated by the surrounding material. Without the rest of the body, cause of death is probably going to be an educated guess. There don't appear to be any ligature marks around the throat. I see several things that point toward decapitation as the cause.'

'Such as?'

'Well, come here for a second. Look at the wound.' Nora reached for the magnifying glass on the tray beside her. 'It's a very clean cut. Look at the way the blood vessels have been sliced through, not torn. Probably a single blow from a fairly sharp blade.' She gestured for him to take the glass, which he did with some trepidation. 'You wouldn't bother being quick about it if the person were unconscious or already dead. And what else could make a person bite down through her own lip like that? She was probably lucky, if that's how it happened. At least it was over quickly. And look at this.' She pointed to what appeared to be a small abrasion on the girl's chin.

'See how the adipocere, that yellowish waxy material under the skin, is exposed here? Looks to me like a small section of the skin has been cut away. That could have been done with the same blow of the axe – or sword, or whatever kind of blade it was that severed her head.'

He must have looked puzzled. Nora leaned forward impulsively to demonstrate, holding her hands behind her back as if they were bound. She lowered her head to the level of the tabletop.

'Look, if I'm on the block, my natural reaction would be to contract, to become as small as possible.' He studied the back of Nora's slender neck, the edge of dark hair that stood out against her pale skin, the small hollow between the tendons that supported her head. How easy it must seem, at first, to sever such a vulnerable connection. But how difficult it must prove, as well, considering the toughness of bone and sinew that must be cut through.

'Do you see how it would happen? If my chin is tucked tight, it comes in line with the blade.' She straightened again. 'We can probably figure out all kinds of things about how she was killed. But the real question is why? This girl is hardly more than a child. The other thing I can't get over is how incredibly well-preserved she is. The lab will check of course, but I can't see any visible evidence of insect eggs or larvae. She must have gone into the bog very soon after her death – which means she was probably killed at or very near the bog.'

'You realize we've probably found out all we're going to about this girl,' Cormac said. He wished there were more as well, but they had to be prepared for reality.

'Yes, I know. But I'm not ready to be perfectly rational about all this yet.'

Should he mention the offer he'd had from Osborne this morning? He could easily drop the whole thing, go on as he had been, finishing his book, preparing to go back to teaching in the autumn. He could see his entire future so clearly down that course. Why did he feel that once he stepped from that comfort zone, he would never be able to return? Then again, what was the point of this or any convergence, if not to create new paths?

'Hugh Osborne asked if I'd be interested in coming back to do a small job for him – a general archaeological survey on a construction site.' A light seemed to spring from Nora's dark blue eyes as she turned to him.

'Oh, Cormac—' she began, then stopped abruptly. 'Please tell me you didn't turn him down.'

'I said I'd have to think about it. It's too much work for one person—'

'I could help. I've got Easter holidays the next two weeks.'

'I couldn't ask you—'

'But you're not asking, I'm volunteering. I want to do it. And going back there would give us a chance to find out more about this girl.'

'She could be a hundred or a thousand years old.'

'And in all that length of time, how many red-haired girls do you suppose have been executed in the vicinity of Drumcleggan Bog?' She touched his hand. 'Look, I'm not trying to press you into doing something you really don't want to do. But Cormac, look into her face and tell me you feel nothing, no obligation to find out what happened to her.'

Dropping his gaze to the dead girl's face, he was again overcome by a familiar, unbidden swell of pity as he answered: 'I can't.'

Even as he spoke, however, Cormac felt the warmth and weight of Nora's hand on his own, and suddenly realized that the strongest obligation he felt at this moment was not to the red-haired girl on the table, but to the living person who stood across from him, her eyes filled with fierce intelligence and compassion. Hers was the unknown story he felt compelled to explore. Above all, he had the strongest craving to hear her speak his name again.

Chapter 7

It was nearly nine when Nora left the conservation lab. She navigated the narrow streets just north of Collins Barracks and pulled up near a pub called The Piper's Chair in Stoneybatter. She had never been in the place, but knew its reputation, and that Cormac Maguire was a regular at its Wednesday night session. The pub itself was a nineteenth-century corner building of no great architectural interest, except that its burnished bar, worn tapestry snugs, and tall windows provided a reminder of dirty old working-class Dublin, and a stark contrast to the trendy, modern bistros that were popping up only a few streets away.

She knew about Cormac's allegiance to this session through their mutual friend Robbie McSweeney – scholar of history, guitarist, and singer, though she wasn't sure Robbie himself would put his occupations down in that order. Had he been born five hundred years ago, she thought, Robbie would surely have been in great demand as a harper in the houses of the aristocracy. According to what he'd told her, the same musicians had been coming to the Wednesday night session here for nearly ten years. She gathered there was a strong West Clare connection in this group, most of the players having come from there, or having parents or grandparents who came from that part of the country. The Piper's Chair was a place tourists were unlikely to find just wandering in off the street, and the regulars liked it that way, because it meant there was little performance pressure and plenty of time for the *craic* and the chat.

Nora found Robbie sitting at the bar, polishing off a prawn cocktail with his first pint. He raised his eyebrows in greeting as he licked the last of the cocktail sauce off his left thumb.

'Hiya, Nora,' he said, pulling up a seat for her, and signalling the barman. 'Will you have a drink?'

'No, thanks, Robbie. I'm just on my way home.'

'So what brings you here to grace our humble presence?'

'I've got something to show Cormac.'

'Oh, so it wasn't music you were looking for, then?'

'Well, that too.' And to try to persuade Cormac to return to Dunbeg, she thought, if he still hadn't made up his mind. She felt a twinge of guilt that she hadn't come clean about her own motivations for returning to Galway, which perhaps had as much to do with Hugh Osborne's missing wife as the red-haired girl.

'You'll forgive me, Nora, but I have to ask – what's all this about a head?' Robbie asked. 'The academic world was abuzz today about you carrying around a severed head in a box.'

'I did no such thing. I took it straight to the lab.'

'God, you make me suddenly grateful I stuck with history,' Robbie said in mock disgust. 'The worst thing I can dig up is a lurid eyewitness account, not an actual corpse.'

At that moment, Cormac came through the door, and Robbie tipped his head to make sure that his friend had noticed her presence as well. Nora could contain her news no longer: 'Cormac, you'll never guess what we found. There was something odd on one of the X-rays.

Right up against the molars on the left side of her jaw. It looks like a piece of metal. Hard to tell what, exactly. We'll do an endoscopic exam in the morning.' She watched the furrow in his forehead deepen. Had he forgotten what he'd said in the lab this afternoon?

'So this head belongs to a she, then? Anyone we know?' Robbie said.

'Not a clue so far,' Cormac said. 'Although Nora's convinced me we ought to try and find out.'

'Well, especially now,' Nora said. 'This piece of metal might be a clue. Robbie, what do you know about beheading?'

'A popular choice, I believe, ranking just after being hanged, drawn and quartered in centuries past. Not a lot of women would have been beheaded, though. You're sure it was an execution, not just a do-it-yourself murder?'

'That's my best guess. It's such a clean cut across the neck. You can see for yourself.' Nora pulled a folder of photographs from her bag and handed them to Robbie, who blanched slightly, but took the file. She was gratified to see his curiosity quickening when he laid eyes on the face of the red-haired girl.

'And no sign of a body?'

'None. Will you help us, Robbie? Find out about any women who might have been executed this way – and why.'

'What time period are we talking about?'

'That's the trouble,' Nora said. 'We don't really know.'

'Probably only the last couple of thousand years,' Cormac said. Robbie looked back and forth, as if trying to decide which one was going to convince him.

'Sure, what the hell,' he said, handing the photos back

to Nora. 'It's not like I've anything more interesting to be doing in the next few months.'

'Thanks, Robbie. You're a dote.'

'Well, put it down to the fact that you're just a bit more fetchin' than he is.'

'Oh, I don't know,' she said. 'But whatever works.'

'We'd better get stuck in there if we're going to, Robbie,' Cormac said. He turned to her. 'Will you stay for a few tunes?'

She hesitated. 'I was really only stopping by—'

'Ah, do, Nora,' Robbie said.

'At least let me get you a drink,' Cormac said. His serious dark eyes had a rather unnerving effect at this proximity, and just past his shoulder she could see Robbie silently urging: *Go on.*

'All right,' she said. 'Thanks.'

Chapter 8

Wading into the session, Cormac negotiated a spot for Nora to sit, on a bench near the window just beside Robbie, where she could be within the arc of the musicians' circle. The evening's repertoire consisted of reels, reels, and more reels, a pattern broken only occasionally by a jig or a hornpipe. He was delighted that Nora had decided to stay for the music. As he played and felt a dozen pairs of feet thumping out the rhythm to the left and right of him, Cormac watched her body move slightly, almost involuntarily, to the same pulse. Toward the end of the evening, at a point where the tunes trailed off, and the musicians reached in unison for their pints, he saw Robbie look sideways at her.

'Would you ever give us a song, Dr Gavin?'

Nora shrank back with a dismissive wave. 'Ah no, I couldn't. Play away there,' she said. Cormac hadn't realized she was a singer. But reticence was the expected response to this first request; coaxing the shy singer was very much a part of the tradition. After a few more words of encouragement from Robbie and calls from the rest of the group, she finally yielded, took a quick drink of whiskey for courage, and leaned forward, clearing her throat and trying to find the right pitch. When she tipped her head up again, her eyes were closed.

The first time I saw my love, happy was I,
I knew not what love was, nor how to deny;
But I made too much freedom of my love's company,
Saying my generous lover, you're welcome to me.

Cormac was stunned by the dark, earthy voice that seemed to pour from Nora's lips. Nervousness caused it to falter slightly, and he could see her eyes flicker under their lids, an intimacy that was almost too much to bear. He closed his eyes, and heard Nora's uneasiness begin to subside as she relaxed. The song picked up strength and fervour like some powerful incantation, spinning a familiar, sad tale of faithless love and abandonment.

So fare thee well, darling, I now must away,
For I in this country no longer can stay;
But keep your mind easy, and keep your heart free,
Let no man be your sharer, my darling, but me.

Oh this poor pretty creature, she stood on the ground,
With her cheeks white as ivory, and the tears running down;
Crying Jamie, dearest Jamie, you're the first that e'er wooed me,
And I'm sorry that I ever said, you're welcome to me.

O happy is the girl that ne'er loved a man,
And easy can tie up a narrow waistband;
She is free from all sorrow and sad misery,
That never said, my lover, you're welcome to me.

There was a brief silence when she finished, then a roar of approval from the gathered musicians, and even from some of the pub regulars who'd hissed one another into silence to hear the song. Cormac sat back in his chair and watched Nora open her eyes, looking as if she'd awakened from some dream to find a whole room full of people staring at her. She seemed astonished, and a little embarrassed, by all the admiring faces leaning in, the hands reaching in to touch her knee, her arm, her shoulder. She looked across at him, but he felt unable to move or speak.

'Time, please,' the bartender shouted over the din. 'Drink up, ladies and gentlemen. Time, please.' There was the usual unwillingness to let the evening end so soon, as everyone seemed determined to remain talking and to stretch out the last pint. Finally the crowd began to disperse, and Cormac was able to make his way toward Nora through the noisy crush of pub patrons just outside the bar. 'Wait,' he said. 'Let me walk you to your car.'

By day, Stoneybatter was a busy thoroughfare lined with dozens of small businesses. But at night, its shop faces were closed up tight with solid metal gates, which combined with blowing litter to give this part of the city centre its nightly guise of a war zone. As they walked slowly down the nearly deserted street, Cormac fingered the wooden flute case he had tucked under his arm, and chanced a sideways glance at her. 'That song was incredible, Nora.'

She smiled. 'Thanks. I was a bit nervous.'

'Where did you ever learn to sing like that?'

'I don't know. Listening to records, I guess.'

'You're joking.'

'Where else? But did you ever get the feeling with a certain tune that it was something you'd been *waiting* to hear? I don't know what it is about old songs. Maybe it's their plainness, or that they're so sad, and so true. And I love the way songs get handed on. It's almost like they're alive, in some way. I'm no good at explaining it. Anyway, here's my car.' She unlocked it with a tiny remote, then opened the door and turned to face him. They both began to speak at once:

'I wanted to ask you—'

'If you'd still be interested—'

Cormac insisted that she speak first.

'I was going to ask if you've decided about going back to Dunbeg,' she said.

'That's just what I was about to tell you. I am going back. I phoned Hugh Osborne this evening. I've a couple of things to do tomorrow morning, then I'm heading out there in the afternoon.'

'And did you find someone to help you?'

'I thought I had a volunteer. Unless you've changed your mind.'

'Oh no, not at all. I have to finish up in the lab tomorrow, but I could probably make it out there by about six.' She stopped thinking aloud and looked directly at him. 'Thanks, Cormac.'

'Not at all. Thank you for the song.' A small gust of wind blew Nora's hair across her eyes. Without thinking, he reached up to brush it away, then let his fingers rest against the soft curve of her cheek. He was startled when she twisted away from his touch.

'No,' she said. 'Please don't.'

'I'm sorry, Nora—'

'It's not you, Cormac – please don't think that. It's just – it's just that I'm a coward.' She finally looked at him again. 'I hope you still want my help tomorrow.'

'Yes, of course I do.' She studied him thoughtfully for a moment longer, then climbed into her car and drove off down the empty street. Cormac began walking briskly back to his own car, realizing that he'd no reason at all to feel hopeful. It had been a most definite rebuff. But he had heard her say his name again – twice.

BOOK TWO

Wound Follows Wound

Wound follows wound that nothing be wanting to fill up the cup of sufferings. The few Catholic families that remain were lately deprived by Cromwell of all their immovable property, and are all compelled to abandon their native estates, and retire into the province of Connaught.

– Father Quinn, a Jesuit priest,
writing to the Vatican from his hiding place
in the mountains of Ireland, 1653

Chapter 1

By the time Cormac crossed over the Galway border at Portumna, the daylong drizzle had turned to lashing rain. The roads and ditches had melted into a watery blur of grey and green, and the poor visibility, along with the steady pulse of the wipers and the random drumbeat of the rain on the roof of the car, had begun to wear on his nerves. The journey was nearly over, he told himself, only ten miles farther. He'd been plagued by second thoughts throughout the trip west, knowing that he'd phoned Osborne for purely selfish reasons, because it meant a chance to spend more time with Nora Gavin. It was too late now to be sorry he'd agreed to the job.

He'd felt at a loss in the weeks since Gabriel's death – uneasy, and unable to concentrate. He remembered the old man's hand at rest on that pad of paper. When the ambulance drivers had taken Gabriel's body away, he'd stayed on, studying the blot of ink that obscured those final words. Of all the indelible details of that strange tableau, this was the image that haunted him. What, if anything, had been in the old man's mind the moment his pen had refused to move? Did he suffer pain? Did he understand what was happening, or was conscious thought simply swept away by the sudden insult to his brain?

They had been together at the site of so many burials,

never venturing to speak about their own mortality. Gabriel must have thought about it. A man couldn't work so intimately with the meagre remains of the dead without contemplating his own passing. But they had never spoken of it. Gabriel must have shared those confidences with his wife; he had been cremated, and there was no religious service, only a memorial gathering at their home in Dublin. The McCrossans had no children, but sitting in their front room among the old man's neighbours, old school friends, colleagues from the university, Evelyn's friends from the world of writing and publishing, Cormac had realized how small his own circle of acquaintances really was.

No one had gained admittance to his unguarded thoughts the way Gabriel McCrossan had. Cormac had in a sense packed his father's bags even before anyone knew that Joseph Maguire was actually leaving Ireland for good. That place in his heart had remained empty until he had met Gabriel. With only one survey course in archaeology behind him, Cormac had signed on for the summer as one of a dozen or so students helping with the excavation of a 2,500-year-old bog road.

McCrossan had had a habit of addressing the students before setting them to work. They'd stood before him quietly, fiddling with their tools, anxious to begin. He'd pace back and forth in front of them, just as he would have done in a lecture hall.

'Now it may seem to you,' he'd say, 'that we're only uncovering a few old waterlogged pieces of timber. But what we're really after is the thinking of the people who put these objects in this place. Their beliefs, their ideals, their intentions are all present with these sodden old logs – along with information about the kinds of tools they used to fell the trees, or to bind them into a trackway, the system of labour it took to accomplish this – and these, ladies and gentlemen, are some of the only concrete clues we have as to what their whole society and way of life was like. I invite you to become the discoverers of what lies in this hallowed ground.'

Cormac remembered voicing his frustration to Gabriel at the slow pace of their work; there was always too little time, too little money and manpower to do the work as it should be done. The ground was teeming with treasure, and vital knowledge of the past was being destroyed every day.

'Aye, certainly it is. You'll get disillusioned very quickly if you begin thinking like that,' Gabriel had said. 'Patience is the first requirement in this job. It's best to remind yourself to just keep digging.'

At Clonco Bridge, Cormac turned off the main route onto the narrow road that ran past Drumcleggan Bog and Bracklyn House. The rain was still pelting down hard. The front gateway at Bracklyn resembled a graceful set of Gothic chess pieces, with arched doorways to either side of the main gate, and ravenlike birds topping each of the four capitals. A nineteenth-century add-on, he guessed, as he turned the jeep down the long gravel drive; the gate's original purpose was assuredly more for ostentation than for defence.

The deep wooded area around the estate's perimeter gave way almost immediately beyond the gate to a circular drive at the front entrance of the house. Within the circle stood a formal geometric garden, separate triangles of rosebushes enclosed by a miniature box hedge. Though the place did not seem uncared for, exactly, the grass was unevenly trimmed and overrun with clover and daisies, and the strict edges of the formal garden had been noticeably softened by time. This approach had once enjoyed better days, and Cormac sensed the effort it took to keep the wildness at bay.

He parked a short distance from the house along the curve of the drive, and sat in the jeep for a moment to see whether the rain might let up. Bracklyn House itself was a well-proportioned Jacobean mansion, much larger than he had imagined upon his first glimpse of it from the road. The building's original function as fortress was still evident, from the thickness of the stone walls and the firing holes in its four-square flanking towers. But the profusion of windows also told him that this house had probably been built sometime in the early seventeenth century, a short period of peace when Ireland's aristocracy began forsaking their thick-walled towers in favour of houses that offered grand vistas of their surrounding lands. Their optimism came about a century too soon, however; some of them would have done better to keep their easily defensible fortresses in the face of the invading English. The country was littered with the burned-out ruins of such houses.

The rain only seemed to be coming down harder; he'd have to make a run for it. Grabbing his bag, Cormac sprinted across the gravel and up the semi-circular steps. He was soaked to the skin, and glad to find the front door unlocked, as Osborne had said it would be. Pushing against the four-inch thickness of oak, he found himself in a formal front hall with a black-and-white marble floor, dark wood-panelled walls, and a huge brass chandelier, under which stood a pedestal table bearing a huge arrangement of long-stemmed red tulips and bright yellow budding twigs. All was still but for the echoing *tock, tock, tock* of a large grandfather clock which stood against the wall at the foot of the massive oak staircase. Cormac set his case down beside the door; he was dripping all over the floor, and didn't want to venture any farther without making his presence known. He tried shouting a couple of hullos, but there was no response, so he began pulling off his sodden jacket.

'May I help you?' The female voice came from above; the accent was English and decidedly upper-class. The woman had begun to descend the last turn in the stairs, and Cormac sensed her dismay at finding him in the front hall of Bracklyn House. She was extremely thin and plain of face, but impeccably groomed, her dark hair swept up at the back and her nails manicured into perfect ovals. She wore a pale brown sweater set and a finely-pleated wool skirt in shades of brown and black, cut in a style that flattered her slender figure. The woman's age was difficult to discern; her angular countenance was unlined, but her ivory skin had a translucent cast, and her hands were beginning to show the first sinuous signs of aging. Cormac imagined that if she were nearer, he might see a fine network of lines radiating from the corners of her eyes. She descended unhurriedly, conveying a sense of urgency without losing an ounce of her carefully cultivated air of decorum.

'I'm sorry, but this is a private home; we don't offer public tours. I'm sure the local tourist office has a complete list of nearby houses that are open to the public.'

She strode briskly past him to the arched doorway and, grasping the iron ring handle with both hands, swung the door open, though it took all her strength. Cormac was unprepared for the hardness in the woman's pale grey eyes. He had just opened his mouth to explain when Hugh Osborne's voice sounded on the staircase behind him.

'I see you've met our guest,' Osborne said, loping easily

down the stairs. He seemed to assume that Cormac had just entered through the open door. 'My cousin, Lucy Osborne; Lucy, this is Cormac Maguire, the archaeologist I told you about. I may have neglected to mention that he'll be staying here with us while he oversees the excavation at the priory.'

An instant transformation took place in Lucy Osborne's eyes. She smiled and extended her hand. As he took it, Cormac was struck by the sinewy strength beneath her cool, dry skin. 'Welcome to Bracklyn House,' she said. 'I do hope you'll forgive my mistake. We sometimes get the odd tourist wandering in off the road. It's not something we like to encourage; I'm sure you understand.'

'I'm sorry I forgot to mention it, Lucy,' said Hugh. 'We only just made the arrangements yesterday. I thought I'd put him in the green bedroom, if that's all right?'

She nodded. 'Yes, quite.'

'You'll find in pretty short order that Lucy runs the household,' Osborne said. 'Things would most certainly fall apart without her.'

Lucy acknowledged this small bit of flattery with a slight, almost imperceptible tightening of her smile. 'I hope you have a very pleasant stay with us,' she said. 'You will let me know if you need anything at all, won't you?' And with that, she turned and disappeared through the doorway under the stairs.

'Excuse me for a moment,' Hugh Osborne said as he hurried after her. All Cormac could hear was a brief murmured exchange, too low for him to make out what they were saying. Osborne soon returned, looking slightly preoccupied.

'Sorry about that. She dreads leaving the front door unlocked, but I refuse to live in a fortress – ironic as that might seem.' He finally noticed that Cormac's clothes were creating a standing pool of rainwater. 'God, I'm sorry, I didn't realize you were dripping. Come on, I'll show you to your room.'

'There's something I really ought to mention right away,' Cormac said. 'I thought it might be a good idea to enlist some help for this project – I hope you don't mind. There'd be no extra expense. I found a volunteer, Nora Gavin – Dr Gavin, I should say – the colleague who was here with me out on the bog.' He watched the shadow of that strange day pass over Hugh Osborne's face. 'I'm very sorry about springing this on you, I should have mentioned it when I phoned.'

'She's arriving here this evening?' Cormac couldn't tell whether Osborne was displeased, or merely trying to work out the logistics.

'She said she might be able to make it by around six. If it's any extra trouble—'

'No trouble at all. I'll just ask Lucy to ready another guest room.'

Hugh Osborne led the way up the massive staircase hung with paintings of richly dressed men from various periods.

'Family portraits?' Cormac asked.

'Rogues' gallery is more like it. The first blackguard, there at the bottom,' Osborne said, stopping to point out the picture of a dark-haired man in a stiff white collar, 'is Hugo Osborne, the first of the family to settle in Ireland. He actually worked for William Petty – I assume you've heard of him – the chap who did the first complete ordnance survey maps of Ireland. They all came here as adventurers, part of Cromwell's grand resettlement scheme in the 1650s. Hugo basically robbed the whole of this estate from a family called O'Flaherty, first getting them shifted west, then making sure the family's only son and heir was shipped off to a life of penal servitude in the colonies. The next chap there beside Hugo is his ne'er-do-well son, Edmund.' Cormac paused in front of a handsome ginger-haired character in a richly brocaded coat and breeches, and was dumbfounded by the resemblance between Hugh Osborne's features – particularly the heavy-lidded eyes and handsomely cleft chin – and those of his distant ancestor, who no doubt had led his own guests up this same staircase four centuries ago.

Chapter 2

At twenty minutes past six o'clock, Nora Gavin pressed the doorbell at the front entrance to Bracklyn House and waited. She felt uncomfortable about meeting Cormac again after last night. The memory made her face burn; she reached up and touched the place his fingers had rested. She'd been completely shocked. And what had she said to him? Something about being a coward? He must think her very odd. Glancing up, she noticed an overhang jutting out from the storey above, and counted three openings above her head, all apparently blocked with mortar and stone. She heard the heavy door open behind her, and turned to find Hugh Osborne framed in the Gothic arch.

'Dr Gavin? We've been expecting you.'

Having only seen him briefly out on the bog, Nora was disconcerted by the impression Hugh Osborne made face-to-face. He was dressed more formally now, and was taller and more powerful than she remembered, with strong bones and a weathered complexion that made him undeniably attractive. The deepset, hooded eyes regarded her with equanimity. But you could look directly into the eyes of a killer and see nothing at all untoward; she knew because she had done it. Osborne obviously had no recollection of her, which was just as well.

'I was wondering about this—' She pointed upward. 'I'm not even sure what to call it.'

'A machicolation. Something the original owners would've installed for dropping stones or boiling water on unwanted visitors. We don't actually use it any more, as you can see.' Nora studied Osborne's benign expression. Getting rid of a body was no simple task – two bodies must be much more difficult. How had he done it? And how had he got away with it this long?

'You're in time for supper,' he said, 'but perhaps you'd like to see where you'll be staying first.' She followed him up the huge main staircase, noting his silent, measured footsteps on the Oriental carpeting beneath their feet. Upstairs, he led her halfway down the central corridor. He pushed open a door and stepped aside, gesturing for Nora to enter. A heavy four-poster bed dominated the room, which was darkly panelled and even more darkly furnished. The windows were draped in a heavy wine-coloured brocade. The effect was impressive, if rather gloomy.

'I apologize if the room is a bit musty. It's been a long time since we had visitors.'

'I'm sure I'll be fine,' she said.

'Good. Supper's in the kitchen – below the hall where you came in; just go through the door under the main staircase.'

Nora heard a knock as she lifted her small case onto the bed. Cormac stuck his head through the open door.

'Thought I heard voices, but I wasn't sure. My room's all the way down at the other end of the corridor. Anyway, welcome.'

'Thanks again for letting me come along. Cormac, I'm sorry about last night . . .'

Even from across the room, she could feel his warm

eyes envelop her. 'Don't worry about it. I was out of line. See you below?'

'Wait, I have something to show you – can you come in for a second? You might want to shut the door.' She reached into her briefcase and pulled out a file as he joined her beside the bed. 'Have a look at those.' Cormac sat on the bed to scan the first few photographs, the documentary shots from the conservation lab.

'Keep going.' He flipped through the prints until he came to several grainy, indistinct images, video stills from the endoscopic exam.

'That's it,' Nora said. 'The piece of metal in the girl's mouth that showed up on the X-rays. You still can't see what it is. But we've got to wait for official approval from the museum before trying to remove it.'

'Any more about the cause of death?'

'Well, Drummond concurred that there's no evidence of blunt trauma to the head. There's also no evidence of strangulation. I told him my idea about execution, and he agrees that it's one possibility, especially given that flap of skin missing from her chin. But he says the remains are too old and too fragile for the definitive tests that would say whether decapitation occurred pre- or post-mortem.'

'I suppose it's as much as we can expect,' Cormac said, still studying the video image. 'May I keep these?'

'Of course.' She hoped her next question wouldn't sound too pointed. 'You've met Hugh Osborne a couple of times now, Cormac. What's your impression?'

'I've hardly seen him since I arrived. I wouldn't say he's overly friendly, but that's understandable. We're only here to do a job for him.'

'Did he say anything about what happened out at the bog?'

'No. The longest conversation we had was about his family, all those portraits on the stairs. Evidently his branch of the family came to Ireland with Cromwell.' A person couldn't have Irish connections and avoid hearing about Oliver Cromwell's legacy: the dispossession and transplantation of Catholic landowners, the half million who died and the thousands more who were transported or sold into slavery in the colonies.

'He said the man in the painting at the bottom of the stairs, Hugo Osborne, got this house and lands from an Irishman named O'Flaherty.'

'I'm amazed that he'd go into all that.'

'It is more than three hundred and fifty years ago, Nora. I don't think Osborne can be unacquainted with his family's reputation, any more than he's ignorant of what people are saying behind his own back now.'

Chapter 3

Nora spent the entire meal studying Hugh Osborne. He'd put together a fine curry for supper, and while she watched the two men eat heartily, Nora found she wasn't the least bit hungry. She was picking at the remains of her dinner when the outside door opened, and a boy about seventeen years of age stumbled into the kitchen. His dark hair was severely cropped, and his dirty sweater, several sizes too large, hung on his slender frame. After a brief silence Osborne said, 'I'm glad you're back.' The boy looked down at the floor and tried to brush past them, but tripped and staggered directly into Nora; his right hand struck her wineglass, which tipped over the edge of the table and smashed to pieces on the flagstone floor. She tried to catch him, but he fell heavily against her, his face pressing into her chest. He seemed to think this was terribly funny, and let out a half-strangled chuckle, filling her nostrils with his volatile whiskey breath.

'Are you all right?' she asked, taking the boy by the shoulders and setting him upright. He swayed, but remained standing.

'Jeremy,' Hugh said, 'please be careful of the glass there.' The boy stood in front of Nora for a moment longer, his dark, glassy eyes staring as though he could barely see her through a haze. Despite being thin and dirty, not to mention flushed and red-eyed from drink at the moment, he was extremely beautiful, in an almost feminine way, with long eyelashes, and flawless porcelain skin.

'Don't mind me,' the boy said thickly. 'Carry on.' He turned and made a shaky retreat out the door that led upstairs.

'I'm terribly, terribly sorry,' Osborne said to her. 'Are you all right?'

'I'm fine. Please, it was nothing, an accident. But maybe we should get rid of this broken glass before anybody steps on it.' Nora stooped to gather up the larger pieces, and as Hugh Osborne went into the hall to fetch a broom, she whispered to Cormac: 'Devaney never said—'

Hugh Osborne evidently overheard her. 'Jeremy doesn't belong to me. He's Lucy's son.' A slight upward movement of Cormac's eyebrows indicated his surprise, and Nora wondered what the mother must be like. While Osborne finished sweeping up the glass, she began to clear away the table.

'Jeremy and his mother live here with you?' she asked.

'Yes,' said Osborne. 'They came here from England eight years ago, after Jeremy's father died. Daniel was a distant cousin; we only met at university. But I never had much in the way of family, so I rather enjoyed having a cousin.'

'What happened to him?' Nora asked. Hugh Osborne looked at her cautiously, as if he'd spoken to strangers once too often and regretted it, but he continued.

'A suicide. He apparently made some rather questionable investments, and lost everything. I gather there was a possibility of criminal prosecution as well. I suppose he couldn't face it. He, ah—' Here Osborne paused, as if he'd momentarily lost his train of thought. 'He shot himself. Jeremy was the one who found him.'

'God help him,' Cormac murmured.

'Everything they had – including Lucy's family home – had to be sold to pay off the debt. She and Jeremy had nowhere else to go, so I offered them a place here. It was her own idea to take up the housekeeping; it's not something I would have asked. And I must say she's been a rock—' Here Osborne stopped, as if suddenly aware that his guests were devoting their full attention to him.

'I'm sorry,' he said. 'I shouldn't burden you with family troubles.' With deliberate care, he placed the last piece of crockery in the sink. 'I'll show you the priory plans now, shall I?'

'I've never been big on pseudo-thatched cottage tourism,' he continued, on the way up the stairs. 'Such a blatant swindle, all of it, and not even necessary. I'm convinced that most people would be interested in a more honest approach to the history and culture of a place, if you'd give them half a chance.'

In his library, Hugh Osborne unrolled a rather unwieldy blueprint across his desk. 'This first drawing is the priory and grounds as they exist now. Here's the area we're planning to develop. The priory itself was excavated about six years ago, and is actually maintained by Dúchas – the Heritage Service. But recent gradiometer and magnetometer readings show areas of disturbed soil here. They're well outside the newer priory enclosure, but very near where we'd planned to put the new buildings. That's what we need to take a look at before we can put in the gas and electric lines to the site.' Cormac was studying the irregular shapes on the drawing, evidently trying to decipher what they could mean.

'This drawing,' Osborne said, pulling a second plan

from beneath the first, shows the existing priory, and the new workshop buildings in the adjacent field. We'll have room for three potters along the west wall, with a kiln here in the northwest corner; metal, glass, and woodworkers here on the southern wall; and weaving studios and dyeworks along the east. The whole complex will generate its own power with solar panels and a wind turbine. Half of this larger building has been designated as a shop for the artists, and the other half as an open public space, where we can serve food but also hold meetings and lectures, or concerts, that sort of thing. We hope to add an interpretive element that will explain the site's archaeology, and eventually a separate interpretive centre focusing on the nearby bog habitat.'

'I understand there's some controversy about Drumcleggan,' Cormac said. 'I've seen all sorts of signs posted along the road. Anything we should be concerned about?'

Hugh Osborne sighed. 'I hope not. Drumcleggan has just been designated as a Special Area of Conservation, to bring us in line with other countries in the European Community. Essentially, that means turf-cutting isn't going to be allowed for much longer. Machine cutting is already banned outright. People around here have always relied on turf for fuel, and it's almost impossible to get them to think about the long-term impact that has on the environment. The government have recently exempted people who hand-cut turf for their own domestic use for another ten years, but it hasn't really assuaged any fears. Those signs have been posted all over the place.'

'A sort of citizens' protest?' Cormac asked.

'I suppose. There's been a whole lot of rumour and speculation, and claims that some boundaries have been changed to suit developers, myself included.'

'And have they?' Nora's question was a bit blunter

than she'd intended, but Osborne didn't appear to take offence.

'No,' he said, 'but tempers are a bit frayed. People around here are sensitive about outsiders telling them what they can and cannot do – and it's understandable enough, I suppose, given their history.'

'What does Drumcleggan actually mean?' Nora asked.

'"Ridge of the skull,"' Cormac said.

'Right,' said Osborne, observing Cormac with the eager anticipation of a man whose obsession has found its way into conversation by happy accident. 'Are you interested in place-names?'

'Interested, but not very knowledgeable, I'm afraid.'

'It's my main area of study, so I'm liable to get carried away. I'll endeavour not to bore you too often on the subject.'

'I'd enjoy hearing more about it,' Cormac said. 'I don't suppose there's very much historical information on the priory itself.'

'Not as much as I'd like. The existing buildings date from the twelfth century. Its most recent incarnation was the family chapel, but there was a fire in 1660, and it was never rebuilt. I have a copy of the old report on file at Dúchas. You can have a look through it if you like.' He dug a thick manuscript from a drawer and passed it to Nora.

> Nothing remains of the first monastery founded here by Saint Dálach, who died around 809. Some time after 1140, the O'Flaherty family founded a priory for the Augustinian Canons for whom the existing church was built in the late 12th or early 13th century, one of several Augustinian houses in the area. After a disastrous fire in 1404, the priory was

> restored on a much grander scale. By the mid 15th century the monastery had become corrupt, and in 1443, the Pope took the priory under his protection. The monastery was dissolved around 1540, but the Augustinian friars returned in 1632 when they subdivided the church, and remained until 1650. A fire in 1660 destroyed the newer complex. There is a fine west doorway inserted in 1471 showing Saint Michael, Saint John, Saint Catherine, and Saint Augustine. Other notable fifteenth-century features include a vaulted rood screen, east window, and portion of the cloister arcade.

'You know, if you don't mind,' Cormac said, 'I think I should fetch down my own maps. I won't be a minute.'

'Great enthusiasm for his work,' Hugh Osborne said to Nora when they were alone.

'He has that.'

'Listen, if you'd like to turn in, do, by all means – don't feel as if you've got to stay here.'

'I'm fine.'

'It's just that we really should go over these drawings if he's planning to begin first thing in the morning.'

'No, it's actually very interesting . . .' Nora said, her voice trailing off as her gaze fell upon a silver-framed photograph of a dark-haired woman and child on the table behind Osborne's desk. The woman's coffee-coloured skin, dark hair, and sloe eyes were reiterated in the features of the child she held facing her. One of the baby's chubby hands reached out to touch his mother's face. Hugh Osborne evidently registered the picture's effect, because when Nora raised her eyes, his frankly wary look told her he knew everything she'd heard about him. 'Yes,' he said. 'My wife and son.'

Nora searched for a hint of denial in his eyes, and found none. They both looked away. She knew that her own countenance too often betrayed what she was feeling. What had he seen in her eyes? She suspected that in future she and Hugh Osborne would observe a polite but measured distance, like two magnets repelled by opposing poles. What exactly had she got herself and Cormac into here? Why had she ever considered it an acceptable idea to stay in this man's home?

'Well, we're very lucky,' Cormac said as he returned with the oversized map book. 'There's quite a lot of detail for this area.' He stopped short when he saw them. 'Have I missed something?'

'I was actually just saying good night. I think I'm going to turn in early.' Cormac looked startled, but said nothing.

'The stairs are just to your left through the next room,' Hugh Osborne said. 'I trust you can find your way.'

'I'm sure I can,' Nora said. She left the library feeling not a little disconcerted at the way the scene in the library had played out, and the way she'd reacted to Osborne's statement. What should she have said? 'I'm sorry'? What words could possibly be appropriate in addressing a bereft husband who was also the prime suspect in his wife's disappearance? The panelled door to her left was dark and heavy, with an ornate iron latch that did not move until she applied all her weight to pull it down hard. The hinges were badly in need of oil. She found herself not in the front foyer, but in another, narrower hallway, panelled with dark wood and dimly lit. This couldn't be right – it wasn't at all like the way they'd come up from the kitchen. Nora tried a door to her right, which led into a dining room furnished with a Baroque-looking table and sideboard, ornately carved with the leering faces of fauns and nymphs. The evening light was completely gone now, and in the gloom, the faces that peered out from the carved wood seemed to take malicious delight in her discomfort. She proceeded cautiously through the room to the next closed door, but when she turned one huge handle with both hands and pushed, nothing happened. She could simply retrace her steps, but that meant crossing the roomful of faces again, and besides, she'd be damned before she'd go back into that library to ask for directions. This was ridiculous. She turned and pushed once more with all her might, and at last the door gave, and sent her stumbling forward.

The room was dark, but she could see from the moonlight streaming in from the windows that the plastered walls were painted a deep shade of scarlet, and that its woodwork, including tall shutters on the windows, had been painted many times over in a glossy white. As in the library, the ceiling was elegantly coved plasterwork, but in this room curls of peeling white paint clung precariously to its surface. The floor was made from broad planks of oak, and the huge Persian carpet that very nearly covered it was threadbare. The room was decorated in a jumble of periods and styles. There were two settees, with slender carved legs, upholstered in gold damask, facing one another in front of a huge stone fireplace. Above the mantel hung a portrait of an aristocratic-looking woman in full riding habit but sans horse. An elaborately carved wooden screen and a large hookah hinted at some family member's military service in India. Along with spoils of empire, this room also held the requisite hunting trophies from a country estate: stuffed pheasants and foxes, even the huge mounted antlers of an ancient Irish elk. Though the estate must undoubtedly be worth some serious money, this room and everything in it spoke of declining fortunes at Bracklyn House.

Nora pushed open one set of heavy double doors at the far side of the sitting room. The stairs had to be close by now; she felt as though she'd been going around in circles. The next shadowy chamber was some kind of office, but much of it was draped in dustcovers. She'd gone several paces into the room when she turned and saw in the darkness before her a pair of large yellow eyes. An involuntary cry escaped her lips. To her left, a door hidden in the panelling opened suddenly, and through it came Hugh Osborne, who quickly crossed to switch on the light. Cormac followed close on his heels.

'Nora, what is it? Is everything all right?'

'I'm fine. I just got lost,' she said, peering at the thing that had startled her: in the light it was nothing but a large brown and yellow butterfly in a bell jar. Nora's eyes travelled upward and around the room. Butterflies – hundreds of them, some as tiny as bees, others with wingspans of nearly ten inches – filled nearly every inch of wall space. They were iridescent blue, and yellow, and brilliant orange, with eye spots and swallowtails, each one pierced through with a pin, neatly labelled and displayed under glass. Such beauty, but the vibrant colours and lifelike poses somehow did not make up for the fact that these lovely insects were all dead.

Hugh Osborne finally said: 'I'd quite forgotten the impression this room can make. My grandfather had rather an avid interest, for an amateur collector. I remember him drilling me on all the scientific names.'

'I've never seen so many,' Cormac said. 'Barring a museum.'

'I'm sure he intended them to end up in some museum, but in later years he lost interest in collecting.'

'What could make him give it up – apart from already having one of everything?' Cormac asked. Osborne hesitated, and Nora watched him study Cormac for a moment, apparently deciding how to answer.

'He'd been away on an expedition, and my parents were on their way to meet him off the boat in Rosslare when their car went off the road. They were both killed. My grandfather hadn't much appetite for anything after that.'

Chapter 4

'It's got to stop, Lucy, before he gets hurt, or – God help us – before he does injury to someone else.' Hugh Osborne's voice was agitated, and Cormac guessed that he was talking about Jeremy. He'd just come from taking another look at the priory plans in the library, and was returning to his room to collect the last of the gear for the morning's dig. He'd reached the landing when he heard voices coming from behind a half-open door at the top. He knew he ought not to be listening in on a private conversation, and yet he felt caught, not knowing whether to retreat or advance.

'I'm very grateful for your concern.' It was Lucy's voice. 'Heaven knows you've tried to be like a father. But most boys Jeremy's age go through a period of rebellion. Your worry is quite out of proportion.'

'He came into the house last night so drunk he could barely stand. Please, Lucy, we have to do something.'

'What can we do? He's not a child any more. I've already spoken to him on this subject more than once.' There was a pause.

'There are very good treatment programmes—'

'I won't have him taken away and locked up. I couldn't bear that, Hugh, I truly couldn't.' Their voices receded suddenly, as if they'd become aware of how loudly they'd been speaking.

Cormac began to climb the stairs once more. His eye

caught a movement in a large mirror just beside the open door, and he could see Jeremy Osborne's dark features reflected in its surface. The boy was standing in a doorway opposite the mirror; he appeared to have been listening as well. His face was deathly pale, and Cormac could see dark circles almost like bruises under his eyes. When Jeremy saw that he'd been observed, he pulled the door shut.

God, the drink was a bastard. What age could that boy have been when he found his father dead? He couldn't be more than seventeen or eighteen now, if that. Cormac remembered his own complex feelings when he was ten, and his almost complete inability to express them. He remembered his hurt and anger when his father had left them, the dreadful helplessness he felt when he looked at his mother's face.

He was sitting on the steps of his gran's house, listening to his mother and grandmother argue below in the kitchen. They didn't know he was there. He'd gone upstairs to get his hurling ball, and couldn't slip out without being seen, so he decided to wait and listen. He pulled out his pocketknife to see if he could prise up a corner of the leather on the ball to find out what was inside.

'And he told you all this in a letter?' He could hear the indignation in his grandmother's voice, her anger boiling over as she stirred the sugar into her tea with a force that threatened to shatter the cup. 'Didn't even have the courage to tell you to your face. And what about Cormac? What about looking after his own son?'

'I've told you all I know, Mam,' his mother said, sounding completely exhausted. 'Must we go over it all again?'

'What business is it of his what they do off in Bolivia—'

'It's Chile, Mammy. People are disappearing.'

'I don't care how much they need him in any godforsaken

country on earth, he belongs here with his family. He'd no business getting mixed up in all that in the first place.' They went on talking, but Cormac listened more to the sound of their voices than the actual words.

They'd received his father's letter a few days before, and he had watched first his mother's anticipation, then her anguish, which she'd tried to keep hidden but couldn't. After about an hour, she'd asked him to sit with her on the sofa. It was very important work that his daddy was doing, she'd said; he was trying to help a lot of people who were in desperate trouble, and he had to stay for another while, he didn't know how long. Daddy had written that he loved them both, but it was far too dangerous for them to be with him, and that at least for now, he had to remain where he was needed. Cormac knew there was more she wasn't telling.

The women's voices floated up to him as he sat on the steps, and he began to realize that his father would never be coming home. He looked down at what had been a perfectly good hurling ball, now a loose flap of leather and a sphere of cork, pitted and gouged from all the places he'd stuck his penknife in it.

The memory unsettled him. He remembered how often as a boy he'd wished his father ill, but it was the kind of misfortune that a ten-year-old child could imagine: that he might trip and fall, or suffer some other small humiliation. He had never actually wished his father dead. But suppose he had? And suppose his father had then died? A suicide must be even worse, he thought, remembering the hours he'd spent trying to divine if there was something he might have said or done that could have driven his father away. No wonder Jeremy Osborne was a mess.

As Cormac slung his map book under his left arm and gripped the worn leather handles of his site bag, he knew that what he saw in Jeremy's face could have been reflected in his ten-year-old self a quarter-century ago. All the wishing in the world had not altered reality, and yet life had not ended. He had survived, and the wounds had eventually scarred over. If there were only some way he could communicate that hope to Jeremy Osborne. But he was here to dig. That was all.

Chapter 5

Nora was waiting for a call from the National Museum when he left the house, so Cormac had set off for the priory on his own. As he nosed the jeep down the shaded drive, he thought about how trees had come to be a sign of privilege in Ireland. The ancient hardwood forests had been systematically destroyed and now the presence of woodland was associated with the walled estates of the English and Anglo-Irish aristocracy. In some cases, the big houses were long gone, and only the trees and walls remained as a legacy of the landlord class. Outside the gates of Bracklyn House, the woodland soon gave way to green pastures on either side. Almost at once, Cormac spied the grey stone ruins of ecclesiastical buildings off to his right and pulled onto the muddy gravel lane that led to the priory. Without all the equipment he had to transport, he might easily have walked the distance in ten minutes. The nearby fields had been fenced for cattle, and a large gate blocked the end of the lane. Osborne had arranged for an excavator to come this afternoon and clear away topsoil before they could begin on the test trenches. Slinging a camera over his shoulder and grabbing a notebook from his site kit, he climbed through the wire fence to have a look at the priory itself before making his walking survey and taking some pictures of the excavation site.

Osborne had said that Dúchas maintained the priory,

but from the state of the place, it appeared to be fairly low on the priority list. Someone had made a rather halfhearted attempt to arrange the fallen stones, and long grass grew up between them. The sweet scent of hay hung in the cool, damp morning breeze. Cormac shut his eyes and took a deep breath, letting his lungs fill with the fragrance. As much as he loved his work and enjoyed living in the city, he missed the sensory feast of the countryside. The ground was soaking from yesterday's heavy showers, but the wind was pushing the clouds steadily across the sky, occasionally letting the morning sun break through. As he entered the cloistered square, he disturbed a flock of hooded crows, which took off in a great noisy, wing-flapping crowd.

Pillared archways were all that remained of the covered walkways, built to protect the monks from the elements as they went from church to work to sleeping rooms. The knee-high remains of storerooms, kitchen, and monastic cells lined the cloister's outer rim. These stones, their worn surfaces incised with patterns, some carved into the shapes of dogs' heads, had been laid by some monastic mason 850 years ago. There was a beauty, a rightness of scale in these old buildings that stirred some aesthetic appreciation in him, and a sense of wonder about the lives of the men who had lived here. Cormac looked into each room as he passed, imagining the robed monks kneeling alongside rude rush beds; working the surrounding fields; sharing a communal meal. At the base of one of the doorways, he knelt to take a closer look at a carving of a fernlike plant he could not name, perhaps six inches in height, its curling, pinnate leaves rendered in shallow relief.

He passed through an archway, its wooden door long ago removed or consumed by fire, and stepped into the nave of a small church. Though it was roofless and full of morning light, he imagined the echoes of medieval prayers offered in the chilly hours before sunrise every day of the year, and conjured the damp, visible breath of the Augustinian brothers as they knelt together in candlelight on these stones. In the niche left by a fallen crossbeam, he glimpsed the small figure of a *síle na gig*, an ancient fertility symbol. This one was typical: a wild-eyed and armless female figure with splayed legs, her hands grasping at the outsized genitalia beneath her grotesquely swollen belly. Why these figures were often found among church ruins was an anthropological conundrum, often taken as a sign that Ireland's pagan past had never really disappeared, only receded, and that Catholicism was only a modern façade on a much more primitive and atavistic religion. After snapping a photo, Cormac recorded the location of the figure in his notebook, and continued on his survey.

An opening at the far side of the chapel framed a small rectangle of green and a larger one of blue sky. Several lichen-covered gravestones tilted into the frame as well. Off in the far corner of the enclosure was a life-sized stone figure of Christ, streaked with rust and mottled with white lichen like the surrounding stones. Its feet were submerged to the ankles in grass dotted with tiny daisies. The left arm was missing entirely, and the right was broken in several places, leaving the iron rods that had once supported stone fingers curled into a rusty fist. Despite its ruined state, Cormac felt the vital energy in the figure's naked torso, the sidelong droop of its head, and found himself strangely moved.

He backtracked to the graveyard. In among the antique graves were fresh stones; their polished surfaces and sharply incised lettering stood out against the weathered slabs from the eighteenth century and before. No doubt Hugh Osborne's parents were buried here somewhere. Cormac crouched by one of the old stones and tried to read the inscription. Vegetation and damp had obscured most of the writing, but he could make out the name, *Miles Gorman*, and the dates, *1604* to *1660*. He reached out to touch the ruffled, papery-dry edges of the yellow-green lichen that bloomed on the stone.

'If you're looking for the Osbornes, they're all under the floor inside.' The gruff voice came from about three graves away. Cormac looked up, shading his eyes against the bright sunshine, and saw Brendan McGann silhouetted against the sky. He was in shirtsleeves, and carried a hay fork. Against the sunlight, Cormac couldn't tell if Brendan's eyes held mischief or malice. How long had he been there?

'Thought you'd packed off home,' Brendan continued.

'I did. But I'm back here on a job. Hugh Osborne's asked me to—'

'That fucking squireen,' Brendan said, his face darkening. 'Never had any use for this land the past twenty years. Then he sends me a letter saying he would be "obliged" if I would shift my cattle from the pasture beyond within two weeks' time.'

'Surely you knew about his plans for the site,' Cormac said. 'He said your sister's been involved—'

'He ought to be leaving this place alone. You can see for yourself how peaceful it is. What we don't need is a lot of tourists coming around, gawping at us and clogging up the roads.'

Cormac found it hard to believe that an increase in traffic was really foremost among Brendan McGann's concerns.

'Seems like this area could do with a bit of help—' he began, but Brendan cut him off again.

'We don't need any help,' he said, looking at the ground, and the vehemence in his voice was suddenly alarming.

'The workshop seems to have a good bit of support,' Cormac said, 'I gather—'

'I don't give a fuck what you gather. If you were a wise man, you'd pack up right now and drive straight back to Dublin and let us settle things here on our own.' His words weren't quite a threat, but the next thing to it.

'As soon as I'm finished here,' Cormac said, hoping he sounded calmer than he actually felt. Did Osborne have any idea of the animosity borne him so close to home?

'No good will come of this,' Brendan said, his muscles visibly tightening. 'No good. You'll see.' Then he turned and tramped stolidly away, leaving Cormac to wonder what kind of hornet's nest he had stumbled into here. There were Osborne's missing wife and child, perhaps the victims of foul play; young Jeremy Osborne's self-destructive bent; and now Brendan McGann's seething hatred of his neighbour. He thought back to the way Brendan had glared at Osborne out on the bog, and the look on Una's face as she defended Hugh against whispered accusations about his wife's disappearance. Maybe that was it – Brendan believed, or a least harboured a strong suspicion – that his sister was involved with Hugh Osborne. And maybe he wasn't the only one – hadn't Fintan said that he wished Una would wise up?

'Hello? Cormac? Where are you?' It was Nora.

'Over here.' He heard her footsteps approaching.

'Sorry that phone call took so long. I should have been here ages ago, I know.' She came around the corner of the church, following the sound of his voice. 'You'll be happy to know it paid off. Dawson's agreed to let us remove the piece of metal that showed up in the X-rays. So that means I'll have to be back for the dental exam on Monday, but you have my full assistance until then.' She paused, waiting for his response. 'Well, isn't that good news? You do want to find out who she is, don't you?' He stood silent and frowning.

'Hello? Cormac?' Nora said, waving a hand in front of his face. 'You haven't heard a word I said.'

'No, I have, I have. But I've just been carrying on a very odd conversation myself.'

'With whom? There's nobody here.'

'Brendan McGann. He's just gone.' Cormac related the gist of his exchange with Brendan, and tried to describe what he'd seen in the man's eyes when they spoke of Osborne.

'So Brendan believes there's something between Hugh and his sister? What do you think?'

'I don't know. Hugh Osborne's a married man.'

'Whose wife has disappeared,' Nora said.

'This is none of our business anyway. Maybe we should give up speculating and try sticking to hard science while we're here.'

They unloaded the surveying equipment from the jeep and, working from the maps Hugh Osborne had provided, began to measure the site and set up markers where the excavator should begin digging. The sound of car tyres on gravel broke the silence, and soon Garrett Devaney approached them.

'How are you getting on?'

'Have you developed an interest in archaeology since we last met, Detective?' Cormac asked.

'Not exactly. I ran into Fintan McGann, and he told me what you were up to out here. I've been going through the old Osborne case file. And I thought with you working out here for a while, and staying up at the house, you might happen to pick up something useful.'

'Do you really think anybody's going to talk to us? We're strangers here.'

'You never know,' Devaney said. 'But what I had in mind was more just keeping your eyes and ears open, letting me know if you notice anything that seems out of the ordinary.' He handed each of them a card. 'The first number is the station in Loughrea, and the second is my home number; you can call at any time.'

'And what should we consider out of the ordinary?' Nora asked.

'You'll know. Why? Was there something you'd like to tell me about?'

Cormac cut in. 'No, Detective, I don't think so, just wondering what you consider strange. Perfectly innocent behaviour might appear unusual if you don't know the background.'

'Indeed. I'm not asking you to betray any confidences, only to keep your eyes and ears open. A woman and a child have gone missing. They may very well be dead, and not one suspect has ever been charged. At this point, I'm willing to follow any sort of lead.'

When Devaney had returned to his car, Nora turned to Cormac. 'You're very cautious.'

'There's a simple explanation for everything we've seen. Lots of farmers get a bit narky about traffic on the roads where they drive cattle. And lots of young lads get maggoty drunk once or twice. Not exactly front-page news.'

'You might feel different if it were someone you knew who was missing. Or dead.'

Chapter 6

Just past midday, Una McGann was working at the loom when she heard a crash from the other side of the house. Brendan was off with Fintan tending the cattle; they weren't due back until teatime, and Aoife was upstairs taking a nap after a long morning of make-believe. She stopped her shuttle to listen, trying to pinpoint where the noise was coming from. Sliding off the long bench seat, she moved quietly to the front hall, and followed the sounds to the closed door of Brendan's room, directly behind the sitting room.

Una threw open the door to find a slightly dazed-looking hooded crow peering up at her from the middle of the floor, black wings shiny against the soft grey of its back.

'Well, Jaysus, Mary, and Joseph,' she said, her surprise melting into relief that it wasn't a more dangerous intruder. 'Just let me get the broom, you dirty bugger, and you'll be outside before you know it.' She closed the door again, and retreated to the kitchen, where she fetched the broom, then opened the front door of the house. As she stepped into Brendan's room, she and the bird eyed one another, each expecting the other to make the first move. The bird turned slowly on its large claws, keeping its head cocked and one shining black eye pointed in her direction.

'Out with you now,' she said, making a sudden lunge with the broom. 'Out that door you go, now.'

But the bird opened its wings and tried to take off inside the small room, fluttering awkwardly over the bed and down behind it. Una gripped the bedpost and gave a mighty pull, then swept the astonished bird along the floor and straight out the bedroom door. Out in the hallway, it began once more to flap, but found the narrow walls too constricting, and skated on its claws toward the open front door, broom straw at its back. Outside, the bird remained grounded for only a brief instant before opening its dark wings and lifting up into the air and away.

Una's heart was pounding. She could not imagine how the bloody thing had got into the house. Brendan was usually so careful about stopping all the chimneys with netting. She returned to his room to put things right. The books on his table were all awry. She knew he wouldn't be at all pleased to know that she'd been in here messing about with his things, crow or no crow, so she tried to replace everything exactly as it had been. She straightened the coverlet on the narrow bed and was about to shove it back against the wall when she noticed a bit of paper sticking out from a hole in the plaster. There was a small hollowed-out place behind the head of the bed, with a folded sheet of paper hanging precariously from it. She smiled at the idea of Brendan keeping a secret place like a schoolboy, and was just pushing the paper back into place when she saw a bit of handwriting that spelled out her own name.

She hesitated, not wanting to intrude upon her brother's privacy, but feeling that she was entitled to read something that bore her name. Slowly she drew the paper from its crevice.

'Éire – Ireland,' the heading ran, 'BIRTH CERTIFICATE issued in pursuance of Births and Deaths Registration

Acts 1863 to 1972.' Everything was written twice, in Irish and in English. 'Ainm (má tugadh) / Name (if any),' and in the space below, 'Aoife.' Her own name was written in the space labelled 'Name and Surname and Maiden Surname of Mother.' The space under 'Name and Surname and Dwelling Place of Father' was blank.

Her first reaction was to tear up this reminder of the day, five years ago, when her daughter was born, a day that should have been a joyous celebration, but instead had been twisted into something shameful by the vaguely disapproving looks of the nurses at the hospital in Dublin. She had never told anyone who Aoife's father was, maintaining that it could have been any one of a half-dozen lads she'd known from university. Her aim had been to shock the prying busybodies, and judging from their looks she had succeeded, but it was an empty victory.

Why would Brendan have a copy of this certificate? And why should he keep it hidden? As she reached in to extract whatever else might be in the hiding place, she heard a small metallic clatter at her knee, and looked down to find a gold hair clasp. She turned it over to find two filigree elephants with their trunks entwined. Holding the clasp in her hand, feeling the weight of it, the roughness of the filigree against her fingers, Una remembered where she'd seen it before.

It was nearly three years ago now. She and Aoife had stopped in at Pilkington's to pick up a bottle of ammonia, which she used as a mordant for her dyes. She'd seen Mina Osborne standing at the counter holding her son, who was a bit younger than Aoife. The child wore a brand-new pair of red wellingtons. Mina Osborne had shifted the child from one hip to the other. The tired little boy had put a thumb in his mouth and reached up the other hand to twine his fingers in his mother's hair, and in this small gesture of self-comfort accidentally touched the clip that held her long black hair in place. The clasp had sprung open, frightening the child, who immediately began to wail, and as the mother comforted him, the hair clasp slid off and fell to the ground at Una's feet. Both women had stooped to pick it up, and Una noticed the intricate metalwork, and its distinctive design of two elephants. *What a beautiful clasp*, she had said, handing it back. Mina Osborne had looked at her so strangely that Una hoped it was not the sight of herself and Aoife that had caused the pain and sadness in those lovely dark eyes. Mina had taken the clasp with barely audible thanks and left the shop. It was the very afternoon she had disappeared.

Una looked down at the clasp in her hand. Two or three long black hairs were caught in its hinge. She reached back into Brendan's hiding place, this time pulling out a pile of carefully folded newspaper cuttings. 'Wife, Son of Local Man Missing,' said one. 'Family Appeals for Aid in Tracing Mother and Child,' read another. 'Gardaí Resume Bogland Search Today,' and finally, 'Gardaí Baffled by Disappearance.'

Why was Brendan hoarding all these things? What explanation could he possibly have? She hurriedly shoved all her discoveries back into the hole, not knowing or caring whether they were in exactly the same place. She nudged the bed back against the wall. Brendan had always been hotheaded; he'd go off by himself when he needed to think, walking the bog or the mountain, or sitting by the lake until he had worked things out or calmed down a bit. He often snapped at her and Fintan. But she'd always believed he was anything but a hard man inside. He could be very gentle with Aoife. She'd lived with her brother in this house for more than twenty years, but did she know him well? Willing her fears not to be true, Una set the pictures on the walls to rights and closed the door to Brendan's room once more. She decided to say nothing about the crow.

Chapter 7

Dunbeg reminded Cormac of his own home place in many ways: the humpback bridge, the small lace-curtained windows on the white, pink, and green pebble-dash houses that lined the only main street. The original Irish name for this place was *dún beag*, 'small fort.' It was possible that there had been no fort here for a thousand years, but the name lived on. A couple of sagging shop fronts stood abandoned, with weeds sprouting in their rain gutters, and a thin layer of soot seemed to cover everything. Even the lowering grey sky contributed to the town's pervading air of pessimism. There had obviously been a recent push to tidy up and present a good face, as evidenced by a couple of freshly painted pub fronts with hanging pots of flowers. But the roar of the Celtic Tiger had yet to be heard here, and Dunbeg was not near any of the main roads so frequented by cars full of tourists. Cormac guessed any holidaymakers here tended to be solitary anglers looking for a quiet spot to fish.

As he pulled to a stop at the kerb, a muscular, short-haired terrier and a shaggy black-and-white sheepdog ambled past, taking turns for a sniff and a piddle at each doorway, a couple of old comrades out on a spree. Cormac climbed out of the jeep and ventured towards a nearby window that displayed a miscellany typical of a small town hardware shop: a pitchfork and spade, wallpaper brushes and paint scrapers, pots and pans, clocks, locks, trowels, dog leashes, flashlights, and fishing poles. A plainly painted antique sign above the window said, 'J. Pilkington.' As he drew nearer, a white placard propped in the window caught his eye; below the quatrefoil emblem of the Garda Síochána, the national police force, was a black-and-white image of a woman and child. The notice was dated almost a year ago. Cormac stooped to read the smaller type. 'In the approach to the second anniversary of the disappearance of Mina and Christopher Osborne, the Gardaí are renewing their appeal for information that would or might help in the ongoing investigation.' The paragraphs that followed gave physical descriptions and details of what the two were last seen wearing. As he read, Cormac became aware of a pair of eyes looking intently at him from the other side of the glass. When he glanced up, the woman inside pretended to be dusting the shelves below the window.

He entered the shop, and as he went about picking up the things he'd need for the dig, had the distinct sensation that he was still being watched, though every time he raised his eyes, there was no one in sight. When he'd gathered all he needed, he proceeded to the counter.

'Can I help you find anything else, sir, or is that the lot?' piped a bright-eyed pixie of a woman. Hers was the face that had been staring at him through the front window. She was thin and dark, and wore a loud polka-dotted black smock. Her wispy haircut further emphasized her elfin character.

'I'll also need a roll of baling plastic and a half-dozen planks of wood, if you have them, about eight feet long.'

'Ah, we do,' the woman said. 'I'll get the young lad to

fetch them out for you.' She stuck her head through the doorway to the back room, and communicated his order to a red-haired boy of about fourteen who was sweeping the floor inside.

'You must be the archaeologist fella who was here before,' said the elf-woman, leaning forward on the till. Cormac smiled faintly.

'I am.'

'Dolly Pilkington's my name. You're very welcome to Dunbeg.'

'Cormac Maguire. I have a letter here somewhere from Hugh Osborne, giving me leave to charge these things to his account,' he said, patting his various pockets to locate the paper.

'Now, don't trouble yourself, there's no need for that at all.' She began totting up his purchases with pencil and paper. 'I don't suppose there's any news on your bog person then?' she asked. 'Oh Lord, you should have heard the rumours flying here a few days ago. Horrible they were, too. Desperate stories about murderers and banshees. There was grown men and women didn't sleep in their beds that night, I'm tellin' you.'

'I heard it was somebody's chopped-off head,' said the freckly red-haired boy, who'd returned with the plastic sheeting and boards.

'This conversation is none of your concern,' said Mrs Pilkington. 'Set those things outside the door, and then back on the broom with you, before I give you a box.' The boy's lower lip jutted defiantly, but he did as he was told.

Cormac was unsure how to respond, knowing that the next person to make a purchase at Pilkington's would no doubt emerge with as much knowledge of the *cailín rua* as he was willing to divulge. But better they should have the basic facts than to let rumours breed. 'We really don't have much information at all at this point,' he said, 'apart from the fact that it's a young woman with red hair.' He searched for the least sensational combination of words. 'And we didn't find her body.'

Mrs Pilkington made a hurried sign of the cross. 'Be the holy mother o' God. Well, of course the first thing we all thought was that it was the pair of them,' she said, pointing towards the placard in the window. 'And wasn't it strange that Mr Osborne was right here in the shop, standing where you are now, when my Oliver came in with the news about a body bein' found in the bog – well, I suppose you're after saying it wasn't a body at all, but we didn't know that at the time, now, did we? Anyway, poor Mr Osborne went pale, so he did, the very same as the colour of chalk, and took hold of Oliver by the shoulders, asking where had he heard it, and where did they say it was, and was he certain he'd heard it right, till I thought he'd shake the life out of the poor lad. And as soon as Oliver answered, he bolted straight out that door, never even waited for his packages or his change. I had to send Oliver round with the parcels and the money this morning, because he never came back for them, not that day, nor the next, isn't that so, Oliver?'

'Yeh,' the boy said glumly, without looking up. Cormac guessed that he'd been called upon to corroborate his mother's story more than once before in this manner.

'Why was it strange that Osborne was here?' Cormac asked.

'Because this is the last place we saw his missus and the little lad before they disappeared,' said Mrs Pilkington. 'Dreadful, isn't it? They used always to be coming in here, you know, a very nice quiet lady she was – a proper Catholic, too, though you mightn't think it to look at her, she was as dark as a black African, that one. And little Christopher. He'd always stop and say hello to me when he came into the village with his daddy. Such lovely manners, he had, for such a small little lad. Do you have any children yourself, Mr Maguire?'

'I'm not married.'

'Well, sure, the want of a wedding doesn't stop them,' she said. 'There's plenty around here proof enough of that. Ah, but you're better off as you are, really, for all the heartache you'd suffer with them.' Cormac glanced over at Oliver Pilkington's bowed head, and wondered what heartache he'd been responsible for thus far.

'What do people make of it – the disappearance?' Cormac asked.

'Depends on them you speak to. Now, I don't hold with gossiping. I'll tell you straight out. It's a sin. There's some round here and they've nothing better to do than sit and natter about other people's misfortunes. For instance,' she said, suddenly lowering her voice, 'there's a few would be delighted to tell you how Mr Osborne's always had a bit of a name for himself as Jack the lad; they say the wife got fed up with his carryings-on, and took the child and ran off. Some look at the money he's to get from the insurance and say she's murdered in the bog and he's the one that done it. Ah God, it's shocking altogether, what people will say.' She gestured dramatically, as if she could bear to talk about it no longer.

'So what do you think yourself?'

Dolly Pilkington's eyes narrowed, and she regarded Cormac as if trying to decide whether he could be trusted. Evidently he passed muster, for she gestured for him to come closer so that she could speak more quietly. 'I can only tell you the same thing I told the police. Missus Osborne was upset over something that day she went missing. You could see she'd been crying her eyes out, poor thing. I don't believe she and the child are still walking this earth,' she whispered, 'God forgive me for saying such a thing. It's just a feeling. But I can't credit the husband having any hand in it. No way.'

'Why not?'

'Because he was standing right before me where you are now when he got the news about the bog. The very spot, and he was absolutely devastated. Nobody could just put on something like that.' Cormac pitied anyone who might try to budge Dolly Pilkington's opinion on the matter. 'Now ask me about some others, and I might be able to tell you a few things,' she continued. 'That cousin of his, she's a quare customer if ever there was one, and the young lad—' She clucked and gasped and crossed herself again. 'So wild! I get down on me two knees every day and thank God my Oliver's not that way inclined.' Sensing another imminent tirade, Cormac tried desperately to steer her off.

'Ah – I wonder, Mrs Pilkington, you seem very knowledgeable. I'm trying to find out whatever I can about the girl in the bog, and I wonder if you could help me locate any local historical records.'

'Well, there's the Heritage Centre over in Woodford.'

'And what sorts of documents might they have?'

'Ah, sure, I wouldn't have a clue. I just know they have loads of Americans going up there searching for their "roots".'

'What about anybody who has a particular interest in the local history or folklore?' He waited while Dolly Pilkington measured his words, and endeavouring not to boast, she said: 'Well, there's nothing happened here in the last fifty years I wouldn't know about, meself, you know.'

'I'm afraid we might have to go back a bit further than that. The bank of turf where the girl was found hasn't been cut in the last hundred years or so, maybe even longer.'

'Is that so? Well, in that case, I'd go and speak to Ned Raftery if I was you.'

'The schoolteacher?'

'The very same – or used to be, I should say, before he lost his eyesight, God bless him. You'd think being stone blind was not a bother on him at all. Why, he was in here the other day, buying a garden shears, if you don't mind, and what do you think he's going to get up to with them things?'

Chapter 8

While Cormac was in town, Nora showered off the muck and sweat of the day's work. They'd only scratched the surface at the excavation site, but her muscles ached from wielding a shovel all afternoon. As the water coursed down her limbs, she remembered the policeman's words: *At this point, I'm willing to follow any sort of lead.*

She dressed and decided to go in search of Cormac; maybe by now he'd returned from the village. The hallway was a twisting maze of right angles, its dark wood wainscoting featuring the same carved motif she had seen in the downstairs rooms, but the wood was cracked in places and looked in need of repair. Just outside her room, however, she noticed an open door leading into a side stairwell. The space was darker, narrower, and much less grand than the carved masterpiece of open stairwork to the ground floor. There was no illumination here, apart from the wan daylight that struggled through a narrow and dusty leaded-glass window on the landing, and not a whisper from above or below. Casting a quick glance back down the hallway, Nora ventured upward.

The few small rooms directly at the top of the stairs seemed to be used for storage. The largest door opened into a long gallery-like space. Unlike the rest of the house, this room was sparsely furnished, and filled with light. About a dozen blank stretched canvases were stacked against the wall, and a large easel draped with a scrap of linen canvas stood in the centre of the bare wood floor. A few finished but unframed paintings leaned against the bits of furniture around the room. Nora stepped closer to the nearest canvas. Its central subject was a pair of detached, slightly abstracted white wings. The painting's surface had the texture of a decaying fresco, and its background was filled with shadowy images of exotic plants and animals behind a veil of golden light. She could make out a few scarlet petals of a flower, the sinuous curve of a snake, and the irregular spots on a leopard's shadowy flank – like a hazy impression of some unreachable Eden. Each canvas was more obscure than the last, until the elements had become completely abstracted, like a dream retreating into the subconscious at the moment of waking. On the easel, she found an unfinished canvas in which she could see the painter's technique of layering and scraping that gave these works their unique texture and depth. The table beside her was filled with tubes of paint and jars full of brushes. Nothing out of the ordinary for an artist's studio, but how curious that most of the items were brand-new, and unused. Nora ran her fingers over the thick bristles of one brush. There were no curtains on the windows, and she finally noticed that this room offered a breathtaking view of the lake, and a small island about a hundred yards from shore.

She paused for a moment. Had she heard something? It came again, the barely audible but unmistakable pitch of a child's voice. The sound seemed to be coming from the stairwell. Nora abandoned the silent paintings, and retraced her steps to the floor below.

She approached the door just opposite her own and tried the handle. Locked. She continued down the hall, until she heard a child's laughter, closer this time. 'No, you,' came a small voice, followed by a low adult murmur. 'No, Mummy, you.' The voice came from a room just past the main staircase, whose door was slightly ajar. Nora knew she shouldn't, but felt compelled. She knocked at the door. No reply. She pushed it slowly open. This room was full of dark, ornately carved furniture, much like her own. There was no one here, but a television in a large corner cabinet was on, and the video image showed the same woman and child Nora had seen in the photograph downstairs. The little boy was older here, a toddler now, sitting on his mother's lap. Her back was to the camera. The mother leaned forward, pretending to tickle the little boy; he shrieked with helpless delight. Who had left this tape running? It couldn't have been Hugh Osborne; he'd been away all day teaching at the university in Galway. That left Jeremy, or Lucy Osborne, whom Nora had yet to meet. She switched off the television and video player, and suddenly realized that she was probably in Hugh Osborne's bedroom. She was paralysed for a moment by feelings of both guilt and curiosity, and had to fight a sudden urge to fling open the wardrobe doors and dig through the chest of drawers. How absurd to think that she might discover something that the police had missed. And yet she couldn't leave, not yet. She walked around the huge four-poster bed, which Hugh Osborne must once have shared with his wife.

What was it that made a person think he could just discard another human being, like something he'd got the best use of and no longer needed? The one thing that she could not begin to fathom was the frightening absence of feeling such an act must require – not even a lack of love or tenderness, but simple fellow feeling. Nora closed her eyes; when she opened them, she saw another door straight ahead of her. Crossing the threshold, she saw that it was a child's room, a nursery. An old rocking horse stood in one corner, sporting a painted saddle on its well-worn hide, and a real horsehair tail. A small table and chairs, a toy box, a brightly painted wardrobe, and a chest of drawers completed the furnishings. The air in the room was cool and musty, as in the studio upstairs, as if it had been closed up for a long time. She crossed to the nearest window and pulled it open, drinking in the freshness of the scented spring air. Only then did she turn and notice the figure in the bed. Jeremy Osborne was much too large for the child's cot, but lay curled up on his side. The coverlet was half-heartedly drawn around him, as if he'd grown cold but couldn't manage to pull it up properly. Abruptly awakened, Jeremy sat up looking slightly disoriented, but also as if he might bolt for the door. He wore the same clothes he'd had on the night before.

'Hello again,' she said, and from the deep flush rising in the boy's cheeks she surmised that he remembered their first meeting all too well, despite his considerable state of inebriation at the time.

'Sorry, I heard the television and didn't realize anyone was in here.' Jeremy said nothing, and looked as if he wished he could disappear. He made a feeble attempt to smooth the coverlet beside him. 'I'm afraid we got off on the wrong foot last night. What if we forget about it, and start again?' Still no response. 'It was you looking at that video, wasn't it?' Jeremy Osborne looked up for the first time, and Nora thought she saw the faint glimmer of hope in his eyes, only to see it abruptly extinguished.

'You must be Miss Gavin,' said a woman's voice from

the doorway. Nora turned to the elegant, smoothly-coiffed woman standing at her elbow. 'I'm sorry I haven't had the opportunity to meet you before; I'm Lucy Osborne.'

'Please call me Nora.'

'What part of America are you from?' Lucy asked. Her cool fingers pressed lightly into Nora's warm palm.

'Minnesota,' said Nora, aware that this probably meant nothing to Lucy Osborne. 'The Midwest. I was actually born in Clare, but my parents emigrated when I was very young.'

'And what made you decide to return to Ireland?' Lucy asked pleasantly, crossing to close and latch the window Nora had left open.

'A temporary teaching job at Trinity College. But I've spent summers here since I was a child. It's always seemed like home to me.'

'I'm sure it has,' Lucy said, with the slightest glance around the room that suggested Nora shouldn't be feeling quite so much at home here. She changed the subject. 'Hugh phoned a short while ago to say that he mightn't make it home in time for your evening meal, so I've taken the liberty of preparing a cold supper for you.'

'That's very kind. Cormac should be back very shortly, if you wouldn't mind waiting.'

The polite smile that crossed Lucy Osborne's face suggested that Nora had a lot to learn about the inhabitants of Bracklyn House. 'Jeremy and I usually take our supper in my sitting room.' Lucy crossed to the bed, where her son sat staring silently at the carpet.

'Are you feeling all right, darling? You look a bit pale.' She pressed the back of a hand to his forehead. He still said nothing, so she straightened his collar, which had got tucked in on itself. The boy's reaction to this motherly gesture was nothing more than a slight shrug of one shoulder, but it did not escape Nora's attention. From below came the sound of a car on the gravel driveway.

'That must be Cormac now,' Nora said.

'If you'd like to go down to the kitchen,' Lucy said. Nora gathered that it was not really a suggestion.

'It was very kind of you to fix a meal—'

'Nonsense, you're our guests,' Lucy said, finally taking her eyes from her son's face. 'Run along, now, my dear.'

As Nora turned to pull the door closed behind her, she caught a glimpse of mother and son sitting together on the edge of the small bed. Jeremy's hands still rested, inert, in his lap. Lucy put one hand up to stroke the hair at the nape of his neck once more, and again, he seemed to tense slightly at her touch. Lucy inclined her head until it was touching Jeremy's, and whispered something in his ear. He made no reply, but nodded twice. Lucy said something more, and although his dark head remained downcast, Nora could have sworn that on the boy's lips played the barest suggestion of a reluctant smile.

Chapter 9

'I don't know about you,' Nora said to Cormac as they were finishing their meal in the kitchen, 'but I find this place depressing as hell. Would you like to go for a walk or something? We've a good hour of daylight left.'

'I was going to try to write up some notes from the dig—' he began, but was stopped by Nora's incredulous look.

'We've put in nearly nine hours today already, and we haven't even had a good look around the place.' She stood up. 'Come on. Aren't you the least bit curious? Have you been down to the lake?' she asked.

'Not yet. Lead on.'

They left by the kitchen door, and walked slowly to take in the magnificent scene. The clouds had broken, and the sun was just beginning to descend, its waning golden light playing on the small, random waves that clapped together on the surface of the lake. A long expanse of green lawn stretched before them, and the forested area that surrounded the lake had been judiciously cleared to afford an almost surreally beautiful vista, a painter's landscape come to life. A hundred yards from shore on a small island stood a tumbling ruin of grey stone. The lawn sloped gently downhill toward the water, where a low shelf of earth blocked the view of the shallow, stony beachfront from the house.

'Look, there's a boat!' Nora said, pointing a short distance down the shore, and Cormac had a sudden vision of what she must have been like as a child, with a curiosity and sense of adventure that remained undiminished all these years later. Before he knew it, she was struggling to overturn the bright blue rowboat, so he leapt down the small ledge to give her a hand. The craft was small, but seemed seaworthy enough.

'Hop in,' he said to Nora, 'I'll shove off.' Once aboard, he set the yellow oars in their locks, then turned the rowboat toward the island, and began to pull against the water with long, steady strokes.

'You're a pretty handy oarsman.'

'We had a boat like this when I was a kid,' he said. 'And I still row a bit, when I have the time. It's a great place to be alone with your thoughts, out on the water.'

Within a moment or two he managed to pull the little boat alongside the island. What a place to live, exposed out here on a treeless, rocky island, at the mercy of wind and water. Some of the earliest settlements in Ireland had been built on islands in the middle of great marshy lakes, timber-fenced earthwork fortresses surrounded by water to defend against raiders. Later had come stone forts like this one, then the Norman-style tower houses, and eventually fortified mansions like Bracklyn House. All built to keep invaders out. All failing in their purpose, until they were piled, one almost on top of the other. Where in that continuum did the *cailín rua* fall? Would she ever have seen what Cormac was seeing now? What name might she have had for this island, this body of water?

The only sounds were the hollow lapping of the waves against the sturdy side of the wooden boat, and the steady creaking of the oars. They came around the far side of the island, and Cormac stopped rowing. From this distance, Bracklyn House was more impressive, more the stately fortress and less the crumbling manor house than it seemed up close. It cast a sharp, looming shadow over the brilliant emerald lawn, and the rough surface of its stone walls looked almost gilded against the faintly purpled clouds of the gathering dusk. One day, it too would be reduced to a ruin like the pile of rubble on the island. It was impossible not to think of all the human lives that had been bound up in the defence, the capture, the possession of this particular parcel of land in the long march of history. And of the lives Bracklyn House contained now, including his and Nora's, which had eventually been touched by that conflict.

He watched her, only an arm's length away in the stern of the boat. She seemed oblivious to his scrutiny, and stared down into the clear water. He was intrigued by the way Nora's dark hair fell softly against her face. What was her story? He studied the hollow at the base of her throat, the way her right hand gripped the boat's rim, the soft curve of her hip on the bench seat, remembering the abandon in the way she'd sung those words: *my generous lover, you're welcome to me.* What he felt right now, looking at Nora, was something even stronger than physical desire – though he felt that intensely, too, he had to admit. But desire was swallowed up in a larger yearning to gain entrance, to wander the rooms and passageways inside her head, her heart, if she would allow him. Of course, that meant throwing open the doors, allowing her into his own hidden places as well. And for the first time in his life, that prospect actually seemed possible.

'Nora—' he said.

'Do you think they're down there somewhere?' she asked suddenly.

Cormac felt his momentary chance dissolve. 'Who do you mean?'

'Mina Osborne and her son.'

'Devaney said the divers never found anything.'

'It's an awfully big lake.' She turned toward him. 'By the way, I met Jeremy's mother while you were in town. I heard a noise down the hall from my room. It turned out to be a video of Mina Osborne and the little boy.'

Cormac remembered the notice he'd seen in the shop window. 'Christopher.'

'Was that his name? Christopher. There was nobody watching the video, but I found Jeremy sleeping in the next room – what looked like a nursery. It was very weird. Anyway, that's when his mother made her entrance. I don't think we hit it off.'

Cormac recalled his own first encounter with Lucy Osborne. 'If it's any comfort, I didn't make a very good first impression either.'

They floated for another while, until the boat gradually drew near the shore, where O'Flaherty's Tower stood in silhouette against the darkening sky. There was no sign of the mob of crows Cormac had first seen around the tower's top.

'I've been wondering about that place,' Nora said, shielding her eyes from the sun's golden glare. 'Know anything about it?'

'Just that it's called O'Flaherty's Tower. They were the landowners here at one time. Una McGann told me it belongs to the estate. And she said it's supposed to be haunted. I don't know any more about it than that.'

'Haunted? And you asked no more about it?'

'Oh, I forgot to mention,' Cormac said, suddenly remembering his conversation with Dolly Pilkington, 'I found somebody who might tell us something about the local history. Ned Raftery, a retired schoolteacher. We'll have to phone up and see if he's willing.'

They had reached the shore again. Cormac turned the oars to stow them, then jumped out to pull the boat up the pebbly beachfront. 'I was hoping we could put in another full day on the dig tomorrow, if you're up to it. But I thought I might take care of some other things on Sunday, as long as you're heading back for the dental exam on the *cailín rua*.'

'The *what*?' Nora asked, and Cormac realized he'd never used that name before, at least not aloud. 'The red girl,' she said. Perhaps he shouldn't be surprised that she had a bit of Irish.

'I suppose we ought to call her something more official, like "the Drumcleggan girl".'

'No, I like *cailín rua*. It's like something from a song,' Nora said, taking the hand he offered her. 'I'm happy to work a full day tomorrow. And I don't actually have to be back in Dublin until Monday afternoon, so whatever you need done on Sunday, I'm happy to pitch in.'

Something in her frank blue eyes disconcerted him, and he had a sudden vision of doors being thrown open. Maybe he wasn't as ready for all this as he'd thought. 'I appreciate the offer,' he said, letting go of her hand. 'But I'm afraid Sunday's personal.'

As they climbed the small embankment, Cormac thought he glimpsed a pale figure in one of the high windows at Bracklyn House, but when he focused on the place again, whatever had caught his eye was gone.

Chapter 10

At half past nine on Saturday evening, Devaney sat at his kitchen table, disgusted that he had turned up nothing in the Osborne file. The truth was he'd barely had a chance to look at it. But this case was always on his mind. No one remembered passing Mina and Christopher on the road from town, so it was possible that they had never returned home. Or that they'd taken a different route, a shortcut away from the road. Hard to do with a pushchair, though, and everyone had seen her with it in the village.

He took a swallow of tea. Christ, he'd give anything for a cigarette right now, to help him concentrate, focus his mind on what was missing. He was going in circles.

Who stood to gain from Mina Osborne's death? Her family in India had money, but the father had supposedly disowned her when she married. That sizable insurance policy might look dodgy, but without a body, Osborne would have to wait seven years to get any money. Besides, everybody said the man was devoted to the wife – but that's what people always said, wasn't it? That's what they'd said about Barney Harrington down in Cork, who'd bludgeoned his wife with a frying pan when she criticized his cooking. The gossipmongers were having a field day now speculating about Hugh Osborne and Una McGann. Perhaps he should find out whether there was any truth to the rumours, and if so, how long the affair might have been going on. If he was going to look into the jealousy angle, why not Lucy Osborne? Say she's living at Bracklyn House for several years, getting on with Osborne like a house on fire, when he suddenly up and marries someone else. Mina's arrival must have been a blow, if Lucy'd ever had any designs on the man. Nothing stayed secret for long in a town like Dunbeg. If there was anything funny going on, Mina Osborne was bound to have found out. Maybe she had just walked away.

He opened the file, flipping past the first few witness-statement forms until he came to a statement taken by telephone from Jaronimo Gonsalves, Mina Osborne's father living in India. He had sworn that no one in the family had made contact with Mina for several years.

He ought to have a word with the parents again, Devaney thought, just to satisfy himself that they had no further information. Better to ring from the sitting room, where he could shut the door and not be disturbed. He checked the spelling again. Gonsalves. What sort of name was that? It wasn't like an Indian name at all – sounded Spanish or something. He carried the file to the sitting room as he repeated the name aloud: '*Gonsalves, Gonsalves.*' The foreign-sounding syllables felt strange on his tongue, but he repeated them until the sound started to become familiar, then picked up the phone. But what would he say? Your daughter is still missing, and we've made a complete bollocks of the case? The parents must be getting on in years. How would it affect them to have the past dredged up again? He pulled the file closer and punched in the number. A rapid *rat-a-tat-tat-tat-tat* on the other end told him it was ringing. A high-pitched woman's voice came on the line: 'Who's calling, please?'

He hadn't bothered to calculate the time difference –

it might be the middle of the night in Bombay for all he knew.

'Who is calling, please?' the tinny-sounding voice repeated, and Devaney cleared his throat.

'Detective Garrett Devaney calling from Ireland. I'm trying to reach Mr Jaronimo Gonsalves.' There was no immediate answer. Had he pronounced the name incorrectly? 'I hope I'm not ringing too late.'

There was another brief pause, during which Devaney imagined his voice travelling to India, as he heard a faint echo of what he had just said on the line. When the woman's voice responded, it sounded slightly weary, but not unkind.

'I am afraid you are too late, Detective. My husband died quite suddenly six months ago. Is there some way that I may help you? Do you have some news of my daughter?' The woman's musical accent gave away the trepidation behind her question, and Devaney cursed the most terrible duty of his profession.

'I'm afraid I have no news, Mrs Gonsalves. I'm just going back over the details, and I wanted to make sure that she still hadn't contacted you or any other family members.'

There was another pause. 'I have not heard from my daughter for the past two and a half years.'

'Excuse me?' Devaney said, thinking he must have misheard. 'Your husband said—'

'When Mina first went missing,' Mrs Gonsalves continued, 'the police spoke to my husband. He told them that he had broken with our daughter when she married Hugh Osborne, three years earlier. And that was true – for him. You see, my husband was a very strict man, a proud man, Detective. He could be very hard. But I ask you, how could a mother who has brought a child into this world, and cared for her, just turn away one day – deny her existence, simply because that child fell foolishly in love?'

'You kept in contact with your daughter?' Devaney's mind was racing; he was sure this information never appeared anywhere in the file.

'Mina and I continued our regular correspondence, without my husband's knowledge, of course. She sent her letters in care of my sister. But they suddenly stopped without warning. One week later, my husband received a call from your Irish police. He thought he spoke for both of us; how could he know he did not? I couldn't go against him. His heart was already broken. I'm only sorry I didn't contact you sooner.'

'And do you still have the letters?'

'Every one.'

'I wonder if you'd be willing to send them to me? There's a chance they might contain some detail that would help us. I will return them to you.'

'Of course, of course, anything I can do.'

'And was there—' Devaney hesitated. 'Was there ever any indication in these letters that your daughter was troubled, or in any way fearful?' He winced, hoping the last part of the question didn't betray his suspicions. There was a brief silence on the other end of the line as Mrs Gonsalves considered his question. God, his reflexes had completely gone.

'If you're asking whether my daughter was afraid of her husband, I think the answer is no. But of course there were things that troubled her. Who among us has no worries? I've no doubt that all these facts are in your files, but when you read her letters, I think you'll understand that my daughter was already carrying their child when she and Hugh were married. I think it remained a question always in the back of her mind, whether they would have married if – well, if the circumstances had been different.'

'I appreciate your frankness, Mrs. Gonsalves.'

'I know you suspect my son-in-law. And I know it's only natural in a case of this sort. But I've come to know Hugh Osborne very well, I think. I'm convinced that he loved Mina and could never harm her in any way.'

'You mean he's contacted you?' This, also, was not in the file.

'Oh, yes. He rang us when Mina first disappeared, but my husband refused to speak with him. But when he heard of my husband's death, he wrote me a letter. We've spoken on the telephone many times since then, and I would say we've become very good friends.' Unfortunately, Devaney thought, this could be either a genuine gesture on Osborne's part, or just a cold-blooded ploy to gain a powerful ally.

'All this happened just when I thought that Mina and her father might reconcile. She'd talked about coming to visit us, bringing Christopher, but—'

'Would your daughter have gone against her husband's wishes? Would she have tried to make the trip anyway, even if he opposed it?'

'I don't know. If she did, she has never arrived home. I would give anything to see my daughter's face.'

A silence fell on the telephone line. 'I'll do everything I can,' he said.

'You'll let me know any news you might discover about my child?' She seemed at once old and young, Devaney thought: young in the way that she referred to Mina as her child, and old in the knowledge that her daughter and grandson were most likely dead.

'I will, indeed. There's one more thing. Would you mind sending the letters to my home address? It's a long story, but the investigation has been transferred to a task force in Dublin. I'm not supposed to be working on the case any more.' As Devaney slowly walked her through the particulars, his heart held tandem hopes: that the letters would contain something useful, and that this decision would not get him booted from the Guards.

'I am getting to be an old woman, Detective. There are days when I am so very tired. But like you, I have not entirely given up hope. I know you will do what you can. Good night.'

Devaney hung up the phone, considering the benediction he had just received. He checked his watch. Nine forty-five. It must be nearly four in the morning in Bombay. When he returned to the kitchen, he found Róisín sitting at the kitchen table, writing in a composition book. Devaney poured himself a whiskey, then joined his daughter at the table, watching her dark head bent in concentration over her work.

'You're up very late, aren't you, Róisín? What are you writing there?'

She shrugged, but didn't look up. 'Nothing. Just things I think about.'

'And what do you think about, *a chroí*?'

'About how everything got all mixed up the way it is.' Devaney felt his heart swell in his throat.

'What we all wonder,' he said, thinking of Mrs. Gonsalves, and admiring the mixture of profound sadness and innocence in his daughter's deep blue eyes. They sat in silence for a moment, studying one another across the table. Róisín returned to her composition book, and concentrated on making a long line of curlicues across one of its thin blue rules.

'Daddy,' she said, when she had finished the last loop, 'do you think I'm too old to start playing the fiddle?'

Chapter 11

The churchyard in Kilgarvan appeared exactly the same to Cormac as it had nineteen years ago when his mother was buried there. The grey stone of the church seemed bleak against the vigorous green of the grass between the gravestones. Both the church and the grass were symbols of endurance, he thought. In the face of weather, time, the rash acts of man, both remained, one bound by tradition, staunchly resisting the forces of change, one engaged in a constant, defiant cycle of death and renewal. He walked slowly along the gravel path through the graveyard, reading the inscriptions, some moss-covered and worn with age, some newly made and sharp as the pain of loss.

He took the first left on the path, to the newer section of the walled-in yard, under a huge beech tree. He remembered hearing the gravediggers cursing as they tried to excavate the spot, running into tree roots as thick as a man's arm, having to hack through them with picks and axes before they could proceed. How well kept his mother's grave was. *Maguire*, read the Irish script on the stone; beneath that her first name, *Eilis*, and the dates. Someone had planted a small bunch of violets below the headstone. The heart-shaped leaves looked freshly watered, and grew in a thick profusion. He knelt on the grass, feeling the unmistakable ache of her absence once again.

She was growing steadily weaker, according to the nurse who looked after her while he was away at college. He had just started his second year at university, as she'd insisted, but on weekends he'd take the train from Dublin or get a lift down to be with her. One Friday in October, he'd caught an earlier train than usual – he was coming down to tell her he wasn't going back to Dublin any more. He was just thanking the salesman who'd given him a lift from Ennis when he saw his mother at the churchyard gate. She was in a wheelchair, and though he was more than a hundred yards away, he knew that the white-haired man pushing the chair was Joseph Maguire. His father. He hung back to observe them; he could see his mother's head tilt, the better to hear the voice that spoke at her ear, and he felt somehow betrayed by the way she looked up at her husband. He was still her husband. They had never gone through the formality of a legal separation. He watched his mother's frail body in the chair, her thin shoulders covered by a sweater and a Spanish shawl. When his parents entered the churchyard, Cormac crossed the street and moved closer to the gate. He watched as they moved slowly up the path. He'd taken the same walk with her only a few weeks ago, when test results had shown that further treatment was useless against the rampant cancer cells, and she had wanted to show him the place she would be buried.

He turned away and pressed his back against the gatepost, trying to work out what to do. He felt a fury of hurt and anger and jealousy. He stepped away from the kerb and began walking blindly until he reached the coast road, where he turned northward, climbed down the rocks, and began trudging along in the sand. He felt ridiculous – he was nearly a grown man, and yet he felt like that confused and abandoned child of all those years ago. He understood when he saw them together that his mother still loved Joseph

Maguire, a man who didn't deserve to be so loved. Why couldn't his father be the one who was dying? He dropped his pack on the sand, fell to his knees, and pitched forward, the pain in his chest feeling as if it would tear his rib cage apart. Hot tears seeped under his eyelids; he tried to breathe, inhaling the salty, seaweed-smelling air of the beach. How long he lay there, he did not know. She was obviously happy to see him. What could he do now but feign gratitude at the old man's return? It soothed him to think of the way things had to be. The wet sand was cool against his face, and eventually he felt a sense of calm returning. He pushed himself to his feet, brushed as much of the sand off his clothes as he could, and slung his rucksack over one shoulder for the walk back to the town . . .

The memory slowly faded. Cormac reached out one hand to touch the letters of his mother's name, then rose from his knees at the graveside, quickly retracing his route back down the gravel path and out the cemetery gate. When he was growing up, Kilgarvan had been just a single, narrow row of houses and a few shops with their backs to the sea. Now holiday homes had succeeded fishing as the main economic force, and modern, sterile-looking developments had sprung up on concrete slabs in hay fields surrounding the town. Tiny flags signified that the natural dunes above the strand had become sand traps in a golf course. He turned onto the coast road, and walked the quarter mile that used to seem endless when he was a boy. When he stopped in front of a two-storey house, now painted yellow with green trim, he was pleased to notice that the rosebushes his mother had tended so lovingly still flourished all around the edge of the front garden.

No one seemed to be about when he arrived home, but a small grey Ford with a car hire sticker was parked in the drive. He pushed open the front door and found his mother tucked up on her favourite antique chaise, her face bright with anticipation, as he had known it would be.

'Cormac,' she said, and in that instant, she saw that he already knew what she was about to tell him. She looked at him with a mixture of hope and pleading. He stood and returned her gaze, hoping that his look communicated understanding, or at least forbearance. The door from the kitchen swung open, and in backed Joseph Maguire, bearing a tea tray. 'I've set three cups,' he was saying. 'I think he's bound to turn up soon—'

He watched his father straighten out of a slightly solicitous crouch. This man was white-haired and rumpled in a professorial way, not at all the image of the dashing, dark-haired warrior he had kept in his head all these years. The two of them looked in unison toward Eilis. Her eyes shone. Speak to each other, *they urged silently.* Say something.

'Hello, Cormac,' said his father, still holding the tea tray and looking slightly ridiculous.

'Hello,' he replied. How many times had he rehearsed this scene, trying to work out what their first words might be, what great deed he might have accomplished to bring his father all the way back across the ocean? Now the moment was here, and he was surprised how little he actually felt. Perhaps he'd spent all the feeling he had out on the strand.

'I was going to tell you, Cormac,' his mother said. 'But somehow we got the dates mixed up, and your father arrived a day earlier than I anticipated.'

'Your mother wrote me,' Joseph said, still gripping the handles of the tray. Only then did it occur to Cormac that this might be awkward for his father as well. 'And we thought it would be best for me to come, to take some of the pressure off you while you're at your studies. It can't be easy travelling such a distance every weekend.'

It isn't, he wanted to say, but the real hardship was going back to Dublin at the end of each visit, knowing that she might not be here when he returned. 'I don't mind,' he said.

Cormac's thoughts were still in the past when the front door of the house opened, and out stepped a girl with pink-streaked hair, dressed in the current fashion, and tottering slightly on platform shoes. As she approached down the footpath, he decided she couldn't be more than about fifteen; her lips were painted a deep shade of blue, and three tiny gold rings pierced her left eyebrow. 'Are ye all right?' she asked. 'Are ye looking for someone?'

'No, I used to live in this house. My mother planted all these roses, and the apple tree in the back garden, if it's still there.'

'Yeh, it's there.' He could sense annoyance as the girl studied him, worried that he'd want to have a look at that, too. She was late for something, he guessed, but didn't like leaving the house with this lunatic hanging about the front gate.

'I don't mean to hold you up,' he said. 'Just wanted to see what the old place looked like.' He wondered as he walked slowly back to the church whether there was an actual physical threshold in the mind, a point at which the past filled up more of one's thoughts than the future.

Chapter 12

On Sunday evening, Garrett Devaney sat in a straight-backed kitchen chair opposite his daughter Róisín. Her head tipped toward her left shoulder, where the body of his fiddle rested, its slender neck cradled in the curve of her hand.

'There,' said Devaney, sitting back. 'How does that feel?'

'A bit strange.'

'It might feel that way at first, but you'll get used to it. It might even feel comfortable after a while. The main thing is to stay relaxed, especially here—' He reached out and pressed gently on his daughter's shoulders, observing how small and thin she felt beneath the weight of his hands. It had been a long time since he'd actually made any sort of physical contact with one of his children. 'Ready for the bow?'

'Yes,' she said firmly.

'All right.' He'd let her tighten the octagonal nut at the end of the bow, and slide the rosin block up and down its length. 'Remember that you must never touch the hairs on the bow.' He guided her fingers around the frog, placing each one where it ought to go, then let her feel the weight of it in her hand, and finally, in her whole arm. 'It all happens with the elbow and the wrist, not the shoulder – like this,' he said, demonstrating with an invisible bow. 'Keep in mind that you're making music, not sawing wood.' Róisín nodded.

'Now the fingering,' Devaney said. Leaning forward, he gently placed his daughter's fingers in the positions she would use to play a simple scale and called out the names of the notes as he did so. He waited for a moment, touched by the sincerity of her gaze as she concentrated on all the strange new sensations. Devaney felt disarmed, utterly defenceless in the presence of this fierce determination.

'Lash away,' he said, and she looked at him with eyes grown round in disbelief. 'Go ahead,' he said, 'make some noise.' She tentatively set the bow on the fiddle strings, where it bounced a couple of times, then pulled, letting the weight of it make a deep, vibrating groan. A small smile and a look of surprise and pleasure crossed her face, then she wrinkled her nose.

'Go mad,' he said. 'Try them all.'

Róisín bent the bow this way and that, testing the sonorous, deep notes, the high, thin sounds she could produce, chording two notes together as she pulled the rosin-laden bow over the strings. He gestured, showing her in mime how to use the full length of the bow, and she followed his example, at least as far as her short arms would allow. Even as he beheld the pleasure she took in these first few sounds, Devaney pictured the hurdles they still faced, and felt suddenly inadequate as a musician, as a teacher, and as a father. As he listened to Róisín's first dreadful attempt at a scale, he thought of Orla and Pádraig, and how he'd missed the few chances he had to be closer to them. He'd better not ruin this – his final chance, as he thought of it – by proving too harsh a teacher.

'Is there any tune you know that you'd like to play?

How about "Páidín O'Rafferty"? You know that one, don't you?' He lilted the first few bars, until the spark of recognition lit up her face.

'That's the tune they play at the end of "Ceili House" on the radio.' Devaney hadn't even realized it, but Róisín was right. She was already listening like a musician, and there was no substitute for that. They worked away at the melody for the next half hour, stumbling painfully through it a few times, until she had the notes and the fingering right.

'Well, how did you like your first lesson?'

'Daddy,' she said, chiding him for teasing her.

'That was it. And what you can do now is to take the fiddle to someplace nice and quiet' – not to mention as far away from human hearing as possible, he thought to himself – 'and practise that tune and a few scales, and get used to it, especially the feel of the bow. We'll try another tune tomorrow.'

She looked slightly incredulous, but nodded anyway.

'And we should see about getting you a smaller fiddle. I'll ask around. Then you can practise whenever you like.'

Róisín held the fiddle and bow in her left hand, and bent at the knees to gather up the case from the table. 'Don't worry, Daddy, I'll be careful,' she said when she reached the door. 'I'm going to practise a lot and be very good, I promise.' She scurried off down the hall, holding the fiddle before her like a prize.

'We'll see,' said Devaney quietly to himself. He resisted the urge to be as enthusiastic as he wanted to be. He'd already let himself imagine playing a duet with Róisín here in the kitchen, a vision that had prompted a curious tightness in his chest.

He turned his attention to a thick file that lay on the

table. For several days he'd thought of almost nothing but the Osborne case, going over and over the details, trying to find a loose corner, a crack in someone's story. There had to be some way in. The opening was here – probably staring him in the face, if he only knew where to look. He tried to focus his mind on Mina Osborne's journey between Point A, Pilkington's shop in Dunbeg, and Point B, Bracklyn House. Where did she stop? Had she gladly accepted the offer of a lift from someone she knew, or been bundled into a windowless van against her will? And what wild creature along that empty stretch of road had been a witness to what actually transpired? Then there was Osborne, somewhere off on the periphery, on his way from Shannon, he said, and the only person in the whole equation who had no one to vouch for him during that time, and he was the one person who had the strongest motive. The best possibilities were still murder or flight. If it was murder, why were items of clothing missing from the house? And whose word did they have that the pair had never arrived home? Only that of Jeremy and Lucy Osborne, who might be looking after their own best interests. They could even be involved in some way. Devaney's head ached. If only he had someone he could use as a sounding board. The details were disjointed from every angle. Nothing seemed to fit – but it must fit one way, and that was the way it had really happened. This kitchen-table detective work was fucking hopeless. He should be out there talking to people, doing something, instead of sitting here getting tied up in knots.

Everything rested on getting to the essence of this fellow Osborne. Some of the statements from people in the village had mentioned his reputation as a playboy in years past, with a whole string of girlfriends – a different one every time he was home from university, people said, and many of them foreigners. So the man had a taste for the exotic. He was also handsome, considerate, apparently well off – on the face of it, exactly the kind of man that women generally adored.

Devaney started sketching out the scenario: Osborne meets Mina Gonsalves while he's over teaching a summer course at Oxford. Nature follows its course and she gets pregnant, so he does the honourable thing and marries her; they settle back in Ireland. Devaney now felt he could see a hairline crack in the perfect marriage. They're reasonably happy, for a time, but then he's back at his old ways. Maybe he'd married her for money, not anticipating that the father might cut her off.

Now that his wife was out of the picture, Osborne had enlisted the support of Una McGann and Mrs Gonsalves. Interesting how it was always the women who believed in his innocence. No doubt if Osborne ever went to prison for this crime, there would be some female trying to rally supporters in his defence. There was nothing quite so dangerous as a professional pity-hound, Devaney thought. A man like that could twist the good nature in people to his own purposes, even have them feeling sorry for him, and trying to rationalize his violent outbursts.

He flipped to the page listing Osborne's assets. For a member of the so-called gentry, the poor sod didn't have much – a modest salary from the university, not many investments, nothing but a couple of small parcels of land and the house. A house like that was always in need of major repairs, not to mention a bugger of a tax liability. What would happen if a man like Osborne got to feeling boxed in by marriage and money troubles at the same time?

All right, supposing Osborne wanted money, Devaney thought, leaning back in his chair. The development scheme could be one way to get it; banks would see a model public/private investment, and no doubt the government ministers in Dublin would piss themselves for the chance to fund such a worthwhile cultural project. But would that be enough? Osborne had no more land to sell off, no other major assets that he could liquidate, except the house and the insurance. When he'd phoned a couple of days ago, Reidy the insurance agent had told him Osborne kept up to date on the premiums after his wife's disappearance. Nothing funny about that; he'd probably been advised to keep paying. If the wife was dead, why not just produce the body? Why drag it out, unless there was something that would point the finger at him, or unless – Devaney sat forward abruptly, and the front legs of his chair hit the ground with a solid thump. Unless there was no body. Unless Osborne's wife and son were still alive. Maybe he really was as devoted as some said. And if he needed money, why not send the wife and kid safely away somewhere, stage a disappearance, act the grieving husband, and collect at the end of seven years? Add the insurance settlement to the development money, and he'd have a fairly tidy sum. Nobody gets hurt, except the insurance company and the banks, and everyone knows they're a bunch of fucking robbers anyhow.

Devaney thought about where a person might hide a wife and child who were supposed to be dead. Ireland, even Dublin, was too small a place to be safe. The logical place to hide a couple of Indians, he thought, would be among lots of other Indians. Mina and Christopher could have been smuggled out of Ireland, but presumably Osborne wouldn't go seven years without seeing them, particularly if he was so devoted. So where had Osborne travelled in the past two years – assuming he'd travelled under his own name? Perhaps he'd left some trail. Credit cards, travellers' cheques, something. There was a major problem with this scenario as well. What would happen at the end of seven years? Supposing Osborne went ahead and collected his money, then what? He couldn't bring the wife and kid back, so what would he do at that point? Sell off the family home, stage his own disappearance, and start a new life somewhere else? All of these same arguments worked just as well in the case of outright murder. They had no evidence to pin any of this on Osborne. But there was that hole in his story, the drive from Shannon to Dunbeg that left nearly four hours unaccounted for. It didn't seem as if anyone had been following the man's movements since that intense period of scrutiny right after the disappearance. If Osborne's statements about the past provided no clues, maybe something in his current actions would.

Devaney heard the faint, scraping sound of a scale coming from upstairs as Róisín tried to coax a few pleasing notes from his fiddle. He wished her success. He wasn't having much himself.

Chapter 13

The red-haired girl's dental exam wasn't due to begin until two o'clock, but Nora Gavin was in the conservation lab at one, anxious to begin. She walked around the table, observing the instruments lying in their trays, the light above the table, and the familiar unwieldy bundle wrapped in black plastic. Immediately following its discovery, the head of the *cailín rua* had undergone a battery of examinations and tests. For the last several days, the remains had been stored at a temperature just above freezing here at the lab, and had no doubt been set out several hours before today's examination was to begin, so that the tissues – and most particularly the jaw muscles – would become pliable enough to manipulate as they tried to extract the object that was lodged in the girl's mouth.

Nora had returned to Dublin Saturday night, after a long and unproductive day with Cormac on the priory excavation. They seemed to be turning up nothing but gravel. And every time she'd brought up Mina Osborne's disappearance, he seemed to wish she'd talk about something else. It was possible that he'd never been confronted with bald-faced deceit, and was actually taken in by Hugh Osborne. The man had a convincing air of sincerity, she had to admit.

But at least Cormac hadn't refused her help on the dig. And so far he hadn't told her to calm down. She could hear a voice from the past – Marc Staunton's voice – suggesting that she take a few deep breaths and try to calm herself. When she'd first met Marc, she had loved his voice, that rumbling baritone she'd first heard through a surgical mask on an operating room visit during med school. She'd been smitten before she ever laid eyes on his face. For a long time, it seemed as if they couldn't have been better matched: he loved music and theatre, they'd read the same books, and had always been interested in one another's medical specialities. And although her parents had never pressured her to get married, she knew they'd adored Marc, and were delighted when he'd introduced her sister to one of his college roommates. That was how she'd met Peter Hallett. The four of them had spent a lot of time together, before Peter and Tríona were married, going out to dinner or a play, spending summer weekends on Peter's sailboat down at Lake Pepin. At times she felt overwhelmed, realizing that all the happiness she'd experienced then was gone now, wiped away like some dream of a life that never really existed.

When Tríona was killed, it was as if Marc had become the self-appointed arbiter of rationality, while she could only feel. He hadn't even heard the patronizing tone he began to use whenever she complained about the lack of news from the police. It was true that she had been utterly consumed by her sister's terrible death; it had been a conscious choice, and one she still didn't regret. But she'd been wrong to trust that Marc would help her, especially when the police started investigating his friend. Little by little, she'd felt Marc's loyalty beginning to shift. First he'd warned her that she was becoming too emotionally involved, and ended up trying to convince her that she was coming unglued, even imagining things that never happened. Her 'obsession', as he referred to it, had finally driven them apart. As she had watched him pack his suitcase with the same meticulous precision he used in the operating room, Nora felt that she had never really known Marc, despite the fact that they had been lovers since medical school, and had lived together for more than eight years. At least she hadn't married him, she thought bitterly. The sound of his voice in her ears made her want to plunge farther into the shadowy thicket of Mina Osborne's disappearance. But why did she presume that she could make a difference this time?

With effort, Nora roused herself. It wasn't even one-thirty yet. She pulled a white lab coat over her street clothes in preparation for the dental exam. As she did so, she noticed the file of written reports that lay on the near end of the exam table. She leaned forward to open it.

> At the postmortem examination on 6 May, Dr Malachy Drummond, Chief State Pathologist, assisted by Dr Nora Gavin, Trinity College Medical School, made the following observations:
> *General:* The specimen appeared to be the head of a young female, approx. 18–25 years of age, found two days previous at Drumcleggan Bog, near Dunbeg, Co. Galway.
> *Preservation:* Much of the soft tissue was remarkably well preserved. The scalp and hair were well preserved on the right side, which had been uppermost in the bog. There was no evidence of injury to the skull. The face was very well preserved; the hair appeared wavy and approximately 40 cm in length, and retained its reddish tint. The eyelids, eyelashes, and eyebrows were all present, with evidence of some tissue remaining in both sockets, the right eye being

visible through the partially open lid. The cartilage and skin over the nose were well preserved. Both ears were present, the right ear in a state of good preservation, the left infiltrated with bog plants. There was a small portion of skin missing from the chin, leaving an exposed area of adipocere and bone. The neck was severed between the third and fourth vertebrae, although it was impossible to tell through naked-eye examination whether this injury occurred before or after death. Report by Dr R. Kinsella, Professor of Radiology, Royal College of Surgeons in Ireland, assisted by Mrs Maire Donegan and Mr Anthony McHugh, Senior Radiographers, Beaumont Hospital, Dublin, on radiograph and CT scan.

Plain Radiographs: Skull: No fracture can be identified. The slightly shrunken brain is well seen. The convolutional markings are clearly identifiable, as also are the cisterns. The ventricles are small, but not greatly distorted, and there is evidence of some air in them. In the lateral projection of the skull, there is a well-defined opacity within the mouth cavity. It is not certain whether this is part of the dental structure, or a foreign body inserted before or after death.

Computerized Tomography: Extensive computerized tomographic images were made of the individual's skull. No fractures are visible in the skull vault. The brain is not greatly shrunken and does not appear to be surrounded by air. The differentiation of grey and white matter can be identified within the dense brain stem extending into the spinal cord. As in the radiographs, there is a well-defined opacity of indeterminate origin, suggesting some sort of foreign body lodged in the individual's mouth.

Report on the endoscopy performed by Dr J. S. Mitchell, Department of Clinical Medicine, Trinity College, Dublin:

The interior of the mouth was very well preserved. The tissues were moist and much less stained than external tissues. They were brownish in colour, and the membranes were not particularly fragile. The object appearing in previous radiographs and scans was present here also, but from its position against soft tissue, it was difficult to discern what exactly this object might be, or any details about its composition.

There was nothing in these reports that Nora didn't already know. She closed the file and slowly circled the table, focusing on the awkwardly wrapped package and imagining the cold horror that waited there. *Who are you?* she asked silently. *What happened to you?* She reached out a hand and rested it on the twisted black polythene. *Tell me.* As soon as the thought flashed through her mind, Nora felt a sudden impulse to withdraw her hand, but couldn't. She felt a pang of heartsickness as strong as any she had ever experienced, and stood with eyes closed, fixed to the spot until the sensation slowly dissipated. She opened her eyes and took her hand away.

Though she had been there dozens of times, the lab's bright light and bare, polished surfaces seemed somehow foreign and strange. *The others will be here any minute*, she told herself. *Get a grip*. She took the X-rays from a brown folder beneath the reports, put them up on the viewer, and switched on the light, studying the location of the 'opacity' that they would try to extricate today.

Ray Flynn, the conservation technician, interrupted

her thoughts, pushing through the door with his camera in hand. He was screwing on the flash attachment and checking to see that it was in working order. 'Anxious to have at it, eh, Dr Gavin?'

'Guilty.'

'You're as bad as my kids at Christmastime.' Flynn pushed back through the door, nearly bumping into Niall Dawson. As assistant keeper of antiquities at the National Museum, Dawson was actually the person in charge of the operation today.

'Hello, Nora,' Dawson said, smiling. 'We'll be getting started any moment now, as soon as Fitzpatrick makes an entrance.'

'What do you think of the execution idea?' Nora asked.

'It's a definite possibility. The electron microscopy shows damage to the vertebrae consistent with use of a blade of some sort. Our problem is that we can't tell definitively whether decapitation took place pre- or post-mortem. We may have to be satisfied with what we have.'

'I know we can find out who she was,' Nora said. As soon as she spoke the words she felt foolish, as though she'd blurted out some secret. 'I know it's completely daft, but I do.'

'You're wishing for something that may not happen. Promise you won't be downhearted when it turns out to be nothing.'

'I'll promise no such thing.'

Thirty minutes later, Barry Fitzpatrick, the plumpish, grey-haired dental lecturer from Trinity, was in the midst of his preliminary naked-eye assessment, speaking with the deliberate, measured tones of a teacher used to dictation: 'The mandible appears to be only slightly dislocated due to postmortem events.' Grasping the crown of the red-haired girl's head, he gently pulled her mouth open, then tried shifting the jawbone, first slightly from side to side, then up and down. 'The jaw remains quite flexible. Because of the remarkable preservation of facial skin and muscle tissue, it will be necessary to open the mandible in order to gain access to the teeth. Mr Flynn, if I could ask you to be ready with the camera as we open the mouth? Thank you.'

Fitzpatrick pulled gingerly at the lower jaw, eventually loosening the red-haired girl's teeth from where they had bitten through her lower lip. He opened her mouth as wide as he could, peered inside, then reached in with a latex-gloved finger to check for missing teeth and molars.

'There appears to be full dentition present, the third molars being fully erupted. The teeth are brown in colour, and there appears to be a complete absence of tooth enamel. Assessment of the individual's age at death is difficult in this case, since enamel provides the most accurate indication of tooth wear. The first molars show slight to moderate wear of the dentine, while the third molars – if you could move the light just a little closer, please, Mr Flynn – show little or no wear. Probable age at death was approximately twenty to twenty-five years. Now, Dr Gavin,' said Fitzpatrick, looking up from his work and wrinkling his nose in an effort to keep his glasses from sliding down any more, 'if you could give me an indication of where we should begin searching for this famous foreign body.'

'It appears to be fairly far back in the throat,' Nora said, pointing to the spot on the X-ray film, 'and closer to the left side than the right.' Fitzpatrick glanced at the negative image, then bent to his task again, using his dental mirror as a tongue depressor.

'I want to avoid damaging the surrounding tissue if I can,' he said, 'but it'll be difficult not to push whatever it is even farther back, unless – Mr Flynn, do you have a very large tweezers of some sort? That will do nicely, thank you.'

It was all Nora could do to keep from pressing next to Fitzpatrick so that she could see what he saw through the magnifying viewer.

'Come on,' he said, coaxing the thing forward, 'this way out. Here it is.' Fitzpatrick lifted the object aloft, and four pairs of eyes beheld a band of finely worked gold, centred with a dark red stone. 'I'd say it was a man's ring, wouldn't you, Dawson?' said Fitzpatrick, clearly delighted with his discovery. They all drew around to examine it more closely.

'Appears to be,' Dawson said. 'And look inside. There's some sort of inscription.' He struggled to make out the letters through the magnifying lens: 'COF, then the number sixteen, letters IHS, another number, fifty-two. Then more letters, AOF.'

That's it, Nora thought, the message she'd known was there. Had this girl tried to swallow the ring, or simply to hide it? What other explanation could there be? What thoughts must have raced through her mind in the last few seconds before she died? Nora looked back to the top of the table where the girl's mouth was still propped open at an awkward angle under the glaring light. She felt suddenly ashamed. 'Gentlemen,' she said, 'if we're finished, hadn't we better cover her up again?'

Chapter 14

The loom's rhythmic sound usually had a calming effect on Una McGann's mind, but tonight she felt slightly on edge. Brendan refused to have a television in the house, so each of them was engaged in some customary evening occupation: Fintan worked at the table, cutting new reeds for his pipes, making an occasional squawk as he blew through each thin piece of cane to test its sound. Aoife knelt on the floor beside him, enacting some story with an unlikely foursome that included a spotted salamander, a winged fairy, an elephant, and a giraffe. Brendan sat apart from them, on a stool near the fire, meticulously grinding a keen edge on one of his half-dozen sickles. He kept a vast collection of old tools in the shed; some had belonged to their father and grandfather, while others came from neighbours who knew that he was interested and offered him their old implements when they ceased cutting turf or making hay by hand, as nearly everyone in the locality had done. His collection included spades and pitchforks, billhooks for cutting ditches, punch forks and hand rakes for thatching, foot *sleáns* and breast *sleáns*. Brendan kept each one shining, never letting the damp turn to rust on their blades.

Fintan waited for Una's eyes to meet his, and his eyebrows raised in a question. He'd asked her advice earlier this afternoon; he was dying to break the news to Brendan about his plans to leave Dunbeg. She'd tried to put him off, saying that now wasn't the time; as long as he wasn't planning to leave until the autumn, there was no point in telling Brendan so soon. He'd only stew about it all summer, she warned. Fintan had disagreed. He still wanted to tell Brendan tonight. She could feel the anticipation in every gesture he made. He'd planned to go to America for years, he'd told her, but only recently had saved enough money to make it possible. He had, enough to live for a few months, anyway, even if he didn't get any work. And a friend in New York had promised to fix up a few gigs for him. Fintan was only two years younger than she was, but tonight Una felt decades older than her brother, seeing him practically bursting with the news.

What would this house be like without Fintan? Una wasn't sure that she and Aoife could remain if he left, but leaving Brendan completely on his own was a thought she had tried to avoid.

She watched her elder brother as he held the sickle against his left knee, tracing the silvery half-moon shape of it over and over again with the pink round of a sharpening stone. Every few strokes, he'd pause to feel its edge against the thick skin of his thumb. It must soothe him somehow, to sit and smoke the pipe and work at these things. How sad that she couldn't really talk to Brendan, and tell him what was in her heart, as she could do so easily with Fintan. But Brendan had always been so serious, trying to act like a grown man by the time he was fourteen years of age. He'd never seemed to have time to play when she was a girl, but then he was six years older than she was, already busy with farmwork when she and Fintan were still small.

Had Brendan ever given any thought to marrying? He'd certainly shown no interest in anyone she knew about. And there weren't many opportunities for a social life in Dunbeg. Brendan was never one for dances or the other usual functions where people could meet. He went to Mass, of course, and he might go into the pub, but he'd always have his pint standing at the bar, nodding wordlessly to the half-dozen other regulars who drained their glasses beside him.

Brendan looked up from the sickle, not at her, but at Fintan, who held a reed up to the light to check its thickness. Brendan looked as if he were about to utter some expression of annoyance over his brother's foolish waste of time, but instead he paused, evidently thought better of it, and returned to his work.

How much had she given up to come back here? She missed the laughing faces of her Dublin neighbours, Celia and Jane. Despite Dublin's grey concrete walls, the graffiti-covered dustbins, the noise and grime of the city, Una had felt warmly accepted, enveloped, even, when she was with them. Celia worked in a bookshop; Jane was a writer. They were as poor as she was, but in a joyful, bohemian way that she always admired but could never quite achieve. Their flat was filled with books, with conversation and cigarette smoke. Perhaps what buoyed her friends was the love they shared, a tenderness forbidden where they came from, but tolerated, or at least ignored in the city, far from the prying eyes and clucking tongues of the villages where they'd grown up. Una had no such close friends in Dunbeg. What a relief it had been to be with Celia and Jane, to feel as if she could let go and say what she really thought. But another part of her spirit had never felt at home in the city. She had missed the smells, the sounds, even the very quietness of Dunbeg, the breathing space one could experience even in a room with several other souls.

That silence, that solitude in company existed for her nowhere but here.

Una looked at her daughter's bright head bent over her tiny tea set, as the child whispered an entire conversation in the various voices of her odd menagerie. Una understood Brendan's desire to keep things as they had been forever. Weren't there times – like this very moment, in fact – that she wished she could spare Aoife all the pain and disappointment of growing up? But she knew that sheltering her daughter from pain would also take away the profoundest joy, like the feeling she'd known when Aoife was born, seeing the damp crown of her daughter's head covered in pale down. The nurses didn't like it, but Una had sometimes unwrapped her completely, to drink in every detail of her compact and perfect naked body. *You must keep the child covered up,* they'd clucked, *she'll catch her death.* As if death itself were contagious. Una had made up her mind to raise Aoife without shame, if she could, and took the greatest satisfaction in seeing her little girl growing up as blissfully alive in her physical self as Una had felt painfully repressed. Her parents had not been entirely to blame for that, she knew. It was the place, the time, and the stifling Catholic morality in the atmosphere they all breathed.

She was glad Fintan knew what he wanted. He had started at the tin whistle, and saved enough money for a set of practice pipes by the time he was thirteen. Brendan considered him lazy, she knew, but Fintan's thoughts were always on the music, to the point of distraction at times. *You can't live on music*, Brendan had often told him, but Una could see in Fintan's eyes the fiercest desire to prove their brother wrong. For years, he'd worked all winter long weaving simple Brigid's crosses to sell to tourist shops in Scarriff and Mountshannon, and he'd saved every penny he ever earned playing music for hire. Hardly laziness. Una also understood Fintan's desire to explore the world beyond a place like Dunbeg, where the future was mapped out for you almost from birth, depending on who your father was, and how much tillable land you owned, and what the people in your family had done for generations upon generations. Tradition could be a prison sentence, as much as a point of pride.

The hidden things in Brendan's room pressed on her heart more each day. There must be some plausible explanation. Surely. So why was she afraid? He'd always been a moody man, but the darkness seemed to have grown worse recently, and she'd started remembering things he'd said or done that troubled her. This morning, rounding the corner of the house, she'd remembered something that had taken place on that very spot nearly twenty years earlier: Brendan, about twelve years old, with a hen whose head he was about to strike off. He held the bird's struggling body between his knees, stretching her neck with his left hand, and chopped the head off with one stroke of the bread knife. He looked up and saw Una but didn't move or utter a word as the hen's body quivered, and then went still. He studied her for a moment, then rose from his crouch, and held out the dripping carcass to her by its scrawny legs. *Here*, he said, *take this to Mam.* She thought he was trying to frighten her, but when she looked up at Brendan's face, there was nothing in his eyes; his expression had been completely blank.

Disturbed by the memory, Una pulled the bar on the loom firmly back, then slid off her bench. 'Come on, Aoife, love, time for slumber.'

'But, Mammy, it's not even dark.'

'No, and it's not going to be, either, until past your bedtime. Don't you want to see where our book takes us tonight?' They'd been reading since the winter, one chapter each evening. Aoife's face brightened, then clouded over again as she considered which prospect appealed to her most at the moment. Una loved to study the landscape of her daughter's face, which was tempered by moods as changeable as Irish weather.

'Come on, upstairs with you now,' she said in a mock-threatening tone. 'Give the lads a kiss.' She stood and waited as Aoife planted her lips firmly on Brendan's whiskery cheek, then on Fintan's. He looked at Una again, and there was mischief in his eyes.

Not now, she mouthed in reply, but Una could see that he didn't plan to heed her advice.

Upstairs in their room, she tore through the bedtime story, prompting Aoife to say, 'Mammy, you're going too fast.'

'Sorry, love,' Una said, slowing her pace, but, as she did, straining to hear what might be passing between her brothers downstairs. The fact that she could hear nothing made her even more tense.

'That's all for tonight,' she said, closing the book at the end of the chapter and giving Aoife a quick kiss. 'Sleep well, my love.'

Una knew the moment she opened the door that the silence below did not bode well. Brendan's voice was quiet, but there was fury in it.

'America, is it? I might have known. Can't wait to get away from us, can you? And not just down the road, you have to go halfway round the world, and it's still not far enough. And how are you going to get enough money to go live in America?'

'I've saved a good bit. And I thought I'd sell off my

share of the farm.' Brendan didn't respond, so Fintan continued: 'I went to the solicitor. He told me that Una and I have equal shares in the farm, the same as yourself. How long did you think you could keep that from us, Brendan? But don't worry, I'll give you a fair price.'

Brendan stood, trembling, with the handle of the sickle gripped tightly in his right hand.

'You fucking *whelp*,' he said, on the last word bringing the blade of the sickle down on the table, where it stuck fast. Fintan scrambled backward, upending his chair, his face openmouthed in shock at what his words had unleashed. Brendan's rage dissolved into bewilderment, then further into remorse. He sagged to his knees, and rested his head against the edge of the table.

'Fintan, you'd better leave,' Una said. 'Just for a while.'

'I'm not leaving you here—'

'Fintan,' she said again, sharply. 'Will you get out? We'll be all right.'

Fintan climbed to his feet, and left hurriedly by the front door. Una stood where she was for a moment, then walked deliberately to the table, where she wrested the sickle from its place. She felt its dead weight in her hand as she opened the back door, walked to the shed, and hung it up among the other tools neatly arranged on hooks above her head.

When she returned to the kitchen, Una saw the door to the front hall closing, and heard Brendan's footsteps treading the length of the hallway to his room. Perhaps it was the relief of not having to speak to him at this moment; she put her hands to her face and drew in a long, gasping sob.

'Mammy?' came a small voice from above. Aoife stood at the top of the staircase in her nightdress. 'Mammy, what's happening? I'm afraid.' Una sprinted up the short flight of steps and knelt to hold Aoife tight.

'It's all right, my love,' she said, smoothing her daughter's hair. 'The boys had a bit of a row, but it's over now. It's all over.'

Chapter 15

Tiny beads of perspiration were beginning to form on Nora's forehead as she walked on the treadmill. She had sublet this flat from a Trinity colleague off in America on a visiting professorship. Although she loved its location on the Grand Canal, and the large windows that looked out over the southwest sector of the city, she had never warmed to its spare, modern space. She did like the treadmill, though; walking put her in a meditative state. She had been at it nearly forty minutes now, relaxing into the steady rhythm, feeling the blood coursing through her muscles, focusing her vision on a place far outside the large plate-glass window. Dublin was still an astonishingly residential metropolis, and she could see far beyond the canal onto the roofs of Harold's Cross and Crumlin, watching the blinking lights appear in the gathering dusk over the city. It was this time of day, and particularly the memory of the setting sun over the Mississippi River bluffs around Saint Paul, that made her homesick for her own home and family. Her parents would both be working right now. She imagined her father checking some experiment in his research lab at the university medical school, her mother listening to the heartbeats of East African women and children, who made up the bulk of her clientele at the community clinic. She hadn't spoken to her parents in more than a week; she should try to remember to phone them before it got too late.

For some reason, she was also remembering a remark that Evelyn McCrossan, Gabriel's wife, had made one evening when they were discussing the progress on the catalogue of bog remains. *When I see those people in the museum*, Evelyn had said, *I always think it's a pity they have to be on display like that. I mean, they're human beings, aren't they? Or were. I always say a little prayer for them.* Nora thought about the *cailín rua*'s matted hair drying against the surface of the examination table. Those tangled strands would remain forever just as they'd been found, wild and uncombed. The circumstances of the red-haired girl's death, combined with the accident of her preservation, meant that she had somehow ceased to be a corpse like any other; she had become an artefact.

After the exam this afternoon, Nora had buttonholed Niall Dawson from the museum to ask him about the inscription they'd found in the ring.

'Well, for one thing, it tells us that whoever owned the ring was most probably a Catholic,' Dawson said.

'How do you figure?'

'The "IHS" in the centre of the date is a liturgical symbol pretty distinctly associated with the Catholic Church.'

'What does it stand for?' Dawson raised an eyebrow. 'I wasn't really raised in the Church,' Nora explained.

He smiled. 'The Christian Brothers used to tell us it meant: "I Have Suffered." But if you want the real story, it was actually a miscopying of "ΙΗΣΟΥΣ", the Greek word for "Jesus", translated into Latin and eventually adopted by the Church as a sort of acronym or monogram. They put various interpretations forward over the years, if I could only think . . .' Dawson scoured his memory. 'The only one I can recall is *Iesus Hominum Salvator* – "Jesus, Saviour of Men".'

'I'm impressed.'

'Yes, well, all that drilling on Christian doctrine obviously made more of an impression than I'm willing to admit.'

'And what about the other initials?'

'I'm guessing it was a wedding ring,' Dawson had said. 'At that time it was the custom for a man to give his own ring as a pledge of marriage. And the two sets of initials with a date would seem to bear that out.'

So if the ring did belong to the red-haired girl, and it was indeed a wedding ring, where had her husband and protector gone? Off to war somewhere? Perhaps he was in the bog beside her, and sooner or later some turf-cutter would eventually uncover his remains as well. The inscription was a break; with a date and a set of initials, maybe Robbie McSweeney could find something more specific.

Nora checked her distance on the treadmill's display; she'd done nearly three miles already, but didn't feel like stopping now. Her thoughts strayed to the notion of marriage, and the custom of rings given as a pledge. What were the words? To love, honour, and cherish. As if it were as simple as a promise.

Devaney had used the phrase 'perfect marriage' to describe Hugh and Mina Osborne – false and reductive words that had also been used to describe Peter and Tríona. Of all the mysteries in the universe, how two people could find continuing joy and satisfaction in one another was one of the greatest puzzles. Even the sincerest attempt at pairing with another human being was bound to involve a delicate balance between conflicting egos and desires, a process that had to be at least as complicated as the two individuals, and perhaps even more so. Who might be able to tell her more about Hugh and Mina Osborne?

A droplet of sweat trickled down and stung Nora's eye, interrupting her train of thought. Why the hell was it that every time she tried to concentrate on the red-haired girl, she always came around again to Tríona – and to the missing woman in the photograph? And why was she so anxious to see Hugh Osborne guilty of murder? She knew next to nothing about the case, only what Devaney had told them, and she wasn't likely to learn any more. She couldn't let another piece of unfinished business chase after her the rest of her life. She pushed the buttons to gradually slow her pace. The dusk was gone, replaced by darkness, and she could see herself reflected in the window. *Leave this,* said the voice in her head. She watched the outline of her shoulders rise and fall with each breath. *Let it go.* She stepped from the machine, feeling as she always did after a long workout: buoyant, as if she walked on air. An answer to the internal voice floated up inside her: *I'll try. I can't promise, but I will try.*

Chapter 16

Devaney sat in the car parked just outside the gate of Bracklyn House. This couldn't really be considered proper surveillance, but it was the best he could do. He'd managed to persuade Nuala to lend him her car, provided he got it back in time for her to meet some clients for a drink. She'd picked out this car on her own, paid for it herself as a point of pride.

He'd never used the car phone, and was fiddling idly with the buttons when a dusty black Volvo wagon came out of the gate. It was Osborne. Devaney waited a few seconds, then pulled out behind the Volvo. He could keep his distance around Dunbeg, aided by the fact that there were not many roads in this part of the countryside. Osborne seemed to be heading north, toward Loughrea. Devaney checked his watch. Seven o'clock. He'd break off when he had to in order to get home by half-nine.

At Loughrea, Osborne turned onto the N6 heading west. There'd be more traffic on this road, less chance of being spotted. He eased onto the highway after the black Volvo, leaving a couple of cars between them. Osborne continued into Galway, following the signposts for the city centre. Devaney nearly lost him on the first roundabout, but caught sight of the car and made the turn at the last minute. He checked his watch again. Nearly a quarter past eight. He should try to call Nuala, let her know that at this rate he might be a few minutes late.

She could always take his car, a point he'd brought up when they'd made the switch. *To pick up clients?* she'd said. He'd gathered it was out of the question.

He lifted the car phone from its cradle, but slammed it down again when he had to turn a corner to keep the Volvo in sight. No use trying until he was stopped somewhere, if that ever happened, unless he wanted to crash the car in addition to being late. He followed as Osborne edged his way around Eyre Square, then pulled into a tiny side street near the docks.

Hugh Osborne parked his car, then entered an unmarked doorway on street level. Devaney would have to drive closer or approach on foot, but either way he'd run the risk of being spotted. He parked about thirty yards away, and waited. He peered up and down the street. No fucking chance of a phone box when you needed one, was there? He looked down at the mobile, and felt the sleek black case with its tiny red and green lights mocking him. How was it Nuala could just figure out all this technology, make it part of her life as she went sailing forth into the world, and leave him standing on the dock? He picked up the handset, held it to his ear. Silence. Maybe you had to press something to turn the bloody thing on. He pushed gingerly on a tiny button marked 'Speak', and a loud dial tone filled the car. He slammed the phone down, pushing buttons furiously to cut off the noise, which must have been audible all up and down the quiet street.

Just then, Osborne emerged from the doorway, looking shaken. He went to his own car and opened the door, but before getting in he seemed to have some sort of a spell, grasping the car door for support, and lowering his head, as if he were going to be sick. And he doesn't even know anyone's watching him here, Devaney thought, unless I've completely blown it. As he retraced the journey, trying to remember if there were any points at which Osborne might have caught a glimpse of him, the Volvo's engine started, and it pulled abruptly away from the kerb. Devaney put his car in gear and followed, hoping Osborne hadn't got too much of a head start. When he rounded the corner, there was a lorry dead ahead, manoeuvring its way into position to drop off a load of empty Guinness kegs. Devaney slammed on the brakes, narrowly missing the man who was directing the lorry, and came to a stop about eighteen inches from its rear end.

'Watch where ye're going, ya dowsy bollocks,' shouted the man, pounding the car's bonnet with his fist. 'You could have fuckin' killed me.' Devaney reversed out of the side street, and went back the way he'd come. Osborne was lost. There was no way to find him again. It was nearly half past eight. If he left now, he could head home and not be more than a quarter of an hour late. But what had happened when Osborne went into that building? He pulled up near the doorway to have a closer look. A thirtyish, sandy-haired man in a leather jacket stood at the door, evidently having trouble with the lock. He tried a second key, and was just trying the third when Devaney came up behind him.

'Closed for the evening, are you?' Devaney asked. The man looked up, startled. His face was narrow, slightly ruddy, and there was a shaving cut just below his right ear. The plaque beside the door read 'Eddie Dolphin, Private Investigations'. Mustn't have had the place for long, Devaney thought, if he's still fishing for the key.

'Why don't you open up again, Eddie, so we can have a bit of a chat?' The man's startled look transformed to wariness, then took on an air of forced nonchalance, the mark of a bad actor. There was something else in the set of his jaw; he didn't want to lose a job, if that's what Devaney turned out to be.

'I was just headin' home. Why don't I give you me card, and you can ring me or come round in the morning—' His manner altered visibly once more, to nervous agitation, when Devaney produced his identification.

'Let's do it now, if you don't mind. While I'm in the neighbourhood.'

Eddie Dolphin opened the door again, and led the way up the wooden steps. He might as well have been climbing to the gallows. When they entered the office, he slumped into his office chair, staring glumly at the cluttered desktop.

Devaney studied Dolphin's demeanour, then looked about, gathering the facts of his surroundings. He took his time, partly to get a firm grasp of his bearings, and the better to prepare Mr Dolphin for questioning. The building had the look of an old barracks: two storeys, single windows at regular intervals. Dolphin's tiny office had two windows, one facing the street, one overlooking warehouse loading areas to the rear, its grimy surface barely admitting a slanting shaft of light from a street lamp. The place smelled of dust and faintly of mildew. The coat of paint on the walls and window sashes was fresh, but carelessly applied. The closet in one corner had evidently been set up as a makeshift darkroom: a large bottle of chemical developer stood inside the door, along with several brand-new computers still in cartons. The rubbish bin was overflowing with empty pint bottles of Guinness and take-away containers. Late nights, Devaney thought as he turned once more to Dolphin, who had begun picking nervously at one of the several piles of papers that seemed to have randomly accumulated on his desktop.

'Has Osborne been a client for long, Eddie?' Devaney asked, crossing his arms and leaning back casually against the door frame.

'Look, I don't have to answer any questions. There's such a thing as confidentiality, you know.' He spoke as if he'd only just learned the word.

'If you're a priest, or maybe a solicitor,' Devaney said. 'You a solicitor, Eddie? I know you're not a priest.' He kept perfectly still, looking mildly at Dolphin. The silence grew.

'About six months.' Dolphin's look was apprehensive, as though he now expected an onslaught of questions. His jaw worked nervously. Devaney kept quiet and waited.

'He came here last winter. Said he wanted me to help him look for his wife and kid. Gone missing. I told him it didn't look good, but—' Dolphin looked up briefly. 'He was a steady client, paid up regular, and I took the job. I did some checking, went around a few places with photos. I've got four kids already, and another one on the way,' he said, a new note of pleading in his voice. 'I needed the work. And there's no one better at finding people. I'd have come up with something.'

'So what was he here for this evening?'

'Somebody sent him a package.'

'What was in it?'

'How should I know?' Dolphin said, contriving to look injured at the suggestion. 'I don't go round opening up packages addressed to me clients.'

'Well, and what sort of a detective does that make you, Eddie? Of course if I wanted to know the answer to that, all I'd have to do is get in touch with my friend Michael Noonan in the collator's office down at Mill Street Station. I'm sure he has a little card in his file with all sorts of information about you.'

'I've done nothin' wrong. For fuck's sake, you can't just come barging in here—' Dolphin spluttered, glancing nervously at the open closet door.

'I've been meaning to give Michael a ring. Haven't seen him in ages. That fella has the most phenomenal memory – never forgets anything. He could give you chapter and verse about every sort of robbery, large and small, that's been perpetrated in these parts over the past five years. Isn't that amazing? You've never seen such a memory.'

'All right, all right,' Dolphin said. 'It was just a fuckin' letter, all right? A couple of pages, handwritten. Going on about "I know what ye're up to, ye bastard, and ye'll never get away with it," and like that. There was something else as well, some sort of metal yoke, I don't know what it was. But he fucked off out of here as soon as he read it. Forgot all about my retainer that was due.'

'Never mind about the retainer, Eddie. Describe this metal yoke for me.'

'It seemed like – I don't know, a brooch or something. Two elephants, like this,' and he pushed his fists together, 'buttin' heads, like.' Devaney froze. Mina Osborne's hair clip. What else could it be?

'How would anyone know to contact Osborne here?' Devaney asked.

'Must have seen one of my adverts. They're not cheap either, them, and it's all come out of my pocket so far.'

Osborne's reaction to the body at the cutaway pushed its way to the front of Devaney's mind. If there was no way to search a whole bog, there had to be some way to force Osborne's hand. He'd put the pressure on around Bracklyn. Lucy Osborne knew more than she was willing to tell. And the lad – Devaney had seen him often enough at Lynch's – might speak out of turn if pressed.

'Look, I've got to get home,' Dolphin said. 'The wife was expecting me ages ago.'

Wife. Jesus. Devaney checked his own watch. Nearly nine o'clock, and he was an hour away from home at least. 'I'll be in touch,' he said to Dolphin. He might be able to find a phone and try to patch things up at home.

He jammed the keys into the ignition. How had it got so late? He darted through the city traffic, keeping an eye out for a phone box, seeing none along his route. Finally, at the outskirts of the city he saw one standing alone at the roadside. He pulled up and leapt from the car, fumbling for coins in his pocket. He lifted the telephone and was greeted by silence in place of the usual buzz, and only then noticed that the cord had been severed. He slammed the receiver down, and trudged back to the car. When he lifted the handle, it took him a split second to realize what had happened. Of all the fucking stupid – the car's security system had locked the doors automatically. This whole adventure was turning into a colossal disaster. He landed a vicious kick on the nearest tyre. Just then a fat droplet struck him in the left eye, then another, and another, and in the space of a few seconds he was wet to the skin in the pelting rain.

It was close to midnight when he reached home. He'd been able to flag down a couple with a mobile within five or ten minutes, but waiting for the locksmith to open the car took a good hour and a half. He'd tried phoning home on the borrowed mobile as well, but no one answered. He was still soaking, and must have been a bedraggled-looking sight when he pushed open the kitchen door. Nuala was sitting at the table with a cup of tea. She gave him a reproachful look that had become all too familiar.

'I had to cancel the meeting. You know, Gar, I'm not

angry for myself,' she said wearily. 'I'm really past that. But you completely forgot you were to take Róisín out to look at that fiddle tonight, didn't you?'

Christ. That's what had been niggling at him all day, the one thing he knew he was forgetting. He sat wearily in the chair opposite Nuala, but she rose from the table, and her look might as well have been a slap.

'She's in bed, but I don't think she's asleep. You might tell her you're sorry.'

He kept silent, knowing any attempts to explain at this stage would only make matters that much worse. She left him sitting there, and each footstep that took her away from him was like a blow to his heart. No case was worth this. He had once felt that they moved in tandem, in everything they did. He remembered drinking in the scent of her as if it were nourishment. The feeling was still there, but it had been buried under the avalanche of practicalities that jobs and responsibilities and life with three children had brought. He felt like rushing after her, tackling her to the ground if he had to, and burying his face in her softness. Instead he took a towel from the cupboard near the cooker, and began drying his hair as he climbed the stairs to speak to Róisín. She stirred when the light from the hall spilled into her room. He sat at the edge of her bed, looking into his daughter's solemn eyes, their pupils large in the murky darkness.

'I'm so sorry, Róisín,' he said. 'I got caught up in what I was doing, and the fiddle completely slipped my mind.'

'It's all right, Daddy. I forgave you right away.' She leaned forward and patted his arm in a gesture of comfort. 'I don't think Mammy has. But don't worry, she will.'

Devaney sat on the side of the bed, looking down at his shoes, trying to imagine how such a thing might come to pass.

Chapter 17

Nora thought she was dreaming when her phone began to ring in the middle of the night. She often had nightmares that ended with a telephone ringing, unanswered, somewhere in the distance, but she gradually realized that this wasn't a dream, and picked up the receiver beside the bed, feeling disoriented and panicky, and nearly deafened by the sound of her own heart clamouring in her chest.

'Hello?' When there was no response, she said again: 'Hello?' She peered at the clock: 12:47. That meant that it was just past seven in the evening at home. She remembered the call she'd received from her father the night Tríona's body was found, and felt a stab of apprehension. When there was still no response, she heard her own tentative question: 'Daddy?'

The voice in the receiver was not her father, but a disembodied, breathy whisper that was neither male nor female: 'Leave it alone.'

'Leave what alone?' Nora demanded. 'Who is this?' For a fragment of a second, her thoughts concentrated on Tríona. She was sure she'd told no one here about her sister's death.

'They're better off.'

'What do you mean? Who's better off?' Nora's brain pitched wildly in its half-conscious state, until she hit upon another possible meaning.

'Do you mean Mina and Christopher Osborne? What do you know about it?' The only response she received this time was the flat-line buzz of a dial tone.

Was it just a crank call, some bizarre accident? And if it was about Mina Osborne, why should anyone call her? Who knew she was even interested? Nora searched her memory, trying to figure out who knew she'd been out at Bracklyn House. She sat in the dark amid the rumpled bedclothes for several more minutes, trying to work out some answers to a relentless torrent of questions. Not least of all, she had to convince herself that the call had actually happened.

It was no use trying to sleep now. Her eyes travelled the room, and rested for a moment upon the laptop sitting on her desk. There was one simple way to find out more about the basic facts of Mina Osborne's disappearance. She crossed to the desk and pressed the necessary keys to connect to the Internet. The *Irish Times* website came up before her, and she quickly went to its archive search. She typed in 'Mina Osborne', but hesitated before pressing 'Search'. What was she prepared to find out? And what about the consequences? She and Cormac might find themselves in trouble if they knew any more. This was her own private compulsion; why drag him into it? And yet he was the one who had agreed to go back to Bracklyn. Perhaps his curiosity was as great as her own. Nora hesitated a second longer, then pressed the button. In an instant, a list of articles appeared. She scanned the headlines:

Concern grows for missing woman and boy
Search is widened for missing mother and child
Woman and child missing for over nine weeks
Gardaí to resume bogland searches today

Search for missing mother and child cut back
Gardaí baffled by disappearance
Osborne critical of Gardaí over handling of case
Women who are dead or missing
Files on missing women are reopened
Gardaí to examine serial killer possibility

She opened the first story, dated almost three years ago:

> Concern is growing for the safety of a mother and child who have been missing from their County Galway home since Thursday. Mrs Mina Osborne and her son Christopher were last seen on Thursday afternoon walking along the Drumcleggan road on the outskirts of Dunbeg.
>
> Garda divers have searched Lough Derg near their home, while 60 people, including neighbours, civil defence, and the Order of Malta have searched a five-mile radius around their home, including bogs and marl holes. Gardaí have talked to a number of people to try to locate the missing mother and child.
>
> Mrs Osborne is of Indian descent. She is described as 5′5″ in height, of slim build, with long black hair and brown eyes. She was wearing an Aran jumper, wine-coloured pullover, purple scarf, blue jeans, and brown leather boots. Christopher Osborne is of mixed Indian and Irish parentage and is described as 2′6″ in height, with black/brown curly hair and brown eyes. He was last seen in his collapsible pushchair, wearing green corduroy overalls, a yellow-and-white-striped jersey, dark blue jacket, and red wellingtons.
>
> Just before she disappeared Mrs Osborne went to the local AIB bank at 1.27 p.m. where she was filmed on closed-circuit security cameras making a

withdrawal. She also stopped at a local shop to purchase a new pair of wellingtons for her son.

Gardaí do not think Mrs Osborne would have accepted a lift from anyone along the walk home, and have no evidence that anyone picked her up. 'She's not somebody who would go off,' said Detective Sergeant Brian Boylan of Loughrea station. Mrs Osborne's husband said she would never make plans without informing him of her whereabouts. Gardaí say there was no sign of a struggle along the road, and that no one reported seeing or hearing anything unusual.

Anyone with information is asked to contact Loughrea Garda Station on (091) 841333 or the Garda confidential telephone number, 1-800-666222.

Nora devoured every scrap of information, alert for any discrepancy, any fissure that might serve at least as a temporary foothold. Looking through the list again, another headline jumped out at her:

Gardaí To Examine Serial Killer Possibility
The Garda commissioner, Mr Patrick Neary, has ordered the setting up of a special detective task force to examine cases of missing and murdered women, and to see if there is a serial killer in this State. The move was prompted by the disappearance on August 12th of Fidelma O'Connor (20), a student nurse last seen walking near her home in Abbeyleix, County Laois. There are similarities between the disappearances, mainly that the women were last seen walking along or near busy rural roads.

What better way to avoid suspicion than to make your wife's disappearance look like the work of a serial killer?

It could work, especially in the absence of any physical evidence. The next article gave a list of all seven disappearance cases that had been reopened. None of the seven women had ever been found. All had been alone when they disappeared. None had had a child with her, except Mina Osborne. Nora remembered Devaney's discomfort about this detail. There was something else as well, she learned from this newspaper account. The seven women were younger: nineteen or twenty, and Mina Osborne was twenty-nine years old. Nora stared absently at the words glowing on her computer screen. It was nearly two o'clock in the morning. She remembered the look on Jeremy Osborne's face when she asked if he'd been watching that video. He hadn't been allowed to answer. If she played it right, maybe she could get the boy to talk.

Chapter 18

Cormac threw off the sheets and sat up on the edge of the high bed. It was no use trying to sleep; he'd be better off doing something else. He switched on the lamp and checked his wristwatch on the bedside table. Twenty past two.

Perhaps he shouldn't have gone back to Kilgarvan. The visit had only dredged up the confusion he'd thought was long past. He'd come back last night, and flung himself into his solitary work at the priory all day long. He should be worn out, and yet his mind would not rest. He had lain in the bed in that hyperaware state that sometimes accompanies sleeplessness, eyes open, trying to make out the looming shapes in the unfamiliar darkness. The room felt airless, despite the window he'd cracked open.

He hoped Nora was getting on all right in Dublin. For a brief second, he allowed himself to imagine her pale neck and shoulders contrasted against the dark green sheets on the bed beside him. He put out a hand and felt the warmth of the place he had lain. *Enough of that*, he told himself. It wasn't that he was a monk. He'd been involved, at various times, with several intelligent, generous women he'd cared for deeply; every one had taught him a great deal. But in each relationship, he'd somehow felt more like an observer than a full participant. He should have felt like a participant, surely. And he knew they had perceived this lack in him, since each one had called it quits before he managed to figure out what wasn't quite right. Now Nora Gavin had managed to unsettle him in a way he'd never been unsettled before. He remembered the expression on her face as she sang, the way her smoky voice dipped and slid so easily through the notes, finding unexpected intervals that had pierced him through. But it wasn't just the beauty of her voice that struck him; he also marvelled at her bravery. Singing unaccompanied must be the next thing to stripping off in a room full of people.

With a sigh, Cormac put on his glasses, and crossed to sit at the table in the tower alcove where he'd laid out all his maps, notes, and photographs of the priory dig. He switched on the table lamp and opened the map book to the page where the village of Dunbeg appeared. Six inches to the mile. The purpose of these maps was to help pinpoint the location of archaeological activity; they showed the subtle curve of every road and stream, tiny lanes and byways that were invisible on any road map, all kinds of ruins and earthworks otherwise known only to farmers and their cattle. He looked at the thin black lines that represented features of the landscape, the built environment, and the empty white spaces between. The excavation at the priory was in just such an empty space. How often had he and his colleagues dug for days, even weeks or months on a site, only to end up filing a report that noted 'nothing of archaeological significance'? What if he and Nora helped Devaney delve into the lives of these people and it turned out there was no reason to do so? What if Mina Osborne had simply walked away? It could have happened that way. Any other possibility meant that someone at Bracklyn House could be involved in murder. Mrs Pilkington said there were some in the village who'd already convicted Hugh Osborne.

Perhaps Brendan McGann was right, and he should just pack it in. But why was Brendan so anxious to get rid of him? Cormac thought of the man's face at the priory. There could be any number of reasons for such ill will, but he wondered whether Brendan could hate Hugh Osborne enough to harm his family . . . Would you listen to yourself? Prattling on like some bloody policeman, he thought. No wonder he couldn't sleep. And they were no closer to solving the riddle of the *cailín rua*, which was the primary reason they'd come back here. Cormac took off his glasses and rubbed his eyes, then leaned forward and opened the window as far as it would go, and switched off the lamp at his elbow. The moon had set, so the darkness was almost palpable. Looking out into the blackness beyond his window, he tried to let a Zen-like feeling of nothingness replace the ticking of his thoughts. He would finish the dig as soon as possible, and be off, and worry no more about this.

He pushed the thought away, focusing once more on the oblong darkness, trying to imagine himself floating in the centre of that darkness, when he saw at its edge, and only for the briefest instant, a tiny speck of light. Cormac quickly put his glasses back on, and strained to make it out again, but no light flickered. The night was still. He waited, feeling his breath flowing in and out. Just as he decided that he must have imagined it, the light appeared again, this time approaching rapidly. The bright spot jogged up and down, like a torch being carried over rough terrain. Then the jogging motion stopped, and the light moved steadily closer, disappearing for a few seconds at a time. It seemed to be moving through the wood that lay to the southeast of Bracklyn House, flickering as it travelled through the trees, then becoming a steady beacon as it skirted the edge of the wood and drew nearer to the house. When it reached what Cormac judged to be a wall at the edge of the back lawn, the light abruptly vanished altogether.

What was it Devaney had said? Anything that seems out of the ordinary. But he couldn't be sure what this was, or whether it had to do with someone belonging to this house. *Leave it*, the voice in his head urged. *Get back into the bed and try to salvage a few hours' sleep*. Instead Cormac switched the lamp on again, threw on a pullover and a pair of jeans, and stepped into his shoes. He picked up the small torch he kept in his site kit, testing the strength of its beam against the palm of his hand. *Couldn't sleep*, he'd say if he encountered anyone. *Thought I'd help myself to a nightcap if that's all right*. He checked the hallway outside his room. All was quiet. He stepped lightly down the carpeted stairway to the foyer and, seeing no one, continued down the stairs to the kitchen. Hugh had cooked them a small supper a few hours ago, and the scent of sautéed onions still hung faintly in the air. The kitchen, too, was dark and quiet, and Cormac began to feel as though he might have dreamt the whole thing. He stood still, listening, then shone his flashlight on the door that led outside. It was bolted shut. He opened the door and stepped outside to look along the back wall of the house. Someone could have entered, he supposed, but gone up by one of the side stairs; there was one set just outside his bedroom, and he guessed that another similar communicating stairwell ran between floors at the opposite end of the house. He felt suddenly foolish at his curiosity, and annoyed with himself for giving in to it so easily. He closed and bolted the door again, and was just turning to go up the stairs to the foyer when he heard the sound of a wooden chair skidding across a stone floor. The noise came from behind a door just to his left, opposite the kitchen at the foot of the stairs. The door was slightly ajar, so he gave it a tentative push, and found himself in a whitewashed stone hallway with several open doorways. A gash of light fell from one.

Hugh Obsborne was sitting at a table, one eye closed in concentration as he threaded a large needle with sturdy white cord. The single lamp on the table cast a warm yellow glow. At his elbow on a workbench were the guts of a book, signatures neatly stacked, and an empty leather-clad cover. A series of different-sized tools, including a variety of awls, presses, and clamps, hung on a wooden rack within arm's reach. The ceiling in the room was quite low, and shiny black panelling reached halfway up the walls; the rest was whitewashed like the hallway, hung with antique maps in plain black frames. To the left of the doorway was built-in shelving, painted glossy black like the panelling, and containing many leather-bound books, which gave the small space the familiar musty smell of a library.

Cormac cleared his throat in greeting. 'Evening.'

Osborne turned on his stool, peering over a pair of magnifying glasses that had slid down his nose. He looked worn, the lines in his face exaggerated by the light of his work lamp.

'Ah, Cormac.' He seemed neither surprised, nor particularly displeased, to see his guest wandering about this time of night. 'Don't tell me that sleep has escaped you as well.'

'It has. I just came down to get something to drink and heard a noise. What's that you're working at?'

'Just putting a sturdier binding on my old copy of *Tom*

Jones. There's some single-malt in the cupboard there to your left; if you'd have a drop, I'll join you.'

Cormac moved to pour them each a measure of whiskey in the pair of tumblers he found beside the bottle. If Osborne had been outside, he'd made a smooth transition. He wore a dark blue sweater and grey wool dress trousers, not the usual kit for knocking about in the woods.

'Oh, by the way,' Osborne said, 'I meant to mention to you this evening that I have to go to London tomorrow on some business. Just for a few days. I hope you and Dr Gavin will be all right here on your own.'

'No bother, I'm sure we'll be fine.' As he poured the whiskey, Cormac found himself checking Osborne's footwear for any traces of mud or dew, but the man's feet were ensconced in a pair of worn leather bedroom slippers. Cormac capped the bottle and held out a drink to Hugh Osborne. 'To books with backbone.'

'Indeed,' Osborne said, 'where would literature be without a spine?'

Cormac sat on a cot against the wall and let his eyes travel around the room. Three butterfly nets, each one larger than the last, stood in one corner. The cot made up one side of a sitting area in front of the small fireplace, along with a slipcovered armchair and a threadbare Oriental rug on the stone floor. A meagre turf fire helped dispel the evening's chill. Despite the few attempts to make it cosy, the room was bare as a monk's cell compared with the heavy opulence of the upstairs rooms. Osborne saw his appraising look.

'I come here often,' he said. 'It helps to have something to do.' He spoke simply, without self-pity. Osborne looked away, and Cormac made no attempt to reply. What could one say to a man preparing to live the rest of his life in uncertainty? Instead, he sat on the cot, glass in hand, and let the silence rest between them for a moment. It was curious that no matter how objectively he might consider the possible role Osborne played in his wife's disappearance, all suspicion immediately vanished when he was in a room with the man. Cormac supposed he'd never make a good policeman for just that reason. When he finally did speak, it was to change the subject, for which Osborne was apparently grateful.

'I've been admiring your maps,' he said. 'They look authentic.'

Osborne nodded. 'That one' – he gestured to the frame hanging above the fireplace – 'was the first comprehensive map of this area, drawn up by Hugo Osborne, the chap in the portrait I showed you upstairs. I think I mentioned he was one of William Petty's men. The story is that he surveyed everything himself.' Cormac stood to peruse the map. According to this drawing, the estate consisted of a large area around the house, and various other small pockets and parcels of land scattered throughout the parish. There was a crude, three-dimensional view of Bracklyn House itself, and the nearby priory, the tower, heavily wooded areas, small clusters of houses, the lake and surrounding bogland, and in the lower right corner, a computation of all the estate's arable lands.

'No mention of Drumcleggan here at all,' Cormac said.

'That's what I first noticed about it as well. Says something about the attitude of the conqueror, doesn't it? Fortunately, the visual detail is spot-on. When you think about it, our vocations aren't all that different. When you excavate a site, you're cutting down through the actual physical evidence of human activity that took place there;

in studying place-names, I dig through layers as well, but they're usually layers of maps and papers, all jumbled up with Irish names, English, Danish, Norman names, some altered beyond all recognition. Bad translations are my greatest challenge.'

'Are all those tapes?' Cormac asked, indicating the rows of white reel-to-reel tape boxes he'd just noticed lining the shelves behind the door.

Osborne was warming to his subject now. 'Yes, my own project. Interviews with old people from the area, on the subject of place-names. It's amazing what some of them can recall, from years and years ago, if only one thinks to ask. And how place-names in particular have a tendency to stick where they've been put down. I'm afraid I've let the project slide recently, but there's a whole lot of valuable documentation there; I'm thinking I should resurrect it one day. You should see some of the blunders being perpetuated on the maps and road signs. If you're going to return to the old names, isn't it important that they be correct, and not just quasi-Gaelic versions of bad translations? At some point it does get down to academic hair-splitting, I grant you, but there is principle involved.' He gave a wry smile. 'Regretting now you ever got me started?'

'Ah – actually, I did mean to ask how you became interested in bookbinding,' Cormac said, consciously playing into Hugh Osborne's self-deprecation. Osborne drained his glass and rose briefly to pour them each another tot. Cormac was relieved that his remark had been received in the spirit in which it was intended.

'At university, actually. I read history as an undergraduate, and was amazed that they'd actually let us handle all those rare papers and manuscripts. The conservator at the library used to let me lend a hand now and again. I set up this workshop a few years ago. Bookbinding is only a sideline, really; maps and documents are my speciality. I do a bit of work for libraries and collectors, partly because it brings in a few shillings, but mostly because I enjoy it. We've a whole lot of old family papers about the place, deeds and records of births, letters from a few historical figures that I think are worth preserving for the stories they tell.' His voice softened slightly, and Cormac felt he was about to receive a confidence that might not have been shared, if it weren't for the hour and their mutual malady. 'All things I'd hoped to pass along to my son, as they'd been passed to me.' Osborne raised his face slightly, and the two men regarded one another for a moment.

Cormac got the sense that he could change the subject a hundred times, but the conversation would turn back to this place time and time again. He regretted harbouring suspicion against this man. He pictured Hugh Osborne as a sea captain lashed to his wheel, staying his course through gales, high seas, and necromancers' spells. After a moment, Osborne returned to his work, and Cormac's eyes came to rest on a large pair of black wellingtons that stood in the shadow of the workbench. Was it his imagination, or perhaps a trick of the light, he wondered, or was their dark surface glistening with wetness?

BOOK THREE

Beasts and Birds of Prey

. . . great multitude of poor swarming in all parts of the nation . . . frequently some are found feeding on carrion and weeds and some starved in the highways, and many times poor children who have lost their parents, or who have been deserted by them, are found exposed to, and some of them fed upon, by ravening wolves and other beasts and birds of prey.

– The Commissioners' Report on the State of Ireland, May 12, 1653

Chapter 1

Distances could be deceiving at night, but looking out from the kitchen window in the light of morning, Cormac could see the edge of the lawn against which the light had seemed to travel last night – or rather, earlier this morning – and he felt he'd judged its path fairly accurately. A small flock of sheep grazed near the lakeshore, some standing, some lying as though their spindly legs had been cut out from under them. He looked farther, past the perimeter of the lawn, to the Bracklyn woods. Rising up out of the branches only a few hundred yards from the house was O'Flaherty's Tower, its ivied walls a shade of green subtly different from the surrounding leaves. From this angle he could see a few wooden roof beams still intact, their slate covering long since robbed to patch holes elsewhere, probably on Bracklyn House itself.

After he'd had his breakfast, Cormac headed to the jeep parked in the drive and deposited the books and tools he needed for the day's work. But the furtive movement of the torch beam – not to mention Hugh Osborne's dew-covered wellingtons – had pricked his curiosity. Instead of climbing in and driving off, he rounded the corner of the house, past the stable that now served as shed and garage, and followed the tumble-down bawn wall that formed the first defensive barrier around Bracklyn House. He tried to imagine living in such a circumspect state of mind, as generations of landowners in these parts must have done, ever watchful for some enemy to come and batter down their doors. Not all that different, he supposed, from the Dublin pensioners shut up in their tiny flats, windows barred and doors bolted with sixteen locks.

He followed the wall, now up to his ankles in thick grass. This patch was one of several to which the sheep had yet to turn their attention. About thirty yards from the lake, the wall came to a crumbling end, no doubt toppled by time and the thick, ropelike vines that snaked over it from the wild wood. He hadn't been careful to make sure no one saw him, but he could just claim that this exploration was somehow related to his business at the priory.

The woods were thick, and the light that filtered through the leaves felt cool and indistinct. It struck him how quickly rampant vegetation could take over any place abandoned or neglected by humankind. The sounds of the wider world were muffled here, soaked up by moss and loamy soil, the carpet of ivy and the green canopy above. What a riot of shapes and textures existed in this monochromatic world. Cormac thought of Una and Fintan playing here as children, of the treasure Aoife McGann had brought home, and understood the attraction a place like this would hold for any child with a vivid imagination. It was the very sort of place that would make you believe in ancestor spirits. How often at the site of some primitive settlement had he tried to conjure up an image of Ireland before it was cultivated – a wild green expanse of forest, lake, and bog, when the people dressed in the skins of animals and plaited their hair and worshipped the sun and the spirits of trees and water?

There was no apparent footpath here, and the thin,

thorny branches that stuck out from the confusion of undergrowth caught at his clothing. He pressed on, and eventually found a narrow trail, or, rather, a place where the ferns did not grow quite as thickly. He stepped over a fallen tree, its bark and fleshy wood being slowly subsumed by a radiantly pale green moss, and as he did so, he heard the distinct snap of a branch. Cormac whirled to see who might be following, but the wood seemed to have closed up behind him. Perhaps it was just paranoia. He turned back toward the tower, listening carefully for any movement besides his own footsteps. The path began to wind this way and that, and Cormac began to understand the reason: he nearly lost his balance when his foot struck a jagged stone embedded in the earth. He knelt and parted the underbrush in several places, finding a handful of similar rocky points within arm's reach. It might be part of a *chevaux-de-frise*, an ancient defensive tactic used around ringforts to prevent easy assault by enemies on horseback. There was the tower, dead ahead, the dark grey stone of its base-batter blooming with lichen and moss. He picked his way carefully through the ankle-breaking stones, then climbed across an overgrown earthwork ditch that might be the remains of a medieval motte. The tower was about four storeys tall and reached above the tops of the surrounding trees; the only windows were arrow loops several feet long but only a few inches across. How dismal it must have been to live in such a place; how like a prison it must have seemed. Above him jutted a square garderobe that flanked a corner, and above that he could see stone corbels made to support some wooden structure long since destroyed. No sign of crows today. Cormac skirted the base of the tower, looking for the entrance doorway, which he discovered on the far side from his approach. The doorway was a simple pointed Gothic arch, above it a carved stone that might have been a family escutcheon, but it was too damaged to make out. The fact that there was a wooden door at all was curious, because the tower looked to be long abandoned. More curious still was the stout, shiny new padlock that hung from a latch firmly anchored to the wall. He lifted the lock and examined the keyhole at its base. Newly made scratches shone where someone had tried to insert the key and missed the mark. Once the door was locked, there was no way into or out of this tower short of scaling the walls.

Why would Osborne want to keep this building locked? The place was in ruins. Probably something to do with liability, preventing local hooligans larking about and getting themselves killed. But why would someone be out here in the middle of the night? If it were some sort of trysting place, that would explain the secrecy. But a trysting place for whom? Maybe he was wrong about Hugh Osborne and Una McGann. If they were involved, they certainly had reason not to be seen together in public. He couldn't imagine Lucy Osborne in a place like this, but what about Jeremy? It could also be someone completely unconnected to this house, some local Lothario who could have claimed this abandoned fortress as a meeting place. If that were the case, however, the whole village would know about it. Dolly Pilkington would certainly know who had purchased such a whacking great padlock, and might even have divined its purpose. Here he was again, acting the policeman.

As he stood at the door, Cormac heard the croaking call of a crow. He turned and saw nothing but leafy greenness all around, heard nothing but the distant shout of a corncrake. Was someone out there, watching him? The teeming silence of the wood gave no answer.

Chapter 2

Nora overslept the morning after the mysterious phone call. She was hurriedly repacking her case for the return trip to Bracklyn when she remembered to check her mobile phone for messages. There was only one, from Cormac, wondering if she would mind picking up a few items for him while she was in Dublin. Robbie McSweeney had a key to the house, and was going to gather up the stuff; she could just collect the bag from him. She erased the message and punched in Robbie's office number. They arranged to meet at Cormac's house.

Coming from the city centre, Nora crossed over the Grand Canal at Charlemont Street and found herself immediately in the heart of Ranelagh. If the daylight seemed a bit harsh this morning, it was probably because the leaves on the trees were still small, still a fresh shade of pale green against the sky. Cormac's street, Highfield Crescent, turned out to be one of those gracefully curved and chestnut-lined Dublin avenues that seemed miles from the cacophonous bottlenecks of the main roads. Robbie hadn't arrived yet, but he was coming all the way from the Belfield campus. Nora studied the face of Number 43, a tidily terraced redbrick row house, with an arched entrance trimmed in leaded glass, one of the thousands of nearly identical Victorian doorways in Dublin. Why did it seem curious to her that Cormac's door was painted a bright, sunny yellow? The fenced front garden was a sharply edged patch of green turf so small that he might easily keep it trimmed year-round with a pair of embroidery scissors. Though she hadn't yet seen the inside, she knew it would be a space very different from her airy, modern flat across the canal. She felt a twinge of uneasiness. It was strange coming here without Cormac's knowledge. Should she have arranged to meet Robbie at his office? She hadn't time to answer her own question when Robbie tapped at the driver's-side window.

'You can wait out here if you like,' he said as she rolled down the window, 'but I was hoping you might come in for just half a minute. I'm dyin' for a mug of tea. And your reward would be the small bit of news I have for you.'

Nora found herself following reluctantly as Robbie pushed open the front door, careful not to knock down the old-fashioned black bicycle that stood in the narrow front hall. 'I'll round up the things he's asked for, shall I, and you can get started on the tea.' After pointing her in the direction of the kitchen, at the back of the house, Robbie disappeared up the stairs, half lilting, half humming a faintly familiar tune. Nora entered the clean black-and-white-tiled kitchen; a table and two chairs stood in the small conservatory that jutted off the back of the house into the walled garden, giving the room a bright aspect, even on this slightly overcast day. She filled the electric kettle, found tea in a tin beside the stove, and prepared two mugs, then checked the fridge for milk. Plenty for tea; she held the bottle to her nose to make sure it hadn't turned. The kettle boiled quickly, and while the tea was steeping, she ventured into the dining room, or what would normally have been used as a dining room, for this place was set up as a study:

bookshelves lined the walls and a large table in front of the window was piled high with books and manila folders that almost obscured the view of the garden. Through an open set of double doors was a sitting room, with a deep leather sofa in front of a fireplace, and a couple of chairs upholstered in Turkish-looking geometric tapestry. The walls of both rooms were painted a ruddy ochre, and at the front of the house was a broad windowseat flanked by two bookcases that reached to the ceiling. The atmosphere was orderly, unfussy, much like the man himself, and yet there were a couple of pieces that didn't seem to fit, like the pillow-covered chaise in the corner at the far side of the fireplace. She tried to imagine Cormac at home here. The stereo cabinet in the near corner was piled high with homemade tapes. Nora scanned them, recognizing the names of some older traditional musicians. She approached the bookcases in the living room. The archaeology titles were no surprise, but Cormac also had quite a collection of books on art history, world religions, architecture, and language. There was a whole section of books on Irish place-names. What was it he'd said to Hugh Osborne? 'Interested, but not very knowledgeable.' Right. She moved to the other set of bookcases, running her fingers along the spines of old editions in Irish, antique collections of Dickens, Shakespeare, and Jane Austen, newer translations of Dostoevsky and Tolstoy, a pile of Graham Greene novels, books of poetry by Seamus Heaney and Patrick Kavanagh. Had Cormac read them all? She was suddenly seized with homesickness, remembering her own precious books, save for the few volumes she couldn't possibly live without, packed up in storage at home in Saint Paul. Seeing this wonderful collection only served as a reminder that nothing in her life was the same as it had been before. She sank down slowly on the window seat and closed her eyes, overcome by a terrible and familiar craving. And what if her need to scrabble through the evidence to find something, anything – what if it never satisfied her emptiness? Nora opened her eyes. She could still hear Robbie's absentminded lilting from upstairs.

A small framed photograph on the mantelpiece caught her gaze. It was Cormac and Gabriel McCrossan, looking up from an excavation pit and showing off a hoard of artefacts they'd just uncovered, looking tired and dirty and immensely pleased with themselves. How was Cormac faring after losing this man he must have considered a second father? Maybe Robbie had some clue about how he was getting on. She set the picture back on the mantel as she heard footsteps on the stairs.

'Find everything all right?' Robbie asked. 'For the tea, I mean,' he added hastily, and from the look that came with it, she knew he was giving her a gentle ribbing for having a look around the place.

'Everything was exactly where it ought to be,' she said. 'Cormac is a very logical fella.'

'Oh, he is,' Robbie agreed, following her into the kitchen. 'Promise you won't hold that against him?'

'Robbie, I'm anxious to hear what you found out.'

'And I'm just as anxious to tell you. But hang on, hasn't he got a biscuit or something to go with the tea?' Robbie asked, opening a cupboard and rummaging around until he found what he needed, an unopened packet of plain chocolate wheatmeal biscuits. 'Doesn't even fancy these, but keeps a few on hand because they're my favourite. Commendable, isn't it?'

'Very touching,' Nora agreed. 'But, Robbie, what did you find out?'

'You understand that what I was doing was only very general research.'

'I do. Go on.'

'Well, it's interesting,' he said, through the crumbs of his first biscuit. 'Beheading was generally reserved for people of some importance. Old-fashioned hanging was considered sufficient for most crimes, and for most criminals, right up through the nineteenth century.' He was warming to the subject now. 'And hanging generally meant slow death by strangulation. I found several reports of people being resuscitated after a half-hour on the rope.' He spoke with some amazement at this fact. 'Of course, we have a couple of Irish doctors to thank for the long drop. They took into account the prisoner's weight, and how much force it would take to break his neck. It was all very scientific; they had tables for calculating the length of the rope. Though it seems the main reason for the change wasn't to put the condemned out of their misery any more quickly, but to spare witnesses the discomfort of watching them dangle.'

'Absolutely fascinating,' Nora said, hoping that her exasperation wasn't starting to show.

'But back to beheading – you'd have to be a fairly high-born person to get your head chopped off. Not only that, but you'd have to have done something pretty terrible, treason or regicide, or something equally heinous. That's why not a lot of women would have been beheaded; I'm having trouble coming up with any actual historical accounts. But – and here's what I found most interesting—' he said, leaning forward, 'starting in the Middle Ages, beheading became a sort of standard punishment for infanticide. I suppose it's always considered the worst sort of abomination to kill a child—'

Nora could hear Robbie's voice continuing, but the

noise in her head crowded it out. There was a dinning sound, like the beating of dustbin lids in her ears. She felt a prickling sensation down her neck and on the backs of her arms.

'Robbie,' she said suddenly, 'we have a date now, or at least a rough time frame. Remember that piece of metal in the X-rays?'

'I do.'

'It was a ring, possibly a wedding ring. And it was inscribed with a date – 1652. How many women could have been executed in East Galway since then? If we were looking for a needle in a haystack, I'd say the needle had just grown larger.'

'Ah, but you're forgetting that a large portion of the haystack itself went up in smoke,' he said. 'Lots of documents from that period were destroyed when the Public Records Office was shelled during the Civil War back in 1922.'

'But surely not everything burned. There are other sources, aren't there? I just can't believe that would be the only place to look. What about the National Archives? Or the Public Records Office in London? And couldn't the initials from the ring help somewhat? Maybe there are marriage records, or at least census records for the area somewhere that could give us a clue.' Nora was surprised at the urgency in her own voice. 'Don't give up on me now, Robbie.'

Chapter 3

St Columba's Catholic Church was a severe-looking grey stone monstrosity, built in the nineteenth century and now serving Dunbeg and several small neighbouring communities. Father Kinsella was evidently just finishing up with the cleaners, a small brigade of nondescript, slightly doughy middle-aged women armed with mops, buckets, rags, and polish. Their beaming faces and collective posture told Devaney that the handsome, curly-haired curate knew exactly the effect he had on female parishioners of a certain age, and felt no compunction about using it – all to the advantage of the Church, of course. Devaney stood inhaling the atmosphere – that mixed scent of furniture polish, incense, flowers, and candlewax peculiar to a church – and waited for the priest to finish with his fan club and herd them off in the direction of the sacristy.

Despite its familiar essence, this modern space felt strange to Devaney, not at all like the ancient and mysterious Church of his childhood. Perhaps it was the changes in the Mass since he was a boy; perhaps it was just that the rituals and accoutrements of faith no longer impressed him.

'Ah, Detective,' Kinsella said, rubbing his hands together like an eager young businessman when he turned and caught sight of Devaney. He paused to genuflect briefly in front of the altar, then came sprinting energetically down the centre aisle to shake hands. 'Garrett, isn't it? I know your family, of course, Nuala and the children, but we haven't had the pleasure of your company.' When Devaney offered no visible reaction, the priest was politic enough to press no further.

'Is there somewhere we could talk that's a bit more out of the way?' Devaney asked, pulling a small notebook from his breast pocket.

Kinsella led the way to the baptismal chapel, and offered Devaney a seat on one of the benches that lined the walls. 'Now, Detective, what can I do for you?'

'I'm going through the file on the Osborne case, talking to some of the original witnesses, just on the chance that anything new has come to mind.'

The priest's helpful demeanour changed to a look of thoughtful resignation. 'I had a feeling it might be that,' he said. 'I try to keep hoping for the best. It's getting more and more difficult. But I do pray for them every day.'

'You said in your original statement that Mina Osborne wasn't a regular parishioner when you first came here.'

'That's right. She only started coming to Mass after Christopher was born.'

'I was surprised to find that she was a Catholic,' Devaney said. 'Coming from India—'

'There's actually quite a large number of Catholics in India, Detective. Ever since the forcible mass conversions by the Portuguese in the fifteenth century. Not the most commendable period in Church history, I grant you. That's when Mina's family would have taken the surname Gonsalves.'

'Strange how they kept the faith, if it was only forced upon them.'

'Yes, that does seem curious, doesn't it? But I suppose

by the time they did have any choice in the matter, it was already something of a long-standing family tradition.'

'I think you said Mina spoke with you the week she disappeared, and in fact had been to see you more than a few times in the previous couple of weeks.'

'Yes, that's right, there were things she wanted to discuss about her own spiritual life, but she was also thinking about her son. Whether he ought to be brought up in the Church.'

'You say *she* was trying to decide. Was there any disagreement between Mina Osborne and her husband on that point?'

'I don't know that I'd call it disagreement. They were discussing options. Christopher was still very young. I don't know that Hugh Osborne had a terribly strong opinion, to tell you the truth. It was more a matter of Mina trying to resolve some questions of her own about her faith.'

'Did she say anything that seemed out of the ordinary, anything to indicate her state of mind? Was there anything troubling her that day?'

'I hope you're not trying to insinuate—' Kinsella began. 'Because I'm certain that Mina would never have harmed herself or Christopher.'

'I'm not insinuating anything; what I am trying to do is to find Mrs Osborne. Please, just tell me what she said.' The edge of exasperation in Devaney's voice seemed to give the priest pause.

'The reason the whole question of religious education had come up was that Mina wanted to take Christopher to India to meet his grandparents. She wanted to be able to tell them, truthfully, that her son was going to be raised in the Church. And her husband evidently had some reservations. There's always tension when the couple come from different traditions. There were a few issues they'd not really resolved before the marriage – one of them was how the children would be raised – but it was nothing that couldn't eventually be worked out. Mina had been estranged from her parents – her father, at least – since she married Hugh Osborne. They'd chosen not to be married in the Church, you see, and it mattered a great deal to her father. His family had always been strict Catholics, loads of aunts and uncles in religious orders; one was even an archbishop, I think. Anyway, Mina believed that such a gesture on her part might ease things with the father. Personally, I think there was more to it than that. We see it all the time. People fall away when they come of age, but when they have children, when they need something to connect with, something meaningful and profound to pass on to their children, they're drawn back to the Church. The pull of tradition is much stronger than we realize.'

'Do you remember exactly what she said?'

Kinsella looked as though he wasn't quite ready to part with the information. 'I've gone over and over our last conversation. It was a couple of days before she disappeared, but I never saw her after that. Just as she was leaving, she said, "Hugh's against the idea now, but he'll come around. He's hardly going to try keeping us here under lock and key".'

'Excuse me, but I don't recall any reference to "lock and key" in your earlier statement,' Devaney said.

'She was only joking, Detective. There was no fear in those words. She'd come to a decision, and was joyful about it.' He added, as if to excuse his sin of omission, 'I knew it would be taken the wrong way.'

Devaney gave the priest a questioning look. 'Anything else you've suddenly remembered?'

'I swear that's the only thing I might have left out of my original statement.'

'Would she have made the trip without her husband's approval?'

'I believe she would have waited. She'd never have deliberately done anything to hurt him. That's why her disappearance has been so troubling. You don't know her, Detective. Mina's spirit was filled with light, unlike any other person I've known.'

Devaney studied the priest's face. 'Sure you didn't fancy her yourself? You wouldn't be the first.'

'Contrary to what you might read in the papers, Detective, there are a few of us who do take the vows seriously. I don't deny that Mina confided in me. I don't even know why, really. I suppose there weren't many people around here she could consider friends. But we were just friends.'

'What did you talk about?'

'Oh, I don't know – books, music, the nature of God, the life of the soul. I think she was just starved for conversation.'

'And she couldn't talk to her husband?' Devaney asked.

'Of course she could. I'm not saying that. But an intelligent person like Mina needs a very high level of intellectual engagement. She told me once that when she came here she couldn't paint all day and all night as she'd done before. I think she needed other outlets.'

'What was your impression of the Osbornes' marriage?'

'I think it was fairly solid, despite their brief courtship. She was certainly committed to the marriage. Of course she knew that her husband had other . . . women friends, before they married. He is somewhat older, and she wasn't completely naive. But I got a sense that—'

'What?'

'Well, she never actually put it into words, but I think she may have had . . . some worries. Probably completely unfounded.'

'Can you recall what it was that gave you that sense?'

'I remember her asking rather pointedly in our last conversation about God's forgiveness of sin. Hating the sin, but loving the sinner.'

'Maybe she was thinking of herself. You know that she was pregnant when they married?'

'Yes. Oh, don't worry, I'm not divulging any secrets of the confessional. She didn't try to hide it. Sometimes I think that may have been the real source of her doubts.'

'You don't believe Osborne had a bit on the side.'

'I don't know, Detective. I can't say I really know the man.' Kinsella looked steadily back at Devaney. 'He comes here, you know. Shows up at an early Mass and just sits in the back. I've tried to find him afterwards, a couple of times, but he's always gone.'

For a brief portion of a second, Devaney thought he glimpsed what failure felt like to a priest. 'Thanks for your time, Father. I think that's all for now.'

'Tell Nuala and the children I was asking for them.'

'I will.' Devaney turned to leave, and was about to push open the door at the back of the church when he heard the priest draw a tentative breath.

'You know, I wonder, as long as you're here,' Kinsella said. 'It's hardly worth mentioning, really . . .'

'What is it?' Devaney asked.

'Well, we've had a rash of petty thefts recently, nothing serious, just somebody nicking offertory candles from one of the side chapels. I know a few candles might not seem like much in the larger scheme of things, but every penny counts in a small parish like this, and it's all quite mysterious.'

'Can you show me where?'

Kinsella escorted him to a small, shadowy chapel just off the altar. A stained-glass window filtered a gloomy light into the alcove, where a painted plaster statue of the Virgin stood upon an altar. A metal crown of stars formed a halo around her head, and a half-dozen flickering candles illuminated her face from below. Devaney suddenly remembered being in thrall to a similar statue as a child. With her outstretched arms draped in that sky-blue robe, her face a portrait of radiant kindness, he had thought her the most beautiful creature he had ever seen. He'd have willingly saved a thousand pennies just to light one candle at her feet. He turned his attention to the priest.

'So this recent theft wasn't the first?'

'The first time was about six months ago, then again a few months later, and finally, last weekend. The candles are usually kept here.' Kinsella indicated an empty shelf below the row of burning votive lights. 'I might not have noticed, even, except that we'd just put out a whole rake of new candles on Friday, and on Sunday morning they were all gone. I've held off saying anything, but now it's becoming a rather regular habit. I'm not sure we'd want to prosecute, but I'd surely like to know who feels the need to steal from the church. It may be a cry for help.'

'How many entrances to the building?' Devaney asked.

'The main doors, of course, and two side doors, one through the sacristy, and the other through this side.' The priest indicated a door just around the corner from where they were standing. 'But that's locked most times, only used for funerals and the like.'

'Do you ever lock up entirely?'

'I'm afraid we have no choice,' Kinsella said. 'I only say Mass here two days a week; I have two other parishes to look after. Unless the cleaners are here, like today, or we have some evening function like a wedding rehearsal, the building is locked up tight. And Saturday evenings, of course, when I hear confessions. I'm almost sure that's when it's happening.'

'Why do you say that?'

'Well, it occurred to me that each of the thefts happened on an evening we had a visit from the "phantom penitent".' Kinsella's face betrayed slight embarrassment. 'Not very respectful, I'm afraid.'

'Why do you call him that?'

'I'm not even sure it's a him,' Kinsella said. 'This person – whoever it is – waits until the last one before him is in the confessional, then comes in at the other side. Never says a word. At first I just waited; I understand it sometimes takes a few moments to order your thoughts. I've tried speaking up as well, but there's never any response. After about five minutes, whoever it is gets up and leaves. I haven't gone so far as opening the door to try and find out who it is.'

'How many times has this happened?'

'I don't know. Four or five times, I think.'

'Could I have a look at the confessionals?' Devaney asked.

'Surely, right over here,' Kinsella said, leading the way to the opposite side of the church.

'Do you hear confessions every week?'

'I do. Always a rush at Christmas and Easter, but there's generally not a great demand.' Kinsella gestured for Devaney to open the door to the confessional and look into the central compartment, which he did, noting the red velvet cushion for the priest, and the small sliding wooden doors. The one to his left was open, and he could see where the confessor heard sins through a grille covered with black cloth.

'I wonder if you'd mind stepping inside for a moment,' Devaney said. 'Which side does the person come in?'

'Always the right side. My right, that is, when I'm inside. Does that make a difference?' Devaney thought he detected a touch of excitement in Kinsella's voice, the kind of enthusiasm an ordinary citizen feels when involved in some aspect of a police investigation – the kind of enthusiasm the police were often better off without.

'It might,' Devaney said. He stood just outside the confessional door, looking up and down the length of the church. 'Who are your regulars?'

'I don't know if I ought to say.'

'It's possible someone might have seen your phantom.'

Kinsella seemed to consider this point. 'There's Mrs Phelan, who lives just beside us here, in the lane. Tom Dunne, since he's been retired, has been coming every week, and Margaret Conway. A few others as well.'

As harmless a bunch of wretches as ever there was, Devaney thought to himself. A hell of a lot they'd have to confess. 'And where do they queue up?'

'In the pews, just opposite. But as I said, whoever it is always waits until the last one of them is inside the confessional before coming in the other side. I doubt whether any of them have seen who it is.'

Devaney opened the door and went into the confessional on the side the phantom penitent used. The last time he'd been in one of these places, he'd been Pádraig's age, a brainwashed altar boy fairly saturated with impure thoughts. He pulled the door closed, to get the full effect. He half smiled at the idea, remembering with clarity the exact moment when he'd rejected the notion of God. It had been no more complicated than flicking a light switch. He'd been better off since. He knelt at the leather-padded prie-dieu, and did not adopt the prescribed posture of supplication, but examined the interior of the tiny space, hearing in his head the whispered sins of multitudes, a running inventory of gossip repeated, losses of temper, drinks taken, as if God were some miserly book-keeper, logging every minor offence. But maybe there were a few major offences as well. What was it Houlihan always said? He could hear his old partner's nasal East Clare accent digging into the pithy syllables: *Debauchery, skulduggery, fornication, and witchcraft. No shortage of them, anywhere you look.* Devaney was aware of dampness on his palms, and he could feel his breath becoming shorter, but he remained in the compartment, the only illumination coming from a small barred opening at the top of the door. He felt the air stopping halfway down his windpipe, no matter how he tried to draw it in. He was starting to feel light-headed, and knew he should get out. He reached for the prie-dieu to pull himself to his feet, and, although he was almost overcome with panic, felt a roughness with his thumb below the ledge. With great effort, he stood, and burst out of the confessional, gasping for air. Kinsella was right behind him.

'Are you all right?' The priest's face showed genuine concern. Devaney sat at the end of the nearest pew and tried to get his breath.

'Touch of a flu coming on,' he said when he was able, wiping his face with the crumpled handkerchief from his back pocket.

'Are you sure? I can phone for the doctor.'

Devaney shook his head vehemently. He wasn't even supposed to be here. And this wasn't the sort of thing he'd want his comrades in the Guards to know about. He went back to the open door of the confessional. He didn't go in this time, but crouched to look under the armrest on the prie-dieu. What he had felt seemed to be letters – initials, perhaps – crudely cut into the wood, probably with a penknife. He had to crawl partway into the confessional to see. He pulled a small torch from his breast pocket and shone it on the obscure spot. It wasn't just initials, but a whole string of letters – *H E K N O W S W H E R E T H E Y A R E*. It took him a few more seconds to make out the separate words: *He . . . knows . . . where . . . they . . . are.* Devaney felt his breathing become shallow once again.

'That's all for now, Father,' he said, rising from his hands and knees, and replacing the torch in his jacket pocket. 'But do me a favour, will you? Don't let anyone in. Get everyone out of the church and keep it locked up until I get back.'

Chapter 4

It was nearly two-thirty when Nora pulled up at the Drumcleggan Priory. She could hear flute music, and the noise of a pickaxe hitting damp soil. All the way out here she had argued with herself about whether to tell anyone about the phone call. In the end, she decided to keep mum unless something else happened. She just wasn't sure what 'something else' entailed. Nora grabbed the file containing photographs of the ring, and made her way to where Cormac was working. His back was to her, so she walked closer, admiring the way he swung the heavy pick. She waited until the sharp point was in the ground before speaking.

'I'm back. I brought the things you asked for.' Upon hearing her voice, Cormac dropped the wooden handle and turned, wiping his palms on his dusty trouser legs.

'Oh, hello,' he said. 'Thanks.' They stood awkwardly for a moment, looking at one another. The day was overcast but warm, and a mist of sweat covered his face.

'I'm making some progress,' he finally said, gesturing to the second set of test trenches, which he'd already excavated down to a depth of about three feet. He must have been working pretty steadily while she'd been away.

'So I see. Anything turn up?'

'Just a few bits of crockery. I'm not very far along with this area.'

There was a pause before they both began speaking at once.

'Sorry,' Nora said. 'You first.'

'No, I insist,' Cormac said.

'All right. That piece of metal inside the girl's mouth – you'll never guess what it turned out to be.' She extended the folder, which he opened to a glossy photo of a gold ring, shown at about five times its actual size, the red stone looking slightly washed out by the flash.

'There's an inscription,' she said. 'You can see it in the next couple of pictures, I think.'

Cormac sat down on the lip of the trench to look through the photos more carefully. 'It's a pretty astonishing find, but what does it tell us? That she wasn't likely in the bog before 1652 – but it could have been any time after that. It's possible that the ring was inscribed in 1652 but not buried with her until years later.' He sounded disappointed.

'At least it's something,' Nora said. She felt slightly perturbed that he wasn't more excited.

'What did Robbie make of all this? I assume you told him.'

'He isn't too hopeful, but he agreed to press on, looking for trial or marriage records. It occurred to me on the way out here that OF could stand for O'Flaherty.'

'Surely. But it could just as easily be O'Farrell, O'Flynn, or O'Fallon as well. We'll never find out conclusively, and we'll just end up running in circles and going mad over all the possibilities.'

'I know we can find out who she was,' Nora said. 'I don't know why I believe it so strongly, I just do. Go ahead and laugh, but I think the ring is some sort of a message. I think it was the only way she could think of to tell us who she was.'

'Anyone could have put that ring in her mouth, even after she was dead. We've nothing to go on either way. You see, we're going mad already, arguing about it. But what if we go and speak to Ned Raftery, the schoolteacher?'

She could tell he was trying to make peace. 'All right,' she said. 'What was it you were going to tell me?' She listened intently as Cormac told about what had happened in her absence: the light in the woods, his late-night chat with Hugh Osborne, and his visit this morning to the tower house.

She said, 'I hope you notice that I'm not in the least bothered by the fact that you went there without me. You're turning into a regular gumshoe.'

His look was slightly sheepish. 'God help us.'

'I think it's time I got my hands dirty,' she said. 'Back in a bit.'

Nora drove rapidly to Bracklyn House, first dropping off Cormac's case in his room, then returning down the broad, carpeted hallway to her own. The house was quiet, but something in the stillness made her uneasy. There wasn't enough life in this place; things got done silently, by unseen hands, and it could unnerve a person. In her own room, she slipped off her shoes and crossed to the bathroom. Before she stepped over the threshold, something caught her eye, and she stopped short. Shards of broken glass lay scattered across the floor. She checked the shelf above the sink. The drinking glass was gone. And yet the jagged shards seemed to add up to more than a single water glass. She looked down at her stockinged feet. Stepping into the room would have been disastrous. Was this really an accident, or some sort of warning? Nora felt a sudden prick of fear as she remembered the whispering voice on the phone: *Leave it alone*. This place was making her paranoid. She should just carry on, and assume it was an accident unless something else happened. She'd seen where Hugh Osborne put the broom after Jeremy's encounter with her wineglass, so she put her shoes back on and ventured downstairs towards the kitchen.

She heard the sound of scrubbing coming from the doorway under the main stairs, and saw a figure in old clothes, down on hands and knees, scouring the stone floor with a hard-bristled brush. The woman's dark hair was caught up in a scarf, but a few stray wisps moved as she worked the brush with one gloved hand in a vigorous circular motion.

'Excuse me,' Nora said. The woman dropped the brush in her bucket with a splash and started to her feet, removing her bandanna in one sweeping motion. It was Lucy Osborne. They stood for an instant in silence. Lucy's humiliation was evident from the rising tide of crimson on her neck, until Nora managed to stammer, 'I'm sorry, I thought you were—'

'Yes. Well.' Lucy Osborne was beginning to regain her composure, smoothing the stray hairs back into place. 'My cleaner, Mrs Hernan, is down with a flu, and these stairs were in sore need of attention, with all the extra traffic through the house.'

'I apologize if I startled you,' Nora said. 'I was just getting a broom – there's a broken glass in my bathroom.'

'Oh dear. I'll be right up to see to it.'

'There's no need. I know where to find the broom.'

Nora left Lucy Osborne standing in the doorway at the top of the kitchen stairs, with the bandanna still clutched behind her back. But when she came back up the stairs a moment later, there was no sign of Lucy or her brush and bucket, except for the faint damp spot on the stone floor.

Chapter 5

After returning to the church and swearing Father Kinsella to silence about this latest development, Devaney shot some pictures of the letters carved in the wood of the confessional and dusted the area for prints. There were no clear fingerprints; plenty of smudgy partials, but nothing of any real use.

When he'd finished at the church, Devaney drove to a spot just outside the gates to Bracklyn House and waited. He saw Dr Gavin's car pull out of the drive, presumably headed towards the priory. About twenty minutes later, he spotted Osborne's black Volvo. He counted out ten seconds, then pulled out of the blind approach and followed.

Tea time came and went as he followed Hugh Osborne to Shannon Airport, but Devaney found he wasn't even hungry. Now he watched through the glass of the departures lounge as Osborne boarded a British Airways flight to London. When the last passenger was gone, Devaney approached the counter where the uniformed reservation agent stood.

'What time does this flight arrive in London?' he asked.

'There's no stopover in Dublin,' the young woman said, 'so it should arrive in Gatwick at nine-fifty.'

Nine-fifty. It might not be too late to call the Badger. Jimmy Deasey, an old friend from his early days in the

Guards, had been called 'the Badger' as long as Devaney had known him, which must be going on twenty years, although it was doubtful whether anyone at all remembered why. Deasey had emigrated to England five years ago, taking up a cushy post as head of security for some high-tech company outside London, but they had kept in touch. Devaney located the nearest coin phone, looked up Jimmy's entry in the tiny book he kept in his breast pocket, and dialled the number.

'Hullo,' said a deep voice, which, despite the loud, thumping music in the background, he thought he recognized as the Badger's.

'Jimmy, it's Garrett Devaney—'

'Hang on. I think you want my da.' The sound of a hand over the receiver muffled the boy's voice as he called, and Devaney could just make out the Badger saying, 'Ciaran, would you ever turn that down? How do you expect to hear anyone over the phone?' The music subsided, and he heard the Badger's voice, but with an unfamiliar, businesslike tone. 'Seamus Deasey here.'

'Jaysus, Jimmy, the lad must be as tall as yourself. It's Garrett Devaney.'

Instantly, the Anglicized inflection disappeared from Deasey's voice, replaced by his own musical Cork accent. 'Ah, Devaney, begod, how are ye getting on? It's been feckin' ages.'

'Ah indeed, don't remind me.'

There was a pause. 'I heard about your trouble, Gar. I'm sorry. It could have happened to any one of us.'

'Thanks, Jimmy,' Devaney said. Another brief silence. 'I'm actually ringing for a favour. I'd never ask, but there's nobody else who can help me out on this thing, only yourself.'

'Not in trouble with another superintendent, are you?'

'Not yet. Although if that fuckin' magpie mentions his spotless divisional record to me one more time . . . I've actually just followed a suspect out to Shannon Airport. He caught a flight to Gatwick, should be arriving there at nine-fifty tonight. I was wondering – I mean, if you've nothing on – if you'd be up for a small bit of—'

'Surveillance?' Devaney could hear the surprise in his friend's voice, and waited uneasily as Jimmy considered the proposal. It was a lot to ask.

'Just see where he goes from Gatwick?' Deasey asked. Devaney had him.

'That's it, just tell me where he goes, who he talks to. Nothing strenuous.'

'What have you got on him?'

'Fuck-all, that's the trouble. But his wife and kid have gone missing, and I can't convince myself that he wasn't somehow involved.'

'Could be interesting,' Deasey said. 'Better give me the lowdown.' Devaney passed along the pertinent information: Osborne's description and flight number. He could hear Deasey scribbling them down.

'Ring me at home, will you, Jimmy?' he said. 'I'm heading there now. I'll be up late.'

As he went home, Devaney timed the drive from Shannon to Dunbeg. It was no more than thirty miles as the crow flies, but there was no direct route, only branching secondary roads up through Sixmilebridge and then east on the Ennis road to Scarriff and Mountshannon. Couldn't have taken Osborne less than an hour and forty-five minutes, providing that he drove without trying to attract attention. Including the walk from the plane, and out to the car park, that would have put him outside Dunbeg at 2.15 p.m. at the very earliest. So, if he had met his wife and son outside the town, taken them somewhere, and still returned to Bracklyn by 6 p.m., as Lucy Osborne reported, they'd have to be somewhere within a two-hour radius. Jesus. That was half of Clare and East Galway. He studied his road map, mentally drawing a circle around Dunbeg. That area included the lake, but it also included some remote and heavily forested mountains along the border. No fucking wonder they hadn't been found. He'd see what the Badger came up with on Osborne's trip to London, then suss him out about checking into that conference Osborne had at Oxford. If he was telling the truth about having to stop for a kip on the way home from the airport, who or what had kept him up so late the night before?

Deasey's call came at a few minutes past eleven. 'Well, that was a dead-easy job,' he said. 'Your client left the airport, took a cab straight to a house in Christ Church. I've got him under obso now. Posh sort of a house for the area; he's standing outside the door. I'll check on the address for you in the morning. These fuckin' mobile phones are great, aren't they? What did we ever do before?'

'Is he letting himself in, Jimmy, or is somebody answering?'

'Hang on, let me get the specs on him. There's a woman answering the door. Looks Pakistani, short hair, about thirty. Seems like he was expected. Big hug; she's kissing him on the cheek.' Devaney felt a surge of adrenalin, as he had in the old days, chasing down a hooligan on foot. When he spoke, however, his voice was calm. 'Are they alone?'

'Yeah,' said Deasey. 'No – now it looks like he's talking to somebody else.' There was a pause.

'What's he doing now, Jimmy?'

'He's just leaned over and picked up a kid.'

Chapter 6

Una McGann had to use all her strength to knead the huge ball of brown bread dough on her kitchen table. The house seemed peaceful at the moment, with the occasional ray of early morning sun coming in, and the wireless tuned to Radio na Gaeltachta, the rhythmic waves of traditional music occasionally interrupted by the faint drone of the news in Irish. But it was a false tranquillity. Since Monday night the atmosphere in the house had been poisonous. Brendan and Fintan went about their work on the farm without uttering so much as a word to each other, and neither would speak more than two words to her. When they got home, each retreated to his room, venturing into the kitchen only when the other was safely out of the way. Brendan was still angry at both of them, and Fintan was furious with her for not leaving immediately – and for forcing him to stay, since he felt he couldn't leave her and Aoife alone with Brendan after what had happened.

Una looked over at her daughter, who'd crept downstairs early and was now slumbering again on the sofa. The sun was beginning to cross Aoife's bright hair, her face so smooth and relaxed in the oblivion of sleep. She was going to be tall, Una thought – unlike her mother. No doubt about that. She felt a surge of anger at Brendan. How dare he request a copy of Aoife's birth certificate behind her back? She'd have shown him the bloody thing herself if he'd bothered to ask. And how dare he think it any of his business who Aoife's father was? That's what he'd been after, she was sure. There was only one person besides herself whose business it was, and that person was Aoife. She would be told when the time came. So far, it hadn't been a problem, but Aoife was getting to the age where such things did matter. In a place like Dunbeg, the label of bastard still carried a lot of weight, far more than it had in Dublin, where half the children in their street had no known fathers at all. She'd better start working out what she would say to her daughter and to the world. Una had once half thought of making up some foreign student – a German, or a Swede, perhaps – who'd been at university when she was there, a short-lived romance with someone now totally out of the picture. There was no danger that such a man would ever resurface, since he was fictional.

That would be the simplest story to tell the outside world, but what about Aoife? She doubted that she could tell her daughter such a lie, but to tell her the truth meant telling everyone, since you couldn't expect a child to keep that kind of confidence under pressure. And pressure there would be; no one could find the weakness in a person's armour like a malicious eight-year-old in a schoolyard.

Brendan's outburst had convinced her that she and Aoife must not be dependent on anyone. That's what had prompted this flurry of activity, in preparation for the market day. Two hand-knitted jumpers, and as much brown bread and seed cake as she could turn out in three days wouldn't bring much, but Una knew she had to begin setting aside something so that she and her daughter could strike out on their own. It would be another year at least until the priory workshops were finished, and that was only working space, no living quarters, as far as she knew. Perhaps she could clean or cook in exchange for a little house or an apartment. She had rejected Fintan's offer to bring them to America with him, knowing that it wasn't what he really wanted, or what she and Aoife wanted either. The few years she'd spent in Dublin had given her a glimpse of a kind of desperation she did not want to see again. At least here you could grow your own vegetables, and the shops in the village, some of them, anyway, would keep a running total of your purchases that you could pay off as you were able. There was slightly more mercy here than in the city, she thought – about some things, not others. She knew people in the village remembered how she'd run away, shamed her family, and shamed them once again when she'd come back with a child in tow. Some still clucked over the fact that she'd only come home for her mother's funeral, though it was more than three years past. There was no way not to be talked about. People in Dunbeg had nothing else of importance to occupy their minds. She could see it in their faces when she entered a shop, hear it in the polite conversation when they asked after Aoife, or remarked on how tall she was getting. People in Dunbeg seemed to have her whole life neatly summed, but sometimes she wanted to ask what they'd bloody well figured out, because it wasn't at all clear to her.

She had two large rounds of brown bread and four half-sized loaves ready to go into the oven. Una took the bread knife and deftly cut a cross in the top of each one, just as her mother had shown her how to do, then quickly shoved the pan into the hot oven. She turned and regarded the mess in the kitchen, the large crockery bowl and table covered with the sticky remains of the brown bread and spilt buttermilk, the open bags of flour and wheatmeal, and she sat down wearily at the table, and rested her head on her arms. A few hot tears trickled off the end of her nose and splashed in the flour left over from where she'd kneaded the bread. The world had fallen asunder, and she had no idea how to put it right again.

Chapter 7

The phone beside his head roused Devaney out of a deep sleep. He rolled over and grabbed the receiver. 'Devaney here.'

'Still in bed. Christ, how I miss dear auld Ireland,' Deasey said. 'I'm calling with news. The least you could do is act surprised, if you can't manage to be pleased this time of the morning.'

'I'm fucking delighted,' Devaney said, sitting on the edge of the bed and squinting. 'What time is it, anyway, Jimmy?'

'Nearly half-nine, ye lazy sod.' Fuck it; nine-thirty, Devaney thought, and nobody had bothered to wake him. That meant he'd already completely missed the station meeting this morning.

'Thanks for ringing, Jimmy. What have you got?'

'Your man's gone into a bank. The receptionist turned out to be a girl from Cavan, so I turned on the auld charm and actually got her to cough up a small bit of information. Seems he was at school with one of the top men there, and you know what chummy bastards old schoolboys are. No word on what the meeting was about, but nobody goes to a bank unless he's got plenty of money, am I right?'

'Or needs money.' Devaney was completely awake now, struggling to put an arm through his shirtsleeve while keeping the phone to his ear. 'Anything on the address from last night?'

'Oh, yeah. Bad news, I'm afraid. Or mebbe I should say no great mystery. Your man's not a bigamist after all. The house belongs to a doctor named DeSouza. Well respected, good clientele. The woman and child were evidently his daughter and granddaughter, friends of Osborne's wife. He always stays with them when he goes to London. Sorry.'

As he hung up the phone, Devaney knew he should have asked the Badger to follow up on Osborne's movements in the days before the disappearance. Why hadn't he just come out with it? The image of the carved letters in the church floated in his groggy head: *He knows where they are.* If somebody knew something, why wouldn't he just come forward? The usual reason was that he'd have to put himself – or someone else – in a compromising position. Who among Osborne's family, neighbours, and business associates might have something to hide? He already knew the answer: everyone.

Chapter 8

Ned Raftery's house was set at a right angle to the road, so that the gable end faced out, and the front of the house faced a walled garden. Nora pulled up in the gravel drive, and Cormac followed as she entered through the black iron gate. Inside, a chest-high boxwood hedge defined the margin of the garden, and against its tiny, dark green leaves grew hundreds of rosebushes. Most were just beginning to bud, but a salmon-coloured climbing rose and several sprays of white shrub roses were already in bloom and gave off the most marvellous scent. Nora leaned in to the nearest open flowers to inhale their sweet, heady perfume, and let out a small, wordless exclamation.

'I'm glad you like them,' a man's voice said. She turned and saw the man she presumed to be Ned Raftery rising from his knees, closing the lock on his pruning shears, and moving toward the sound of her voice. His clouded eyes seemed to look straight ahead.

'They're wonderful,' Nora said. 'I'm drunk on that fragrance, I swear.'

'And people wonder why a blind man bothers growing flowers at all,' Raftery said, smiling.

'We haven't met. I'm Nora Gavin.' She was unsure whether a handshake was in order until Raftery put out his open palm, on which she placed her own. He brought a fresh-cut rosebud from behind his back and presented it to her.

'Welcome, Dr Gavin. And Professor Maguire as well, I presume, welcome.'

'Thank you for taking the time to speak with us,' Cormac said.

'Not at all. I'm not sure I have any knowledge that might be useful to you, but you're welcome to whatever I've got locked away up here.' Raftery tapped his forehead. 'Please come in; I'll make tea.' They waited for him to step onto the path before them, and followed as he ushered them into the house.

Just inside the front door was a long room. At one end, near a large fireplace, sat four well-used upholstered chairs; bookcases, crammed with volumes old and new, crowded the walls. A heavy oak trestle table with eight chairs divided the sitting area from the open kitchen, and a huge cookstove stood where the opposite fireplace used to be.

Raftery followed an obviously familiar path to the kitchen, where he put the kettle on to boil, and set about cutting some white soda bread studded with raisins, using his left hand to reach across the knife blade and gauge the thickness of each slice. Nora and Cormac each took a seat at the large table.

'Fintan McGann mentioned that you were his teacher,' Cormac said.

'Ah, Fintan. Bright lad. I tried to teach him something about history, but even then he didn't care about anything at all except the music. He's getting to be a tasty piper, wouldn't you say?'

'Very decent,' Cormac agreed. 'He was playing some great notes at the session last week.'

'That was a mighty night, wasn't it? Well now, you're

here to find out something about our local history,' Raftery said, bringing over the bread on one plate, a lump of butter on another, and a couple of knives. He drew out the chair at the end of the table, and lowered himself into it. He must have been about sixty years of age, clean-shaven, with grey hair standing up a bit off his forehead. He was a burly man, with short legs and a long, barrel-shaped torso. He wore a button-down shirt and a sweater with a hole in one elbow, heavy brogues on his feet. More the look of a labourer than a schoolteacher, Nora decided.

'We're trying to find out anything that would help us identify the girl from the bog,' she said. 'I assume you've heard about her – seems like everyone has. We know it's a long shot, but we've just come across something that I hope could be a significant clue.'

Raftery's face was impassive; his eyes seemed to fix their sightless gaze on the other end of the table. 'Go on.'

'There was no sign of her body anywhere about. Just the head. Since then we've been able to do a fairly thorough examination. She was about twenty to twenty-five years old, with long red hair. From the damage to the vertebrae, we think she was beheaded, most likely with a single blow from a sword or axe. Now the recent development is that inside her mouth, we found a man's gold ring with a red stone. There was an inscription: two sets of initials, COF and AOF; a date, 1652; and the letters IHS set in brackets at the centre of the date.'

'We're still waiting on radiocarbon results,' Cormac said, 'so we've started to do some historical research on beheading. Then Nora discovered this ring, which gives us a possible date – a place to start at least.'

'Our reasoning is that she'd probably been in the bog no earlier than 1652, since that's the date on the ring, although it could have been any time since then.' Nora looked at Cormac and shrugged. She'd known he was right, even though it annoyed her.

'So you're looking for the record of a trial, or an execution, or perhaps a marriage record of some kind,' Raftery said. He considered for a moment. 'You realise that 1652 was smack in the centre of the Cromwellian resettlement. There was pretty significant upheaval all over Ireland. Catholic Church records from that time are sketchy. Civil records, especially something as serious as an execution, might be another matter, it's hard to know. Have you checked the National Library or the Archives?'

'We have a friend in Dublin who's working on that now,' Cormac said. 'You were recommended as a person who might be able to tell us about the local history.'

'As I used to tell my students, there is no history but local history. And some of that is written down, and some of it lost, and a good bit of it is carried in what you might call the collective memory of ordinary people, whether they realize it or not.'

'What was happening here in 1652?' Nora asked. 'I only have the most general knowledge of the transplantation. What was that time like for the people living here?'

'You've heard the expression "to Hell or to Connacht"?' Raftery asked. The kettle began to boil, so he rose and moved slowly to the stove, poured the steaming water into a battered tin teapot, and returned with it to the table to let the tea steep as he continued. 'That was the choice many people were given, so they were on the move. For modern comparisons, think of the ethnic cleansing of Bosnia in the early 1990s, the "reeducation" camps of Southeast Asia. Catholic landowners were being uprooted and shifted west, and when they proved understandably slow about going, Cromwell gave them a deadline. They had until the first of May in 1654 to relocate to whatever lands they'd been granted in Connacht. And the English were building garrisons and fortifications along the Shannon to keep them there.' Raftery's voice was relaxed, but he was completely engaged with his subject. 'There was terrible starvation where the English troops went about burning and cutting down the corn, and most ordinary people had to subsist on potatoes. Bands of refugees – entire extended families – were wandering the roads, so an order came down to transport the children who had lost their families, and the women who could work, to the colonies in America. Between the fighting, famine, transportation, and the plague, Ireland lost more than half a million people in the space of about two years. Wolves became so plentiful that the government issued an official order in 1652 prohibiting the export of wolfhounds, and they paid a generous bounty – five pounds for the head of a he-wolf, ten pounds for a bitch. Heads of priests and Tories – the Irish word for outlaws – usually brought a good price as well. This part of Galway was considered a border area, so despite the fact that Connacht had officially been reserved for the Irish, the landowners in what the English called "riparian" areas – along the coasts and navigable rivers – were displaced for security reasons.'

'Including the O'Flahertys?' Nora asked, with a sideways look at Cormac.

Raftery considered. 'Yes, including them. Most of the lands around here belonged to various branches of the Clanricardes, the Norman family also known as the de Burgos, or the Burkes. They managed to hang on, despite the fact that they were Catholics. But there were a few smaller landowners as well; the O'Flahertys of Drumcleggan were among them. You'll find a great number of O'Flahertys out in the west country, but there was one branch of the family that still held lands here. It was Eamonn O'Flaherty who built the big house at Drumcleggan in the 1630s – only to be evicted twenty years later. He was granted a parcel of land further west, but died soon after being relocated.'

'And the Osbornes took over his lands,' Nora said.

'That's right,' Raftery said, pouring the tea now. 'Hugo Osborne was granted the entire estate at Drumcleggan, which was considered a vulnerable location along the border. He rechristened it Bracklyn House. But O'Flaherty's son became a rather notorious outlaw; he kept an armed band of men above here in the Slieve Aughty Mountains, and attacked various English garrisons in the locality. Even mounted a rather ill-advised armed raid on Bracklyn House – when the Osbornes were all away, as it turned out. Young Flaherty was eventually captured and sentenced to hang, but because he and his men had committed no serious outrages, he was transported instead – or Barbadosed, they called it.'

'Do you happen to remember when he was transported?' Nora asked. Raftery got up and crossed carefully to one of the bookcases filled with file boxes.

'I used to have a copy of the transport manifest here somewhere, if I can find it.' He felt the face of each box in turn. 'I think it may be in this one, if you'd like to have a look.' He set the file on the table, and Nora opened it eagerly, scanning through the photocopied documents until she found a thick sheaf of handwritten ledger entries. She handed Cormac half the pages, and began scanning the list of names, ages, and what looked like occupations. She suddenly experienced an almost hallucinatory image of the hand that penned these lists, and instinctively grasped the fact that these simple quill scratches represented multitudes of uprooted, ravaged lives.

'Is there a date at the top of those pages?' Raftery asked.

'November 1653,' Nora answered. She scanned a few more sheets, before turning toward her companions. 'Hang on, this could be him. O'Flaherty. Aged twenty-seven. Outlaw and thief. Transported for life. Do you know anything else about him? Did he have a wife? Is there any way to find out?'

Her barrage of questions left Raftery looking a little nonplussed, but he smiled. 'I'm not sure there's any documentation. The story I've always heard is that he ended up on the Continent somewhere, as a mercenary. A sad tale, but not uncommon. I'm not sure now whether or not he was married.'

'Nothing else?' Nora asked. 'What was his name?'

'Sorry, didn't I say? Cathal.' Raftery paused. 'He was known as Cathal Mór because of his great height.'

'Cathal O'Flaherty – COF. You can't tell me it's just coincidence,' Nora said to Cormac, feeling a flush of victory. 'The date is right. The location and the initials are right. So if our red-haired girl is his wife, and supposing she is, there's no record of her being transported as well. And if he was only transported for his crimes, why would she have been executed?' She heaved a frustrated sigh.

'Has anybody collected songs from this locality?' Cormac asked. 'It seems like a famous outlaw might be deserving of a song or two.'

'I'm not sure there's any formal collection, but you

know, for those sorts of things—' Raftery hesitated a moment, frowning.

'Yes?' Nora perked up slightly at the prospect of advice.

'There's no one better than my aunt, Maggie Cleary is her name. Lives in a little townsland called Tullymore up the side of the mountain. Now I have to warn you, she can get a bit narky. She has good days and bad, and it's come to the point where the bad are beginning to outnumber the good. But when she's on, there's no one can tell you more about the families around here. And she has loads of songs – hundreds. You never know. If you just chat to her awhile, show her some attention, she likes that. A naggin of whiskey wouldn't go amiss either.'

Chapter 9

Half-eleven the following morning found Cormac and Nora hard at work on the excavation site. Banks of low grey cumulus clouds scudded across the sky from west to east, and a damp breeze from the ocean blew in over the mountains. Resting for a moment on the spade handle, Cormac thought about his own life, and what might remain of it in three hundred, eight hundred, or a thousand years: items he'd lost down the floorboards, or hidden so no one else could find them, until he, too, had lost track of their existence. He identified with the hoarders of earlier ages, burying and protecting their precious possessions, and then – whether through faulty memory, migration, or death – unable to reclaim them.

He looked down to the end of the trench at Nora. Her job was once again sifting through the rubble with a large sieve, looking for artefacts: pottery shards, glassware, bits of slag, or the telltale green of corroded bronze. As far as artefacts were concerned, early Christian sites like this one usually yielded little more than the bones of slaughtered animals, and a few bits of broken crockery. Much of what would have been used in this sort of community was organic material that would have decayed long ago. Still, one never knew what one would find. Though no ruin existed at all above ground, there was bound to be evidence beneath the surface, some clues to the methods of construction or the industrial activity that took place here. And there were always the middens, of course, rubbish heaps where each layer contained a valuable cache of information. That was the beauty and mystery of archaeology to him. Each site had to be treated as a potential treasure, each step in the excavation undertaken with the same scrupulous care, in case valuable artefacts – or even more important, valuable details – might be lost or overlooked. He was not just undertaking this work for the present, but also for future generations, who might come to see some larger pattern in the discoveries that he and his contemporaries were now making that wouldn't reveal itself for another fifty or a hundred or two hundred years, and perhaps then only if the previous research was thorough and meticulous. The soil samples he took today would be sieved back at the lab for microfossils, insect remains, seeds, plant matter. They still used many of the same techniques when excavating by hand, looking with the naked eye for layers and horizons, but so many new microscopic and chemical analysis techniques had been developed in the last few years, not to mention new types of sampling and scanning technologies, things Gabriel had never even dreamed of when he picked up the trowel.

Cormac looked down to the other end of the trench, where Nora was working, kneeling in the dirt with her sleeves rolled up. Grey dust clung like mist to her dark eyebrows. She was about four feet away from him, concentrated on her work, searching through the damp soil with a trowel, then dumping the gravel into her growing pile of debris. Cormac decided he quite liked being here, the only sounds the scraping of the spade, the thump of each panful of soil, the occasional distant croak of a disgruntled crow.

'Do you ever get tired of turning up nothing?' Nora asked. 'All this work, to find nothing but four solid feet of sand and gravel? What keeps you going, inch after bloody inch?' Strange how she seemed to know exactly what he'd been thinking.

'The potential, I suppose, the hope that something might turn up. Your work must have a good bit of drudgery as well, all those thousands of straightforward textbook cases before you get to the one really interesting anomaly. Isn't it this part, the sifting through the ordinary that makes breakthrough moments all the more memorable?'

'You're right, of course,' Nora said, 'but remind me again what we're looking for.'

'Artefacts from any period, of course, but also evidence of any structures, layers of ash or charcoal that might give us dates or horizons for the occupation of the site. Refuse pits, slag heaps, any specific waste from human activity. Communities like this often served secular needs as well as spiritual ones. We're looking to see what this spot can tell us about the events that took place here, and in what order.' He continued talking as he pulled a slip of paper from his clipboard and wrote a number on it, then impaled the paper on a three-inch nail in the wall of the bank. 'I will admit it's frustrating, trying to get clues about a whole culture from what you can see through a couple of what are essentially peepholes. But put our peepholes together with the peepholes from all over the country, and a larger picture begins to emerge. And who says we're turning up nothing?' He gestured toward the bank of clay in front of him. 'See how the coloration of the soil changes here? And see this thin layer of black between? That's charcoal. Evidence of human habitation. With a little more work, we can even tell what kind of wood they burned. You have to learn how to look at it.' He put down his spade and came to sit beside Nora.

'Look over there,' he said, gesturing toward the landscape across the road, 'and tell me what you see.' Nora lifted her head, and gazed toward the horizon of hay fields and pastureland.

'Cattle, grass. Lots of yellow flowers. Why, what do you see?'

'Look again,' Cormac said. 'Straight ahead.'

'I see a hill. Is this some sort of a trick?' Cormac said nothing, but watched her face as the rounded knoll that rose out of the canary-coloured sea of dandelions, the shape she had no doubt first seen as a natural feature of the landscape, took on an altogether different profile. He knew that all at once she could see that it was too round, too regular to be an ordinary hill, and one end was cut out, almost like the entrance to a mine shaft. He watched appreciatively as her mouth dropped slowly open, and she turned to face him once more.

'What is it?'

'Could be the remains of a ringfort, or a burial mound.' He was pleased that the discovery had made such a profound impression.

'You're giving me goose bumps,' she said.

'I swear that wasn't my intention.'

They worked for a while in silence. 'You know, Raftery said it might be a couple of days before he can get his aunt to speak to us,' Nora said. 'There must be something else we can do in the meantime.'

'What do you propose?'

'Well, we could go to the heritage centre you mentioned, see what kinds of records they keep. We could try bribing Robbie with biscuits to dig up all he can about

Cathal Mór O'Flaherty.' She paused, but he sensed there was more.

'And . . .'

'Well, what I'd really love is a look inside that tower house. Are you any good at picking locks?'

'Hang on. I'm not going to go breaking in somewhere.'

'How else are we supposed to get in?' Nora asked, dumping out the sieve and banging it on the ground to dislodge the last bits of pebble and clay. 'There isn't exactly a welcome mat at the door. I suppose you're waiting for an invitation.'

'You realize that if you insist I'll have no other choice but to go along, if only to keep you out of trouble.'

'I'm perfectly happy to go on my own,' Nora said. 'I might have to, if you're going to be squeamish about it—'

Cormac raised a finger to his lips to signal silence, and Nora clamped her mouth shut and listened. She heard nothing but the harsh *aic-aic* of a corncrake.

'There's somebody here,' Cormac said under his breath. 'Up in the cloister walk. Keep working. Maybe we can get whoever it is to come out.' They busied themselves at their work again, stealing an occasional glance toward the cloister wall.

'Let's walk back to the jeep,' Cormac said quietly. 'Slowly. You go first. Create a distraction. Cut through the cloister at the near end, here, and I'll go to the far end. Unless whoever it is wants to climb out a window, he'll be stuck in the middle.' As he spoke, Cormac wondered if he was a physical match for Brendan McGann, if it came down to that.

Nora nodded and stood up, brushed the knees of her jeans, and spoke loudly enough that the eavesdropper could hear. 'Well, I can't wait any longer for lunch, I'm ravenous.' She walked a diagonal to the corner nearest where the jeep was parked. 'I believe our choices today are plain cheese or cheese and tomato.' She had reached the end of the cloister, and turned to find Jeremy Osborne pressed against the wall at the far end of the corridor. He looked at her, and turned to retreat, but by then Cormac had come up behind Jeremy and received the tackle solidly, catching the boy by the shoulders.

'Hold up there,' Cormac said gently. 'No need to run.' Jeremy was wresting his arms away from Cormac as Nora came up behind him. 'Hello, Jeremy,' she said, and he turned to look at her again. Out here in the daylight, how fragile he looked, she thought, with the same large eyes, pronounced cheekbones, and pale, translucent skin his mother had. His features were more pleasing, however, and his cheeks still had the youthful high colour Lucy's had lost. Something in the way he moved reminded Nora of a skittish horse, and from what she'd seen of this boy with his mother, he was not unused to bit and bridle.

'What are you up to?' she asked, hoping that the glimmer of friendship she'd once seen in his eyes could be coaxed back if they used gentle words, and avoided sudden movement.

'I wasn't spying,' he said. 'I came to help.' Nora looked at Cormac and raised her eyebrows in silent exclamation.

'That's great,' she said. 'I'm sure we can find plenty for you to do. Nice of your mother to spare you.'

Jeremy's eyes met hers for an instant. 'I'm here on my own.'

'Well, we can certainly make use of you,' Cormac said. 'Always good to have an extra pair of hands. You don't mind being a general dogsbody, do you? I'm afraid that's the only position available on this dig.'

'I don't mind.'

'Can I show you what to do?' Cormac led the boy over to the trench, while Nora went to the jeep to get their lunch pack; she really was ravenous. When she came back, she watched them for a while: Cormac, his voice quiet and confident, was explaining what they were about, what Jeremy should look for, and how he was making a record of everything they found. This was a side of him she hadn't seen: Cormac the teacher, down on one knee, demonstrating the proper way to sift debris, letting the boy try it, then praising him for a quick study. Jeremy was hunkered down on his heels like a child, filling the pan, sifting through it with his fingers, and methodically dumping the gravel into the small pile she had started.

'Well, now you're fully broken in,' she said to Jeremy, 'how about some lunch? We've plenty of food.' She could see the boy hesitate slightly before accepting. They settled on a patch of grass a short distance from the trenches and Nora began passing the sandwiches, then poured them each tea from a flask. Cormac took out his pocketknife to cut a pair of green apples so the three of them might share. The sky was overcast, but behind the clouds they could tell the sun had climbed to its place at the top of the sky; the day was growing more close by the minute. They'd been saved from sweltering thus far by a gentle but steady wind that seemed to roll down from the mountains in the west.

'Ever work on a dig before?' Cormac asked. Jeremy shook his head, and Nora was struck by the mannerly way the boy swallowed his food before answering.

'I used to come and watch, when they were working on the priory,' he said, 'but they'd usually run me off. Didn't want me messing about, I suppose. I was only a kid.'

'You must be finished with secondary school,' Cormac said. Jeremy nodded. 'Are you thinking about going on to university?' Though it was asked without judgment, this question seemed to make the boy uncomfortable. He started methodically uprooting handfuls of the grass that grew beside him.

'I've still got exams. I'm not sure yet what I want to do. Mum says I ought to be learning something about how to run an estate,' Jeremy said, his voice betraying how little he thought of such an occupation.

'What are you interested in, Jeremy?' Nora asked. His eyes met hers, and for a second she thought she saw something in them vaguely akin to an accusation. Then they dropped to the ground again, to the rapidly balding patch beside him.

'I – I don't know,' he stammered. As though that were something to be ashamed of, Nora thought, at his age. She could see his ears begin to burn a bright crimson.

After lunch, they continued working a good three and a half hours until tea time. Cormac took a break from his spade work to take some photographs showing the general progress of the dig and to check levels. Jeremy acted as his assistant, holding the meter staff in place to mark the depth of the trenches, and the scale of variances in colouration. As the afternoon wore on, the breeze died down, until there was hardly a breath stirring. Nora stopped to take a long drink from her jug, then tipped her head down and poured some of the lukewarm water over the back of her neck. As she stood straight again and mopped the extra droplets with her bandanna, she found Jeremy Osborne staring at her. When their eyes met this time, he did not look away, and something in his look made her inordinately self-conscious. Nora turned away and knelt to gather up her tools. She remembered helping the sodden young man to his feet the night they met, and wondered whether he might have acquired an unhealthy yen for her. If that was the case, she'd probably only encouraged it, chatting away like that the afternoon she found him asleep in the nursery. How could she get him to talk to her now? She had had no business fuelling any adolescent fantasies. Nora suddenly remembered the breathy voice on the telephone. Could the words of warning have come from Jeremy Osborne?

Chapter 10

Nora had been surprised when Una McGann and her daughter stopped by the dig Friday to ask for a lift into town on Saturday morning for the market, but she'd agreed, partly out of curiosity. The market was just gearing up this time of year, Una said, but there were small baskets of new potatoes, early hothouse strawberries, flowers, peas, lettuces, white and brown hen eggs, duck eggs. No one made cheese any more, but there were homemade sausages and black and white puddings, along with household goods like rush brooms and baskets.

Saturday morning arrived damp but mild. Nine o'clock seemed late for a market to open, Nora thought, as she approached the McGanns' house. She hoped she wasn't late. Through the open window, she could see the little girl, Aoife, skipping in a circle around the kitchen table and hear Una counting aloud, no doubt totting up how much her wares would bring. The little girl's voice broke in: 'Mammy, Mammy, can I get a bun from the sweet shop, can I please, Mammy?'

Una's reply was short: 'I'm still counting, Aoife, can't you hush?'

'Mammy, Mammy,' Aoife was pulling on her mother's hand now. 'I think she's here. I think she's here.' Una withdrew her hand in annoyance, and Aoife, who had been pulling with all her strength, went sprawling backward. There was a moment of horrified silence before the child began to whimper, and Una dropped to the floor beside her.

'I'm sorry, I'm sorry. I'm just so tired, Aoife. I'm not angry with you.' When Nora came to the open door, Una was kissing her daughter's head, and rocking back and forth to calm them both.

'Hello,' Nora called. 'Anyone home?' Una was helping Aoife to her feet, and wiping her eyes with the back of one hand.

'Are you all right?' Nora asked. Una looked frayed, but she patted her daughter's hand and said: 'We're grand now, aren't we? Nora, could you manage a few of these bags? Aoife, you take a couple as well.' Una herself picked up the heavy box full of sweet cakes, and followed them out the door.

When they arrived in Dunbeg, the market vendors were still setting up: Travellers setting out cheap mobile phones and garish rugs next to farmers selling brown eggs and wild heather honey. Una shared a stall with a few fellow artists, some of whom had finished work to sell, and some, like herself, who sold whatever they could. Aoife hung on her mother's conversations with fellow vendors though it was clear, from the number of times she had to be asked to stop touching the goods and to be careful not to knock things over, that she was getting underfoot.

Nora pulled Una aside. 'Aoife and I could take a little excursion, if you like, down to the tearoom or something. At least until you're set up.'

Una's face revealed a mixture of gratitude and relief. 'That would be brilliant. Wait, I'll give you some money,' she said, reaching for the small pouch that was slung around her waist.

'Oh no, my treat, please. But maybe we'd better ask Aoife what she thinks of the idea.'

Una made her way over to where the little girl was strumming the fringes on a whole rack of Indian scarves. Nora observed their conversation from a short distance, then saw Aoife running toward her, face aglow with anticipation.

'Mammy says you and I can go off on our own.' She slipped her hand into Nora's. So much for her fear that the child wouldn't want her as a chaperone. A quick wave and they were off, with Aoife pulling her through the streets like a tugboat towing an ocean liner, her small feet beating double time on the pavement, stopping occasionally to share a tidbit or a confidence.

'There's Declan Connelly,' Aoife confided to her at one corner. 'He chased me once, with his manky old dog.' They barged past a nameless pub; Hickey's garage, with two petrol pumps stuck in the kerb and a shop window full of bicycle tyres; the newsagent's, with windows full of faded postcards and HB ice cream posters. Aoife slowed her pace when she was within sight of her ultimate destination, so that she could get the full effect of the colourful half-curtains, and the homemade sign depicting cream-filled cakes and apple tarts. A signboard leaning by the door said, *Teas, Coffees, Confections.*

'Shall we go in here?' Nora asked. Aoife nodded wordlessly, as if mesmerized, and made a direct line for the case, which displayed a variety of cream buns, as Nora spoke to the girl at the counter: 'We'll have one white coffee, a currant scone, a glass of milk, and—' She looked at Aoife. 'Whatever my friend here wants.' The little girl perused the case carefully, finally selecting an enormous, greasy-looking bun piled with whipped cream and with a radioactive-looking cherry on top.

Nora shuddered inwardly. She let Aoife choose a table by the window while they waited for the server. As they sat at the bare table, she felt herself the object of the child's frank scrutiny. Aoife sat back in her chair.

'Do you love Cormac?' she asked.

Nora was dumbstruck. Aoife went on: 'I asked Mammy if you did, and she said she didn't know, I'd have to ask you.'

'Well, he's very nice,' Nora said, but could see that this answer was not definite enough for her interrogator.

'Would you want to marry him?' Fortunately for Nora, the server approached with a tray. The dreadful cream bun looked even larger on the table than it had inside the display case. Aoife had a fork, but couldn't resist dipping immediately into its crown of stiff, buttery cream with her index finger, carefully avoiding the cherry. Watching her, Nora was overwhelmed by a sense of loss, remembering outings just like this one that she'd shared with her niece. She hadn't seen Elizabeth for almost four years; that had been the price of her conviction that Peter Hallett was guilty of murder.

'I'm going to marry someone,' Aoife declared, as if the admission might make it easier for Nora to confess her own true feelings.

'Are you, really?'

'Yes. His name's Tomás Ó Flic, and he plays with me sometimes. We have tea' – her voice took on a conspiratorial volume and tone – 'only it's not real tea, it's pretend.'

'What's he like?' Nora asked. Elizabeth had made up scores of imaginary friends when she was small, and Nora had loved asking her about them. She'd always been intrigued by the idea that children had such an instinctive buffer against loneliness.

'Well, he's twigs all in his hair, and sometimes he's a bit smelly. That's because he never washes himself and he lives under a tree in the woods.'

'And what do the two of you talk about?'

'Oh, he never says anything at all,' Aoife said. 'But sometimes he brings me things. He gave me this.' Licking the cream expertly from between her fingers, she reached into a pocket and brought out a flat, pale stone about the size of a 10p coin.

'It's beautiful. May I have a closer look?'

Aoife hesitated before handing it over. 'Do you promise to give it right back?'

'Oh, I promise,' Nora said. She turned the stone over in her palm. It was a highly polished piece of rose quartz, not something you might find in nature. She handed it back, and felt the slightest twinge of queasy doubt, wondering if she should press any further.

After replacing the precious stone in her pocket, Aoife concentrated briefly on the mountainous portion of cream bun left on her plate, then slumped back in her chair and scrunched up her nose. 'I have something to tell you, Nora. I can't eat any more of this. And there's something else as well.'

'What's that?'

'You forgot to answer about Cormac.'

Chapter 11

While Nora was at the market, Raftery had phoned to say his aunt would see them this afternoon, and Cormac had taken down a rather elaborate set of directions to the old woman's house, though she lived less than five miles from Dunbeg. Now the road to the townsland of Tullymore stretched before them like a green tunnel, its walls composed of leafy ditches strangled with ivy, its vaulted roof the arching branches of trees.

'Do you think Jeremy was disappointed that we didn't ask him along?' Nora asked as she turned the car down a narrow lane at the end of the sheltered road.

'He didn't look happy about it. But we can't completely monopolize his time.' Nora felt the same way; it seemed they'd had hardly a minute without Jeremy's company for the past couple of days. 'There's another turn up here,' he said, 'left at the T-junction.' They were beginning to climb the side of a hill now, with flowering blackberries growing thickly on the steep slope to their left.

'I'll be amazed if we can find our way back,' Nora said. 'And I'm trying to convince myself that this Mrs Cleary might just remember some story from over three hundred years ago.'

'It's a long shot, but it's not actually impossible. Some of the airs I play are at least that old. Don't forget, our *cailín rua* was an actual person who might have lived no more than two or three miles from where we are right now. You'd be surprised how long things remain exactly where they've fallen; the same applies to songs and stories. Just passed on, one person to the next. And a bold attack on English settlers, or a beautiful young woman losing her head – whatever the reason – are just the kinds of things somebody might have set down in a song.'

'I'm wondering whether we shouldn't have brought the jeep,' Nora said as the road began to narrow. She had to downshift twice; by the time they reached the summit of the hill, it was only a lane with a grassy ridge growing down the middle. The land to either side of the road was a treacherous combination of football-sized stones and spongy pasture.

They crept down the far side of the hill, and turned once more, when Cormac said: 'Well, according to these directions, we should be there.' Nora stopped the car, and they looked around. At the far end of the road, some three hundred yards distant, stood a freshly thatched house with tiny windows, its whitewashed walls and yellow roof gleaming in the afternoon sun. As they drove closer, Nora could see that the half-door stood open.

'Looks as if we're expected, anyway,' Cormac said as they climbed out of the car and approached the house. 'Hello?' He rapped on the open door. 'We're looking for Mrs Cleary?'

An old woman's croaking voice came from the dark, cool interior of the house. '*Tar isteach.* Come in.' Cormac entered first, and Nora followed. After the brightness of the day, her eyes took a moment to become accustomed to the gloom. She could dimly make out an old lady sitting beside the open fireplace at the far end of the room, propped up in a tall, uncomfortable-looking upholstered chair. She was small-framed and thin, and wore a plain wool skirt, a crisp white blouse, and a cardigan. Age accentuated the hawklike curve of her nose, and the bony, arthritic hands that gripped the chair's arms further underscored the avian impression. Despite the warmth of the day, a turf fire glowed orange in the grate.

'You'll pardon me if I don't get up,' she said. 'My daughter should be in the scullery there, just getting the tea. Rita – Rita, where are you?'

'Quite all right, Mrs Cleary,' said Cormac, taking a small bottle out of his coat pocket. 'I hope you were expecting us. My name is Cormac Maguire, and this is Nora Gavin. We've brought you a drop of whiskey.' He advanced a little cautiously, knelt beside the chair, and pressed his gift into one of the bent hands. The woman's wrinkled face brightened as she fingered the bottle. Nora could see that she had the same milky-white eyes as her nephew.

'I'm pleased to meet you,' Nora said. The old lady cocked her head at the sound of an American voice.

'What's the matter with the Irish girls, then, Maguire?' she asked abruptly. Nora's cheeks burned with embarrassment.

'Dr Gavin is a colleague, Mrs Cleary. We work together.'

The old woman ignored him. 'Well, sit yourselves down, the two of ye. Rita – where is that lazy girl? She was to put the kettle on for tea.' She gestured vaguely toward a table arranged against the wall, where the tea things were laid out. 'And I'd have a drop of that whiskey now, meself.' Cormac took the bottle from her, and handed it to Nora, who found a glass on the table into which she poured a generous shot.

'We appreciate you taking the time to see us,' he began,

venturing to sit on the edge of a chair across from Mrs Cleary.

'Ah, sure, what's a useless old woman like me got besides time?'

From the door of the scullery came the voice of the 'girl' to whom Mrs Cleary had referred; she must have been nearly seventy. 'Now Mammy, go away out of that, you're not useless. You're enjoying a well-deserved retirement.' Rita Cleary was quick to gather what had gone on in her brief absence. 'You haven't already been passing remarks on these nice people, have you?' To Cormac and Nora she said: 'I hope you can bear with her. She usually loves visitors, but I'm afraid she's been in a rather unpredictable mood this afternoon. Go on and sit down there. She'll be fine as long as I'm here to keep an eye on her.'

Cormac and Nora sat down again. 'Here's that whiskey now, Mrs Cleary,' he said, taking the glass from Nora and guiding it to the old lady's hand. 'Do you mind if I record our conversation?'

'Do what you like,' she said.

He fished in his pocket and drew out a tiny tape recorder. 'I'm not sure if Ned mentioned what we're looking for, Mrs Cleary. Any songs or old stories you may have heard over the years about a famous outlaw from these parts, or perhaps a young girl who was beheaded. Perhaps some story about a famous murder, or someone being executed for a crime.'

Mrs Cleary smiled and took a tiny sip of the golden liquor. 'I don't know when I've had so much attention. First the crowd from Radio Éireann coming down last week to record me, now the likes of you. I'll have to start charging by the hour.' She looked pleased with herself, but Rita crouched down beside the chair, took the old lady's hand and stroked it as she said in a soothing tone: 'Now, Mammy, you remember it was a long time ago that the men from the radio were here. It's more than thirty years ago. You know that, don't you, Mammy?' The old lady looked sorely put out, and the volume of the daughter's voice dropped as she addressed them, somewhat apologetically, still holding her mother's hand. 'She usually doesn't start getting like this until much later in the evening. It's possible she's a bit tired.' Nora was beginning to wonder if they were on the wrong track entirely, but surely Raftery wouldn't have sent them out here if he'd known the trip was going to be a waste of time.

'This girl – what's she got to do with you?' Mrs Cleary demanded sharply.

'Well, nothing personally,' Cormac replied. 'We just happen to have dug her head up a few days ago in Drumcleggan Bog.'

'Red-haired, was she?'

'How did you know?' Nora asked.

Mrs Cleary pursed her lips. 'People talk. No secrets around here.'

'Would you have many red-haired people around these parts?' Cormac asked.

'Well, there were a fair number, in certain families. The Clearys – my husband's family – the Kellys, and the McGanns always had a good deal of ginger-hair amongst 'em. Not them all, now, but always a few.'

'What was significant about red hair?' Nora asked. She knew it supposedly indicated a hot temperament, but maybe there was more.

'My father always said meeting a red-haired woman at the gate was terrible bad luck. Ah, you never know but they might have powers. With cures and curses, the evil eye and such.'

Nora realized she hadn't asked Robbie specifically about what might happen to a young woman suspected of practising witchcraft.

'We found a ring as well,' Cormac said. 'It had some initials inscribed inside, COF and AOF, and a date, 1652. We're hoping it might help us find out who this red-haired girl was. Do those initials mean anything—'

'And supposing you do find out who this girl is? What difference will it make?'

'Well, no difference at all, I suppose, in the grand scheme of things,' Cormac said, accepting a steaming cup of tea and a biscuit from Rita.

'I think we feel – responsible,' Nora said. 'At least I do, to try to find out who she was, and how she came to be there. You might feel the same, if you'd seen her.' Nora realized her blunder, but did not apologize.

The challenge in her words had a strange effect on Mrs Cleary. The old woman's eyes narrowed; her lips curved into a scowl, but she seemed to be considering. They waited.

'I know nothing about any red-haired girl,' Mrs Cleary muttered.

'Nora's got a suspicion that the initials OF might stand for O'Flaherty,' Cormac said. 'Ned was telling us about the last of the O'Flahertys from these parts, a young fella called Cathal Mór, who was transported to Barbados. You wouldn't happen to know anything about him?'

Mrs Cleary's right hand grasped the arm of the chair as she thought. Her clouded eyes were downcast as if focused on some scene from the past. The left hand, which held the whiskey glass, rested slackly in her lap. For the first time, she seemed a little hazy, worried about something. 'I used to remember it all. Used to hear the auld ones talking, and I remembered things. People came to me. It's all gone now . . .'

'Perhaps we could call around another time,' Cormac said. The old woman gave no response, but her daughter nodded from across the room, and he switched off his tape recorder. What else could they do? He gently took the glass from Mrs Cleary's hand and set it on the table beside her. All hint of her former peevishness was gone, replaced by pitiful confusion. 'Rita,' she said. 'Rita, where are you? I'm thirsty.'

Nora was just turning her key in the ignition when they heard a voice calling sharply from the doorway: 'Mr Maguire, wait! Come back.' Rita ushered them back into the dimly lit room, where they took their former places on the straight-backed chairs beside the old woman. This time the daughter sat down beside Mrs Cleary, and stroked her hand.

'Now, Mammy, you were just singing a bit of something just there, do you remember? A little snip of a song you used to know.' She hummed a fragment of melody, and patted the old lady's hand in time, as Cormac silently pushed the record button again, and Mrs Cleary squeezed her eyes shut in an effort of concentration. Then the old woman opened her mouth, and from it came a voice as sinewy as old leather. There was nothing of conventional beauty in this voice, but it lay on the ear and invaded the chest in a way that no youthful, thrushlike strain could equal.

As I walked out one evening,
In the springtime of the year;
I overheard a soldier bold,
Lamenting for his dear.

For fourteen years transported,

To the Indies I was bound;
But to see the face of my one true love,
My escape I lately found.

Says I be not uneasy—

Here the old woman's voice faltered, but the daughter held her hand fast, bringing it forward in a slow circular motion in time to the song, almost like the piston arm on a locomotive. Nora watched, fascinated, as Rita continued humming the melody: '"But tell to me your true love's name",' she prompted. Something clicked in the old woman's head. She began again:

Says I be not uneasy,
Nor troubled in your mind;
But tell to me your true love's name,
And her dwelling you shall find.

He gave to me his true love's name,
A burning beauty bright;
But if I should tell of her sad fate,
Broad day would turn to night.

Your true love lies a-sleeping,
Her dwelling is the clay—

Again she stumbled, and again the daughter's low voice kept the music going until the old lady had cleared enough cobwebs from her memory to deliver up another few lines:

For the slaying of her new-born babe,
With her own life she did pay.

He bowed his head and tore his hair,
And with grief was near o'er ta'en;
Crying they've murdered thee my own true love—

This time the singing ended abruptly. '*Sin é*,' said the old woman. 'That's all. Ah, there's more, but I've lost it now. I can't—'

'It's all right, Mammy,' said Rita. 'Whisht now; you did grand, just grand.'

'You got the best part of it,' Cormac said. 'Not to worry.'

'That was wonderful, Mrs Cleary, really,' Nora said. The sound of her own voice grated on her ears, and she knew that she could never truly be a part of what was happening in this room. It was not the first time she'd felt it. There was an intimate form of communication taking place here, an exchange from which she was excluded, cut off by the broad chasm of culture and experience. The sound of Mrs Cleary's ancient voice and the image of the grieving soldier in the old lady's song merged with the red-haired girl and the vision of Tríona's smiling face, and Nora felt filled again with the terrible, aching sadness that had overcome her as she stood alone in the lab with the red-haired girl.

'Well, Mrs Cleary, we don't want to be wearing you out,' Cormac finally said. 'Perhaps we could come back and visit another day. Thank you so much for talking with us.' The old lady had warmed to Cormac now, and clearly didn't want him to go. She reverted to her cranky persona in an instant.

'Do what you like,' she said, waving a hand indifferently. 'Makes no difference to me.'

Cormac could see that Nora was upset as they left Mrs Cleary's, so he didn't speak until they were some distance down the road: 'Sorry, that was a bit rough. Are you okay?'

'Not really. I'm thinking of that old woman sitting

there day after day, with all that inside her – doesn't it overwhelm you sometimes, Cormac? All that's been squandered and lost?'

'But it's not all lost. That's what I've been thinking about as we're digging at the priory. Things do remain. People carry on, without even knowing. You can't kill that, as hard as you might try. It's almost like something embedded in our subconscious, like a virus, that only shows itself in certain conditions. Sounds daft, I know, but doesn't it make sense, when you think of all that's managed to survive? I hear it all the time, Nora. I hear it in your voice.' He watched a solitary tear spill down her cheek.

'Oh, bloody hell,' she said. They were going uphill now, and she was struggling with the gearshift. 'Bloody buggering hell.' Neither of them saw the sheep until it was nearly too late.

'Look out!' he said, and she swerved instinctively to avoid hitting the animal. The car veered wildly as she tried to maintain control, then landed with a thud as the left front tyre skidded over the edge of the small embankment. 'Are you all right?'

Nora nodded, and let out her breath. Cormac peered out his window, testing to see whether the movement would cause the car to tip further. When he was satisfied that it wouldn't, he cautiously opened the door and climbed out, circling the car to assess the situation.

'It's not too bad,' he said. 'I might be able to push us back up onto the road. Put the gearbox in neutral, would you?' He pressed his back against the passenger door, grasping the bottom edge of the door, braced his legs, and heaved. He could feel the car rock slightly, so he heaved again, to no avail.

'It's no good,' Nora said. 'You can't do it alone. I'll give you a hand.'

'The ground's a bit soft to get any traction,' he said, looking down at the high grass that brushed against his thighs. 'I doubt if even the two of us would have much luck, but come on.' They positioned themselves with their backs to the car, on either side of the front wheel well, and began to shove. 'If I'd been watching the road—' Nora said. With the sudden force of the push, her feet slipped out from under her and she disappeared into the wet grass.

Cormac dropped to his knees and parted the thick blades with his hands until he found her lying on her back about halfway down the embankment. Tears streamed down her face, and her body shook as though wracked with sobs, but when she opened her mouth, the sound that floated upward was a silvery peal of laughter. He couldn't blame her; the whole situation was ludicrous. She lifted her arms and, seeing that they were coated with mud, dissolved into helpless laughter once more.

Cormac sat back on his heels. 'This isn't going to work, is it? Come on, then. I suppose we can walk back.' She grasped the hand he held out to her, and Cormac pulled her toward him, and didn't stop until he was kissing her, cradling her dark head in his hands, aware only of her vital electricity and the soft warmth of her lips. He let her go and sat back abruptly. 'I'm very sorry,' he said. 'I had no right.'

'No,' she said. They were both breathing hard. He struggled to stand, but felt her hand grasp the front of his shirt. She held him there until the distance between them began to close again, ever so slowly. He felt her eyes travel across his face, intimate as a touch, and this time he tasted her salt tears, the gritty smudge of mud on her chin, the softly perfumed whiteness of her neck. But the image of the pair of them on their knees in the ditch must have been too much; she had to pull away to release another helpless whoop of laughter. 'Oh God, I'm sorry,' she said.

'It's a good thing I'm not easily offended. But I'm afraid you're alarming the sheep.'

Chapter 12

Devaney rapped on the kitchen door at Bracklyn House. Through the small squares of wavy glass, he could see a figure approaching.

'Mrs Osborne? I hope I'm not disturbing you,' Devaney said when a slim, dark-haired woman opened the door. 'There was no answer upstairs. Detective Garrett Devaney.' He presented his identification, which she studied with interest.

'I'm afraid my cousin Hugh is away at the moment, Detective. I assume he's the one you've come to see.'

'Actually, you're the person I had hoped to find at home today,' Devaney replied.

Lucy Osborne returned his level gaze. 'I'm at home every day, Detective.'

'I wonder if I might ask you a few questions. Please, continue whatever you were doing. I won't take up too much of your time.' She led him down the hall to a room where she was in the midst of doing some flower arrangements. Devaney positioned himself on a stool across the table so that he could watch her through the spray of roses as she worked.

It was Lucy Osborne who spoke first: 'What can I do for you, Detective?'

'I just had a few questions about Mina Osborne's disappearance.'

'I thought Hugh mentioned that the case had been

given over to some sort of national task force.' She knew about the referral. Devaney saw that he'd better tread carefully.

'That doesn't necessarily mean the local police have given up. Besides, the task force are all the way over in Dublin. It's our duty to be their eyes and ears in the community.'

'I understand that you had no control over what people would say when that' – she searched for the right word – 'that person was found in the bog. But I must tell you, I don't think it'll do any good to stir things up all over again.'

'It's an ongoing investigation.'

'Of a non-existent crime. Hugh's wife left him, Detective. It's unfortunate, certainly, but what possible concern can it be to the police?'

'That's why I've come to you. In the past, most of the attention has focused on Mr Osborne as chief suspect, but I'm wondering if we haven't been overlooking some of the other, perhaps less sinister possibilities.'

'And just exactly how may I be of help? I have nothing to add to any of my earlier statements. I'm sure they're in your files.'

'I'm trying to find out more about Mina. Her habits, her usual routine, her circle of friends and acquaintances. I'm trying to get closer to who she was, to see if that might not shed some light on the case.'

'I'm not sure I can be of any assistance to you. We were not close.'

'Still, you lived in the same house for several years.'

'It's a very large house, Detective.' The woman's manner softened. 'I don't mean to be unhelpful, but we led almost completely separate lives.'

'But surely you could offer a few details about how she spent her time here.'

'Well, it was clear to me from the start that she wasn't remotely interested in the running of the household, and it was just as well. I can't imagine—' Lucy Osborne evidently couldn't stop herself picturing the disaster that would have befallen if Mina had been interested, and gave a small shudder. 'Neither she nor Hugh was much use at that sort of thing. She did have some ability as a painter, I believe, though her work was never really to my taste. Hugh set up a studio for her at the top of the house, but the smell of paint evidently disagreed with her. And after the child was born, she rarely ventured up there. The place is strewn with half-finished canvases.'

'If she wasn't painting, what did she do?'

'I believe she was a great reader. Always leaving piles of books about the house.'

'And who were her friends? Did she socialize much with anyone in the town?'

'I'm not sure she had any friends here. She did have ties in England, of course, school friends and the like, but—' Lucy Osborne hesitated. 'The only person I remember her seeing on a regular basis was the priest, I can't recall his name.'

'Father Kinsella?'

'Yes, that's it. She may have mentioned him from time to time.'

Devaney's thoughts leapt back to the letters in the confessional: *He knows where they are*. Maybe he'd been too hasty in assuming that the 'he' in this case referred to Hugh Osborne. What if it meant the person on the other side of the confessional wall?

'Was Mina happy here?'

'I was not in her confidence, Detective.'

'But perhaps you have an impression about how she and her husband were getting on at the time of her disappearance.'

'I'm afraid I'm not in the habit of prying into other people's private affairs. I believe they were reasonably happy.' She paused briefly. 'At least they always seemed so, in spite of the obvious . . . difficulties when people from such dissimilar backgrounds decide to marry.'

'What difficulties would you say they had, in particular?'

'Nothing of any great consequence. But a child always complicates matters, Detective. Especially when the parents come from such divergent worlds.'

'Surely a child can learn from both,' Devaney said.

'But the tragedy is that he can never really belong to either. Wherever he goes, such a child will always be an outcast. My view of the situation may sound harsh, Detective, but it's based in reality. The world can be a pitiless place.'

Devaney remembered what little he knew of this woman's circumstances, and considered her statement for a moment. 'Did they have any disagreements about how to bring up their son?'

'I never heard them argue.' Her reply left the question open, to be asked again another way, even as it condemned indiscretion as a sin.

'But you felt there might be some tension on the subject?'

'I really couldn't say.'

'And at the time of the disappearance? Was there any particular point – even a seemingly minor one – that remained unresolved?'

Lucy Osborne stopped her work. 'Detective, I'm not about to feed any false impression you may have that my cousin was not completely devoted to his wife. It simply isn't true.' She had finished the first arrangement, and started in on the second, clipping the end of each flower before dethorning it and wrapping it in wire.

'Of course, I'm not sure I can say the same about her.'

'Go on,' Devaney said.

'On the night before she went away,' Lucy said, and he sensed she was measuring the weight of each word as she twined the green wire along the stem of a rose, 'I did happen to overhear her on the telephone; I assumed she was speaking with Hugh. I could tell she was upset, but then she was often emotionally overwrought. I couldn't hear what she said, but I wouldn't characterize the conversation as an argument.'

'How would you characterize it?'

'I thought there was a note of disappointment in her voice. I couldn't say any more than that.'

'Would you call your cousin a possessive man, Mrs Osborne?'

She fixed him with an ironic look that said she wasn't that easily fooled. 'So, you haven't entirely given up on him, Detective? But to answer your question, no, I would not. If anything, Hugh was always far too willing to give up his own ways to please his wife.'

'And what about Mina? How do you think it would have affected her to learn that her husband had other women?'

'I'm not stupid, Detective. I know what people have been saying about Hugh and that McGann woman. But it isn't true.'

'How can you be so sure?'

'Hugh was devoted to his wife. Rather foolishly devoted, as it turned out.' It struck Devaney at that moment:

throughout this entire conversation, Lucy Osborne had never once spoken Mina's name. It was always 'she' or 'my cousin's wife', and Christopher was 'the child'. He wasn't sure why this disturbed him, exactly, but he filed it away.

'Have you any idea of Mr Osborne's financial situation?' Devaney asked. 'For instance, who would stand to inherit the estate right now if something should happen to him? We know he'd made provisions for his wife and son, but if she's cleared off, as you say, maybe he's had second thoughts.'

'He hasn't chosen to share any information with me on that subject, Detective, and it's really none of my business. My son and I are only guests in this house.' She rearranged a rose stem to turn the bloom outward, then reached for a spray of greenery that would serve as the final touch, snipping the long stem into shorter sprigs, adding them to the arrangement, and adjusting the balance here and there with an expert's quick, decisive motion.

'That reminds me, I'd also like to speak to your son, if he's here,' Devaney said. Lucy Osborne stiffened, and Devaney at once saw the cause. In her haste, she had pricked her finger on a hidden rose thorn. A droplet of bright red blood fell onto the wooden tabletop.

'Are you all right? Can I help?'

'I'm quite all right, Detective,' she said, pinching her injured finger to stem the bleeding. Devaney noted the large diamond on her left hand while she fished in the drawer of the table for a bandage. Lucy Osborne was evidently prepared for such occurrences, and had the wound bound up in a few seconds.

'You asked about my son. I believe Jeremy is over at the priory today, helping with the excavation. Now, if you would excuse me, Detective, I must get these flowers to the church.'

From where he stood in the sacristy at St Columba's, Garrett Devaney could see seven or eight people sitting at some distance from one another in the pews just beside the confessional. Father Kinsella had gone into the central compartment a few minutes earlier, and was just hearing the first confession. The faces in the pews were familiar to Devaney. They were mostly older women. He could see Mrs Phelan, one of the regulars Kinsella had mentioned, Mary Hickey, and Helen Rourke, all charter members of the Father Kinsella fan club, who might gladly make up sins for the opportunity to confess them to the handsome young cleric.

He thought of Kinsella, sitting there in the darkness of the confessional. It must be strange listening to the petty jealousies, the slights and counterslights that made up the multitude of sins, dispensing novenas and Hail Marys like a village doctor treating numberless cases of flu. Though he never felt it himself, Devaney imagined that the urge to confess must be strong. When he first joined the Guards, every time there was a particularly horrible crime reported in the papers – the sort of act that made people cringe even as they soaked up every available repellent detail – a smattering of false confessions would turn up. Most were from people who were desperate for attention or delusional, who once might have harboured thoughts of committing such a crime, and felt they ought to be punished for even imagining such a thing.

The words from the confessional swam once more to the forefront of Devaney's consciousness: *He knows where they are.* What if Kinsella had succumbed to the desires of the flesh? If he and Mina Osborne had so much in common, perhaps he had helped her to disappear. And if indeed he had, that might explain why she hadn't contacted her mother. But Kinsella hadn't appeared the least bit ruffled when he discovered the carved letters; on the contrary, he'd seemed intrigued. Still, it was worth looking into.

Mrs Rourke was just shuffling into the confessional when he noticed another figure in the side chapel, head bent over clasped hands. When the man raised his head, Devaney could see that it was Brendan McGann. Brendan had never been a cheerful-looking man, but he looked particularly troubled at the moment. What was he waiting to confess? The McGanns were Osborne's nearest neighbours. Devaney vaguely remembered talk of Brendan objecting to the development at Drumcleggan Priory. Squabbles over land, no matter what the cause, had a history of escalating into the bitterest of disputes. He considered McGann's darkened countenance once more, and decided that this, too, might be worth checking out.

Chapter 13

There was no one in the foyer at Bracklyn when Nora and Cormac returned from their outing, and she was still feeling a bit light-headed from what had taken place out on the Tullymore road.

'Hey, don't you think we'd better take off our shoes, at least?' she asked, as Cormac seemed ready to head straight up the stairs. 'I've already had a complaint about extra traffic muddying up the floors,' she whispered.

'Oh, right.'

'My bloody laces are too tight now. I can't get them undone.'

'Here, let me try,' he said. Jeremy came through the door at the top of the kitchen stairs just as Cormac was kneeling to have a look at her muddy shoelaces; her hand rested lightly on his shoulder.

'Hello, Jeremy,' Nora said, then watched as the boy's expression changed from pleasure at their return, to surprise and bewilderment at their dishevelled appearance. 'I'm sure looking at the state of us, you're probably glad you didn't come along after all.' He didn't reply.

'Near miss with a sheep,' she continued. 'The car went right off the road.' Something in Jeremy's face made her acutely aware of the mud on her back and elbows, and the dark patches on the knees of Cormac's trousers, and how they might easily be misconstrued. From the sudden heat in her face, Nora knew that she was blushing deeply, but there was nothing she could do to stop it. Jeremy's looks, and his silence, only made matters worse. She nattered on about how they were finally rescued by a trio of farmers. 'Three brothers by the name of Farrell. Hauled us out of the muck with a chain. Michael was good enough to give me an old potato sack from the back of their car, to keep from getting my upholstery muddy.'

'Too late for your upholstery, I'm afraid, but it did save the car.' Cormac must be completely unaware of what was happening here. Perhaps he hadn't seen Jeremy's accusing look as he dealt with the laces. But why did he have to pick this moment to demonstrate his sense of humour? Cormac went on: 'We'll be down for supper as soon as we've changed, Jeremy, if you'd like to join us.'

Nora watched the boy's eyes flicker from her face to Cormac's, and watched with a sinking heart as the hurt began to harden in them, and his jaw muscles began to tense in the slight concavity of his cheeks. He was just a boy, and everything mattered so much when you were young. Cormac looked evenly at Jeremy. Could he really have missed all this? Retreat seemed like the best strategy at the moment; they could talk later.

'Well, lads, I'd love to stand here chatting, but I've *got* to get rid of this mud,' Nora said. 'See you in a bit.' She walked between them, holding her mucky shoes aloft.

'Will you come down and have supper with us?' Cormac asked again. This time the boy offered a barely audible response, which seemed to satisfy, because Cormac began to follow a few steps behind her. As she turned on the landing, Nora could see Jeremy standing in the foyer with his hands in his pockets, following their movement up the stairs with a new coldness in his eyes.

Jeremy did not come down to the kitchen for supper. As

she and Cormac lingered over their evening meal, Nora alternately suffered twinges of guilt for perhaps having alienated Jeremy, and small surges of gratitude for time alone with Cormac. He had not even so much as brushed against her while they were preparing the meal, and neither of them had mentioned the momentary madness that overtook them on the road from Tullymore. They both seemed to be engaged in an elaborate game of avoidance, but the question that loomed – at least in her own mind – was not whether such a thing might ever happen again, but when. And yet she wasn't even quite sure how she felt about it. She wasn't ready for things to progress any further than they already had. There was so much Cormac didn't know.

'You've never told me how you came to be so interested in bog bodies,' he said, taking a dripping plate from her as they washed and dried the supper dishes.

'I guess it started with the summers I spent with my grandparents in Clare. My grandfather used to cut a bit of turf, and I was always fascinated by the things he turned up in the bog. Nothing spectacular, mostly small chunks of waterlogged wood that looked like they'd only been cut the day before. He showed me once where he'd come across the outline of a fallen tree. The wood was completely gone, but it had left a kind of ghost image in the turf.

'Then when I was about fourteen, I decided to do a school paper about bogs. I stumbled across a book in the library that had these incredible black-and-white pictures of Tollund Man.' She paused. 'You know Tollund Man, the famous bog body from Denmark?'

Cormac nodded. 'I certainly know of him, although we've never actually met.'

'Isn't he incredible? To see his face, down to the

worry lines and the eyelashes and the chinstubble, so perfectly preserved after two thousand years. That was it for me. And the more I found out, the more interesting it was. Why was he naked? Why was his throat cut? And why was that noose around his neck? I started digging for everything I could find about bogs – archaeology, biology, chemistry. Even when you understand the science of bog preservation, it's still pretty mysterious, the way unsaturated fatty acids are gradually replaced by saturated fatty acids with two carbon atoms less. So the body's organic compounds aren't broken down in the usual way, but chemically transformed.' She pulled the stopper in the sink and watched the last of the soapy dishwater as it slipped down the drain.

'Are you all right, Nora?'

She nodded. 'Just thinking.'

Nora climbed the stairs from the kitchen with Cormac following behind her. When they reached the main foyer, the only sound was the loud, steady ticking of the grandfather clock.

'Dead quiet, isn't it?' Cormac said.

'A bit too quiet, I think I'm just going to head upstairs to bed.'

He made no reply, but followed as she turned to go up the main stairs. They had just come to the landing when Cormac spoke: 'Hugh gave me a very nice bottle of single-malt that I was thinking of cracking open for a nightcap. I don't suppose you'd care to join me?'

She stopped and half turned to him: 'I don't know, Cormac . . .'

His voice was quiet. 'It's only half-ten. Come and sit with me for a while. Maybe that willie-the-wisp I saw will show itself again tonight.'

Nora still hesitated, struck by the thoughtful expression in his eyes. She found herself wondering whether the slight and rather appealing pronouncement of his lips – the muscle she knew professionally as the orbicularis oris – came from playing the flute. 'Single-malt?' she asked. He smiled. 'Maybe you could play that tape of Mrs Cleary for me again.'

A few minutes later, Cormac was lighting the fire in his room, and Nora was tucked into a heavy leather armchair just beside it. 'You know, I wonder if we shouldn't have tried to find Jeremy,' she said as Cormac handed her a heavy tumbler containing a small amount of golden liquor. She lifted the whiskey to her nose, and enjoyed the dusky scent of turf smoke that rose from the glass.

'My guess is that he would hate anyone fussing over him,' said Cormac as he settled into his chair opposite her. 'Whatever it is will blow over. Wait and see.'

'And how did you happen to gain such insight into adolescent psychology, if you don't mind me asking?'

'If I know anything about a mixed-up young lad like Jeremy,' Cormac said, 'it's because I was once just like that myself.'

'And what had you so confused?'

He drummed his fingers on the arm of his chair, then moved to the fireplace again, to gaze down into the flickering light.

'Oh, you know, typical bewilderment of a young fella leaving home and finding out he isn't quite as smart as he'd reckoned he was. And then my mother was very ill. She died the following winter. She was the only real family I had at that point; it was like being cut adrift.'

'God, Cormac, how awful. How old were you?'

'Nineteen. I don't know what would have happened if Gabriel hadn't thrown me a lifeline.'

'I had no idea you and Gabriel went that far back. I saw the picture on the mantel—' Nora suddenly realized she hadn't told Cormac about being in his house. 'You must be truly missing him.'

'I am.' Cormac's face was still turned away from her, but she could hear the note of desolation in his voice. 'The strange thing about Gabriel was that he had no children – I'm not sure whether that was by choice or by chance – I don't know how he knew so much about being a father.'

'What happened to your own father?' She could feel his embarrassment at the question, and wished she could withdraw it.

'Maybe we'd better talk about something else,' he said. But when he looked at her, Nora could see that he was at war with himself, unsure whether to venture into that uncharted, dangerous place. 'I've always told everyone he was dead.'

She wasn't prepared for this response. 'He's not?'

'No.' Cormac seemed to be trying to form the words in his head. 'When I was nine, he volunteered for a few weeks at a South American mission run by an old friend, and became very involved in the human rights work they were doing. He went back again, and happened to be part of a delegation visiting Chile when the generals took over. The six weeks he was supposed to be there turned into six months, and after that, I think my mother knew he wasn't coming back. It was hard for both of us, but especially for her, I think. She could never be officially angry with him; the man was a humanitarian hero.'

Cormac knelt and reached for the poker to stir up the fire. 'He did come home for a time when my mother was ill, but after she died he went back to Chile. I've tried to put myself in the place of all those people who lost someone. It's hard.'

'Where is he now?'

'He came back to Ireland two years ago, to his family place up in Donegal. He wrote me when he was coming home, but I couldn't – I haven't seen him since the funeral.' She understood now that this was the first time he'd ever told anyone the whole truth.

'Cormac, I'm sorry.'

'Yes. Well. It's my own choice.' He changed the subject. 'Would you like to hear that tape now?'

'I would.' She didn't want to press him any further. Was he sorry that he'd told her all this? 'Maybe we can keep an eye out for your willie-the-wisp while we have a listen,' she said. 'Where were you when you saw it – just there in the alcove?'

'Yes. But listen, if you're coming away from the fire, you'd better have this.' He pulled a small blanket off the bed and draped it around her shoulders.

'Thanks. Won't you be cold as well?'

'I'm very warm,' said Cormac, and he pressed the backs of his fingers to her cheek to prove the point.

'So you are.'

Nora sat with her knees pulled up to her chest on one of the deep, cushioned windowledges in the tower alcove as Cormac pushed the button on the tape recorder. They sat looking out into the darkness, listening to the background noises of conversation and chairs being rearranged. The sound of Mrs Cleary's croaking voice affected her almost as much the second time she heard it. When the old lady's song ended, she asked: 'Why wouldn't the song just say the girl's name?'

Cormac switched off the tape. 'Too dangerous. Besides, at the time, everybody in the locality would know who it was talking about. Lots of songs were written in code. It was pretty common convention during dangerous times.'

'I suppose you're right, like all those allegorical songs with the veiled references to Napoleon coming to save Ireland. Robbie has a song that doesn't mention the lady's name, only gives a cryptic anagram of her initials – I'm still trying to figure it out. But you know, there are a couple of things that don't fit. Mrs Cleary's song is about a soldier transported for fourteen years, and Cathal Mór wasn't a soldier; he was an outlaw, and transported for life. And the song says, "they've murdered thee", but there's pretty good evidence to say our red-haired girl was executed – she couldn't be both.' Nora had been slouching in the windowledge, but now sat forward abruptly to peer through the glass.

'What is it? What do you see?' Cormac joined her at the window.

'It's just the new moon. There, do you see it?' She murmured under her breath: '"I see the moon and the moon sees me—"' To her surprise, Cormac joined in: '"God bless the moon and God bless me".' He was close beside her, and his warm breath stirred in her hair. There was something strange about the sound of their voices joined in the darkness, as if this harmless, whispered prayer were a sort of spell or incantation. Perhaps that's what it was, an ancient attempt to harness the frightful power of the moon, and to use that power for good and not for mischief. Nora shivered, and suddenly felt anxious having him stand so close. If she weren't careful, the voices of reason and temperance could so easily be drowned out by the sound of her own pulse. And yet for some reason, she couldn't move.

'Nora? Could I ask you something?' She didn't answer,

but could sense his unease as he sat down beside her on the deep windowledge. 'That very first day, when we were out on the bog, something Devaney said seemed to upset you.'

The silence between them grew, but he waited, unmoving. He'd shared with her his most private thoughts, things he had never revealed to anyone else. What could she do but answer?

'It wasn't anything Devaney said,' she began. 'At least not at first. It was the red-haired girl. My sister Tríona had the most gorgeous red hair, masses of it, thick and wavy. I was always so envious. When I was twelve, and Tríona was seven, I had to brush her hair every morning before school. It was one of my chores. I grumbled a lot, but I secretly enjoyed it. You've no brothers or sisters?'

'No.'

'Those five years between us were like a gulf at the time. They seem so insignificant now. When I saw that red hair coming out of the turf . . . Everything that reminds me of Tríona also reminds me that I was at least partly responsible for her death.'

'Why would you think that?'

'Because I was the one who convinced her to leave her husband, and the very next day she disappeared. It wasn't just coincidence, Cormac. When I had to identify her body, the way I knew that it was Tríona was all that lovely red hair. I couldn't look at her face, you see, because she didn't have a face any more.'

'Ah Jesus, Nora.'

'And I was the only one who knew it was Tríona's husband who killed her. I knew it. The police believe it now as well, but they can't do anything. He's been questioned, but there's never been enough evidence to arrest him. It turned out that Tríona never told anyone but me about how Peter got some sort of twisted pleasure from hurting her. She said she was too ashamed to tell anyone. He was smart enough never to raise a hand to her in public. Why should anyone suspect him? He's rich, he's handsome, he's on the boards of dozens of worthy charities. He had everyone actually feeling sorry for him because of the theory he put forward, that some crackhead carjacker must have killed my sister. He swore she never once mentioned leaving him, so that made it my word against his, and lots of people started to think I was crazy. He told the police that he and Tríona spent the evening at home, then she went off to the health club for a massage the following morning and never came back. Her car turned up in a car park four days later. Her body was in the boot.'

'And there was nothing to link her husband, no physical evidence at all?'

'Nothing, despite the fact that he had no real alibi. Through all of it, I kept telling myself that I didn't want revenge, that all I wanted was justice. I'm not even sure what that means any more. When Tríona's case was put in the drawer with all the other unsolved murders, Peter filed the claim on her life insurance. Of course the insurance company denied it, since he was still the main suspect, but he sued and they eventually had to settle out of court. He took the money, and he took my niece, and he moved as far away as he could get. I haven't seen Elizabeth for nearly four years; she'll be eleven in October.' Nora paused and looked up at Cormac. 'She's already lost her mother, and I would gladly have taken her father away as well. If I'd had a chance in hell. But it seems I didn't.'

'Is that why you're here?'

'Desperately trying to patch together what's left of my life and my sanity.'

'I'm so sorry, Nora.'

'I might have been okay about the red-haired girl if Hugh Osborne hadn't shown up, looking for his missing wife. With no alibi, and no evidence against him.'

She could see by Cormac's expression that something had finally clicked into place. He hesitated. 'It seems unfair to assume that Hugh Osborne is guilty when we don't have all the facts.'

'Then why not help me find some? We could just as easily exonerate him.'

'Nora, we can't just go charging through people's lives like – I mean, maybe the light I saw out there is somehow related to Mina Osborne's disappearance, but there's a better chance it's not. It must have been so terrible to lose someone like that; I can't even begin to imagine. But they're two totally separate situations. You can't let your own anger and frustration make you jump to conclusions about people. You must see that.'

'I saw something in his eyes, Cormac, the first night I came here. I can't even describe it, except to say it was almost a challenge. Like he was saying: "Prove it," right to my face. You were out of the room at that point. You didn't see.'

'I just wonder how much of it can be put down to the fact that you want him to be guilty.'

'Next you'll be saying that I've come unglued.' As she spoke, Nora found the elevated pitch of her voice disconcerting, almost unrecognizable.

'I don't think that.' Cormac's voice softened. 'Jesus, Nora, I don't. It's just—' He reached for her, but she pushed past his hand and crossed to the door, shedding the blanket he'd given her. When she reached for the door handle, she felt Cormac's hand cover hers. 'Please, Nora, you don't have to leave.'

'I do.' Her voice was even. 'Please let me go.' Cormac removed his hand from hers and took a step back.

When she was alone in the hallway, Nora slumped against the wall and drew in a long breath. What the hell was going on with her? Everything he'd said was perfectly rational. Hadn't she been telling herself the same things over and over again for the past few days? She'd become so bloody defensive, and nobody deserved that, least of all Cormac. Remembering his gentleness, Nora felt overwhelmed by a sudden, hollow ache of desire. At precisely the same moment, she heard a clattering noise in the stairwell only a few feet from where she stood.

She pushed open the stairwell door. 'Who is it? Who's there?' No one. But someone had been there, watching her – perhaps watching them. When she turned to go back to the hall, her foot struck something that rolled and clinked against the wall. She stooped to pick it up – an empty whiskey bottle. As she made her way down the hall to her own room, Nora raised the bottle briefly to her nose, remembering her first chance meeting with Jeremy Osborne, and the same sweet, strong whiff of his breath against her face.

Instead of enlisting their help, she'd managed to alienate both Cormac and Jeremy in the space of a single day. She was especially sorry about Cormac. Why did everything have to be so complicated? Nora's stomach was in knots as she switched on the light in her room and dropped the whiskey bottle in the bin. She lingered by the door another few seconds. Something felt wrong. She scanned the room, looking for anything out of place; her eyes came to rest on the bed. The cover was disarranged. Had Jeremy been sleeping in her room this time? She crossed to the bed, threw back the covers, and had to stifle a cry.

Atop a pile of dirt and leaves lay the rotting carcass of a large crow. The bird's dead eyes were dull and sunken in their sockets; its large claws grasped empty air. The broken glass might have been an accident, but there was no mistaking the warning in this message.

Her first reaction was to phone Devaney. But as she rummaged through the pockets of her jeans, looking for the card he'd given her, Nora realized that calling the policeman meant that she and Cormac might have to leave this house before they discovered anything. Probably exactly what the perpetrator wanted, and she wasn't about to be so easily manipulated. And that meant calling Devaney was out of the question.

Who could have done this? And more to the point, why exactly was someone in this house trying to scare her off? Hugh Osborne was out of town – gone to London, he'd said – and she wondered whether the story was true. She also remembered Jeremy's cold look, and wondered whether he'd been upset enough to pull a prank like this.

Nora returned to the bedside and looked down at the crow. The filthy thing was crawling with maggots. She couldn't just leave it here, not if she was going to have to spend the night in this room. She gathered up the corners of the sheets and carefully rolled the bedding into a tight bundle. Then she opened the casement as far as it would go, and pushed the whole thing out of the window into the garden below, and turned to face the room again. Sleep seemed impossible, and it was cold in the room. Nora wrapped herself as best she could in her raincoat and settled onto one of the sofas near the fireplace, contemplating what she ought to do next.

Chapter 14

Una McGann was awakened by the sound of pounding at the front door. She hurried down the stairs in her nightdress and bare feet, and stood on the other side of the door, unsure who was making the commotion. Then she heard Brendan's voice.

'Una, open the door, I've dropped my key. Una!' She stood frozen to the floor, trying to work out how to respond. He pounded again, with the flat of his hand.

'Una! Let me in. I know you can hear me. Come on, open the fuckin' door.'

'Hush, Brendan, you'll wake Aoife.' It suddenly dawned on her what was wrong with him. 'Brendan, are ye drunk?'

'S'none of your fucking business how I am. Open up, I said.' He gave the door a vicious kick, and then another. 'I built this fuckin' door with my two hands; you've got some fuckin' neck using it to bar me.'

'I can't let you in when you're like that. You're frightening me. And you needn't bother trying the back door. It's locked as well.'

She winced as Brendan swung wildly at the door, but its stout wood received a rain of blows from his fists and feet without so much as a shudder. There was a brief respite, and she could heard him moving away from the door. But her momentary relief was shattered when she heard an explosion of breaking glass against the door and the side of the house. He must have brought home a few bottles from the pub. Una sat crouched on the floor, her arms clasped around her knees in a posture of self-protection, and though she knew the door would hold against this onslaught, the sound of each heavy pint bottle hitting the house made her jump. Fintan appeared beside her, dresssed only in his underpants. 'What's going on? Is that Brendan? What the fuck is he up to?' They listened, but could hear no more than a low muttering from beyond the door. Fintan lifted a corner of the curtain in the kitchen and peered outside. 'It's all right. He's heading off.'

'Brendan's drunk. He's drunk, Fintan. He never drinks.'

'We'll leave him until he's sober. He can go sleep in the shed.'

'Fintan, what are we going to do?'

'He's just angry about us wanting our shares of the farm. He'll get over it. We can't let it change what we've planned.'

'There are things you don't know, Fintan.' She looked at him, but couldn't find the strength to speak.

'Tell me. Una – you must tell me what it is.'

'Come,' she said, and led him down the hall to Brendan's room, where she pulled the bed from the wall, and showed him the hiding place she'd discovered on the day of the bird's intrusion. She reached in and lifted up some papers, searching for Mina Osborne's hair clip. It was gone.

'It was here, I know it was. I held it in my hand.'

'What?' Fintan asked.

'A hair clip. It belonged to Mina Osborne. I know because I saw her wearing it on the day she disappeared. And there are a whole lot of cuttings about her in here as well. Fintan, what are we going to do?'

Her implication took a moment to sink in. Una could see him resisting the notion, as she had, denying the possibility even as he remembered the look in Brendan's eyes when the sickle blade had sunk into the table only inches from his own head.

'No, there's no way,' he said, shaking his head. 'He's our brother. You must be mad.' Despite his protestations, she could see the idea burrow in and take root. But the fact that Fintan now shared this dreadful knowledge did not make it weigh any less on her own heart.

Chapter 15

Nora was startled awake by a knock at the door of her room. She was momentarily disoriented, but the memory of the crow crashed back into her consciousness.

'Are you all right, Nora?' It was Cormac's voice. 'It's after ten. Nora?' The handle moved, and she hadn't time to react before he opened the door. He understood immediately that something was wrong, and quickly approached her.

'Nora, what's happened? Are you all right?'

She hesitated. It all seemed so strange now. 'I'm fine, Cormac.'

'Then what's—' He gestured toward the stripped bed.

'When I came back here last night, I found something.'

'What? Please tell me.'

'A dead crow.'

'Jesus, Nora.'

'I didn't want to raise an alarm. What good would that do? So I—' It seemed too bizarre in the light of day. 'I threw it out the window. Bedding and all.' She got up and crossed to the window. 'I know it was dead, and it wasn't going to hurt me, but—' She stopped short. There was no sign of the crow, or its litter of bedding and dead leaves. She knew Cormac saw it too.

She turned to him. 'It did happen.'

'I believe you. But Nora, why didn't you come get me?' She found she couldn't say a word, but could only look at him. Cormac put his arms around her, and neither of them spoke for a few moments. Then he asked: 'Do you still have the card Devaney gave you?'

'What can he do now? I've nothing to show him.'

'But he asked us to tell him about anything out of the ordinary, and I think this definitely qualifies. Please, Nora.'

'I left my mobile out in the car.'

Cormac led the way downstairs. There was no one about, until they met Hugh Osborne at the front door. He looked strangely at them, and said: 'I'm very sorry.'

At first Nora wondered how he knew about the crow, until she saw the cars parked in the drive. Cormac's jeep was in the worst state, its windscreen and rear window smashed in, and all four tyres completely flattened. The whole thing had been smeared with mud, now dried into patterns showing the sweep of the vandal's arm. The final insult, a fresh pile of manure on the jeep's hood, had begun to dry in the morning sun; flies buzzed about in a swarm. Her own car had fared somewhat better: although it was streaked with the same thick brown muck, and appeared to have a couple of punctures and smashed headlamps, at least the windows were still intact.

Nora couldn't help noticing that there was, in fact, a great stillness in the air – like the deep quiet she always imagined upon a battlefield after the calamitous noise of war. It was as if the morning itself could not countenance the violence done here lately. There was nothing but the mute testimony of the two ruined vehicles to bear witness to what had passed.

Chapter 16

Devaney was at Bracklyn House not more than five minutes after he received the call from Dunbeg Garda station. He arrived to find Osborne, Maguire, and Gavin on the gravel drive with the damaged vehicles. Osborne's Volvo was parked nearby, without so much as a scratch.

'Thank you for coming so quickly, Detective,' Osborne said. 'I just got in from London this morning, and came home to this. We haven't touched anything.'

Devaney took a closer look inside the jeep. Bits of safety glass lay scattered all over the vehicle's interior. A load of surveying equipment was still in the back; he'd have to ask to make sure nothing was missing. A blue and white vehicle pulled up beside him; it was Declan Mullins from the Dunbeg station. The scene-of-crime officers would have to come from Galway, so it would be a while before they arrived.

'I'll start the interviews here in the house,' Devaney said.

'Right, sir. What'll I do, then?'

Devaney found himself envying the eagerness in his young colleague's freshly scrubbed face. 'Mark off this whole area and don't let anyone touch anything. Get the scene-of-crime boys set up if I'm busy when they arrive. And see if you can't get the vehicle owners to give you an inventory of what was in them, to make sure nothing's missing.' He suspected that Gavin and Maguire knew more about the inhabitants of Bracklyn House than they had so far been willing to divulge. Perhaps this turn of events would prompt them to be a little more forthcoming. He spoke to Osborne first, in the library, while the other two waited outside.

Hugh Osborne had taken an early flight and driven up from Shannon this morning, he said, and arrived at about twenty minutes past ten. Devaney asked him about security around the house. The front gate was never locked, never even closed. The house only had the two entrances, the big front door, and a smaller door in the kitchen round the back. Lucy always made sure both doors were locked and bolted before she went to bed. Neither of the visitors had keys, since Lucy was generally here during the day, when they would be coming and going.

'I don't want to alarm you unnecessarily,' Devaney said, 'but I'm not concerned about this only as a property crime – it's fairly serious as property crimes go, but I'm more concerned that this might be some sort of personal threat. Can you think of anything that's happened recently – even something that might have seemed harmless at the time – anything at all that might have angered someone connected to you or your guests?'

'I can't imagine, Detective. I've not had any unpleasant dealings with anyone. Maguire's here doing a small job for me, the excavation at the priory, and Dr Gavin's just lending a hand. They've been around just over a week, and they'll be finished in another few days. The work they're doing is all very routine in the course of any development.'

'You haven't run into any opposition to your project?'

'Nothing explicit.'

'What do you mean by "explicit"?'

'Well, no one has come right out and voiced any opposition. I mean, we've all seen the placards posted everywhere, all that nonsense about bog evictions, trying to stir people up with incendiary language. Knowing some of my neighbours, it's hard not to take those as indirect criticism. I know they mightn't believe it, Detective, but I had nothing to do with Drumcleggan being put up for the list of conservation areas in the first place. I supported the move, but I had no part in the decision.'

'So you're saying there's no relationship at all between your project and Drumcleggan being named a protected area?'

'Actually, I wouldn't say that, Detective. The bog does adjoin the property I'm trying to develop. It's not in the immediate plans, and I've not discussed it with anyone yet, but eventually I hope to offer some environmental education programmes centring on Drumcleggan. We'd be foolish not to do so. It's an amazing resource.'

Not to mention a dead handy place to get rid of a couple of bodies, Devaney thought. He changed the subject. 'You've been away. Where?'

'London. I had meetings with my solicitor and with the group that's going to handle the additional financing on my redevelopment plan.' Devaney pictured the name the Badger had given him, of Osborne's banker friend, written in block capitals a few pages back in his notepad, and made a mental note to ring London and check the story. He'd get Mullins to check out British Airways to make sure Osborne had been on the early-morning flight.

'As far as you know, there's no apparent connection

between this incident and the disappearance of your wife and son?'

'I've been struggling with that question myself, Detective. I can't think of any possible connection.' He sat back in the chair and sighed.

'You'll let me know if you think of anything further.'

'Of course. Surely this had to have been just some local hooligans,' Osborne said. 'Some of them can't resist taking the piss when they're drunk. It's happened before. Not recently.'

Devaney looked into Hugh Osborne's bloodshot eyes. 'You may be right,' he said. 'I hope that's all it was. I'll see the professor next.'

Cormac Maguire had heard nothing in the night. 'Dr Gavin and I were out all afternoon; we came back to the house sometime between five and six. We washed up and cooked a meal, and afterwards we sat and talked in my room until about midnight.'

'And then?'

'And then Dr Gavin left and went back to her own room.' There was something more he wasn't saying. Why not? Devaney decided to try another approach. 'What about Bracklyn's other residents? Where were they all last night?'

'Hugh probably told you he was away in London; he just got back this morning. Lucy Osborne's pretty much kept to her room since we've been here; I haven't seen her at all except on the afternoon I arrived. I did see Jeremy twice yesterday, both times only briefly.'

'I happened to be here yesterday afternoon myself. The boy's mother told me he was helping you and Dr Gavin,' Devaney said.

'He has been helping with the excavation, but he

wasn't with us yesterday. We took the afternoon off to visit a Mrs Cleary.'

'Ned Raftery's aunt?'

'Yes, that's right. Ned told us she might be able to shed some light on the story of that red-haired girl from the bog. We didn't bring Jeremy along. Didn't think he'd be interested, I suppose. He sort of latched on to us, Nora and myself, a few days ago, and started helping out with the dig. Apparently hasn't many friends his own age. He might have felt left out, but that's hardly enough to provoke such a vicious attack.'

'When did you say you last saw him?'

'Early evening, when we got back from Mrs Cleary's. I asked him to join us for a meal; he said he would, but he never showed up.'

'No one thought twice about him going missing?'

'He may have been with his mother. I can't say I know what the boy's usual behaviour is.'

'You've no idea why anyone would want to do something like this? Could it have been intended as a warning?' Devaney could see that he'd struck a nerve.

'A warning about what, Detective?'

'Maybe someone doesn't like the idea of yourself and Dr Gavin being here. Perhaps someone who doesn't want this development to go through. Can you think of anyone who'd object to Osborne's plans for the site?'

'But in that case, why interfere with Dr Gavin and myself? We've nothing to do with whether or not the project goes through. And there's no equipment missing. Surely if someone wanted to delay the work at the priory, they could have just stolen or damaged the equipment. Or sabotaged the site.'

'Maybe delay wasn't enough. Maybe someone wanted to bring it to a stop.' Devaney pressed further: 'Did you know that the priory land abutted Drumcleggan Bog? And that it's the subject of a rather heated dispute at the moment?'

'Hugh did mention it, but only once, when we first arrived. I'd seen the signs posted along the road – you know the ones I mean – and when I asked what they were about, he told me, but didn't seem particularly worried. Then the day after we arrived, I was out at the site. Brendan McGann and I had a few brief words. He's evidently not keen on the plans for the priory. He said if I were smart, I'd pack up and go home to Dublin, and not get mixed up in things that had nothing to do with me.'

'Why didn't you mention this before?' Devaney asked.

'It just seemed like idle talk. Bluster.'

'What's your impression of Brendan McGann?'

'I've only met him a couple of times. He seems to me an unhappy sort of man. Doesn't like Hugh Osborne; that much is very clear. But you live here, Detective; you probably know the why of it better than I do.'

'I appreciate your honesty,' Devaney said. 'As I told Osborne, in all likelihood this isn't related to his wife's disappearance, but until we know more, we can't rule anything out. May I offer some advice to you and Dr Gavin? Mind yourselves – this may not be an isolated incident.'

'No.'

'Was there something else you wanted to tell me?'

'When I went to call Dr Gavin this morning, she told me someone left a dead crow in her room last night. We were actually on our way to phone you when we found the cars. I only hestitated telling you because I didn't actually see the thing – it's probably better if you ask her directly.'

'I will,' Devaney said, excusing him.

Dr Gavin was eager to talk. Devaney indicated one of the overstuffed armchairs. 'Shall we start with last night? Just describe what happened from, say, late afternoon onward. Whatever you can recall.'

'Cormac and I came back from Mrs Cleary's about five-thirty, I suppose. We had a bit of a mishap on the road, so we were both pretty well covered in mud. I had a bath, and Cormac got cleaned up as well. Afterwards, we had supper in the kitchen, then sat in Cormac's room and talked.' Both of them were holding something back about that conversation, Devaney thought. 'I must have gone back to my room around midnight, I think.'

'And where were Lucy and Jeremy Osborne?'

'I don't know. I didn't actually see anyone.' She stopped suddenly. 'I thought I heard someone in the stairwell when I came out of Cormac's room. But when I looked, there wasn't anyone there, just an empty bottle on the floor.'

'What sort of a bottle?'

'A whiskey bottle. I threw it away when I got to my room.' Devaney waited. 'I could tell there was something wrong; the bed was rumpled. When I pulled back the covers I found that someone had left me a message. There was a dead crow in the bed. My first thought was to call you—'

'You should have.'

'Yes, I know. But whoever left it there meant to frighten me, and I wasn't about to give them any satisfaction. So I threw it out the window.'

'Excuse me?'

'I wrapped it up in the bedsheets and threw it out the window. And when I looked out this morning, it was gone.'

Devaney felt a sharp twinge just behind his eyebrows. 'Who would want to frighten you?'

'I'm not sure. But I don't think it was the first time. I got a strange phone call when I was home in Dublin last Monday. It was late at night, and the person – I couldn't tell who it was, or even whether it was a man or a woman – just said, "Leave it alone. They're better off".'

'You're absolutely certain those were the words?'

'Yes, I'm sure. I tried to get the person to say more, but whoever it was hung up.'

'Is there anything else you can remember from the past few days, any little thing that seems amiss or odd in any way?'

'When I came back from Dublin a few days ago, I found broken glass all over the floor of my bathroom. At the time, I thought it must have been an accident. Now I'm not so sure. When I went to get a broom to sweep it up, I came across Lucy Osborne, down on her knees scrubbing the floor in the front hall. All done up like a cleaning woman, head scarf and everything. I don't know, it was just odd. She said her cleaner, Mrs Hernan, was down with a flu, but for some reason, I don't really know why, I didn't believe her. It was something in the way she handled the brush and the bucket – like she was used to it.'

'Let's go back to the crow for a moment. Whoever put it in your room had access to this house. Hugh Osborne says he was in London last night and didn't get back until this morning. If his story checks out, that leaves Lucy or Jeremy, and why would either of them want to warn you off? What have you been doing here?'

'Nothing. I've done nothing to provoke anyone, unless—' Dr Gavin began absently fingering the brass nail heads that stood out on the arm of her chair. She continued:

'I was wandering around upstairs one day – by the way, did you know there's a painting studio way up on the top floor?'

Devaney nodded. 'It's Mina Osborne's.'

'I came downstairs when I heard a child's voice – it turned out to be a video of Mina and Christopher Osborne. And I found Jeremy sleeping in the next room, a nursery, in a child's bed. That's when Lucy came in. She wasn't happy to see either of us in that room.' She paused again, and Devaney could see that she was wrestling with whether to tell him any more. 'Cormac probably told you that Jeremy is helping with the work at the priory. I've caught him a couple of times, staring at me.' She sighed. 'He may be upset because he thinks Cormac and I don't want him around.'

'And do you?' Devaney asked. She was flustered by his question, and coloured deeply. 'I don't mean to pry; it's important that I have all the facts.'

'We weren't actually trying to get rid of him. I just can't see Lucy Osborne putting a rotten animal carcass in someone's bed; it's so completely out of character. I wish I could be so sure about Jeremy. But he doesn't strike me as the kind of kid who'd go around bashing things. And the other thing is, if the damage to the cars was meant to scare us off, it was a pretty poor job, since we can't leave without them.'

Devaney was with her on that point. It seemed unwise to assume that all of the previous night's events were somehow related.

When he opened the door for Dr Gavin, Devaney found Lucy Osborne sitting in the foyer, waiting to give a statement. Although her windows faced the drive, she had little to add.

'I'm a very light sleeper,' she said, 'and normally would

have been awakened by the slightest noise in the yard, but I hadn't slept well for a couple of nights previous, and decided I'd take one of my tablets to see if I couldn't get a decent rest. I'm very sorry not to be more help. Have you any idea who would do such a thing?'

'Have you?'

'The local villagers are nothing but ruffians, the lot. I wouldn't put this sort of thing past any one of them.' She got up to leave the room.

'You do a lot of gardening, Mrs Osborne?'

'Flowers are my passion, as you may have gathered.'

'I suppose you always get a few animal pests disrupting the beds – moles and birds and the like.'

'A few. We manage to deal with them. The crows are a terrible scourge. I had to resort to poison, but that seemed to take care of them.'

'Poison? So what do you do when a dead crow turns up in the garden?' He watched for any change in her demeanour, but saw nothing.

'Jeremy takes care of it for me.' Then she stopped, puzzled by his line of questioning. 'Why are you asking me all this?'

'Just routine. I want to make sure I speak to all the potential witnesses. If your son is outside, would you mind sending him in?'

'I'm afraid he's not here, Detective. He was running an errand for me this morning and hasn't returned yet. But he should be back any time now; I'll tell him you're waiting to speak with him, shall I?' Devaney now understood why Lucy Osborne had so eagerly volunteered: she hadn't a clue where her son was. Just then the library door opened slowly, and Jeremy Osborne's dark head peered cautiously around it.

'Hugh said you wanted to see me—' When the boy saw

his mother, he turned his face away automatically, but the movement was not quick enough to keep her from seeing the cracked, swollen lip and the darkening bruise on his left cheek. Lucy Osborne's alarm was instinctive; she stepped protectively between Devaney and the boy.

'Jeremy, what on earth happened? Did someone hurt you?' Devaney could see her inspecting her son's face and frame for any other injuries. The boy's face and clothes were clean, as were his hands, though the knuckles were swollen and abraded.

'I'm all right. I slipped climbing over an embankment when I was out.' As Lucy searched her son's face, Devaney saw ordinary motherly concern, but something else as well: wordless entreaty, supplication. He realized that at this moment, for the first time since he had met her, Lucy Osborne seemed completely bereft of her usual and formidable lines of defence.

'Thank you for your statement, Mrs Osborne,' Devaney said. 'I'll just finish up with Jeremy here, and then be on my way.'

'I'd like to stay, if you're going to question my son,' she said. The boy looked pained.

'There's no need. This isn't a formal interview, just a couple of routine questions.'

'Nevertheless—'

'I'll be all right, Mum, don't worry.' Devaney thought they'd have a harder job getting rid of her, but Lucy Osborne withdrew without another word. He gestured for the boy to sit on the sofa, and placed himself in the chair facing. Jeremy's eyes travelled nervously to the door a couple of times, as Devaney began jotting down a few brief notes in his book.

'Sore head?'

The boy's eyes snapped toward him. 'Sorry?'

'I asked if you had a sore head.'

Jeremy studied him curiously. 'You have to watch yourself with the whiskey,' Devaney continued. 'Only takes a few before you're stone mad. You're better off on the beer at your age.' Jeremy took this fatherly advice with a trace of suspicion, but Devaney could see that underneath the brusque exterior, the boy craved this kind of attention.

'Why don't you tell me what you were up to last night, Jeremy? Don't worry, it's strictly between ourselves at this point.'

'You'll have to put it down in there,' Jeremy said, looking at the notebook.

'That's right. But nothing goes into any file except a formal statement, if that becomes necessary. You may be sure I don't pass this round for people's mothers to read. Were you down at Lynch's again last night?' Jeremy shook his head wordlessly, and Devaney could see the dim memory of the evening coming back to him in the successive waves of shame, anger, and disappointment that washed over his face. Devaney leaned forward and spoke as gently as he could. 'Where were you, Jeremy?'

The boy's eyes were on the patterned carpet, his voice was barely audible. His long fingers picked at a thread coming out of the seam of his black jeans, and Devaney could see that his nails had been bitten to the quick. 'I nicked a bottle Hugh keeps in his workshop. I remember having a few drinks from it, but I don't know what happened then. I woke up this morning in the woods.'

'So what you told your mother about slipping on the embankment—'

'I couldn't tell her I'd been out all night.' The pathos in his voice was sincere. 'I'm not supposed to be drinking. She gets worried enough as it is.'

'So you don't know how you happened to get those – souvenirs?'

'No.' Jeremy gingerly touched his broken lip, and winced. Well, fuck me if he isn't telling the truth, Devaney thought. If he did do it, the scene-of-crime boys might soon have the evidence; drunks weren't normally careful about not leaving prints.

'And you know nothing about a dead crow turning up last night in one of the bedrooms upstairs?'

'No!' The boy appeared genuinely taken aback, even horrified by this bit of news, and Devaney pushed a little further.

'Maguire tells me you've been helping him with the excavation at the priory.'

'Well, I'm finished with it.' Hurt and anger flashed in the boy's eyes.

'And why's that?'

Jeremy Osborne looked down, and tried valiantly to regain control of his emotions. When he'd succeeded, he raised his face to address Devaney once more: 'Bloody boring work, isn't it?'

Chapter 17

Devaney wasn't sure what he expected to find out by speaking to Brendan McGann. He remembered what Maguire had told him, of McGann's veiled threats at the priory. The information didn't surprise him; everyone knew Brendan had a short fuse, and bickered with his neighbours – over livestock gates left open, property markers and fences, the usual small irritations between farmers. Devaney would wager that every perceived indignity, every slight that Brendan McGann had suffered over the years had been banked and kept alive in his belly like the embers of a turf fire. Eventually, those things either ate away at you from the inside – he had seen it happen to his own father – or they came bursting out. On the murder squad, he'd seen the consequences of the latter far too often.

Brendan's statement in the Osborne case file had been true to form: few words, grudgingly delivered. He'd offered no alibi for the time of the disappearance, said he'd been driving cattle home from pasture. Devaney pulled into the drive, feeling the Toyota vibrate dangerously as it rumbled over the cattle grid. Jesus, something was going to fall off the fucking car any minute. No one answered when he rapped at the door, which was shut, and locked, when he checked the handle. Something popped under his foot, and he looked down to see several shards of dark brown glass on the footpath.

Looked like a piece of a broken Guinness bottle. He flipped it aside, and was just stepping away from the door when he saw Brendan McGann round the corner of the house, wiping his hands on a bit of a rag.

'Devaney,' he said curtly. It was a greeting.

'How are ye, Brendan? Thought I might have a chat with you about what happened last night at Bracklyn House.'

'What happened there? I've not been to town today.'

Now there was a strange thing, Devaney thought. For all his roughness, Brendan McGann was known as a regular churchgoing man, and he'd been to confession last night. 'Bit of a shemozzle over a couple of motorcars.'

'And I'm meant to know something about it, am I? I'll tell you once and for all, anything going on at that house is nothin' to do with me.' Brendan jerked a thumb in the direction of the shed. 'D'ye mind? I'm in the middle of something here.'

'Maybe I can give you a hand,' Devaney said. Brendan's face was expressionless; he said nothing, but turned on his heel and headed for the shed. When Devaney reached the door, he could see that Brendan had been struggling to get a new tractor tyre on a rim and could probably use his help.

'Fine collection of old tools you have here,' Devaney said, kneeling to hold the wheel rim steady, and looking about him at the astonishing assortment of hay forks, scythes, thatching tools, and *sleáns* that hung from the walls and rafters of the shed. 'By Jaysus, I haven't seen a billhook like that in years. It's the very same as the one my father had. You still use all these?'

'I do. Lift.'

As they wrestled the tyre upright and laid it down again, Devaney's nostrils took in the smell of turf mould and damp, and yet Brendan's tools seemed wondrously untouched by rust. Given the right provocation, Devaney imagined any one of these gleaming metal blades could cut a person's throat as cleanly as they severed slender stalks of oats and hay. Brendan strained to pry the tyre over the rim, and Devaney was close enough now to smell the sour reek of sweat that came off the man, mingled with his stale, beery breath. Strange. Everybody in town knew McGann wasn't much of a drinker. On the rare occasions he was seen in the pub, he had a quiet pint or two on his own, and then went home. It took more than a couple to leave you stinking like a brewery the next day. As he held the tyre in place, Devaney cast his eyes around the shed once more. His eyes grew accustomed to the dim light that made its way through the one tiny window, and he could see a makeshift cot in the corner, with an ancient straw mattress. His eyes returned to Brendan, registering the creases in the man's clothing and the few bits of dirty yellow straw that clung to the back of his shirt.

'I stopped to see if you saw or heard anything out of the ordinary last night,' Devaney said.

'No,' Brendan replied. He must have seen Devaney's chagrin at the curt answer. 'I stopped for a jar at Lynch's last night. Left around nine. I saw no one coming or going, and went straight to bed when I got home.'

'Is there anybody who might vouch for you? Your sister wouldn't be at home by any chance?'

'No.'

'Well, that's all right, I can talk to her later. She's fairly involved with Osborne's new craft workshop, isn't she? But you're not too keen on it yourself, I understand.' Brendan just looked at him, and Devaney's eye was attracted to a stack of plastic bucket lids that stood on the workbench behind him. These plain, white rounds were identical to those used in making the signs that had appeared on the roadsides around Dunbeg.

'Some people say you have good reason to resent Hugh Osborne,' Devaney said. 'They say—'

'It's no secret I don't like the bastard,' Brendan interrupted, the volume of his voice rising ever so slightly. 'That's not against the law, and the reasons for it are me own. But I was home in bed last night, Detective.' Brendan gave the iron another mighty push, and the massive tyre finally snapped into place on the rim. 'And you'll never prove otherwise. I'm obliged to you for helping me here. But I've nothin' more to say.'

Chapter 18

After the cars had been towed away, Hugh Osborne proposed a trip to the excavation site.

'I've been so busy, I hope you don't feel as though I've been ignoring your work,' he said as he drove them the short distance to the priory. 'I'm really interested in how you're getting on, that is, if you don't mind showing me around.'

'Of course,' Cormac said. They each took a hand carrying some of the equipment, and when they reached the site, Nora began to set up for the day while Cormac gave Hugh a guided tour of the several trenches they'd dug so far.

'At the moment we're working on an area that appears to have been some sort of midden or rubbish dump. Archaeologically speaking, middens are like treasure troves. They have so much information, not just for the purpose of dating a site, but about what people ate, what kinds of tools and vessels they had, all kinds of details about their everyday lives.' Cormac jumped down into one of the pits just barely within earshot, and Hugh crouched above him to have a look.

The day was overcast, with a strong wind pushing billowy, moisture-laden clouds eastward. Between gusts of wind, Nora heard Cormac's murmuring voice and watched him point out for Hugh the dark layer of a charcoal deposit, and the brown stain that marked where a wooden support had been sunk into the soil. He also showed Osborne the sheets they used for describing what turned up in each test pit.

'What we're doing here is really keyhole archaeology,' Cormac was saying. 'It's like trying to do a big three-dimensional jigsaw puzzle without any picture to go by.' Hugh was standing with his arms crossed, asking the occasional question and nodding appreciatively. Nora could see that they had become friends, and worried what would happen if it turned out that Hugh Osborne had been involved in his wife's disappearance.

She hadn't even told Cormac the worst part of her story last night. That her parents wouldn't do anything to help convict Peter Hallett, despite the suspicions and the intensive police investigation, despite everything she told them about what the man had done to their own daughter. Her father simply refused to listen, and had taken an adamant position on his son-in-law's innocence. Nora could see that her mother had instinctive doubts, but wouldn't allow herself to contemplate any action as long as Peter had sole custody of their only grandchild. *Please try to understand, Nora,* she'd said. *We've already lost Tríona. If we do anything, anything at all, he could take Elizabeth away from us as well. Forever. And then what would we have?* But he had taken Elizabeth away. So what did they have now?

Nora watched the two men deep in conversation in the far trench. Cormac was right: they knew little about Hugh, and still less about the circumstances of his marriage and family life. He seemed like a decent guy on the surface. But so did a lot of disturbed people. What was that expression her gran had? She could see the old lady's shrewd eyes, the set of her lips as she pronounced the words: *Street angel, house devil.* The first time she heard those words was the moment Nora realized there were plenty of things grown-ups never told children. Who could say that Hugh himself hadn't lost it and smashed up their cars? He said he'd only returned this morning, but the guy looked like hell, as if he hadn't slept at all. It was all very well to go about their work and to keep telling themselves that they weren't really involved here, but they *were* involved. Deeper and deeper, it seemed, first with the anonymous phone call, and now with all the events of last night.

Hugh took his leave, and a few minutes later, Cormac was in the trench they'd begun at the rubbish dump, about four feet down, wielding the pickaxe with a ferocity Nora hadn't seen before.

'Cormac, did you tell Devaney about that light you saw out at the tower? I couldn't really say anything; you're the one who saw it.'

'No. That is, not yet. I'm not sure it's significant.'

'He's supposed to decide what's significant. That's his job.'

Cormac was silent for a moment. 'I asked Hugh about the tower.'

'What?'

'Just now. I asked him about the tower. Why it's locked up. He said he didn't want kids climbing around in there and getting hurt.'

'Did you tell him you'd been out there?'

'No.' He stopped digging and looked up at her. 'I'd like to go back. Just to have another look.'

'I'm coming with you this time.'

He pressed his lips together and nodded briefly. Nora could see the clash of conflicting emotions in his face, doubt and curiosity battling his sense of loyalty and fair play. He had obviously thought about everything she said the night before. She felt somewhat guilty for tarnishing his opinion of Hugh Osborne, but as she studied the warring impulses that passed over Cormac's dark features, a sense of elation washed away any regret.

Chapter 19

Delia Hernan's house was on a small lane off the main road about a mile past Drumcleggan Bog. As Devaney approached he observed the general air of neglect about the place. The whitewashed stones that lined the path were out of place; the choppy hedge in front was overgrown, and thick moss grew on the tile roof. He knew Mrs Hernan had been widowed over the winter, but it looked as if the place had been suffering for at least several years. Devaney had heard there were a couple of sons off in England who didn't often get home.

Mrs Hernan didn't seem at all surprised to find him at her front door. While he took a seat at the kitchen table, she began to fuss about making tea, and Devaney used the opportunity to look around. The house had a look of hire-purchase shabbiness about it: the loud wallpaper, the wobbly chairs, the cracked oilcloth on the table where he sat, the cheap, faded souvenirs from Ireland's holiday spots, even the new strip of flypaper that hung from the smoke-stained ceiling next to a bare lightbulb. The patterned linoleum on the floor was worn away in places, and the lace curtains that hung in the windows had not been white for many years. A yellow enamel cooker in the corner had been scrubbed clean in spots, but remained blackened with sooty grease around the edges. Three pots of busy lizzies on the windowsill pressed their faces to the light outside and shed their shrivelled blossoms onto a growing pile on the floor. The room felt closed in, its warm, damp air permanently flavoured by decades of cigarette smoke and the sour smell of cabbage. He spoke over the sound of running water as she rinsed the teapot in the tiny makeshift scullery off the kitchen.

'I'm here to ask about your work at Bracklyn House. How did you first come to be working there?' Mrs Hernan emerged from the scullery with the teapot, into which she spooned a great quantity of loose tea from a tin, and then filled with water from a huge steaming kettle that rested on the corner of the cooker. She was a plump, full-bosomed woman of about sixty, with a frizz of mouse-brown dyed hair about her face. The fingers of her right hand were stained and leathery from nicotine, and she was apparently unaware of the cigarette ash that clung to the front of her shapeless woollen skirt. As she spoke, Mrs Hernan went about slicing several cuts of brown bread and thickly slathering them with butter.

'My Johnny, God rest him, always did the firewood for the house. Shortly after Missus Osborne – the elder Missus Osborne, that is – and her young lad arrived over from England, Mr Hugh asked my Johnny did he ever know anyone who'd be interested in helping out with the cleaning once or twice a week. I went there the very next day. Of course yer wan thought she was in charge, acting the grand lady, but I told her, seeing it was Mr Hugh that paid me, it would be him that gave the orders. Oh, she didn't like that. Not one bit.'

'And when Mina Osborne came to Bracklyn?'

'Ah, now, she was a dote. Always very lighthearted. And a real lady she was, too, but not above pitchin' in now and again, not her. The little lad, Christopher, was a pure angel, used to love going around with me while I was cleaning. I'd give him a bit of a rag—' Mrs Hernan's voice quavered, and tears sprang to her eyes. 'I know it's dreadful to think the worst. I can't help meself.' She shook her head and sighed. 'And Mr Hugh has taken it terrible bad, poor man.'

'How would you say they got on, Hugh Osborne and his wife?'

'Ah, a pair of lovebirds, those two. Couldn't get enough of each other, if you know what I mean. Are you married, Detective?' Devaney nodded. 'You know yourself, then. Of course they hadn't been married terribly long when the baby came along. I suppose they were still getting used to each other, like. I'm sure everyone has their ups and downs. They might have had a few small disagreements now and again, but they never went so far as throwing the delft or any such thing like that – not like meself and Johnny. Oh, Janey, we used to go at it sometimes. And I'd surely know if they had. You learn an awful lot about people from what's in their bins, I always say. I'm trying to think now if I ever heard them arguing at all. There was one time I heard her giving out to him about how much work he was doing, leaving her alone there in the house. And he said he understood how she felt, but they needed the money.' Mrs Hernan swirled the pot around a few times and poured the tea. Devaney opted for two spoons of sugar and plenty of milk.

'So you were working at Bracklyn at the time Mina Osborne and her son went missing?'

'Not on the very day. We had to get the bus, you see, Johnny and me, up to the doctor in Portumna that day.'

'That reminds me. How's your flu?'

'What flu?'

'Lucy Osborne mentioned to someone that you weren't able to come and clean at Bracklyn House last week because you were down with a flu.'

Mrs Hernan was stunned. 'Well, of all the – I never had any bit of a flu in me life. And as for the reason I wasn't there last week, she should know bloody well enough – it's nearly three months since I was sent packing.'

'By whom?'

'By herself, Mrs High-and-Mighty Lucy Osborne, who do you think? She's a right bitch, that one, accusing me of stealing. I never was so insulted in all me life.'

'What did she accuse you of stealing?'

'A scarf belonging to Mr Hugh's wife. I never took anything. Now, I'm not saying I never opened a drawer or two while I was cleaning, but I never took anything, and I'll swear it on me own mother's grave.'

'Why did she think you'd stolen it?'

'That's what I'd love to know. When I showed it to her, she starts givin' out stink, accusing me, running me out of the house like a common thief before I can even tell her where I found the feckin' thing.'

'Was there something strange about that?'

'Well, didn't I find it in young Mr Jeremy's room while I was hoovering under the bed? Stuffed under the mattress, it was, as if he was trying to hide it, like.'

'But you never mentioned that to his mother?' Devaney asked. Something about this didn't sit right, but he couldn't say what, not just yet.

'How could I? I was out the door with her foot up me backside before I could get a word in.'

'And you didn't find any other items of clothing?'

'No, nothing else. And you may be sure I got down on me two knees and looked everywhere under the bed.

What was her young fella gettin' up to with a lady's scarf? That's what I'd like to know.'

'You've not mentioned your dismissal to anyone?'

'And have her spreadin' lies about me? No, thank you. Better to say nothin' at all, turn the other cheek, as Our Lord said to do. Ah, ye couldn't pay me to set foot there ever again.'

Devaney changed his tack: 'Mrs Hernan, how would you say the Osbornes get on with their neighbours?'

'Ah, sure, not great. But Brendan McGann's always been a bit mad, if you ask me. And you could see his sister playing the innocent, trying to sink her hooks into Mr Hugh the minute his poor wife was gone. She's got some awful neck, that Una McGann. No shame at all. Oh, it'd sicken ye.'

'What gives you the impression she's out to snare Hugh Osborne?'

'Sure, didn't I see them often enough when I'd be coming and going on me bicycle, her getting a lift off him, or chatting to him through the window of his car? This was going on all the time, mind you, even after he was married. But she'll never get him, not for all her tears and her sweet smiles.'

As he took his leave and filled his lungs with the fresh air outside Mrs Hernan's house, Devaney had a claustrophobic vision of her sitting in that room day after day, drinking tea and chain-smoking, boiling bacon and cabbage for her dinner, marking the hours until *Coronation Street* came on the telly, and winding the clock at bedtime so that it would continue slowly ticking away the remaining minutes of her life.

Chapter 20

'Have you got a torch?' Cormac asked. Nora patted the pocket of her jacket. It was Monday evening; they had put in almost a full day at the excavation, and were now on their way to the tower, before Hugh Osborne returned from Galway. The late afternoon was as the day had been, overcast but temperate, with a faint taste of the lake in the air. But for the occasional birdcall, it was quiet as they made their way along the demesne wall toward the woods. Nora led, with Cormac following close behind.

'Watch where you step as we get closer,' he said. 'You could break an ankle if you aren't careful.' He'd been solicitous since yesterday morning, and hadn't wanted her to stay alone in her room last night. She'd finally persuaded him that she'd be fine on her own, but decided that she didn't mind his consideration. They had travelled about a hundred and fifty yards when she stopped. Through the thick cover of leaves and branches, she could just make out the tower's outline. Cormac was pointing out some of the tower's features when he suddenly fell silent.

'What is it?' she asked.

Cormac raised a finger to his lips, then pointed wordlessly to the door of the tower. The hasp was open, as was the padlock, which dangled from the staple.

'What should we do?' she whispered. He gestured to

her to keep back against the wall, then indicated that he would approach the door. Cormac looked behind him, and picked up a stout tree branch that lay near the cleared area, turning it to find the surest grip, and using the cudgel to push against the stout wooden door. To her surprise, it swung open easily, as if the hinges had recently been oiled. There was no response from inside, no sound or movement, so they exchanged a glance, and began to walk slowly through the doorway. It was dark and damp inside. The narrow slits in the thick walls didn't let in much air or light. Cormac's torch beam revealed a stone stairway that wrapped around the room and disappeared up into the heavy, cross-timbered ceiling. Nora reached in her pocket and switched on her own torch, whose light fell on a stack of large books and a pile of woollen blankets that lay on the dirt floor to one side of the room. She nudged the blankets with her foot, and saw that one was not a blanket at all, but a large shawl or something similar, shot through with gold threads. The floor looked as if it had been swept. Beside the blankets stood a crate covered with what appeared to be puddles of melted wax and burned candle-ends. In fact, there seemed to be half-burned candles everywhere they could see: a few tapers and pillars, but mostly tiny votive lights. A jumbled pile of brand-new candles lay on the crate nearest the makeshift bed. As Cormac turned, his torch flickered over a stack of crates against the far wall, and he trained the beam more carefully to see what was there.

'Nora, look at this.' She added the light of her torch to his, illuminating what appeared to be an orderly collection of small animal bones: among them she recognized long-toothed skulls of rabbits and sturdy-snouted badgers, the delicate skeletal remains of stoats and birds.

The next crate held the road-flattened carcass of a fox, with its bushy tail intact, and the severed wing of a crow, with its jet-black feathers fanned outward.

'What do you make of all this?' Cormac asked.

'I don't know. Hey, what are those?' Nora shone her light on several large sheets of paper that lay on the floor beside Cormac's feet. He crouched to examine them.

'Sketches,' he said.

Nora knelt beside him, and they each took a handful of curled and water-stained sheets to sort through. She could make out the recognizable shapes of animal skulls and bones, done in thick lead pencil, but the lines were wildly expressive, as though the artist had tried to memorize the contour of each object, and had put pencil to paper with closed eyes. There were dozens of sketches, compulsive repetitions of the same objects. Nora picked up and studied one of many distorted outlines of the crow's wing. 'Who could have done these?'

'Just what I was – wait a minute, look.' Cormac shone his torch slowly up the wall. Nora added her light as well, and each of them turned slowly in place, until their torch beams revealed that most of the wall space had been covered with huge abstract images of bones and eyeless skulls, on a background of twisted organic shapes – jagged lines, curving contours, and spirals of dark purple and dusky blue, interlaced with wide, wriggling swaths of metallic gold. Seeping moisture had caused some of the paint to come away in places, and from its thickness, they could see that the walls had been obsessively layered with paint over time. At the foot of the stairs lay a jumbled pile of empty cans, rags, and petrified brushes. A few spray cans and tins of paint, obviously used, stood on one of the crates nearby. Of all the things they had imagined when the door remained locked, the tower house as some kind of makeshift studio was not even among the considerations. And yet here it was before them.

'God, Cormac, this is so weird. But it's kind of wonderful as well.' Nora began perusing the volumes that lay by the makeshift sleeping area. 'Bird books, lots of art history,' she reported, then pushed the stout wooden door shut. The back of it had been painted in the same fashion as the walls, but in the midst of the paint was a large colour plate of an icon depicting a Black Madonna and Child.

'Cormac, have a look at this.' There was no answer but a startled cry and a flapping, scuffling noise, and Nora swung her torch around just in time to perceive that she was under attack. She threw both arms up to protect her head, and felt a sharp scrabbling and a gust of wing beats against her face and hands as she flailed the torch in an effort to shake free. Cormac grabbed hold of her sweater and pulled her to the ground.

'Keep down!' he whispered fiercely as the random flapping continued above their heads.

'What the hell is that?'

'Just a bird. I'm afraid I dropped my torch. Which way is the door?'

'Behind me here,' Nora said. They scrambled out into the fresh air and light, and sat for a moment with their backs pressed against the tower's sloping base, gasping for air.

'I should have warned you,' Cormac said. 'This place seems to be a sort of rookery, I suppose you'd call it. There's a whole flock of crows nesting in the top of the tower and the trees above.'

Nora rubbed her pecked fingers, then reached up and felt the scratch on her forehead. 'Here, let me see that,' Cormac said. He knelt beside her and tipped her head back to examine the wound. 'It's not too deep. You'll mend.' He sat back on his heels and crossed his arms. 'Well – we've seen inside, and we don't know anything more than we did before. But I'm willing to call Devaney if you think we ought to.'

'Let's think about this for a minute. Somebody uses this place to make pictures. That may be a bit strange – I'd even go so far as to say creepy – but it's not illegal. And if it is Hugh—'

'But he already has a sort of workshop in the house,' Cormac pointed out. 'So why would he come all the way out here? And in the middle of the night? It doesn't make sense.'

'Well, who else could it be? He put the padlock on and presumably has the key – although I suppose it's easy enough to pick that sort of a lock.'

'Dead easy. What about Jeremy?'

'I don't know,' Nora said. 'Could be anyone who knows about the tower.'

'So have we any reason to phone Devaney?'

The Madonna and Child image flashed through Nora's consciousness. She hadn't really had a chance to examine it closely. Apart from some overpainting, there was something else strange and disturbing about the picture, but what was it? With effort, she might be able to conjure up the image that had only imprinted itself briefly on her brain in all the pandemonium. She closed her eyes and willed herself to remember. If she wasn't mistaken, the eyes of both mother and child had been cut out rather crudely with a knife.

'You know,' she said, 'I think we might.'

When they returned from their expedition to the tower, Cormac found a note slipped under his door. He read it in a glance, and hurried down the hall to Nora's room.

'Message from Ned Raftery,' Cormac said when she'd answered his knock. She was daubing at the scratch on her forehead with antiseptic. 'Just says to ring him back; he may have found something on our red-haired girl.'

'I might have had something for you earlier,' Raftery said, when Cormac had him on the phone, 'but I had to ask someone to read through some of the boxes of old papers I have here. I don't know if I mentioned that I'd done a history of the Clanricardes some years back. I got to thinking, and wanted to check through some of the material. I knew that Ulick, the marquess of Clanricarde – he was the son of Richard de Burgo, who built Portumna Castle – wrote a memoir that was published a hundred years after his death. He lived from 1604 to 1657, so that puts him in roughly the same time frame as your red-haired girl, if she was indeed married in 1652.'

Cormac covered the mouthpiece on the mobile and called out to Nora: 'Come, quickly, I think you'll want to hear this.' She came and stood beside him, and Cormac tried to hold the phone so that she could hear as well.

'There was nothing in Ulick's own memoir or letters,' Raftery said, 'but what I found was a letter Clanricarde received from one of his neighbours, a Charles Symner, in the spring of 1654. Symner mentions attending the execution of a young woman named Annie McCann, convicted of killing her newborn child. The date on the letter is May twenty-third. It's not much, but Symner makes particular mention of the young woman's wild red hair.'

Chapter 21

On the phone, the young Garda sergeant had reminded Devaney of himself nearly twenty years ago, and he could hear the distinctive cry of a newborn in the background as they spoke. They settled on meeting in a pub on the outskirts of Ballinasloe. Donal Barry had been the man assigned to Bracklyn House during the original search for Osborne's wife and child over two years ago. Devaney knew he was grasping at straws here, but he'd begun to feel as if he was getting somewhere. Sooner or later, something would tip. That's the way it was with cases like this. Keep scraping away, like a file on metal, and eventually someone's story would weaken and give way. The hard part was sussing out where the vulnerable spot might lie.

Devaney got a pint and stood at the far end of the bar. Soon a strapping young man of about twenty-five came in. He was over six feet tall, clean-shaven, with fairish curly hair and a rugby guard's muscular build; he wore jeans and a heavy plain blue pullover.

'Devaney?' the young man said.

'Mr Barry.' Devaney held out a hand. 'Thanks for coming. What'll you have?'

'Same as yourself.'

Devaney lifted his near-empty pint and held up two fingers to the barman. 'You were posted at the Osborne house during the various searches and the original interviews,' he said. 'And I wanted to get your impression of the situation there.'

'I thought the case had gone up to the task force in Dublin.'

Devaney frowned. 'It has. But my superintendent evidently doesn't see how this one sticks out.'

'Don't tell me – Brian Boylan?' Barry's tone was one of disgust. 'What a fuckin' toe-rag.'

Devaney found himself warming to the young man. 'I can't say I disagree. Now, I don't quite know how to put this: was there any angle that ought to have been pursued and wasn't?'

'I knew from the start the whole kidnap scenario was a fuckin' waste of time,' Barry replied. 'I mean, the boys generally know when there's something up, don't they?' He meant the Provos, the Provisional IRA, and he was right. They were sometimes the first to volunteer any information they had on criminal cases – provided they weren't involved. A bit of community-mindedness went a long way in the propaganda war. 'There was nothing on the telegraph about this one. Boylan wasted a whole lot of precious time on it, though.'

Devaney was impressed both by the young man's powers of observation and his common sense. Apparently Barry hadn't actually participated in any of the interviews, which was a great pity; Devaney was sure the lad would have got more out of the witnesses than his superiors apparently had.

'What did you see or hear that didn't get into the official reports?'

'The trouble with this case was always the lack of a really good motive,' Barry said. 'The most obvious suspect, the husband, has a motive all right – the insurance money – but then why bother with the whole disappearing act? It would make more sense if the wife's body was found right away. I was never sold on the husband.'

'There's a neighbour who might have a motive as well. Brendan McGann. Thinks Osborne was messing about with his sister.'

'Ah, those rumours have been flying for years. I know Brendan – mad as a snake, but canny. I'm not saying he couldn't have done it, of course. He's got a wicked temper. But Brendan's more likely to goad people into killing each other than topping anybody himself. I never knew why they didn't spend more time on that cousin.'

Devaney's ears pricked. 'The boy?'

'Well, he was another right head case. But no, I meant the mother,' Barry said. 'Something quare about that one. A bit too – precious, if you know what I mean. I can't think why they didn't shake that tree a little harder.'

'Tell me more about her.'

Barry thought a moment. 'After a day or two sitting in that chair in the front hall, I got to be invisible. Part of the furniture, you might say. She'd make tea and sandwiches for the detectives when they were doing interviews, bring up these trays loaded with food, and straight into the library with them, as though—' he hesitated slightly '—well, almost as though she were part of the investigation herself. I don't know, I'm not puttin' it very well, but it was like she got some sort of thrill out of being there, so close to it all, and having to mind Osborne while he was in such a state.'

'Did you get the impression there was anything between herself and Osborne?' Devaney asked.

'I can't say for certain. Nothing obvious. I do remember one day she thought they were being too hard on him, asking too many questions. Well, she reared up. Fairly chased 'em out of the place.'

'And she never made you tea and sandwiches?' Devaney inquired with a sideways glance.

'She did, of course. But I had mine below in the kitchen, not above with the great men. I'll tell you what else bothered me: she was the one who kept pushing the notion that the wife had just scarpered. I mean, there were things missing, clothing and so forth, a couple of suitcases, right? But anyone in the house would have had access to those things, and could have nicked 'em before we even searched the place. Had three fuckin' days to do it.'

Devaney felt foolish; he had never stopped to consider that fact. Put it together with the scarf Mrs Hernan found under Jeremy's bed—

'Listen, I have to be heading off,' Barry said, draining the last of his pint. 'Sorry. I promised the wife I wouldn't be late. New baby.'

'You've been a great help. Let me know if you think of anything else.' Devaney watched Barry's broad shoulders push through the door as though it were made of cardboard, and imagined him stooped over, changing the nappy on a tiny infant. There was a father who hadn't missed the delivery of his child, Devaney thought. He took another drink from his pint. Barry had helped uncover another side of Lucy Osborne, one he had never fully considered before. He'd been concentrating all this time on one motive, money, and never settled long enough on one of the other overwhelming human motivations – jealousy. He remembered Lucy's vague disapproval, even disparagement of Mina Osborne as she stood before him, arranging those flowers. If she did have her eye on Osborne, was that enough to make her get rid of his wife? She's there for years with her son, getting used to the idea that this little arrangement could go on forever, and what does Osborne do? He goes off on a summer course and brings home a pregnant wife. Must have been a shock, to say the least. Lucy and Jeremy get shunted aside, while he starts a new family. But what could have triggered a murderous impulse? In Devaney's experience jealousy usually had a trigger point, sometimes brought on by drink, or seeing the person with someone else. Devaney cast his mind back again to the flowers, and focused on Lucy Osborne's finger wrapped in a bandage. Was it just coincidence that she'd slipped and injured herself at the very moment he'd happened to mention her son?

The pub door opened, and who should appear again but Donal Barry. 'There's one more thing I forgot to mention,' he said, coming up beside Devaney and leaning forward on the bar. 'Probably nothing, but you never know. There was one day when I was in the kitchen, one of the very first days after the disappearance. Lucy Osborne sets a plate of biscuits in front of me, right, and all of a sudden the stone drops right out of her ring. Huge fuckin' diamond. And along with it comes a little shower of dried clay. I think nothin' of it, and she brushes it away, sayin' something about how she'll have to give up digging in the garden.'

'What's so strange about that?'

'My mam's a great gardener. Colossal. Never gets the clay out from under her nails. Now, hanging about that place, I saw Lucy Osborne working in the garden plenty of times. And she always wore gloves. Always. That woman wouldn't get her hands dirty for nothin'.'

* * *

After Barry left, Devaney checked his watch – ten minutes past five. He'd have to head off if he was going to make it to Dunbeg before Pilkington's shut for the evening. In asking around, he'd found Dolly Pilkington had a small fiddle that might work for Róisín, and he had promised to come by the shop this evening to have a look at it.

Mullins had dutifully phoned this morning with the information he'd been checking. The scene-of-crime unit had found no complete fingerprints on the vehicles at Bracklyn, and nothing was missing from either car. This was going to be one of those cases where they'd never be able to prove who the perpetrator was – but they had to look as though they were making an effort. Mullins also reported that Hugh Osborne had indeed been on the seven o'clock British Airways flight from London on Sunday morning, just as he said. Fine. There was no reason for him to interfere with his own project. Maguire had a point: if whoever it was wanted to stop the priory development, why not actually put a spanner into the works at the site itself? Besides, there was fury in the way the damage had been done, Devaney thought. This wasn't just some calculated, bog-protest publicity stunt, it was personal. So why target a couple of strangers? Could they just have been in the wrong place – too near the real target? What was it Osborne had said, that his car might have been damaged as well if he'd been at home?

And then there was Dr Gavin's mysterious dead crow. He didn't want to disbelieve the woman, but he'd checked all around the house and found nothing to support her story. He agreed with her assessment of Jeremy Osborne: the boy's destructive tendencies seemed more inward- than outward-directed. But his mother was terrified that he'd actually done the damage; you could see it in the way she looked at him. What did that say about how they were getting on? The word *overprotective* wasn't strong enough for Lucy Osborne.

And then there was Brendan McGann, with straw in his clothes, broken Guinness bottles on the footpath, and a story about coming straight home to bed after the pub. Devaney made a mental note to have a word with Dermot Lynch tomorrow at the session, to ask if there was anything unusual about Brendan's behaviour Saturday night.

Devaney pulled up in front of Pilkington's just as Dolly was locking up the old-fashioned double doors. She opened them again to greet him. 'How are ye, Detective? I was just thinking you weren't going to make it.'

'Sorry, Dolly – busy day.'

'I heard about the goings-on at the big house yesterday.' She clucked and shook her head. 'Shockin' – I'd be terrified, livin' in a huge wreck of a place like that. Have you any idea at all who did it?'

'We're pursuing a few lines of inquiry,' Devaney said. It was what he always said, even when they had caught the doer of the deed red-handed. Besides, if he told Dolly Pilkington anything, he could be sure the whole town would have some version of it in a matter of minutes. Oliver Pilkington's head appeared from around the corner of the back room, as he looked to see the person his mother was addressing. He squeezed past them and busied himself sweeping out the shop, sticking close enough to hear what they were saying.

'Ah, sure, we'll never get so much as a midge's dinner out of you, will we, Detective?' She opened the small fiddlecase on the counter. 'Well, here it is. Poor Oliver hasn't a note in his head – sure, you may just as well try teachin' music to a lump of stone. Try it out there, if you like.' Devaney picked up the diminutive fiddle and put it to his shoulder, leaning his head over the body the better to hear its voice as he pulled bow across string.

'Got a good tone.' He plucked the strings, and held the instrument up to the light, to check the varnish and the straightness of the neck and sound post. 'Could I have Róisín try it as well, to see if it suits her?'

'Surely. Keep it as long as you like, Detective.'

Devaney set the fiddle back in its case and began to examine the hairs on the bow. 'You've lived in Dunbeg a long time, Dolly.'

'Born and reared.'

'I imagine you hear both sides of every quarrel. Like it or not.'

'Ah, there's some of that, you know. The secret of staying in business is listening to what people say and keeping it to yourself.' She nodded wisely.

'So you might have heard a theory or two about what happened at Bracklyn House last night.'

Dolly Pilkington's face lit up, and he knew she was about to ignore her own sage advice. 'You won't have to look very far to find the culprit.'

'Is that so?'

'Maybe only as far as across the road, they say.'

'I understand Brendan McGann's dead against the development at the priory. Can't be easy when his sister is keeping company with your man.'

'Keeping company, indeed,' Dolly snorted. She glanced at Oliver and leaned forward. 'There are some saying he's going to sue.'

Devaney must have looked blank. 'For maintenance,' she said, and raised her eyebrows. 'For the child.'

'His sister's child?'

Devaney heard a snigger and saw Oliver Pilkington's gingery head lift slightly. 'Sure, everybody knows Aoife McGann is Hugh Osborne's bastard,' the boy said, and almost before the words were out of his mouth, Dolly had whirled and delivered a resounding slap to the back of her son's head. Oliver dropped his broom and made a dive away from his mother to avoid another clout, then stood a short distance away, rubbing his head and scowling.

'Go away out of that, you dirty boy,' she said, brimming with indignation. 'I won't have that kind of talk in here.' It was plain that Oliver had heard this very phrase on his mother's lips, and was shocked to be dealt with so severely when he simply repeated it. Devaney was sorry to make the boy suffer for his benefit.

'It's a few years ago, now, but you know how people go on,' Dolly Pilkington said. She offered a sniff of disapproval. Devaney's mind began turning over this new information. Of course he'd heard the current whispers around the town about Hugh Osborne and Una McGann, but he couldn't believe he hadn't heard the whole story. Even the children of Dunbeg took it as fact. Perhaps his own children. He thought of Brendan's bowed head and clasped hands as he sat in the church pew, of the crude letters carved inside the confession box. If Una McGann had a child by Hugh Osborne, that might put Mina's disappearance in a whole different light.

Chapter 22

When Devaney returned home with the fiddle, he found his daughter Orla reigning over the kitchen, wearing a baker's apron that nearly wrapped twice around her slender waist. She'd been on a French cookery kick for the last fortnight, ever since she got home from a school trip to Normandy, and the family were all beginning to put on weight from the cream sauces, herself excepted. Now she was trying to show Róisín how to make a rose from a tomato, which his younger daughter undertook with the same earnest concentration that she brought to every task. The aroma of onions and seared meat reminded Devaney that he'd forgotten to eat lunch.

'Begod, Orla, that food smells mighty.' He lifted the lid off a saucepan and breathed in the fragrant steam. 'What is it?'

'Get out of that, Daddy, you're not supposed to take the cover off while it's cooking.' She sounded a bit like her mother. 'It's *Suprêmes de Volaille Véronique avec Riz à l'Indienne*,' she continued, with a perfect French accent, apparently anticipating his grimace at such a reply, because she quickly translated: 'Chicken and grapes in cream sauce, with curried rice.'

'With the hunger that's on me now, I'd eat the Lamb of God. Mammy home yet?'

'She's on her way.'

'Orla, this is impossible,' Róisín said. Devaney felt her frustration, and appreciated the way her face brightened when she saw the fiddlecase under his arm.

'Daddy, you remembered. I knew you would.' She quickly abandoned her bruised-looking tomato and began circling around him, hungry for a look at the new instrument. He set down the fiddle and noted the parcel beside it on the table, bearing a large number of foreign-looking stamps.

'That came for you in the post today, Daddy,' Róisín said. 'Where's it from?'

'From India,' he said.

'What is it?'

'Just my work, Róisín.' Satisfied with that answer, his daughter shifted her attention to the new fiddle, and he watched with pleasure as she traced her finger around its curved sides, and tried out the instrument as he had done.

When Nuala arrived home, Orla's feast was ready. The girls had laid the table; now they lit candles and poured wine, and they all actually sat down and had a meal together – like a real family, Devaney thought – for the first time in months. Even Pádraig tore himself away from his PlayStation battles long enough to sit and wolf down some food and trade a few good-natured barbs with his sisters. The phone rang at one point, and Devaney half rose to answer it, but Nuala threw him a look that said, *Let it ring, just this once?* And so he had. Probably for one of the children anyway.

He caught Nuala looking at him curiously several times. Why was he pushing himself so hard, when it seemed so simple, so easy to be here? The feeling, like the wine, seemed to warm him like a candle-flame from the inside. It lasted all through the supper, through the fiddle lesson he gave Róisín, watching her fingers take their positions for a new tune. It hadn't worn off by the time he and Nuala went to bed, and as he watched her undress, he imagined stopping his wife's fingers as she reached for the zip on the back of her skirt and undoing it himself. But even in his imagination, he was clumsy, hesitant, unsure of how she would react. Sitting on the edge of the bed removing his shoes, he watched as she slipped from the skirt and hung it in the closet. As she lifted the silky blouse above her head, he imagined reaching out and pulling her toward him, until he could drink in her subtle fragrance, feel the warmth of her breasts and belly against his face, the ever wondrous softness of her pale skin. There was nothing to stop him from doing so, nothing but the deadening force of habit and his own fear. As Nuala climbed into the bed beside him, pulled the duvet over her shoulder and plumped the pillow, the same way she did every night, the distance between them had never felt so great. He reached up to switch off the light.

When he did pull her against him during the night, he was amazed how easily it all happened. Why had he hesitated so long? For the first time there was no terrible urgency in their lovemaking. In its place, Devaney was aware of a new kindness in the way they touched one another; he felt they were once more moving in tandem as he heard Nuala's voice whispering urgently in his ear. At the sound, he awoke abruptly from his dream to find her breathing softly beside him. Devaney had been here a thousand times before, suspended on the point of indecision, and wondered what would happen if he were to touch his wife the way he had in the dream. Disconcerted by the thought, he quietly slid out of bed and went downstairs. It was just after one o'clock, and the house was completely silent.

When he switched on the light, the package from Mrs Gonsalves awaited him on the kitchen table. It was done up in striped brown paper, with clear Sellotape, his name and address in a curious, old-fashioned hand. He hesitated for a moment, then got scissors from the drawer and sliced open the end of the bundle. As he did, a pile of tissue-thin gold-and-green-edged airmail envelopes slid out onto the tabletop. There must have been almost a hundred letters in all. It would be best to read them in order, starting with the oldest first, and so he dug every one out of the package and began organizing them by the dates on the postmarks.

He had not learned much about Mina Osborne from the case file. Despite the photos, the physical description, the witness statements that described the kind of person she was, he did not have a complete sense of her. It was typical of witnesses in a disappearance like this to offer vague descriptions that didn't even begin to capture the complicated character of a human being. Even her husband's attempts to draw a detailed portrait seemed to come up short. The fuller picture of Mina Osborne did not start to emerge until he opened her first letter home. 'Dearest Mama,' it began. He thought of the mother's voice echoing on the telephone line, and could almost imagine the sound of Mina's voice from the way she wrote. 'Give Pa an extra kiss tonight. Maybe someday you may tell him it's from me.' That was the only reference she made to being cut off by the father. She promised to write often, and from the looks of the stacks of letters on his table, she had kept that promise. He carefully reinserted the letter in its dated envelope and moved on.

Mina offered vividly detailed descriptions of every room at Bracklyn House, no doubt in case her mother would never have the opportunity to visit. She marvelled at its age, the comfort of its furnishings, the profusion of books in its library, the sweetness of the roses in the garden. The newly married Mina also painted a glowingly affectionate portrait of Hugh Osborne, and shyly confided to her mother the surprise and delight she found in being married. Devaney felt his face flush as he realized it was an indirect way to tell her mother how much she enjoyed sex. 'I'm glad after all that you persuaded me not to join the Sisters of Mercy. I was so keen on it, too. How did you know it wouldn't be the right thing?'

But if her view of Hugh Osborne was softened by love, she was able to observe other people with a less clouded eye: 'Lucy is not the warmest person, I'm afraid, but she's put on a brave face and is obviously making an effort to get used to me. I sometimes catch her staring, when she thinks I'm not paying attention. I know that my arrival has changed things for her, but I hope one day we may become friends.' Of Jeremy, she wrote: 'He's such a sad, beautiful boy that I feel like weeping when I look at him. At times he's not like a child at all, so serious and thoughtful. But sometimes I also get a feeling he longs to be held and comforted like a child again.'

Subsequent letters contained details about Hugh's teaching, how her work in the studio was coming along, the progress of the herbs she'd sown in the kitchen garden, the dismal lack of variety in the fruits and vegetables available at the little market in Dunbeg. There was always a lively description of whatever book she was reading at the moment. Devaney was amused by her fond characterization of Father Kinsella: she genuinely liked him and valued their exchange of ideas, especially on spiritual matters, but Mina Osborne was also aware of the effect the handsome young priest had on most of his female parishioners. The picture that emerged from the letters was that of a highly intelligent young woman, acutely observant, and yet somehow completely guileless. She knew so much, saw so much, but remained almost painfully innocent about the motivations of those around her, interpreting their actions as if all shared her open-hearted spirit.

In the first few letters there was scant mention of the child she carried. And only once did she express apprehension about having a child so early in the marriage, before she and Hugh had come to know one another sufficiently. But as the pregnancy progressed, Mina began to provide her mother with more regular updates on doctor visits, and marked how her own enthusiasm and energy for painting and letter-writing seemed to flag.

'I sometimes feel quite depressed when I don't have the inclination or the energy to work,' she wrote. 'But then I consider the millions of cells dividing inside me, and I think that nurturing a new life is one of the supreme acts of human creativity.'

Devaney tried to keep in mind that he was looking at Mina Osborne's life in a drastically telescoped, condensed fashion, and also through the medium of letters, which could lead to a somewhat heightened impression of reality. He found a noticeable gap in the letters just before Christopher was born to about six weeks after. No doubt learning to care for a newborn left little time for the kind of expansive letters Mina was used to writing, but he made a note to ask the mother if they'd had contact by phone during that time, or if there really had been no communication at all.

The next letter contained photographs, fuzzy close-up

shots of the tiny newborn Christopher, all wispy curls, plump cheeks, and tiny slits of bright, dark eyes. Mina acknowledged her long silence, and promised she would not neglect letter-writing again. She described the surreal days and nights following her son's birth, the blur of feedings, the sudden seesaw between wakefulness and fatigue, and the intensely physical experience of motherhood.

Mina's letters began to grow more relaxed again as the weeks went by, as she and the baby got used to one another. Her husband's presence began to fade ever so slightly into the background, details about his academic work displaced now by Christopher's exploits, the walks Mina took with him in the pram. Hugh occasionally stayed late in Galway to work, a thing that seemed to disturb her somewhat. Ordinary adjustments, Devaney thought. Jeremy began to have a larger role in her letters as well, growing curious about the baby, and becoming involved in his care. 'He's very gentle,' Mina wrote, 'and looks so sweet holding Christopher with a nappy over his shoulder.' Devaney tried to picture this from what he'd seen of the boy, and had trouble conjuring the image in his mind. Jeremy would have been what age then? About fourteen, he reckoned. Christopher's sitting up on his own, his first tooth, his first steps were all documented in the letters, along with photos showing him asleep in his cot, long dark lashes lying like shadows on his cheeks. There was nothing so far that seemed remotely disturbing or out of balance. Hugh Osborne was only mentioned in the most loving terms. In one letter there was mention of a dust-up about Jeremy going to Mass with Mina. From what she said, Devaney gathered that the boy's mother didn't approve and had evidently put a stop to it. Later missives confirmed what Kinsella had said, that Mina was anxious to reconcile with her father. The separation from home and family seemed to weigh upon her more heavily as Christopher grew.

It was nearly five o'clock when Devaney reached the last few letters; there was a note clipped to the last two: 'Received these after October 3.' That meant Mina mailed them just before she disappeared. Devaney opened the first one and read the now familiar hand, searching for some hint, some trace of information in the words, or between the lines, but all he found was astonishment about the rate at which Christopher had grown, a mention of Hugh leaving for a conference in Oxford, and Mina's hopeful spirit continuing to press toward reconciliation with her father.

'The subject of our visit remains under discussion. Hugh still thinks it would be ill-advised, but he doesn't know Pa. You and I know Papa's secret, that he's not really the hard man he pretends to be. How could the embrace of our beautiful, innocent child not change his heart?'

Devaney slipped the last letter back into its envelope. Did she not have a clue what people in the town were whispering about her husband and Una McGann? He supposed she could have been ignorant of the town's idle gossip. Or simply unwilling to discuss such a subject with her mother. There was not enough in these letters to implicate Osborne as a suspect, nor anything to suggest Mina Osborne had simply run off.

It was only then that Devaney recalled the telephone ringing during the meal. He picked up the receiver and heard the broken signal indicating a waiting message. The call had not been for the children after all, but for him: Dr Gavin, with news that she and Maguire had found something that might be of interest, and asking him to ring back. Fucking hell. He'd told them to ring at any time.

Devaney looked at the letters and photographs stacked on the table before him. As he gathered them into the envelope, and climbed the stairs toward his bed, he contemplated the lightness, the seeming insignificance of this small package that held a few scant remains of Mina Osborne's earthly existence.

He snapped awake when the phone rang. It was still dark, and he heard Nuala answer from her side of the bed. 'Yes, he's here,' she told the caller. His first thought was that it might be Dr Gavin, but it was Brian Boylan's voice on the line.

'We've got a lucky break on your arson case, if you're interested.' The superintendent's tone made Devaney think someone might have tipped him off on the Osborne thing.

'What's happened?'

'Night watchman in Killimor caught your firebug – up to his eyeballs in petrol.' Wonderful, thought Devaney, just what he needed. Some gombeen with a torch stumbles onto the arsonist at work, and in the process manages to make the officer in charge – himself, as it happened – look like a totally incompetent gobshite. But it wasn't as if Boylan had very far to go to be convinced on that score anyway. He could tell the superintendent was waiting for a reaction.

'Well, apprehending the suspect is really the main thing, isn't it, sir?'

'We'll need you up in Killimor as soon as possible,' Boylan said.

'I'll be there in twenty minutes.' Devaney turned to his wife, slipped an arm around her, and kissed her lightly on the temple. God, she was so warm, and she smelled wonderful. 'Nuala, I've got to go.' Her voice was slurred with drowsiness. 'I missed you, Gar. I woke up and you were gone.'

'I was downstairs. Couldn't sleep. I was doing a bit of reading.'

'Mmmm,' she responded, and pulled his arm around her more tightly. Devaney cursed Brian Boylan and the Killimor firebug as he gently extricated himself from her grip.

Chapter 23

Hugh Osborne insisted on driving them to the session on Tuesday evening. As Cormac looked over at the tall figure in the driver's seat, he could feel a difference in the way Osborne had engaged with them in the past couple of days. Had he seen them coming back from the tower yesterday evening, or perhaps overheard Nora leaving the message for Devaney? Or was Cormac letting his attraction to Nora colour his assessment of the whole situation? Then he remembered the violence to the cars, and in the pencil strokes of the sketches in the tower. They had done the right thing in phoning Devaney.

'How's the work coming along?' Hugh Osborne asked.

'We should be able to finish up by the end of the week, I think,' Cormac said.

'Good, good, that's good. We'll be able to move ahead, then.'

'You will. There's nothing significant enough to hold up the plans.'

Nora had been conspicuously silent, but finally spoke up from the back seat: 'I'm sure you'll be glad of a little peace and quiet once we're out of your hair.'

They drove in silence the rest of the way to Dunbeg. As they climbed out of the car, Osborne said: 'Give me a shout when you're ready, and I'll come collect you.'

The punters were three deep at the bar at Lynch's.

From the dark suits, Cormac guessed there was a crowd in from a funeral up the road somewhere, and from the look of them, decked out in brand-new Aran sweaters and tweed caps, a tour bus full of Yanks as well, stopping in for a pint and a bit of the local colour, God help them. The air was already thick with smoke, and the din of voices overlaid with tipsy laughter. The players were in their corner, with full pints but instrument cases shut tight, no doubt waiting for a bit of a lull in the commotion. Cormac surveyed the half-familiar faces and nodded to Fintan McGann, who lifted his glass and shrugged. No sign yet of Devaney.

He turned to Nora, and had to shout to be heard. 'What'll you have?'

'Small whiskey and a glass of water.'

'Nora!' came a voice from a few feet away. 'Over here!' She turned and scanned the crowd, until she recognized the jubilant face of a fair-haired, bearded giant of a man making his way toward her.

'Gerry!'

'How are ye, gorgeous?' The man's merry blue eyes seemed to devour Nora; it was only then that Cormac noticed that she was wearing a touch of dark lipstick, and that the clean soap scent of her hair lingered in the air before him. Despite the crush of the crowd, the man proceeded to lift Nora off her feet and plant a sloppy kiss on her neck, which she wiped away in mock disgust.

'God, Gerry, you're an awful messer. Do you know Cormac Maguire? Gerry Conover.'

'Delighted to meet you,' Conover said, straightening up and grasping Cormac's hand. 'Nora's told me nothing about you at all, but I'm guessing that's a good thing. She has to keep a few secrets from me, I suppose.'

'Don't make me sorry I came down here, Ger,' Nora said. 'What are you doing here?'

'Ah, it's a sad occasion.'

'Are you part of the funeral, then?' Cormac asked.

'I am. We buried my uncle Paddy this afternoon. Ninety-four years old, God rest him. We're giving him a good send-off.' The drinks arrived, and Cormac handed Nora her glasses over the heads of their fellow bar patrons.

'Do you mind if I steal her away?' Conover asked. 'I'm dyin' to show her off to the relations.'

'Be my guest,' Cormac said.

'Back shortly – maybe you can find Devaney,' she shouted into Cormac's ear as Conover lifted her whiskey glass and led her away by the hand through the crowd.

Cormac took a long swallow from his own pint, and wondered how long he could stick the noise level. He ventured over to Fintan McGann, who moved down to offer a seat on the bench.

'Welcome to the Wild West,' Fintan said. 'Jaysus, didja ever see the bate of it?'

'Do you suppose anyone's actually going to play?'

'Well, I am, funeral or no funeral, and Yanks or no fuckin' Yanks. Got the machine there, yourself?' Cormac patted the flute case he'd stuck in his coat pocket. He could see Ned Raftery down the way. The woman beside Raftery waved to catch Cormac's eye, and asked her neighbour to pass a folded piece of paper down to him. This must be a copy of the letter Raftery had promised. The blind man raised his glass. Cormac made another quick scan of the room, but Nora was nowhere to be seen.

It was nearly half-ten by the time Devaney arrived. Cormac quickly drained his glass to indicate that he'd come up to the bar for another drink and a chat with the policeman. From where they stood, leaned over the bar, Cormac could see Nora at the centre of Conover's group, the funeral party. As he described to Devaney what they'd seen in the tower, his eyes kept returning to the sight of Conover's arm draped casually around her shoulder. He heard Devaney's voice, but his attention was elsewhere.

'Sorry?' Cormac said, turning to him. 'What was it you just asked me?'

'No sign of whoever it was had been in the tower?' Devaney repeated.

'None that we could find. But we got chased out of the place by a belligerent crow.'

Devaney pulled at his chin. 'I'll have to think about this. It's all right for you to be going out there, but for me to go stickin' my nose in, it's probably got to be more – official, if you like. But I'm glad you told me. I'll check it out as soon as I can. Right, seeya.' The policeman took his drink and his fiddlecase and plunged into the crowd. Cormac knew Devaney was aware of who might be observing them,. and was determined to make their conversation brief.

'*Ciúnas*, ladies and gentlemen, *ciúnas*!' a booming voice shouted over the noise. 'Let's have a bit of quiet. We're going to have a song.' A silence fell, broken only by a few drunken giggles, until the singer began, and Cormac immediately recognized Nora's voice. He squeezed through the crowd to where he could see her better.

Through bushes and through briars,
I lately took my way,
All for to hear the small birds sing,

And the lambs to sport and play.

I overheard my own true love,
His voice it was so clear:
'Long time I have been waiting for
The coming of my dear.'

Cormac watched Nora's upturned face as Conover grasped her hand between his own burly paws, and all the carousers sat with bowed heads and closed eyes as they listened to the sound of her liquid voice:

Sometimes I am uneasy,
And troubled in my mind,
Sometimes I think I'll go to my love,
And tell to him my mind.

But if I should go unto my love,
My love he may say nay,
And if I show to him my boldness,
He'll ne'er love me again.

Through bushes and through briars,
I lately took my way,
All for to hear the small birds sing,
And the lambs to sport and play.

There was a brief silence when the song finished. Gerry Conover lifted Nora's hand to his lips and kissed it. 'By the Jaysus, that was gorgeous!' he shouted, and the spell was broken; everyone could go back to drinking and swearing and telling stories at the top of their lungs.

Nora eased her way past a pair of black-suited mourners and made her way to Cormac. Her face felt flushed and damp from the heat of the crowd, and she fanned herself with both hands. 'Did you see Devaney?'

'He says he'll check it out as soon as he can,' Cormac said. 'Listen, I was thinking of heading off. You can stay, if you like. I'm sure Gerry would see you home.'

'I'm sure he would, but I'm fed up with this place.'

'I was going to walk back. You don't have to come along.'

'Ah, but I want to.'

The night was fresh and cool after the stifling atmosphere of the pub. They were a good way outside the town before either of them spoke.

'Did you get that letter from Ned Raftery?' she asked. Cormac patted his breast pocket. 'And have you read it?'

'I was waiting for you.'

'I didn't think it'd be so black out here. I didn't even think to bring a torch.'

'I dropped mine at the tower.'

Nora felt something brush against her legs, and stumbled over a sturdy branch lying across the roadside. Cormac reached out to keep her from falling. 'I'm all right,' she said. 'It's only a stick or something.'

'Take my hand.' She hesitated briefly, then slipped her hand into his. As his warm fingers enfolded hers, Nora wondered if Cormac understood what it meant for her to actually feel safe with someone. They were passing by the tower, and she could barely distinguish its ivy-shrouded outline against the inky night sky.

'I suppose you've known Gerry Conover a good while.'

'Only about three months. We met in Dublin when I started going down to the singers' club at the Trinity Inn. That's where I first met Robbie as well, before I realized that you and he and Gabriel all knew each other. Sometimes I'm still amazed at what a small world it is here.' She knew that wasn't really what he was asking.

'Gerry's a lovely guy,' she continued, 'but he's a singer, you know, and I'm finding that I'm more partial to flute players. I'm not even sure why. Maybe I'm just a sucker for a nice embouchure—'

She couldn't say any more, because Cormac had pulled her close and was touching his lips to hers, at first gently, then more urgently, until Nora felt dizzy, even slightly delirious.

'Let me stay with you tonight,' he said. 'I can't stand the idea of leaving you alone in that room again. I'd sleep on the sofa.'

'You wouldn't have to do that, Cormac.'

'I don't want to take advantage.'

'You wouldn't be taking advantage. You'd be welcome.'

She took his hand once more, and they turned into the gate at Bracklyn House. Their feet made a rhythmic crunching in the gravel as they ambled up the long drive.

Cormac tried the front door. 'Locked. We'll have to ring the bell.'

Now that their feet were silent, Nora could barely hear a faint noise in the distance, like a motorboat propeller idling underwater. 'Cormac, do you hear something?'

His hand dropped from the bell. 'I hear it. Seems to be coming from the garage.' The old stable building where Hugh Osborne kept his car was set perpendicular to Bracklyn House, thirty yards from the doorway, but they both covered the ground in a few seconds. Through the window on the side door, they could see the black Volvo inside the garage, enveloped in gauzy clouds of exhaust. Cormac tried the doorknob.

'Locked.' He used one elbow to break the glass, then reached in to unlock the door. The billowing fumes made them both cough as they made their way to the car. 'See if you can find a way to open the garage door,' he shouted as he pulled at the car door. 'This is locked as well.' He searched around the floor for something heavy enough to break through safety glass, and finally came up with a sledge from the corner. She couldn't see him swing it, but heard a dull thud and the rain of shattered glass as it fell into the car. Cormac pulled open the door and struggled to lift the slumped figure from the driver's seat. It was Hugh Osborne.

'Turn it off,' he said, 'then come and help me.' Nora reached in to switch off the ignition, and heard something roll off the seat onto the floor. She felt around the floor mat until her fingers closed on a small plastic cylinder, and held her breath as she read the label. She ran quickly to where Cormac was kneeling over Osborne's still form.

'Cormac, let me have a look at him; he may have taken sleeping tablets as well.' She held up the pill bottle. It was empty.

Chapter 24

Two hours later, after the flashing lights had disappeared and the ambulance had taken the unconscious Hugh Osborne off to hospital, Bracklyn House was quiet again. Lucy had rung for the ambulance and insisted on going off to hospital with Hugh. In all the chaos, Jeremy was nowhere to be found. Unable to sleep, Cormac lay on the sofa in Nora's room, revisiting the troubling events of this night and the past few days. He looked over at her, lying on the bed, and saw that she was asleep. Nora was convinced the case was closed, that Osborne would confess if and when he ever awakened. Cormac didn't feel sure. He'd begun to regret this whole episode, everything that had taken place since he had answered the phone call in Dublin and agreed to come to Dunbeg. Well, almost everything. He couldn't regret coming to know Nora better. He still felt a certain kinship with Hugh Osborne, despite Nora's suspicions about the man. He also felt bound to Jeremy Osborne, in whom he could see so much of his younger self. But how much of that understanding was real, and how much was based on illusion?

Responsibility. His father had felt it for complete strangers more than for his own family – the people for whom he should have felt truly responsible. Cormac had always told himself that he wanted no part of his father's abstract notion of responsibility. But wasn't that what had brought him here in the first place? What was the word Nora used in talking about the *cailín rua*? Obligation. He had understood exactly what she meant, and felt it acutely when he first laid eyes on the girl's small ear exposed in that cutaway. The thought of it pierced him through, along with the memory of the expression in Hugh Osborne's haunted eyes out on the bog, and Nora's laughing, tearstained face on the road from Tullymore. He felt exhausted, and lay very still.

The next moment he was awakened by Nora's voice in his ear. 'Cormac. Cormac, there's someone out there. I saw the light.' What was she was talking about? The tower. She was talking about the tower. And then she was out the door. Cormac threw off his blanket and stepped hurriedly into his shoes, fully awake now. He couldn't let her go out there on her own. He only realized he'd forgotten his glasses as he left by the kitchen door.

Nora was about fifty yards ahead of him. He watched as she vanished beyond the end of the demesne wall, and followed, unsure whether to call out or keep silent. He plunged into the brush at the place he'd seen her disappear, only conscious of the danger she was in, not of the branches that whipped at his chest and face. He ploughed through the wood before stumbling and falling hard, his ribs taking the brunt of the blow against a jagged stone. The pain in his side took his breath away, but he got up and forced himself to continue through the rocky maze of the chevaux-de-frise, until he came to the tower house. Nora stood outside the door, and as she swung it open, a golden light spilled out and seemed to surround her. The glow came from a hundred or more flickering candles inside the tower. Each of the tiny flames cast a wavering light, and the undulating shapes on the walls seemed to take on life and movement, an effect further exaggerated by his astigmatism. He stood for a moment, transfixed, before stepping inside. Jeremy Osborne sat at the foot of the stone staircase, arms wrapped tightly around his knees, rocking rapidly back and forth, as if he were in a trance.

'Jeremy,' Cormac said, 'are you all right?'

The boy looked up. The wavering light accentuated both his thinness and the recent bruises, and the naked panic in his face. He picked up the first weapon he could find, a screwdriver, from the floor at his feet.

'Get out – get out!' he screamed, backing slowly up the first two steps. 'You're not supposed to be here. No one's allowed in here!' Nora seemed about to speak, when Jeremy flung the screwdriver, which bounced harmlessly against the door behind Cormac's head. Jeremy spun around and scrambled as fast as he was able up the crumbling stone stairway. Cormac followed, taking the steps two and three at a time, until he was suddenly engulfed in darkness.

'Jeremy,' he called. 'Jeremy, wait.' The sound of footsteps continued, and Cormac could hear Nora shouting to him as well as he continued climbing blindly to the top of the tower, panting and dry-throated when he came out upon the battlements. The sky above was clear, and in the dark he could just make out the edge of the steep roof and the silhouettes of spindly weeds that sprouted from the cracks. He slid against the stone wall, stepping sideways cautiously; there was no telling when any of these floors or walls might give way, rotted as they were by centuries of neglect.

'Why did you have to come here?' Jeremy's anguished voice cried from beyond the pitched roof beams.

'Jeremy, I'm sorry if we startled you. Everything's all right.' There was nowhere to run, only a narrow circular walkway around the battlements, and Cormac stayed where he was. He didn't want to lose access to the stairs below. Again he heard Nora's voice, more urgent this time: 'Cormac, you've got to come down.' He smelled the smoke in the same instant that he heard her voice. 'There's a fire – I can't put it out. Cormac!'

'Jeremy, did you hear? We're in danger if we stay here.' He inched along the wall, feeling his way with one arm, thinking he might be able to bring Jeremy along if he could only reach him. There was no time to lose. The smoke from below was getting thicker. He could hear the roar and crackle of the flames, and then a strangled cry from below.

'Nora, are you all right? Nora?' he shouted over his shoulder through the battlements, searching for her figure through the acrid smoke that billowed from the stairwell, filling his lungs and stinging his eyes.

'I'm here,' she shouted. He could hear that she was outside now, safe. 'I'm all right. Jeremy, please come down. You can still make it.'

Cormac had edged his way around the top of the tower, moving toward the spot where he'd last heard Jeremy's voice. 'Come on,' he said. 'There's no more time.'

Cormac pictured the melting candles on their wooden crates, the dozens of paint tins, the stacks of books and papers and the rotting beams that would begin to catch fire any minute. He knew that once a fire started, a tower house was little more than a giant chimney, its windowless walls containing and encouraging the flames upward until they burst out the roof. He was counting the seconds until it happened. Why did the boy delay?

'Leave me,' Jeremy shrieked. 'Everything I do, everything I touch is fucked. It's fucked. Just leave me.' He held his head in his hands, rocked his body against the wall in terror and despair.

'I can't do that.'

The heat from the fire was becoming intense. There was no way they could go down the stairs now. Cormac pressed himself to the wall, and as he did, what was left of the tower roof gave way, crumbling into a gaping pit of fire below them. Jeremy let out a howl through clenched teeth, and pushed himself from the wall, as if to pitch himself headlong into it. Without thinking, Cormac lunged forward and seized the back of the boy's shirt with one hand, nearly losing his balance, and pulling with all his strength until Jeremy's full weight slammed back against him, knocking the wind from his chest. And with the force of the blow, time seemed to telescope. The spaces between seconds allowed an almost unbearably acute perception of each sensation as it passed through him. He was conscious of the grinding sound of stone and mortar giving way, sharp pain and snapping tree branches, then falling, falling into darkness, and the earth seeming to meet him too soon, with a shuddering thump. And then silence. A most pure and sublime silence roared in his ears as he struggled to take a breath.

Then Nora was beside him, close, touching his face, saying: 'Cormac, Cormac!' Her horrified face was upside down, and he wanted to laugh, but found tears starting to his eyes instead.

'Can you breathe? Just try to breathe. Please breathe!' He took a gasp of air, and began to cough. Nora turned her attention to the motionless shape beside him. 'He's alive,' she said. 'I've got to go for help. Don't try to move.' She hesitated only a second before disappearing into the woods.

Beside him, Cormac could see Jeremy's eyes flutter. The boy's lips moved as though he would speak.

'No,' Cormac said. 'Lie still.' Jeremy made a noise that was like a gurgling cough. Cormac desperately tried to remember what to do, but he couldn't seem to think straight. He struggled up on one elbow, wincing in pain, and put his ear down to the boy's lips, hoping he wouldn't pass out himself. He heard a whisper.

'They're here,' Jeremy said. 'There's a place underground.' He paused to gather what strength he could. 'She knows,' the boy muttered urgently. 'She knows. She'd never tell—' He lapsed into unconsciousness. Cormac felt himself sinking as well; his head drooped until it rested against Jeremy's chest.

BOOK FOUR

Heaps of Bones

It is a grievous situation that has befallen Ireland
Wild blows heaped upon her by ruffians
Her nobility struck to the ground, unable to rise
Her heroes now heaps of bones.

– Irish poet Dáibhí Cundún, 1651

Chapter 1

When Cormac awoke, it was daylight, and Nora dozed in the chair beside his hospital bed. He wanted to speak, to let her know he was awake, but his head felt huge and thick. She stirred, looked about for a second, as if she didn't quite remember where she was, then pulled her chair up to the bedside and put her face close to his. The mark of the crow's sharp claw had begun to heal, but there were fresh, raw scratches where brambles had cut her face, and he dimly began to recall what had taken place. It seemed so long ago now.

'Shall I call the nurse?' she asked. He tried to shake his head no, but couldn't manage it. He winced instead, then licked his lips and tried them out.

'Never should have had those fifteen pints,' he mumbled. She took his hand and smiled, but her chin wavered slightly.

'Please don't. This is all my fault,' she said.

'It's not.' He tried again to move.

'Lie still, Cormac.' He liked the sound of her voice, the way she said his name. 'The doctor said you have a mild concussion, and some nasty bruises – but no fractures, which is a miracle. The tree branches must have helped to break your fall. And you're only slightly singed from the fire.' Cormac looked down at white gauze bandages on his left arm and hand.

'Jeremy?'

Nora looked down. 'He's badly hurt. Broken bones, some internal bleeding. A possible head injury – it's too early to tell.'

'Has he said anything?'

'He's been unconscious.'

Cormac closed his eyes to consider what he should do. He opened them again, and said: 'Nora, could you find Devaney for me?' The strain of the last twelve hours showed in her eyes, and it seemed to Cormac that she finally understood his reluctance to be drawn into this story, as if he somehow knew from the beginning what would be asked of him. He sank back into a half-sleep, and in what seemed like only a few seconds, Nora was back with the policeman at her side.

'Hell of a night,' Devaney said. 'You and the young lad are lucky to be here. Osborne likewise. You needed to see me?'

'I did,' said Cormac. His own voice sounded strange and far away in his ears. 'Jeremy said something last night – at the time I hadn't a clue what he meant, but I think I do now.'

Devaney's voice was quieter than usual. 'Go on.'

'He said: "They're here. There's a place underground."' Cormac watched as the substance of the words struck his listeners. Neither apparently had any doubt as to whom Jeremy's words referred.

'Oh God, Cormac,' Nora said, and sank into the chair beside his bed. Devaney's eyes closed, and his lips were set in an expression of disappointment and finality.

Cormac felt exhausted, and had to close his eyes as well. But there was more. He tried to remember what it was, though his head was pounding like a bass drum. 'I think he said something else as well. Something like: "She knows. She'd never tell."'

Devaney's voice was sharp. 'Are you sure? "*She* knows? *She'd* never tell"?' Cormac could hear the words stick in the policeman's throat.

Chapter 2

By the time Devaney had phoned in the request for a full-scale crime scene detail to meet him at Bracklyn House, he was already playing out the next few days in his head: the cameras flashing, and tarps rigged to keep away rain, the barriers set to fend off the prying reporters who invariably descended. Before he left the hospital, it might also be prudent to check on Hugh and Jeremy Osborne, and put a couple of the local lads on duty outside their rooms. The boy's words finally gave them something to go on, but still left open the question of responsibility.

What had prompted Hugh Osborne to try the ultimate escape? A suicide didn't fit with any way Devaney had figured the case. If Osborne wasn't guilty, maybe he just couldn't go on any longer. And if he was, perhaps he saw things beginning to unravel. When Devaney stopped at the door, Osborne was turned on his side, facing away from the corridor. A thin cotton blanket was drawn up over his shoulders, but there were no restraints. Nothing to keep him from walking away – or to keep him from doing himself further harm, Devaney thought.

'He's sleeping now,' whispered the young nurse who came up behind him. 'Just as well. When he wakes up he'll have a right bugger of a headache.'

'How's he getting on?'

'Are you a friend?' The girl's porcelain skin was lightly

freckled, and her green eyes fixed him with a compassionate gaze. He looked away.

'Acquaintance.'

'Much improved this morning, but the doctor says they're going to keep him another day or two for observation. Carbon monoxide can have some rather nasty effects, and they don't want to let him go too soon.'

'I see – thanks,' Devaney said. He'd see what turned up at the tower before he had a chat with Hugh Osborne. Two young Garda officers approached, and Devaney took them aside.

'What are your names?'

'Molloy,' said the first young officer.

'O'Byrne, sir,' said the second.

'I want you to stay here as my eyes and ears. Molloy, you'll stay with Hugh Osborne. Try to be as unobtrusive as possible.' When he saw the blank look on the young man's face, he added: 'Blend in. O'Byrne, you can come with me.'

Jeremy Osborne's status was still critical. Devaney approached the room where the boy lay propped up in bed with his left leg and arm in casts, and his head swaddled in bandages. Jeremy's face was distorted and discoloured by bruises, and a breathing tube was taped to his open mouth. Beside him, his mother sat upright in a chair, as if by keeping straight, she could hold her son back from the brink of death by sheer force of will. Lucy Osborne's whole body turned toward Devaney as he entered the room. Her dry eyes seemed to overflow with pain, but the rest of her face remained masklike, frozen into a stoic calm.

'I blame myself,' she said. 'If he had stayed near me, I might have kept him safe.' Her eyes flickered to the Garda officer beyond the door. 'What's going on?'

'It's just routine. Until we have the full story of what happened last night,' Devaney said. 'I promise he won't be in your way.'

As he drove to the tower, Devaney thought of Mina Osborne's letters, and of the mother in India, waiting patiently for news. People knew that the person they loved was dead, but let themselves be deluded, buoyed up for a while on the notion that what their gut was telling them could be wrong.

Maguire's second bit of information had given him pause. *She'd never tell.* Could mean she'd done it, or they'd done it together. But it could just as easily mean that the boy and his mother had stumbled across the evidence, and – for whatever reason – decided to keep quiet. He should have realized the boy knew something, should have pushed him more at the interview about the cars. But there wasn't time now to worry about all the possibilities; he had to find out whether Jeremy Osborne was telling the truth.

As Devaney pulled up at the side of the road near the tower, the file on the passenger seat of his car slid forward, and some of its contents spilled out onto the floor. He reached over to gather up the sheaf of scattered papers. Among them was one of the photographs he had taken in the confessional at St Columba's. Devaney put the car in neutral, and took a moment to look closely at the picture. There were the carved letters, crudely made, but clearly legible: HE KNOWS WHERE THEY ARE. He had been very nearly convinced that Brendan McGann carved them, as a silent accusation against Hugh Osborne. But as he looked at the photograph once more, his eyes returned to the first mark – it wasn't a letter at all, but an empty square, more deeply gouged than the rest. It could be a mistake, but whoever made the mark could also have changed his mind, and wanted to destroy what had originally been there. He tried to find any evidence that it had once been the letter S. As in SHE KNOWS WHERE THEY ARE. Whoever carved those words wanted so desperately to tell someone, anyone, to relieve the burden of guilt, but couldn't muster the resolve to do it out loud. Another idea struck him. Of course. Jeremy Osborne had to be Father Kinsella's candle thief; Dr Gavin had said the tower was full of candles. If Jeremy was the messenger, who was the subject of his message, and why had he changed it? Or could someone else have found the message and altered it to suit his own ends? Devaney remembered the praying figure of Brendan McGann in the side chapel of the church. One thing at a time, he told himself, and braced himself for what he was about to do.

It was late afternoon before the scene-of-crime officers arrived. The grey day had grown more overcast and a soft rain had begun to fall. There was a mechanical quality to the work entailed at a crime scene, what to Devaney always seemed a small amount of comforting routine in the face of horror. He stood in the woods near O'Flaherty's Tower, surrounded by a drone of activity: scene-of-crime officers in their white suits, and policemen in yellow rain gear. The fire brigade had succeeded in dousing the flames last night, but the tower had been reduced to a blackened and empty shell, with a few stout timbers high up that had partially withstood the blaze. Even in the rain, small plumes of smoke still wafted from the rubble, a dangerous mixture of fallen stones and charred, splintered wood. In daylight it was readily apparent where the firemen had trampled through the thick undergrowth, and the bright green of the rain-slick leaves leapt out against the tower's blackened bulk.

The boy had said, *They're here*. However, if there was some sort of underground chamber in the tower, the entrance was well hidden, and Devaney wasn't surprised that no one had discovered it during previous searches. Once they'd cleared the rubble from inside the tower, the dirt floor was solidly packed, and showed no evidence of having been dug up. Likewise, the team could find no areas of disturbed earth around the building's perimeter. Why should it be easy? Devaney thought. Every way into this case had been a hard road; why should this, even though it seemed the final step, be any bloody different? He was feeling the raw, edgy effects of too many hours without sleep, but couldn't force himself to leave. Even when the passage had not been located by nightfall, he stayed and watched the team press on under the glaring white of the floodlights. When daybreak came, they switched off the lights. The sky had cleared, but they still had found nothing.

At mid-morning, a police vehicle pulled up on the roadside near the tower. Molloy, the young officer he had placed outside Hugh Osborne's room, approached.

'It wasn't my idea, sir. He insisted.'

'Who is it, Molloy?'

'Osborne, sir. Dr Maguire and Dr Gavin are with him.'

Devaney watched as the three passengers emerged from the car. The effects of his fall were evident in the careful way Maguire moved, but he was trying to put on a good front. Beside him, Osborne also moved slowly, not from any apparent physical injury, but like a man mesmerized. He looked only at the white-garbed officers as they went about their work. Dr Gavin followed behind the two men; her dubious expression told Devaney what she thought of this impromptu expedition. He stepped in front of them.

'I'll have to ask you not to go any further just now,' Devaney said. Hugh Osborne just looked at him blankly.

'We'll stay right here,' Maguire said, 'if that's acceptable.'

Devaney nodded, then pulled Dr Gavin aside. 'Are they all right?' he murmured, tipping his head in Osborne's direction.

'Neither of them should really be up and about, but they wouldn't stay in the hospital. Cormac insisted on telling Hugh what Jeremy said. I tried to convince him that it might not be a good idea. Hugh Osborne is still your chief suspect, isn't he?'

'Unless we find evidence to the contrary. But we're not making much headway here.'

Maguire approached and spoke in a low voice: 'If I might offer an idea?'

'By all means.'

'Well, it looks like your team are assuming the underground place and its entrance to be somehow connected to the tower. But people tend to build on the same places over and over again. It may very well be a souterrain or underground chamber left over from some previous settlement or fortification that's older than the tower. Have you got a piece of paper or something?' When he'd got it, he hastily sketched the tower, and marked the locations of the various earthworks.

'We're here.' He pointed to the spot on his crude map where he and Devaney stood, about twenty yards from the tower. 'Do you see the area of raised earth all around us here? That's where I'd begin, within that circle. The entrance is bound to be pretty well concealed.

It might save time to use that ground-probing radar you mentioned, if you have access to some equipment.'

Osborne refused to leave the scene; he hovered, sometimes sitting quite still, sometimes standing beside the yellow tape the scene-of-crime unit used to mark the perimeter, but his silent presence did not appear to disturb the officers as they went about their methodical work. It wasn't until mid-afternoon, when they'd got the loan of radar equipment from a surveying firm in Ballinasloe, that the team were able to make any progress. The readings showed a solid slab about four feet below the surface, within the circle Maguire had shown them. They called in earth-moving equipment, a small backhoe that trampled the vegetation that lay in its path like some prehistoric beast. Fortunately, the operator was an artist, a man who could control the heavy steel excavation bucket as though he were measuring tea for the pot rather than a half-ton of soil. The sound of metal scraping on stone came from the trench, and a voice said: 'He seems to have hit something here, sir.' Devaney peered into the pit. He could see several large flat stones. One of them suddenly gave way and collapsed into the chamber below, taking with it loose soil from the surrounding banks.

'All right,' Devaney shouted. 'Hold up. That's enough.' He sent one of the young Guards to fetch Maguire.

'You've more experience than we have with uncovering this sort of structure,' he said when the archaeologist arrived. 'I wonder if you'd mind advising us on how to proceed.'

Chapter 3

Dressed in a regulation white suit and mindful of his bruised ribs, Cormac climbed carefully down into the chamber while Devaney and the rest of the team remained at the edge of the excavation. At the bottom of the ladder, he switched on his torch and peered into the darkness. The walls were exquisite dry-stone construction, battened to support the heavy lintels. At the end nearest the tower, a slab of sandstone had been cut into an archway to support the roof. As he admired the workmanship of the builders who had put these stones in place more than a thousand years earlier, Cormac suddenly realized what a terrible contradiction existed if the bodies of Mina and Christopher Osborne were indeed hidden here. Souterrains were common enough features of ancient ringforts, but in addition to their function as storage vaults, they often served another very particular purpose – to protect a settlement's most vulnerable inhabitants: its women and children. The entrance creeps were often built purposely small so that a grown man could not fit through.

Everything he could see was covered with a thin layer of dust. He could smell putrefaction. As he slowly let his beam track across the small room, Cormac could see nothing but grey shadows and shapes. *Wait.* He turned his light back to where it had just been, and stared at the pattern that began to emerge. The eye is quick to detect the stamp of human presence in the seeming chaos of the natural world. Beneath the dust, half buried in soil and rubble, he had perceived the diamond motif and raised cable of an Aran sweater. He focused his beam on that spot, and the shapes began to make sense to his eye and mind. He could see a body lying on its right side, back toward him. Near the figure's left hip, his eye began to comprehend the meaning of another form. It was the sole of a child's tiny wellington. He turned to the company standing above him, and didn't have to say a word. They could read what he had seen in his face.

No one noticed that Hugh Osborne had moved gradually closer until he was standing among the crime scene officers at the edge of the excavation. Before anyone could stop him, Osborne had jumped down into the souterrain and seized the torch from Cormac's hand. Devaney held up a hand to signal his fellow officers to hold off for just a moment. Osborne fell to his knees at the entrance to the hidden chamber, and drew a deep breath. Then he looked inside, and what he saw made him release that breath; with it he seemed to release all the hope and fear and anticipation he had held in for so long, to let it all go with a faint sound that was halfway between a moan and a sigh. And when the nightmarish vision before him persisted, and did not fade away, he finally sank slowly downward, and the torch, still switched on, tumbled from his hand. No one spoke or moved until Osborne himself finally broke the silence.

'Thank you – thank you for finding them,' he said in a hoarse voice to the air before him. Then he rose somewhat unsteadily and looked vacantly around him, as if unsure of how to climb out of the chamber. 'I'll go now,' he said. 'You know where to find me.' A couple of officers came forward to help him out of the souterrain, and Devaney signalled them to escort Osborne back to the house. Cormac climbed up the ladder, and sought Nora's face in the crowd. She brushed away her tears as he approached.

Chapter 4

Cormac had just set a mug of tea in front of Hugh Osborne when a rap sounded at the kitchen door. It was Una McGann. She must have heard the news in the village; it hadn't taken long for the story to travel that far. Osborne didn't rise to meet her, but instead lowered his head to the table and covered it with his hands, in a gesture of the most abject helplessness. When she placed a hand gently on Osborne's shoulder, Cormac realized that Una was the first person to offer any expression of sympathy, and he felt ashamed. Then the door banged violently open.

'You fuckin' bastard,' roared Brendan McGann, advancing toward Una and Hugh, his face blotchy with rage. 'Your wife's not yet in her grave and you're back making a hoor of my sister. Get out of my way, Una. Get out of the way!' He seized his sister by the shoulders and pushed her roughly aside, then turned his attention to Hugh Osborne, who half stood, blinking in disbelief. Brendan McGann landed a fist to his jaw that sent Osborne sprawling backward onto the table, and the sugar bowl and mugs of tea smashing to the stone floor. 'Come on, you fuckin' hoormonger, get up and fight.' Osborne was stunned, and staggered forward, but before Brendan could throw another punch, Cormac hooked Brendan's arms from behind and pulled him away.

'Well,' Brendan shouted, 'what have you got to say for

yourself, Englishman? Spittle trembled at the corners of his mouth.

Una rushed to steady Osborne, then whirled on her brother. 'What right have you to come in here flinging accusations? You know nothing about what's between us. Nothing. I found those things you had hidden away, Brendan, all the cuttings, Aoife's birth cert, and the hair clip – Mina's hair clip – and I said nothing. I couldn't believe you would harm anyone, but I don't know any more Brendan, I don't know you.'

As he listened to her words, all the fight drained from Brendan McGann's limbs, and Cormac gradually released his hold.

Brendan spoke quietly: 'You think I – ah, Jaysus, Una, you actually believed that I could hurt a woman – and a child? I found it,' he continued, his voice breaking. 'I found that clip in a fuckin' jackdaw's nest, Una, I swear it. And the other things, you can't blame me for being suspicious, people see him giving you a lift every day along the road, and you turn up pregnant, what were we to think? We're not stupid. And to top it, he goes off and gets married, and leaves you and Aoife to get along as best you can. It tears at me to see you working so hard, and him sitting up here in his big fuckin' house, telling people what to do, not willing to fork over a few shillings for his own flesh and blood. He's the one you want to mind, Una, not me.' His finger jabbed toward Osborne. 'Ask him how his wife and son ended up dead. Ask him.'

Osborne still looked dazed as he wiped blood from the corner of his mouth. He seemed completely bewildered, but as he studied Brendan's defiant expression, a light began to dawn. 'You sent the hair clip. And that letter accusing me, to the private detective's office in Galway.

And you sent Mina a letter, too, didn't you?' Brendan's eyes shifted guiltily. 'Didn't you? Just before she disappeared. Lucy gave it to me the other night; she said she found it only a couple of days ago going through some of Mina's books. When I phoned home that night from the conference – she seemed so distressed, but she wouldn't tell me what was troubling her. It was that vicious, cowardly letter. You made her believe that I'd betrayed her, and I never had a chance – you sick bastard—' This time it was Osborne's anger that boiled over, and he made a savage lunge for Brendan's throat.

'Stop it, stop it!' Una screamed, using all the strength she possessed to get between them and push the two men apart. She turned to face her brother; she was trembling with outrage, and spoke only inches from his face. 'Hugh is not Aoife's father. Do you need to hear it again? Sometimes I wish to Christ he were, but he's not. But he was the only person who befriended me when I got pregnant, the only person who noticed or cared that I was so miserable and confused. Just so you know, Aoife's father was one of my teachers at university. I should have known better – and I went away, Brendan, only because I was ashamed to think what a fuck-wit I'd been. Hugh knew what people were saying about us all these years. He put up with all the looks and the whispers because I asked him not to say anything. Are you satisfied now, Brendan? Are you fuckin' satisfied?'

'Why didn't you come to us, Una? To Mammy and me? Why did you have to go to a stranger? We'd have looked after you, Una. We'd have helped you.' The hurt in her brother's voice appeared unfeigned, but Una's face was incredulous.

'You know it wouldn't have happened that way, Brendan. I'm sorry for everything I've done. I know you went through an awful time with Mammy, and I am sorry I wasn't there to help you. But I can't regret having Aoife, I can't. And I came back here in spite of all the small-mindedness and suspicion, because I wanted my daughter to have a home and a family, Brendan. You and Fintan are all that we have, God help us.'

Brendan's hands moved feebly at his sides. 'Una—'

'Your apologies are no use to anyone at this stage. Go home, Brendan. Will you just go home?'

He turned to leave, but stopped at the open door, and looked outside as he addressed his final words to Cormac. 'I'll pay for the cost of repairs to your cars. I got drunk. Lost the head.' That was the sum of Brendan's confession. He pulled the door closed, and was gone.

Una knelt to pick up the pieces of shattered crockery that littered the floor. Now it was Hugh Osborne's turn to comfort her. He stooped and took the pottery shards from her hands and set them on the table, then lifted Una to her feet and put his arm around her. Initially she resisted, but could not hold back a choking sob as he sat her down beside him on the bench beneath the windows. Cormac and Nora worked together without speaking to finish the task Una had begun, mopping up the milk and tea, sweeping up the spilled sugar, collecting broken bits of crockery and disposing of the debris in the bin. By the time they were finished, Una had pulled herself together; she and Hugh Osborne now sat side by side on the bench, linked only by hands clasped on the seat between them, each staring into the chasm of the past.

Chapter 5

As he drove to the postmortem in Ballinasloe, Devaney remembered how his prediction about inquisitive reporters had come true the previous afternoon. The first was an ambitious young man from the *Sunday World* who had to be escorted from the scene to keep him from crossing the barriers they'd set up near the road; next came the RTÉ camera crew. At least Devaney was spared dealing with them. As the superintendent in charge of the investigation, Brian Boylan was only too eager to be quoted in the papers and on the television news. Of course Boylan had nothing to say, apart from confirming what everyone already knew, that human remains had indeed been discovered at this site, and that it remained to be determined whether there was a connection between the discovery and the Osborne case or any other unsolved disappearances. He also didn't tell them that the police had found a collapsible pushchair, a pair of small blue shoes, and Mina Osborne's handbag, or that a .22 rifle had also been recovered from the souterrain. As he'd watched his superintendent bask in the television lights, Devaney had imagined the modesty with which Boylan would eventually take credit for shepherding the investigation to this juncture.

Once in Ballinasloe, he drove around the back of the hospital to the mortuary. He'd always dreaded postmortems, and the familiar queasiness started even before he'd parked the car. He got directions to the autopsy room, and found Malachy Drummond just outside the door. Drummond was a thinnish man, balding and bespectacled, known by colleagues for his trademark dickie bows and his appetite for good food and drink. His face had become familiar to the general public from coverage of crime scenes on the television news, but Drummond took this exactly for what it was, a kind of spurious quasi-celebrity that had nothing whatever to do with his actual work. To his colleagues in the police, what Drummond did bordered on the repellent, but the man himself had earned their respect for a professional demeanour and methodical work habits tempered by consideration for the dead. He always referred to his charges as 'the lady' or 'the gentleman', despite the often undignified circumstances of their deaths.

'Detective,' was his laconic greeting to Devaney. 'Sad business, this, a young mother and child. Very sad.' Devaney had enough experience of the man to know he actually meant it. 'I have a few things I want to show you.' Drummond led the way into the autopsy room, where Devaney was relieved to see that the bodies had been covered.

'With dental records we were able to confirm the identity of the young lady – she is Mina Osborne, without a doubt. And the cause of death seems fairly clear.' Malachy Drummond picked up long tweezers from a metal tray, and held up for Devaney's inspection a slightly misshapen rifle pellet. 'I found this inside the braincase. But there was neither entrance or exit injury to the skull itself, which tells me a couple of things: one, that she was not shot at close range – which would rule out a self-inflicted wound, and two, that the bullet probably entered the body through soft tissue – the eye, for example, or perhaps the mouth. Difficult to tell with such an advanced state of decomposition.'

'And the child?' Devaney asked.

'With the remains almost completely skeletized, it's hard to say. No apparent knife or bullet wounds, no blunt injury. The only evidence of trauma is a hairline skull fracture, but that doesn't appear severe enough to have been the cause of death on its own. However, as I said yesterday, the position of the bodies certainly suggest that they were moved to the location where they were found. I'm ruling both as homicides.' Drummond must have heard the small sigh that escaped Devaney's lips. He added, gently: 'From the nature of his injury, I'd venture to say the little lad was probably unconscious, Detective, whatever ultimately happened to him.'

Devaney himself wasn't sure why the information about Christopher Osborne triggered such an emotional response. He had worked on scores of murders, and had always been able to maintain his objectivity. Lack of sleep, it must be. He straightened. 'Thanks, Malachy. I'll look for your report.'

As he walked down the corridor from the mortuary to the main hospital building, Devaney tried to work out a scenario in which the different causes of death would make sense. He'd had no preconceptions about what might have happened; why did these facts, taken together, seem so strange? Even after the bodies were discovered, he had wondered about the possibility of a murder/suicide. Such things were not unheard of. But Malachy had found that Mina Osborne's injuries were definitely not self-inflicted. They'd have to get a ballistics test to find out whether the gun found in the souterrain was the same one that fired the fatal bullet. So how did Jeremy know where the bodies were, unless he was somehow involved? The boy didn't seem like the type to plan and commit two murders all on his own. Maybe he had witnessed something. Devaney's head began to ache from the smell of antiseptic, and from the thoughts that kept tumbling against one another in his brain. Christ, he'd give anything for a cigarette.

He turned down the corridor that would take him past Jeremy Osborne's room, where he pulled aside a passing nurse.

'Any news on the Osborne lad?'

'Sorry, there's been no change.'

Through the large window, he could see that Lucy Osborne still kept her vigil. She hadn't been home since Jeremy had been brought here, but sat silently beside her son. In all the times he'd been to check on the boy, Devaney had never seen her sleeping, and yet she somehow managed to maintain her usual fastidious appearance, despite having to wash in the public lavatory down the corridor. He had not divulged to anyone, even his own colleagues in the Gardaí, where the break in the case had come from, but with the burgeoning media attention, there was no way Lucy Osborne could have missed hearing about the recovery of the bodies. No doubt she was trying to block it from her mind, concentrating fiercely on her son.

Chapter 6

The day after the scene-of-crime officers had finished and packed off back to Dublin, all that remained was the flimsy barrier of yellow tape staked around the perimeter, wrapped around saplings in the now torn-up woodland at Bracklyn House. Cormac had come back out here looking for Nora; there was no sign of her in the house, and he wanted to let her know he was going to work on the excavation site. He stepped up to the edge of the souterrain, thinking that this secret place, this nest of concealment had ultimately succeeded too well in its purpose.

Nora was sitting with her knees drawn up to her chest and her back up against the wall of the souterrain. A torch lay just out of reach beside her on the clean-swept dirt floor. She didn't look up. 'I had to see it for myself,' she said.

Cormac eased himself down into the souterrain and sat down a couple of feet from her. Nora's right hand held a jagged piece of stone, and for an instant she seemed unsure what to do with it. Instead of flinging it, as he had thought she might, she began to scrape at the dirt floor beside her, almost unaware of what she was doing.

'I've been sitting up there for days, watching all this, thinking about Mina Osborne,' she said. 'I wonder if she even knew she was in danger.'

Cormac said nothing, only watched Nora's hand scrub

a shallow trough in the earth with the stone. She finally spoke: 'The night she was killed, I thought my sister would be safe with me. I thought I'd finally succeeded in convincing her that the way Peter treated her wasn't right. That she didn't deserve it. Elizabeth was away for the weekend with my parents. Tríona called to tell me she had packed a bag, everything was set, and she was finally walking out. She was going to be all right; she and Elizabeth were going to stay with me as long as they needed to. But do you know what else she told me just before she hung up the phone? That underneath it all, even though she couldn't live like that any more, that a part of her still loved him. I think she tried to tell Peter what she'd told me, and he finally snapped. Nobody can prove it, but I know, I know that's what happened. He couldn't keep her, so he made sure she would never be her own, separate person, or anything more than his pathetic victim, forever.'

The surface of the floor had begun to break apart beneath the steady scouring of the stone, but Nora didn't seem to notice until her fingers brushed against a tuft of ragged cloth that stuck up from the loosened soil. As Cormac watched, she brushed away the soil to uncover a bundle of what looked like rough-textured woollen homespun. When she carefully lifted the top layer of frayed and moth-eaten fabric, a tiny, fragile-looking skull lay exposed on the surface of the soil, its empty sockets upturned toward the sky.

'Cormac,' she whispered. 'This is a newborn baby.' He experienced a kind of slow-spreading horror at the realization that Mina and Christopher Osborne might not be the only victims entombed here, merely the most recent. 'Help me,' she said, and began to scratch at the surface of the soil again with the rough edge of stone.

'We should get the Guards.'

She paused only briefly to scan his face. 'I'm not stopping now.'

'At least let me get some tools. Please be careful, Nora. Let me show you what to do.' He hurriedly reached up to the bank above their heads and felt around for the handle of his site kit. He handed her a trowel, and used another himself to help clear away bits of soil and animal bones, until the infant was completely uncovered, and what was clearly recognizable as an adult's elbow joint protruded from the earth beside it.

Within the space of a few minutes, they'd uncovered almost the entire right side of an adult human skeleton, curled around the bundle containing the remains of the child. They really ought to stop now; the standard protocol in the discovery of any human remains was to inform the Gardaí immediately. But Cormac knew he'd have a job convincing Nora on that point. Besides, these bones were too old to be of any concern to the police, he was certain. At least a dozen skeletons like this turned up every year, as building foundations were excavated and pipelines and sewage schemes were launched; such discoveries had become almost routine in a place that had been so densely populated for so long.

'See how the surrounding material is full of bones and broken shells?' he said. 'That probably means this area was used as a midden; people had to live in these places for extended periods if they were under siege, so they needed not only a stock of supplies, but also a place to get rid of rubbish. It seems like these two weren't just left in the souterrain, but were actually buried here. Though I couldn't tell you why.'

About two inches from the adult skeleton's flexed knee joint, Cormac's trowel suddenly came in contact with what appeared to be a small patch of metal just under the surface of the clay. He quickly scraped away the dirt and gravel to expose one side of an oblong metal container, about the size of a small bread box and rather ordinary-looking. With further digging, the box turned out to be a sort of coffer or strongbox, now heavily corroded from being buried in damp soil. It was decorated with nail heads and secured around with two heavy iron bands. When he finally had the whole thing excavated, Cormac could see the remnants of leather handles on either side that had rotted through, and the rusty padlock that secured the vaulted lid.

'Maybe something in here can give us an idea who they are,' he said.

Nora could perceive that Cormac was speaking, but his words didn't register. She had seen hundreds of human skeletons in the course of her career, but each time, she couldn't help being struck by the beauty and ingenuity of the form, the strength and flexibility in the triangular bones of the spine. She was studying the way the soil had infiltrated the child's chest cavity, cradling the breastbone, ribs, and collarbone. She knew how difficult it was to tell whether an adult skeleton was male or female without precise measurements of the pelvic bones, though this one being found in the company of a newborn child increased the probability that it was female. Nora knelt over the mute remnants of what might be the second mother and child hidden in this dark place, and understood from the posture of the whitened bones lying before her, now exposed to the light, that again there had been no laying to rest here, no ceremony, but another hurried inhumation cloaked in secrecy. All at once she began to experience the same prickling sensation she had in the lab the day she was alone with the head of the *cailín rua*. 'Cormac,' she said, 'do you realize what we haven't found?'

Nora worked feverishly to remove compacted soil until it was clear that no skull was attached to the end of the adult's spinal column. She quickly counted the vertebrae, careful not to touch the bones themselves for fear of scratching or damaging them. A normal human spine should have seven cervical vertebrae; this individual was missing the first three.

'My God, Cormac, this could be our red-haired girl,' Nora said, then almost immediately reversed herself. 'No – that would be just too fantastic.'

'Of course it would. But I don't know why it should be. The girl Raftery told us about – Annie McCann – who was executed, she was from around this place somewhere. And what would have become of her body after the execution? You wouldn't very well bury a convicted murderer in the churchyard with all the proper Christians.'

If by some remote chance this actually was the *cailín rua*, why would someone take the trouble to conceal her body in a souterrain – with the corpse of the infant she'd presumably murdered? Of course none of it made logical sense. Nora's head ached, and her shoulders finally began to feel the crushing weight of the last few days' events. She looked down at the child's tiny skull, and tried to imagine what little effort it would take to stop the breath of such a helpless creature. It would be over in a few brief seconds. Is that how this child died, when its mother's touch turned murderous? The infant's empty orbits stared up at her, unanswering, and Nora felt suddenly cold, kneeling in the damp, shaded corner of the underground room.

Chapter 7

Malachy Drummond had returned and confirmed Cormac's assumption that the remains found in the souterrain had indeed been buried there for several centuries. Now Cormac sat with Nora in the evidence room at the Loughrea Garda station. They were waiting for Niall Dawson from the National Museum, who was coming down to have a look at the strongbox and to take it and the skeletal remains with him back to Dublin.

'You're very quiet this morning,' Cormac said.

'I'm just thinking about how thin the line is between thinking about doing something and actually doing it. And once it's done, how everything changes.'

'We have nothing to be sorry about, Nora. If you and I had never come here, Mina and Christopher Osborne would still be missing. All we did was to help uncover what was already done.'

'I know, I know. I keep telling myself that. But the way I went about things here only ended up causing extra pain, to you, to everyone. It's ironic that the whole point of coming back here was supposedly to find out more about the *cailín rua*, and we haven't even managed to do that.'

'Hang on,' Cormac said. 'We found that bit of a song. Raftery found the story of an execution that fits the dates. And we should know within a few days whether the skeleton from the souterrain belongs to our red-haired girl. That's an incredible amount of information, Nora. What more could we possibly learn?'

Her eyes pierced him. 'That she didn't do it. That she didn't murder her own child.' As Cormac studied Nora's face, he knew that she was also thinking of Hugh Osborne. The awful uncertainty over the whereabouts of his family had been replaced with an even more dreadful probability – that one or more of the people they had come to know in these few days at Bracklyn might be involved in a double murder. The thought had been weighing upon him as well.

Devaney had remained tight-lipped about the post-mortem results, but he and his fellow detectives had begun intensive interviews, particularly of Hugh and Lucy Osborne. They had put out additional public appeals for witnesses and information about the day of the disappearance, but as yet no one had been charged. Cormac couldn't help thinking that nothing would be resolved as long as Jeremy remained unconscious, the words he'd spoken at the tower as much a mystery now as when he'd uttered them. They were all waiting for the moment when the boy would awaken – if he awakened at all.

A few minutes later, Cormac stood by with Nora and Devaney as Niall Dawson launched his examination of the strongbox from the souterrain. Dawson began by taking several photographs of the unopened coffer. He gently tried to work the ancient lock with a thin tool, teasing flakes of rust onto the table below. After a few seconds, the lock cracked apart and fell to pieces in his gloved hand.

'Probably wonderfully strong when they put it on,' Dawson said as he lifted the lid. 'Hmm. Seeing what's in here may help in dating the box quite precisely.' After taking a few photos of the undisturbed contents, he lifted out a slightly concave paten, and a chalice, both of which appeared to be made of pewter or some similar metal. The chalice was set around with uncut stones. The next object was a crucifix, about eight inches long, made of wood, with a crude metal Christ figure.

'See how the arms are very short? Makes it easier to hide up your sleeve, a handy trick if you're saying a Mass somewhere you oughtn't. These weren't items to be caught with – unless of course you felt compelled to risk your neck. So that presents a dilemma: you shouldn't really destroy them – that would be sacrilege – but you can't risk anybody finding the bloody things either. So you bury them, and pray for times to change.'

At the bottom of the coffer was a book that looked badly damaged with age, its warped calfskin cover embossed with red and gold. Dawson's gloved fingers opened the pages at random. It appeared to be a Latin Bible with woodcut illustrations and initials. From the quick appraisal Dawson gave the book, Cormac surmised that he had apparently seen at least a few others like it.

'Italian imprint, published in 1588,' he said, opening the volume to its flyleaf. 'That means the National Library will be at least wanting to take a look at it.' He turned to Devaney. 'I'm not sure what you were looking for, Detective. These items have some historical interest, but they're not all that rare. There's nothing of great monetary value here, if that was a concern. The Bible is worth a couple of thousand at most. You'd find objects of this sort in many local historical museums around the country.'

'I appreciate you coming all the way from Dublin on

short notice,' Devaney said. 'It's good to be clear about what we have.'

'Not at all,' Dawson replied.

'Niall,' Nora said, 'I wanted to ask if you've found out any more about the ring.'

'I'm afraid it's out of my hands. The decorative arts department have possession of it; they might be able to tell you more.'

'Why would it go to them? I thought "decorative arts" meant vases and furniture.'

'Well, the general rule,' Dawson explained with a wry grin, 'is that if an artefact is found in bits it comes to Antiquities; if it's intact, it goes to Decorative Arts. But you didn't hear that from me.'

A young Garda officer stuck his head in the door. 'Excuse me, Detective Devaney? O'Byrne's just phoned from the hospital, sir. Jeremy Osborne has come round, and says he won't speak to anyone but you.'

Chapter 8

When Devaney arrived at the hospital, he could see a medical team hovering over Jeremy Osborne's bed. O'Byrne, the young officer posted at the door, eagerly filled him in on what had happened: 'I wasn't in the room, sir, but I could hear everything that went on. His mother was in there with him, like she has been all along, and you could hear him rustling in the bed, like. "Jeremy," says she, "lie still. I'll get the doctor." Well, I can't leave me post, so I flag down a nurse and says to her: "Get the doctor, yer man's awake inside in the room." I go in, and the next thing you know he's screaming bloody murder, and telling me to get her out, get her out, he doesn't want her here, and she's trying to get him to whisht, and he just gets worse, roarin' and shoutin' and carryin' on till the doctor arrives and sends us both out into the hallway until they get him settled down. Then the mother tries to go in, but he's at it again, and the doctor tells her to stay out if she wants what's best for the lad. That's when I rang you.'

'Where's the mother now?'

'Over there, sir,' O'Byrne said, indicating her with his eyes. Lucy Osborne sat upright in a chair in the corridor outside Jeremy's room. Devaney thought he could finally detect the strain beginning to show in her face.

'Mrs Osborne, I understand that your son wants to speak with me.'

'I should be in there with him,' she said, rising and moving toward the door. Devaney stepped into her path.

'I'm afraid that's not possible.'

'You don't understand. Even before the accident, he wasn't well.'

'I'm sorry, Mrs Osborne, but we're allowed to question him alone if he's over seventeen. I'll have to ask you to wait here. Maybe one of the nurses would get you a cup of tea or something.' When he turned away, Devaney could feel her eyes drilling holes in his back.

The nurse was taking Jeremy Osborne's pulse. He looked dreadful, his face still bruised and swollen under the bandages, but Devaney could see relief in the boy's eyes as he dutifully kept the thermometer under his tongue. After the nurse left the room, Devaney closed the door and drew a chair up on the far side of the bed. Through the window, he could see Lucy Osborne's anxious face as she strained to catch every gesture, to comprehend what was being said behind the glass, and found himself praying fervently that he could play this thing right. It might be his only chance.

'Hello, Jeremy. This is Garda O'Byrne,' he said, indicating the uniformed officer. 'I do have to caution you that you're not obliged to say anything unless you wish to do so, but whatever you say will be taken down in writing and may be given in evidence. Do you understand that, Jeremy?' There was no response. 'I have to make sure you understand.'

Jeremy's voice cracked as he answered: 'I understand.'

'We uncovered the bodies of Mina and Christopher Osborne three days ago, in an underground passage near the tower house, just as you said.' He watched the boy's face crumble. 'Why don't you tell me what happened, Jeremy?'

'Why did he have to stop me? Why couldn't he just let me die?'

Devaney imagined that the boy was referring to Maguire, who had prevented him from leaping into the fire. 'Maybe he saw someone worth salvaging.'

'You don't understand. I killed them. I killed them both.' Jeremy Osborne looked at him, and Devaney could see the effort it had taken for the boy to speak those words aloud, and how much more it was going to take to finally give the full story. He waited, and Jeremy's eyes closed once more. The silence grew until it filled the space. Finally, Jeremy began to speak again; Devaney had to lean forward to hear his faint whisper:

'I had my birthday the end of September. Mum gave me a hunting rifle, an old one that belonged to my granddad. She said she didn't want me to be afraid of guns just because of – because of what happened to my father. I never even touched a gun before. She said to wait until someone showed me the proper way to use it, but I took it out anyway. I was only going to shoot at birds; ah Jesus, I never meant—' Jeremy's face screwed up again, and Devaney simply waited once more, wishing this could be over.

'I went up to the tower. It was foggy, and when I heard something move, I fired.' It was clear he was reliving those endless seconds again, as he had every day, every night for almost three years. 'I thought it was a bird.' The tears were spilling down Jeremy's face now. His eyes focused not on Devaney, but a place somewhere on the ceiling of the hospital room, where the scene seemed to play itself out before him. Devaney could see it as well: mother and child arriving home from the village, the little boy, wearing his new red boots, climbing from the pushchair and leading his mother on a chase, or a game of hide and seek at the edge of the woods.

'I thought it was a bird. But it was Mina.' He recoiled at the memory. 'I don't know what she was doing there. Her eye was gone, it was all blood—' He reached up as if to touch her face before him, and his hand stopped in mid-air. 'And then I saw she'd fallen on top of Chris. He wasn't moving.'

'What did you do next?' Devaney asked.

It was a moment before Jeremy could respond. 'I don't remember, I just knew they were dead, and I had to cover them up,' he said, and even before he finished speaking, Devaney knew the last part was a lie. Everything the boy had said to this point had the ring of truth in it; why would he begin to lie now?

'Nobody knew about that underground passage, only me. I used to hide there. I dragged them inside, and closed up the entrance, covered it with stones. That's why the police never found it.' Though he was nearly exhausted, the tears had stopped, and Jeremy's voice had taken on a hard edge it hadn't had before.

'Are you saying that you hid the bodies all on your own? That no one helped you?'

'No. There was no one else. Only me.'

'If it was an accident, Jeremy, why didn't you come forward?'

'I don't know, I don't know – I was afraid.'

'What about the gun, Jeremy? What did you do with the gun? And the pushchair?'

The boy's face suddenly betrayed confusion, and his breath began to catch in his throat. 'I – I don't remember. You're trying to confuse me.' Devaney saw his chance and took it, not looking up to see whether Lucy Osborne was still watching.

'Listen, Jeremy, I have reason to believe that someone helped you, at least in the covering up. Why don't you just tell me how it really happened?'

'I've told you. No one helped me. No one.' If anything, the boy looked even more abject and miserable than he had before he'd relieved himself of his awful burden. You think you've got rid of it, but it doesn't go away, Devaney thought. It never goes away.

'Then tell me, Jeremy, why would you have said: "She'd never tell"?'

'I said that?' The boy looked horrified.

'You did. Maguire says you told him there was a place underground, then you said: "She knows. She'd never tell." You don't remember that?'

'No. I never said that.'

'I see. Let's go back to Christopher. The postmortem shows he had a hairline skull fracture, but the pathologist says that alone wouldn't have been enough to kill him. How did Christopher die, Jeremy?' Devaney moved closer to the boy, spoke softly, close to his ear. Jeremy's hands and feet began to move, and Devaney hated himself. He knew he must stage this as carefully as a performance, must persist in probing until he could sense the gnawing horror in the boy's insides, and see it in his terrified eyes. 'I'm thinking it probably wasn't very difficult to smother him. He was small, and not very strong. Maybe he was unconscious, and never even struggled. What did you do? Did you just put your hand over his face? What did that feel like, Jeremy? What does it feel like to stop a helpless little child breathing until his heart stops? Until you know that he's really and truly dead?'

Jeremy's body was writhing weakly among his bed-clothes, as he tried to resist the dreadful words, the even more terrible images they conjured up. 'No, that's not how it was. She fell – oh, Jesus, help me. Somebody help me—'

That was the moment at which Lucy Osborne, who had been watching through the window, could restrain herself no longer. She opened the door and came to stand beside Devaney's chair.

'Get away from my son,' she warned in an icy voice. 'I know what you're trying to do. Leave him alone.' When Devaney stood to address her, she slapped him hard across the face. He took the blow, but seized her arm before she could strike him again. For such a slight woman, Lucy Osborne was phenomenally strong, and at first only her eyes gave away the fury she had managed for so long to contain. Then she began to laugh breathlessly, almost hysterically, and Devaney felt his stomach heave as he stood between overprotective mother and sheltered son, and only dimly began to realize that he'd had the whole thing backwards all along. The relationship between parent and child had been distorted beyond all recognition, and it was Jeremy who'd been protecting his mother, not the other way around. Devaney suddenly knew that the scene as he'd played it out for Jeremy didn't come close to the real atrocity that had taken place that day in the woods at Bracklyn House. As he stood facing Lucy Osborne, her wrist gripped tightly in his hand, he had to extinguish a savage desire to stop the laughter, to strike the woman to the ground and pummel her until he could make it stop. He looked into her eyes as he spoke the words of the official caution again, slowly and carefully, as a way to calm himself. Then he let go of her arm.

'What's the matter, Detective?' she asked in a strangely mocking tone, as if she knew what had gone through his mind. 'Hasn't my son broken down to your satisfaction? Hasn't he played his part well enough in your precious search for the truth? I'll give you the truth.' She spat the word with a venomous contempt.

'No, please, no,' Jeremy pleaded, but there was no stopping Lucy Osborne now.

'I'm the one you want. My son didn't know what he was doing; the shooting was a complete accident. He came into the house raving: "I've killed them, I've killed them." He kept saying it over and over again.'

'Please stop,' Jeremy implored once again.

She reached out for her son's hand, and stroked it as she addressed him: 'Hush now, don't say any more. I have to tell them, darling, don't you see, they're going to take you away unless I do, and I can't let them do that, I can't.' Then she turned back to Devaney and began to speak slowly, deliberately, and seemingly without emotion: 'All I could think at first was that our chance to get home again to England was ruined. I had been planning it for so long, working out the details, and now this would destroy everything. But then I began to see how it all might work. If we could manage just to stay calm and handle ourselves well. There wasn't very much blood at all, not like Daniel. We didn't have much time. Hugh might be back at any moment, so we had to find a place to hide them, just until I could think things through. Jeremy told me about his underground room. I had him run and get a spade from the shed, and then—' Her eyes stared into the past. 'I was looking down at the child. He was quiet, but I could see a pulse, just there.' She raised her fingers to her own throat. 'I had to make it stop, don't you see? It was so small, so insignificant. And all I could think was that this boy was in the way, he was the one minor obstacle that now stood between

Jeremy and the dream I'd always had for us. We had to get back to our home at Banfield. We'd made the mistake of losing it once before, you see, more than three hundred years ago, but we got it back then, and we could get it back again now. We were so close. I don't suppose it means anything at all to you, but I wasn't about to let five hundred years of my family history at Banfield come to a full stop just like that. I couldn't be responsible for that. So all I could think was that this child must die – and after that it would be easy, so easy.'

Jeremy Osborne's face was filled with revulsion, but his strength was gone and he could not pull his hand away from his mother's grasp. Lucy continued, her voice now absolutely cool and deliberate: 'And then I thought how fitting it was, in a way, because of all the people who had tried to take Jeremy away from me, it was this child, this filthy little kaffir who'd most nearly succeeded. I said to him: "It's really for the best, don't you see? There's nothing left for you here, you poor, motherless mongrel." What I did was an act of kindness.'

Devaney pictured the boy arriving back with the shovel, to find his mother's hand covering Christopher's face. 'Is that how it happened, Jeremy?' he asked.

'I don't know. I don't know.' The boy's face was twisted with anguish. Here was the real reason Jeremy had not come forward, though he had nearly died trying to keep that terrible truth within himself. It had been too late to do anything for Mina, but Jeremy had suffered torture for over two harrowing years, thinking that he might have saved Christopher.

But Lucy wasn't finished. 'After that, there was only Hugh, and he was so bloody weak – like all the Osbornes. He let himself be convinced – under the circumstances – that the estate ought to go to Jeremy if anything happened to him. That's what he told me Sunday evening, that he'd gone to London to change his will. He even believed that it was his own idea all along.'

Lucy Osborne's eyes grew larger, and the words came faster and faster, spilling out in an unstoppable torrent: 'I knew no one would question a suicide, the way he'd carried on. It was almost too easy, putting the sleeping tablets in his tea. I knew the real difficulty would be in getting him out to the car, but the garden cart worked very handsomely. But that meddling pair ruined everything. That wretched American, prying into every corner, using Jeremy to get at me. I tried to warn her off, get rid of her – I told her on the phone, leave it alone, they're better off. The broken glass was far too subtle; she just swept it up. Finally, I put that horrible dead thing in her bed, but she still wouldn't leave us alone. That's why it had to escalate, why Hugh's suicide had to happen that night, when they were supposed to be out for the evening. And if only—' The memory of this failure seemed to cause physical pain, and Lucy Osborne's bony fingers clawed at the bedsheets like talons. Her eyes brimmed with hatred and disgust. 'If only they'd arrived five minutes later, Jeremy and I would be shot of this godforsaken country and on our way home again. And none of you could have stopped us.'

Devaney had heard his share of confessions. He'd seen plenty of suspects finally crack under the pressure of questioning. But he had never witnessed anything quite like what had just taken place here.

Lucy's face softened again as she turned to her son and took his hand. 'This is not your fault, darling. You did so well for so long. I know it was difficult. Whatever happens to me, you mustn't blame yourself.' With gritted teeth, Jeremy wrested his hand from his mother's grip, and turned away from her, wracked with broken sobs. Devaney wasn't sure the woman realized that her son had been lost to her quite some time ago.

'Lucy Osborne, I'm arresting you for the murder of Christopher Osborne, for the attempted murder of Hugh Osborne, and for concealing evidence in the death of Mina Osborne. It would be in your best interest to speak with your solicitor as soon as possible. You can phone from the station. Do you understand? Mrs Osborne?'

Lucy ignored him, and reached out to stroke her son's hair. 'You haven't been well, my love. Not well at all. You rest now, darling. I'll be back soon.'

Not for about thirty years, Devaney thought. 'I'd be obliged if you and Mullins would take Mrs Osborne to the station,' he said to O'Byrne. 'I'll be there shortly – there's something I have to do first.'

Devaney was crossing Drumcleggan Bog when he saw Hugh Osborne's black Volvo heading toward him. He leaned on the horn; though Osborne had been driving fast, he managed to slow down and stop, then reversed until the two cars were side by side.

'I had a message about Jeremy. Is he all right? What did he say?'

Devaney looked into the man's eyes and felt the words tearing at his throat as he tried to speak. Maybe it would be better if there were other people around. 'Hadn't we better go somewhere it's easier to talk?'

'Tell me now, Detective. Please. There's a place where you can pull off the road just ahead. I'll turn around.'

Devaney nodded once, and drove off the road to the place Osborne had mentioned, a small peninsula of solid ground that jutted out into the bog. He looked through the windscreen at the black voids of the random cutaways and the little clumps of footed turf as the first drops of rain began to spit from the low, shifting blanket of clouds that moved in from the west. And he knew that Hugh Osborne had been telling the truth all along. That ridiculous story about stopping to rest along the road from Shannon was not merely lame fiction but cruel fact. It meant that Hugh Osborne would have to live the rest of his life with the knowledge that he'd been asleep only a few miles from home as his wife and son had been killed. Devaney thought as he opened the car door and felt the freshness of the mist on his face how strange it was that this chapter of the story at least would reach its end here in the bog, almost exactly where it had begun. And it struck him that there was nowhere to hide in this place of banishment – neither tree nor stone nor bush as far as the eye could see, nothing to provide shelter from the wind, and from the rain when it came.

Chapter 9

Alone in her room, Nora counted the time: it was nine days now after the tower fire, and just a week since the discovery of the souterrain. Cormac's work at the priory was finished, and they would be leaving Bracklyn House after the funeral tomorrow. They were alone in the house at the moment; Hugh Osborne had looked exhausted this morning, but he'd insisted on driving on his own to collect his mother-in-law at Shannon, and they hadn't been able to dissuade him.

She found Cormac in his room, packing for the journey. 'I just spoke to Hickey, the garage man,' she said, sitting on the bed where he was arranging the items in his case. 'My car's good as new, but they couldn't get all the parts for yours. Drivable, he says, but you'll have to get the rear window replaced when you get back to Dublin.'

'I was actually thinking I might not go straight home,' Cormac said. He paused a moment before continuing. 'I was thinking of heading up to Donegal for a few days.' He hesitated once more, but this time looked up at her. 'You could come with me.'

This sudden fit of spontaneity took Nora completely by surprise. She studied his face for a moment before responding. 'I have to get back to Dublin; I've already missed a week of classes as it is. You're probably better off on your own, anyway. I imagine you and your father will find plenty to talk about. How's your head, though? Are you sure you're all right for driving?'

'I'll be fine.' He shoved his case aside and sat down beside her, then reached for her hand, and pressed his lips to the inside of her wrist.

She tried to withdraw her hand. 'I'm going to be kicking myself as it is, but you have to bloody well make sure of it, don't you?'

'Nora, what's bothering you?' He didn't let go, but held her hand fast.

'I was so wrong about Hugh. I heard what I wanted to hear, and I came here ready to hang him. The worst part is that he's been so forgiving.'

'It wasn't just you; everyone suspected him. The police—'

'Everyone but you.'

'Maybe it seemed that way. On the inside, I'm afraid I wavered too.'

'I keep wondering what's going to happen here, Cormac. Devaney said we might be called to testify, if the case actually goes to trial. I hope it doesn't come to that. I wonder if Jeremy could survive going to prison. And if he isn't charged, or gets a suspended sentence? Devaney said it's a possibility because he was underage at the time. Where will he go?'

'Hugh told me he wants Jeremy to stay on here – if and when he's released. He knows what happened wasn't the boy's fault.'

'It sounds very noble, but the whole idea is fraught with disaster. How could he not be reminded every single day of what Jeremy did? And how can Una McGann possibly go on living in the same house with her brother?' Nora said. 'Fintan's going off to seek his fortune in the States. For Aoife's sake, how can she even think about staying there?'

'I know we've been through an ordeal with Hugh, and with Una these last few weeks,' he said. 'But it's not as if we even really know them. Maybe Hugh Osborne has more forgiveness in him than you or I could ever imagine. Maybe he needs Jeremy as much as the boy needs him. Maybe Una will decide to leave home. They'll have to find their own ways through this, Nora. They will. But I don't know that we can help them.'

She had imagined that finding answers should impart at least some small sense of satisfaction, and yet that feeling was absent. She knew that they would all carry on, as human beings had always carried on, as automatically as their hearts carried on beating, their lungs continued taking in and expelling breath. Sometimes without thinking or feeling, sometimes invaded by despair. Why then, after helping to unearth the truth of this place, did she feel so compelled to do more? What more was there? Maybe Cormac was right, maybe they had reached the end of doing.

'Come here to me,' he said, and whether it was the warmth of his arms, or the roughness of his face against hers, she did not know, only that she needed the solace he offered, and responded instinctively to his touch until they were tangled together on the high bed. All Nora could hear was their ragged breathing, and she felt herself falling, borne downward into a maelstrom, a potent confusion of feeling.

Downstairs, the single deep note of the doorbell sounded in the front hall. Nora pulled away and slid off the bed. 'What the hell are we doing? What were we thinking? I'm sorry, Cormac.' As she left the room, she heard his carefully packed case go crashing to the floor.

Chapter 10

Devaney stood outside the front door at Bracklyn House, bearing the brown paper envelope containing Mina Osborne's letters. When Nora Gavin answered the door, he said: 'I just dropped by to see Mrs Gonsalves.'

'We're expecting them any time. You can wait if you'd like.'

Devaney stepped inside, and caught Dr Gavin eyeing his package. 'Just some letters,' he said. 'From Mina Osborne to her mother.'

'You've read them?'

'I have.'

'What was she like?'

Devaney considered for a moment, thinking of the Mina Osborne he'd come to know a little, remembering the intelligence, thoughtfulness, and compassion that radiated from her letters. He had wondered the same thing, and yet what was the point of such a question, since none of them, not even her mother or her husband, had really known, or would ever know? Mina Osborne had become a void, an absence in the lives of those she'd left behind. The paltry words that he might use to sum her up would be based only on a few lines of handwriting. He was aware that Dr Gavin was watching him with a curious expression. 'I'm afraid I can't really say.'

Maguire seemed rather subdued when he joined them, and Devaney got the distinct sense that he'd interrupted something when he'd rung the doorbell.

'Detective,' Dr Gavin said, 'we've been wondering what's going on, and maybe you could enlighten us. Cormac and I have read the papers and heard lots of things second- and third-hand about Lucy Osborne's confession and the charges. We'd rather not be asking Hugh.'

'I'll tell you what I can. According to what Jeremy told us, his mother had become obsessed about getting back her home place in England. She'd started writing rambling letters to her solicitor, and was scheming about ways to get it back. She evidently got it into her head some time ago that the Osbornes collectively owed her for the loss of her family home. Who knows if she would have done anything on her own, but when the shooting occurred, an opportunity presented itself, and the more she thought about it, the more she began to see eliminating this branch of the Osborne family as the main chance for herself and her son. With Mina and Christopher out of the way, she accomplished two things: she eliminated Hugh Osborne's lawful heirs, and put her own son in their place. Hugh Osborne would be a rich man when he got the insurance, when his wife was declared legally dead. But once Hugh made Jeremy the beneficiary in his will, there was no reason to wait. All she had to do was to see that something happened to Hugh, and she and Jeremy would be secure. Osborne's own policy might not have paid if he committed suicide, but Jeremy would still stand to inherit Bracklyn House, not to mention the life insurance on Mina Osborne.'

'How did it all start to unravel?' Dr Gavin asked.

'Jeremy told us that he and his mother removed

suitcases and clothing from the house to make it look as if Mina had simply run away. He was supposed to burn it all, but he hung on to a few items. Then a couple of months ago the cleaner, Mrs Hernan, found one of Mina's scarves under his mattress – and when Mrs Hernan brought it to Lucy's attention, she was sacked. Evidently Lucy forced Jeremy to burn the scarf – this time in front of her, to make sure it was done properly – and that's when he felt he had to find a way to tell someone. He tried to keep away from his mother, ended up practically living out at the tower – he started stealing food, and all those candles he had were nicked from the church. Between the drink and camping in the tower like an outlaw, it's not hard to see why Jeremy seemed to be the one who was going mad.'

'Do you know anything more about the charges, Detective?' Maguire asked.

'We got word today from the DPP – that's the Director of Public Prosecutions. Lucy Osborne is charged with one count of murder for the death of Christopher Osborne, and one of attempted murder against Hugh Osborne. If she's judged competent to stand trial – and they cautioned that it's a big "if", considering her current mental state – she could receive a life sentence on those charges alone. And she could get an additional sentence for concealing evidence. At this point, Jeremy's up on a single charge of involuntary manslaughter for the death of Mina Osborne, but the DPP says he'll most likely receive a suspended sentence, given the circumstances of the case, and his age at the time.'

'The thing I don't understand is why Hugh didn't say anything about Lucy giving him sleeping tablets,' Dr Gavin said.

'He says he has no memory of anything that happened

after he went down into the workshop – he can't even recall Lucy bringing him tea.'

'Surely he must have figured out that he didn't end up in that car by himself,' she said.

Devaney hesitated, remembering Hugh Osborne's explanation when he'd brought up the same point himself during questioning. *When you've thought as often as I have about what it would be like – to go out to the car, turn it on, and just go to sleep*, he'd said, *it's somehow not at all surprising to find out that's exactly what you did.* If it weren't for Lucy's admission, Devaney thought, the man might still consider himself an unsuccessful suicide.

The sound of voices cut short their conversation as Hugh Osborne came in with Mrs Gonsalves. Devaney heard the voice he'd come to know on the telephone, and wondered how the woman's grace and dignity could seem completely undiminished by the length and grim purpose of her journey. He watched her dark eyes alight upon the package in his hands.

'You must be Detective Devaney,' she said.

'You know one another?' Osborne asked.

'We've spoken on the telephone,' said Mrs Gonsalves, clasping Devaney's outstretched hand. 'Detective, I'm so grateful for all you've done on my daughter's behalf. And my grandson—' Her voice faltered, but her eyes were steady. Devaney held out the precious brown package.

'Thank you for returning Mina's letters,' said Mrs Gonsalves as she received it. 'I know you understand how I treasure them.'

Devaney begged off staying for tea. He had done his duty in bringing the package. Upon reaching home, he could hear a few faint, wobbly fiddle notes as he got out of the car. Róisín was in the kitchen, tentatively picking out a tune; he could barely recognize the first few bars of 'Páidín O'Rafferty'. He watched through the kitchen window as Nuala came in, kissing the top of her daughter's studiously inclined head as she passed.

'That's starting to sound lovely, Róisín, keep at it. Remember what Daddy said, and don't try to play too fast. I've got to go out—' Nuala stopped when he opened the door. Devaney felt frozen on the threshold, couldn't force himself to speak or to step into the house. Róisín stopped playing, and Nuala came and stood in front of him.

'Are you all right, Gar? Why are you home in the middle of the afternoon?'

He wanted to tell his wife that for the first time in a long while he could see her so clearly, so entirely, every curve and eyelash and tiny line, as clearly as that first time they had slept and awakened together, but he found himself unable to speak.

'Garrett,' she said, 'why won't you come in?' Her touch was enough to break the spell. He stepped forward and sat down facing his daughter across the table. Nuala seated herself beside him.

'Listen, Daddy, I've nearly got it off,' Róisín said brightly, launching into a halting jig tempo once more, barely getting through the *A* part of the tune.

'Isn't she coming along?' Nuala asked, still searching his countenance for some inkling of what was going on. He felt them standing on opposite sides of a threshold, if not of understanding itself, then at least a willingness to understand one another again. Nuala reached up and touched his face. 'I'm going to call the office and ask Sheila if she wouldn't mind taking a couple of appointments for me. I won't be a minute.'

When Devaney looked across the table at Róisín, he saw a reflection of his own bewildered countenance in the bottomless depths of his daughter's eyes.

Chapter 11

The funeral Mass for Mina and Christopher Osborne took place two days later at St Columba's in Dunbeg. Standing in the back of the church, Devaney watched a small clutch of reporters gather outside the gates, no doubt hoping to get a few shots of the grieving family, to be served up on the evening news with some of the more sensational facts of the case, all intoned with the usual air of affected solemnity. They'd have a good show; the whole village had turned out. Hugh Osborne was already in the front of the church with Mrs Gonsalves. Devaney suddenly realized that in their conversations, he'd never even asked Mina's mother her Christian name. He watched the mourners shuffle slowly past: Delia Hernan, Dolly Pilkington with her three eldest, Ned and Anna Raftery, all the women he'd dubbed charter members of the Father Kinsella fan club. Una McGann and her daughter sat among them, purposely removed from Osborne, Devaney noticed, and he could see the looks from all around her that measured the distance exactly. Una's brothers were there as well, Fintan sitting upright beside her, and Brendan kneeling in one of the back pews with his head bowed, and a rosary knotted through his thick fingers.

Devaney was still standing inside the door, wishing in vain for a cigarette, when Brian Boylan approached. Boylan was all spit and polish today in one of his expensive suits, as if he'd come here to work the crowd – and so he had, Devaney thought cynically.

'Just wanted to say well done, Detective,' Boylan said in a confidential tone. 'Very well done indeed. A sad case, but good to have everything resolved.'

'Sir,' was Devaney's curt reply. He didn't feel he deserved even this brief congratulatory nod. Though he probably would have cracked it eventually, the fact of the matter was that the bloody thing had fallen right into his lap. *When are you ever going to learn to ease up*? asked the voice in his head. Whatever way the answers had come, the thing was finished.

A heavy rain lashed down all during the service, and by the time the Mass was over the television cameras had dispersed. The showers had all but stopped when the mourners reached the burial site, but the sun seemed to dodge in and out behind still-threatening dark clouds that occasionally let go a sporadic drizzle. Mother and child were interred in the same casket, in a corner of the ancient churchyard at Drumcleggan Priory, in an area slightly separated from the rest of the burials. The church had been full to the rafters, but here at the priory Hugh Osborne stood solemnly by the graveside, arm in arm with Mrs Gonsalves, and the only others in attendance were Father Kinsella, Cormac Maguire and Nora Gavin, Una and Fintan McGann, Devaney himself, and the undertaker's men.

After the rain, the air smelled of freshly-turned clay, and it struck Devaney that there was nothing illusory about this burial: no carpet of artificial turf covered the mound of earth that had been dug by hand from the grave; the unpretentious wooden coffin was lowered into the ground on stout ropes by two labouring men in shirt-sleeves. Seated on a folding chair at the graveside, Fintan

McGann strapped on his pipes and, when the holy water had been sprinkled and the last prayers said, lowered his head and began to play an air – a lament whose simple, dignified melody contained the purest distillation of grief. After they all filed from the churchyard, Devaney turned to watch the workmen as they shovelled the wet clay into the grave, listening to the damp, rhythmic scrape of the spades, and the sound of the soil hitting the coffin with a hollow thud.

Chapter 12

Back at Bracklyn House after the interment, Cormac noted how the noise level dipped for the slightest fraction of a second when Hugh and Mrs Gonsalves entered the front hall, just as it had the night he saw Osborne ducking through the door at Lynch's pub. The mood here was decidedly sombre and yet this usually silent house took on a different, almost unrecognizable demeanour when filled with the buzz of conversation. It was clearly the first time most of these people had seen the inside of Bracklyn House, and he could see their eyes gauging its proportions, and their frank astonishment at its general state of disrepair, the age and shabbiness of the furnishings. The doors to the formal sitting room were open wide, the chandeliers managed to glitter through their thin veil of dust, and the huge dining table and sideboard were laden with plates of homemade ham and salad sandwiches, dark fruitcake, and currant scones. The combination of homeliness and grandeur struck a discordant note.

Hugh led Mrs Gonsalves to a chair beside the dining room windows. Una brought her a cup of tea, and tried to press some refreshment on Osborne as well, which he refused. Mourners began to file past. 'Sorry for your trouble,' Cormac heard them murmur in low voices as they leaned down to Mrs Gonsalves, or solemnly shook Hugh Osborne's hand. How strange to see the modern-day citizens of Dunbeg, whose tenant ancestors no doubt spent lifetimes tugging their forelocks in the presence of the Osbornes, greeting the current owner of Bracklyn House as though he still exerted some sort of control over their lives.

As he moved about the rooms, Cormac wondered where Nora had got to, and saw her talking to Devaney in a corner of the library. Going about his work, Devaney always seemed so self-assured, but here he had the uneasy look of a man not used to socializing, at least in situations where there was neither pint nor fiddle in his hands. When Cormac approached, they were talking about the *cailín rua*.

'So you're hoping the bones from the souterrain will come up a match?' Devaney asked.

'Malachy Drummond is helping us with it right now,' Nora said.

Cormac addressed Devaney: 'We found some evidence that the red-haired girl from the bog might have actually been—' he lowered his voice, not wishing under the circumstances to broadcast such news to every soul within hearing '—executed for the murder of her newborn child. But Nora doesn't believe it.'

'I realize we may never find anything conclusive,' Nora said. She looked through the open door into the dining room, where Hugh Osborne stood by the window, accepting condolences. 'I just think we ought to get all the information we can.'

Chapter 13

The morning after the funeral, Nora was packing her case when her mobile phone began to chirp. It was Malachy Drummond.

'I have some interesting news,' he said. 'First, the skeletal remains of the adult from your souterrain were a conclusive match for the head found at Drumcleggan Bog. The vertebrae matched exactly, as did the blade marks on the bones. I'm as positive as a pathologist can be they're the same person.'

'I knew it,' Nora said under her breath, and at the same time, she felt slightly ill as she thought of the *cailín rua* putting a hand over her infant's mouth and nose until it lay still. She didn't know if the murdered child was a boy or a girl. There was no mention of its gender in the account Raftery had provided. 'Thanks, Malachy, I appreciate you taking the time.'

'Hang on. That was only the first bit; there's more. The museum has some sort of arrangement with one of our colleagues at Trinity. McDevitt's his name, a chap from the genetics department. He's working on a database of mitochondrial DNA. Anyway, he came to take a sample from your two specimens while I had them in the morgue, and we got to talking about his research.' Nora was listening, but her mind was already turning over the possibilities in what Drummond was about to reveal.

'It's fascinating stuff. In addition to DNA, he's also collecting surname information. Taken in conjunction, his data will eventually produce a map of genetic diversity in Ireland, as a first step in making inferences about population origins. I told him you might have evidence about this girl's identity, and he said he might like to phone you about it when you get back. I gave him your office number; I hope you don't mind.'

'No, that's fine, Malachy.'

'So as we were working, I told him the whole story, how this young woman's head had been found in a bog, and that you'd turned up evidence that she may have been executed for the murder of her child, very possibly the same infant who was found alongside her in the souterrain.' Drummond paused for breath. 'I thought no more about it. But then McDevitt phoned me, just a few minutes ago, with some very curious results. The mtDNA sequences of these two individuals were completely different. There's no possibility that they were mother and child. They're not even distantly related. Isn't that curious?'

Nora couldn't answer, as her mind tried to take in the enormity of what she had just heard.

'Hello, Nora? Are you still there?'

'Malachy, you're sure that's what he said? Not related?'

'He said the evidence couldn't be more distinct.'

'How is that possible?' She wasn't really talking to Drummond, but trying to fix the contradictory information in her mind. 'So if the child wasn't hers, whose was it?'

Nora carried her case downstairs, where Cormac was waiting for her, and Hugh Osborne walked them out to the cars in the drive. Cormac's jeep still bore a few scars from Brendan McGann's attack; the rear window was temporarily repaired with clear plastic sheeting.

'I owe you both so much,' said Hugh Osborne. 'I've spoken to Jeremy. He's going to come back home here when he's released. I know it may be difficult, but I can't just abandon him. Mina would never have wanted that.'

'If there's anything at all that I – that we can do—' Cormac said.

'I fear I've already asked far too much.'

BOOK FIVE

An Account of Innocent Blood

We are come to ask an account of the innocent blood that hath been shed.

– Oliver Cromwell, 1649

Chapter 1

At 9:15 p.m. on a rainy Thursday night the following November, Cormac Maguire slouched on the sofa in his sitting room, reading. The front window was streaked with rain, but a small turf fire glowed in the grate, and he realized that he had never before experienced such a remarkable feeling of fullness and serenity.

Six months ago, feeling wrung out from a week of difficult conversation with his father, and weary after the long drive from Donegal to Dublin, Cormac had pulled up in front of his own house. He'd sat in the car for a while, studying the dark windows, contemplating whether he could ever return to the solitary life he had studiously built for himself behind them. The car window had been open just enough to admit the seductive scent of some unidentifiable flower. Whether it was the prompting of that sweet fragrance itself, or the prospect of the different sort of life it suggested, Cormac did not know, but he'd turned the key in the ignition and made his way through the narrow Dublin streets until he arrived outside Nora Gavin's flat.

She opened the door as if she'd been expecting him. The time that followed was almost like a dream now. A smile tugged at Cormac's lips when he remembered that those three intoxicating days with Nora were the first time he had felt not like a bystander in his own life, but a full participant. Now he looked down at her stretched out beside him with her head resting in his lap, appreciating the warmth and the intimate landscape of her body, the curl of her ear, the soft wisps of dark hair against her pale skin. This sleep was a good thing; she was exhausted. In the months since they'd returned from Dunbeg, she had kept searching, digging through records of Irish assizes and transportation records at the National Archives in Dublin and the Public Records Office in London, trying to find out more about Annie McCann and Cathal Mór O'Flaherty. Her search had so far borne no fruit, and it seemed at this point that she was completely stuck. Cormac tried to imagine the energy Nora had devoted to the investigation of her sister's death, and knew that she'd not given up in that quest either. He no longer believed that evidence of the *cailín rua's* true story existed, but he'd stopped trying to convince Nora. He found her tenacity extremely touching.

The phone on the desk began to ring, but Nora appeared to be sleeping soundly, and he decided to let the answerphone pick up rather than disturb her. After the tone, he heard a familiar deep voice: 'Ah, Cormac, it's Hugh Osborne. Something's turned up here I think you and Dr Gavin would be interested in seeing. I was phoning to see if you might come down for the weekend – and if you'd bring along any information you've got on the red-haired girl from the bog.'

Chapter 2

The charred tower house was the first thing Nora spied through a tangled veil of wet black branches. Next spring the ivy would twine its way up the walls once more, but now in the bleak and waning November afternoon, it was a gaping ruin, collapsed even further by the rotting damp that had set in on its ancient, blackened timbers. The crows had reclaimed it as their own. Cormac craned his neck to see through the rain-streaked windscreen, and she slowed to a stop to give him time to absorb the picture as well.

'It's all right,' he said. 'Drive on. I was just thinking of the first time I saw that place.'

Hugh Osborne greeted them at the door looking red-eyed and slightly dishevelled, as though he'd slept in his clothes. 'Come in, come in. The place is in a bit of a state. I was up late last night digging through old papers. I've just made tea.' They followed him down into the kitchen, which, like the front hall, seemed different somehow from the last time they'd been here. Nora realized, taking in the sight of unwashed breakfast dishes, an open box of Weetabix on the counter, and the wrinkled linen towel slung through the handle of a drawer, that what the room lacked was the pristine tidiness of the days when Lucy Osborne had reigned at Brracklyn. The house was by no means grubby or squalid, just lived in. She wondered if Cormac perceived the change as well.

'I realize I may have sounded rather cryptic on the telephone,' Osborne said as he poured them each a mug of tea. 'It's to do with that red-haired girl from the bog. At least I think it is. But now, please, you must tell me everything you know about her. I want to feel as if I'm in full possession of the facts.'

The way he phrased it made Nora think he was preparing to make a decision. 'Well, it was fairly clear from the start that the girl had been decapitated,' she said, 'and closer examination told us it was probably done with a sword or an axe. So that brought up the possibility of execution.' Nora reached into her briefcase and brought out the first photographs of the *cailín rua*, taken at Collins Barracks, and laid them on the table. Osborne flinched slightly, but forced himself to look. It occurred to Nora that this was only the second time he'd laid eyes on the face he had searched so anxiously out on the bog. He'd been too overwrought to grasp the full horror of her image at that time; she was simply not the person he sought. But Nora could see that something had happened since then, something that led Hugh Osborne to contemplate every detail of the grim visage that stared back at him from the photo.

'At first we had no idea about a date of death,' she said. 'We had just done the preliminary exam when I found this unusual image in an X-ray.' She placed the X-rays, the endoscopic video stills, and, finally, the colour photographs of the ring on the table before him. 'It turned out to be this ring, inscribed with the initials COF and AOF, and a date, 1652. That gave us a time frame and a clue about her identity, but no real information about why she might have been killed. We started to speculate about why a young girl might have been executed.'

Osborne's expression grew more disconcerted as he studied the picture of the ring. 'Go on,' he said.

'We went to see Ned Raftery, because we'd heard he knew a lot about local history. We told him about the ring, and he told us how the O'Flahertys of Drumcleggan were transplanted, and about the son, Cathal Mór, who was shipped off to Barbados.'

'But he knew nothing about any execution,' Cormac said, 'so he sent us off to his aunt, Maggie Cleary.'

'And what we got from her were some fragments of a song,' Nora said, 'about a man who comes home from the Indies in search of his wife, only to find out that she's dead years ago, executed for the murder of their newborn child. Then Ned Raftery phoned to say that he'd found an account of an execution in Portumna in 1654,' Nora went on. 'A young woman named Annie McCann had been convicted of killing her illegitimate child, and was beheaded for the crime.'

'And of course we were getting frustrated,' Cormac said, 'because none of this was really conclusive proof, just fodder for speculation.'

'Nothing was conclusive, until we found these remains.' Nora hesitated in producing the black-and-white images of the skeletons *in situ*, remembering the adult's body curled around the infant's tiny frame.

'Please,' Osborne said. 'Show me.' She set the picture down, and saw a jolt of recognition in his eyes.

'Malachy Drummond, the state pathologist, was able to determine that the adult skeleton from the souterrain belonged to the red-haired girl from the bog. We thought we'd found Annie McCann and her child, the one she'd supposedly killed. But I kept going back to the words of Mrs Cleary's song: "They've murdered thee my own true love." How could she be executed *and* murdered?'

'At that point, we thought we'd exhausted all the physical evidence,' Cormac said. 'But a researcher from Trinity did some DNA typing on the remains from the souterrain—'

'His research analyses mitochondrial DNA,' Nora explained, 'which is matrilineal; it's identical in a mother and child. But the sequences on this woman and child didn't match, which means they weren't related.'

'The radiocarbon results on the red-haired girl finally came back, and they confirmed the mid-seventeenth-century date, although 350 to 400 years is right on the borderline where the C-14 becomes too recent to be extremely reliable,' said Cormac. 'So what we're left with is a really confusing set of facts. The red-haired girl could very well be this Annie McCann, who may or may not have been married to someone with the initials COF. It seems clear that she was executed for murdering her child, but the infant found with her was not her own. None of it makes sense.'

'No,' said Osborne, 'it makes perfect sense. Come with me.'

They followed him upstairs to the library, where the far corner looked as though it had been ransacked. A safe hidden in the bookcase was open, and boxes of papers were piled about it, what looked like very old legal documents, some still daubed with sealing wax.

'I've been going through the family records,' Osborne said, gathering up some papers and motioning for them to sit on the sofa in front of the fire. 'You'll understand why when you see this. There's some stuff that goes all the way back to the O'Flahertys.' He spread a photostat of an ancient, creased sheet of paper on the table before them. The handwriting was small and cramped, and there was something of an antique flourish in the shape of the letters.

'What is it, Hugh? Where did it come from?' Nora asked.

'Remember the strongbox found in the souterrain? And the book that was found inside it? The thing sat at the National Library for months, until someone finally had time to look at it. And when they were doing a closer examination, this document evidently slipped out from the binding. Someone at the library was kind enough to send me a copy, since the book was found on the property here.'

'It looks like some sort of confession,' Cormac said.

'Read on,' Osborne said.

'From a priest. He confesses swearing a false oath in denouncing the Catholic faith. If he hadn't, it says, his choices were being killed or being sent to Inisbofin.'

'Inisbofin?' Nora asked.

'Island off the Galway coast,' Hugh Osborne said. 'Cromwell's place of exile for priests.'

'Look here, he mentions a second false oath.' Nora began to read aloud, stumbling over photocopied patches of mildew and strange spellings:

> *I had been called upon to attend the lady of that house, who was suffering through the bitterest pangs of childbirth, and by chance discovered whilst crossing the bog a young woman of the locality, known as Áine Mag Annaigh (known as Áine Rua on account of her red hair), herself appearing verie great with child. She entreated me to come to her aid, and told how she had made the arduous journey on foot from Iar-Connacht, the far West country, travelling always*

by night, for fear of English soldiers. I carryed her with me to Bracklyn house, hopeful that she might secure lodging and succour from the servants there. My Christian duty thus discharged, I attended the chamber where the mistress Sarah Osborne was being delivered of her firstborn. The lady was much weakened by the ordeall, which had gone on for fully halfe the night, and would continue on (tho we were not to know it at the time) another twelve houres hence. The lady was at last deliver'd of a boy child she named Edmund, a poor weakling who scarcely mewl'd or cryed. Alas, the child grew weaker by the houre, and at last expir'd. Nigh on to midnight, or sometime therebye, the mistress heard a lusty mewling from afar, and made as if to fly from her childbed for to seek it out. She howl'd most piteously and carry'd on in such manner until the master promised he would fetch the child. He prevaild upon me to assist him in this task, for his lady was past all reason, past all care, and truth be told, nigh unto madness with the childbed fever, and could not be dissuaded. I was sent to fetch the child of Áine Mag Annaigh when infant and mother lay in slumber. When I approached, the lady Sarah Osborne put aside her own dead child and snatchd the living from my arms, and began to give it suck and strok't its brow. 'Take that away,' says she of the dead infant, ''tis but a changeling. Now I've found my own dear babe at last.' Her husband tryed in vain to coax her from this conviction, but none would have the babe from her. 'I would fain learn,' says Osborne to me, 'about the wench below.' 'She is unwed, sir,' says I, but I confess now it was a cruel lie. For had I not wed her, not a twelvemonth hence, to young Flaitheartaigh of Drumcleggan?

'Wait a minute,' Nora said. 'If Áine Mag Annaigh and the Annie McCann from Raftery's account are the same person, then our red-haired girl was definitely married to Cathal Mór.'

'She was,' Hugh Osborne said. 'Keep reading.'

Indeed the marraige had been not much favoured by his father, the maid being but a servant in their house, but I did agree to wed them secretly. But in the evil time that followed, the English soldiers drove the old Flaitheartaigh from Drumcleggan, and banished him to Iar-Connacht. The streams of Gaillimh flowed red with Irish and English blood, and wolf and carrion crow grew stout upon the flesh of murdered priests. I myself was forced to sweare an oath, to renounce the Catholic faith and all its teachings. And alas, when next I heard of young Cathal Mór it was not that he had flown to France, as I advised, but that he was took as a rebel gainst the English, and transported to Barbadoes. All this I knew when I answered thus: 'Her child is but a bastard, sir, and has no father but the Lord God in Heaven.' Osborne tooke this news, whereupon he compelled me to press upon the girl the body of his own dead child, all wrapt in rags, and swear on oath it was her child had perish'd in the night. But when I did as he bade me, the girl flew into a heated rage, and bolted from the house. She began travelling the roads, clutching the lifeless infant to her breast, and pressing upon all passersby the tale of injustice wreaked upon her and her child, the lawful son of Cathal Mór Ó Flaitheartaigh.

To stop her tongue, Osborne next proposed in secret that the two of us should swear the wench had smothered her own bastard. A miserable, deserted creature half mad with grief, he reasond, who would credit her denial? In truth I fear I did not know the man till then. And how dared I oppose him, miserable as I was in my own wretched, damned plight? Osborne made haste to the sheriff for to report the murder, and I was to act as his witness that we two had seen the girl with her hands round the infant's throat. I could not save her except by inviting my own destruction, and that of Hugo Osborne and his lady wife.

And so it came to be that Áine Rua Mag Annaigh was arrested and charged with her child's foul murder, and brought before the assizes, where she was swiftly convicted and sentenced to die by the sword. Within a fortnight she was spirited to the place of execution and her head cleft from her shoulders with a single stroke. When I entreated the sheriff's men to grant me her wretched corpse for burial, they enform'd me that her head had been took by Hugo Osborne off the block. I know not where it lies.

This secret chamber was known to me from earlier days, when I was oft hid here by old Flaitheartaigh, and much use have I made of it since in this latest fearful time. I brought her here, my fear being great that Osborne, in his wrath, would cause her corpse to be disinterred, were she buryed in any rough patch of unhallowed ground. And so within this ancient, private place, along with my forbidden priestly goods, I have entombed the remains of Áine Rua Mag Annaigh. And against her breast I have lodged the hapless infant Edmund Osborne, who drew mortal breath but for an houre.

My confessors all are dead or banished. I therefore confess to whomever shall find this writing that I am a weak and worthless man, who have been hindered by mortal fear from revealing the wicked dealings in which I have played so villainous a part. I dare not seek absolution. I can never rest, for I am haunted by the face of that flame-haired creature, bound upon her knees, and the piteous cry that leapt from her as the swordsman did his evil work. If any person ever find this document, I do heartily beg your prayers, and those of all good Catholics and Christians. I go to my grave beseeching God's mercy upon my eternal soul. Mea culpa. Mea culpa. Mea maxima culpa.

The paper was signed 'Miles Gorman', and dated the twenty-fourth of May 1654. Hugh had waited in profound stillness for them to finish deciphering the words he must have read over and over again. Nora looked up and saw him sitting in the chair across from them, waiting for a reaction with an anxious, guarded expression. 'My God,' she said, 'if this is true—'

'If it's true, then the last three hundred and fifty years of my family's history is built upon an act of judicial murder,' Osborne said. 'Hugo and Sarah had no other children. That's what all these papers are; I spent half the night digging up the whole family tree.'

'And all those portraits on the stairs—' Cormac said.

'Only the first one, Hugo, was actually an Osborne. The man they called Edmund Osborne was the son of Áine Rua and Cathal Mór O'Flaherty, if this Miles Gorman can be believed. That's the question I keep asking myself. Why would he lie?'

A commotion of voices came from the front hall, and Aoife McGann appeared at the library door. 'We're here,' she announced, then retreated, and returned with Jeremy Osborne in tow. A profound change had come over the boy: his hair had grown out into dark curls, and his hollow cheeks had filled in. Jeremy actually looked healthy, and appeared both pleased and embarrassed by Aoife's attention, especially in present company.

'How are you, Jeremy?' Nora asked.

He glanced at her. 'All right.'

'It's good to see you,' Cormac said. The boy's eyes flashed as he checked to see whether the remark had been made at his expense; when he found it was genuine, he seemed at a loss to respond.

Una stood at the library door now. 'As long as you've still got your coats on, you two, how would you like to go and get me some potatoes out of the kitchen garden? About a dozen ought to do.' Aoife seized Jeremy's hand once more, and pulled him after her before another word was spoken.

'God, if I had only half her energy,' Una said. 'Will you come down to the kitchen, so we can talk and chop at the same time?'

Una put the men on the onion and garlic detail at the table, while she and Nora took on washing some greens. 'You're going to ask me how things have been since you left,' Una said as she stood beside Nora at the sink. 'It's been hard. Hugh won't admit it, but he still doesn't sleep at night. Jeremy's been doing much better, but he may need more help than we can give him. Hugh's trying, he really is. We all are.'

'Any word about Lucy? Does he ever see her?'

'No. She's in a special hospital unit at Portlaoise. The psychologist says it may be better for now that he not see her.'

'Aoife seems to have great time for him,' Nora said, watching the small fair head, the arms gesturing as the child both directed and assisted Jeremy, who was digging for potatoes with a spade in the raised vegetable bed outside the kitchen window.

'She's delighted to have a playmate since Fintan's gone away,' Una said. 'And I really think Jeremy dotes on her as well. He really has come a long way. He goes to see the counsellor faithfully every week. It's going to take a long time, but I know Hugh's right – I know there's goodness in him.'

'It'll get better,' Nora said, hoping her words carried the weight of conviction. 'Are you still living at home? I hope you don't mind me asking.'

'We're still there. Brendan's calmed down a lot since you were here. He's realized that Fintan leaving wasn't the end of the world, and he's hired a young fella to help him out with the farmwork. I think it helps knowing that even if Aoife and I should leave, we wouldn't be going far. I don't think I could ever leave this place entirely.'

Hugh Osborne came over to set his plate of chopped garlic on the counter beside them, and stopped to give Una's hand an affectionate squeeze before returning to the table. Nora could see that Una was both pleased and a little discomfited by this gesture.

'Hugh's asked whether Aoife and I might like to come and live here. I still haven't decided what to tell him. But sometimes we actually do feel like a family.'

'It seems to me you both deserve a little happiness, after all that's happened.'

They worked for a moment in silence. Nora glanced at the two men, wondering whether Hugh had mentioned anything to Una yet about the confession, and the astonishing twist it put in the whole Osborne family history.

'Una, I was wondering – the name Mag Annaigh

wouldn't by any chance be a variation of McGann, would it?'

'Oh, aye, all those names, McCann, McGann, MacAnna, makes no difference, sure, they're all just different spellings of the same name. Why do you ask?'

'Just curious. We think we may have found out who our red-haired girl was after all.'

Chapter 3

When the supper was finished, the dishes washed and dried and put away, it was getting close to Aoife's bedtime, and Hugh Osborne offered to walk Una and her daughter home. As they were leaving, he turned and spoke to Jeremy: 'Why don't you show Nora and Cormac what you're working on while I'm gone?'

The boy's expression didn't change, but he led them to the room on the ground floor directly across from Hugh's workshop, and switched on the lights to reveal a spacious whitewashed studio, its walls taped with rough pencil sketches. On a table against the near wall was a miscellany of twigs and leaves, a fox pelt, and a collection of feathers. Nora started slightly when she noticed a large hooded crow, awakened and blinking in the bright light, on a perch in the corner.

'Don't worry,' Jeremy said, approaching the bird and gently stroking the feathers on its belly. 'He won't hurt you. He's only an old pet. But he's very smart.'

Nora began to peruse the paintings. This work was not at all like the desperate splashes of paint they'd seen covering the walls of the tower, she thought, but it did retain a certain measure of the raw expression they'd witnessed there. Jeremy leaned against the wall by the door with his hands in his pockets, trying to affect a look of bored nonchalance.

'You did all these?' she asked. 'They're really wonderful.'

The boy shrugged. 'Hugh thinks it'll keep me from topping myself.' There was a glimmer of the old defensiveness in Jeremy's tone; he obviously wanted a reaction.

'And does it?' Cormac asked.

Jeremy deflected the question. 'There's something seriously wrong with this one,' he said, lifting the nearest canvas up for them to see. 'I can't figure out what it is. What do you think?'

'I don't know,' Nora said. She perused the finished and nearly finished pieces, looking closely at the intricate layering of paint on the canvas, and remembered wandering through the silent studio upstairs, surveying the veiled, dreamlike images of wings, strange tropical plants and exotic animals. These pictures shared with Mina's work a certain technique that suggested dappled light and shadow, though the subjects were the ordinary flora and fauna of the Irish countryside: the owl and the woodcock, the fox and the wren. And, Nora noticed, in nearly every composition, some representation of a crow. In one piece only the bird's beak and bright black eye intruded into the lower corner of the frame; in another, the tip of an open wing seemed to brush the edge of the canvas.

'Jeremy,' Nora asked, 'did Mina teach you anything about painting?'

The boy had been studying her, with his hands still in his pockets, bouncing slowly against the wall. When she asked the question, the bouncing stopped, and he looked down at his feet. 'I used to watch her up in the studio. She showed me how to draw, looking at the thing you're drawing, not at the paper. She said it was a way to find out how you really saw things.'

'These are wonderful, Jeremy. And I'm not just saying that; I really mean it.'

'Would you take one?'

'I'm sorry?' Nora said.

'If I gave you one of these pictures, would you take it?'

'I'd be very honoured.'

Jeremy pushed off from the wall and waded through his paintings, searching for something suitable. The piece he selected wasn't the largest of the canvases, but one of the most sophisticated and abstract compositions. 'Take this one,' he said. 'It's the best.'

'I'd like to give you something, Jeremy.'

'It's not for sale. Take it as a gift, all right?'

Chapter 4

Hugh Osborne had laid a fire in Cormac's room, but the air was still brisk; a sharp November wind whipped around the house, occasionally creating a low, howling noise as it gusted against the leaded windows in the corner tower. He wondered whether Nora's bedroom was as chilly as this one. Neither of them had raised an objection when Osborne put them in separate rooms, the same ones they'd occupied last spring. Cormac was just regretting that fact when he heard a soft rap, and saw Nora's head peer around the edge of the heavy door.

'Cormac, it's absolutely freezing in my room. Could I please, please, warm my feet on you?'

'I was just about to come and ask you the same thing.'

'God, it's just as bad in here,' she said, making a dash for the bed and pulling the coverlet up around her shoulders. 'Well, if the cold does prove fatal,' she said through chattering teeth, 'at least we'll be together. What? Why are you looking at me like that?'

'It's nothing.' He switched off the lamp and slid under the duvet beside her. He lightly traced the pale outline of her face against the dark bedding, and studied her lovely features, which were now and again illuminated by firelight. 'It's just that I once imagined you in this very spot. And now that you're actually here, it's proved a very rewarding sight.' He twined his limbs around hers, feeling her body begin to relax into his as she absorbed some of his radiating warmth. 'Go ahead, put your feet on me.' He let out a sharp, involuntary noise when her icy toes made contact with his calves. 'Jesus.'

'Sorry,' she said. 'Can you stand it?'

'Barely. But you'll warm up soon enough.'

'Cormac, do you think Áine Rua and Cathal Mór ever slept in this room?'

'Not out of the question, I suppose.'

'I know it sounds crazy, but I can feel a difference in this house,' Nora said. 'What was here is gone, and it's as if some benevolent spirit has taken its place.'

'The ghost of the *cailín rua*?'

'Don't be making fun,' she warned. 'It's nothing that specific, I just feel something different.'

'I'm not making fun,' Cormac said, pulling her closer. 'I feel it too. And it is rather eerie how you finally got your wish, to see the red-haired girl absolved.'

'The strangest thing is that I knew she would be, just don't ask how I knew. I can't get over the fact that she walked all that way from the west, trying to find him. It must have been more than fifty miles, and if she had the baby when she arrived here, she must have been very pregnant. To make that journey alone – I've been thinking about her walking all that way. How did she know which way to go? Where did she sleep? And when did she find out that her husband had been transported? She must have been fierce, don't you think, to try to tell what they did to her? Even when they cut off her head, she found a way to outwit them. She never gave up, not ever.'

'Reminds me a bit of someone I know.'

'What was it that you and Hugh were talking about just before we came upstairs?' she asked.

'He wanted to know what had become of the *cailín rua*. I think he's been thrown off balance a bit,' Cormac said. 'You can't blame him. If what it says is true, that confession is the single thread that unravels his entire family history.' No, that wasn't quite right. The thing was far from being unravelled; in some ways it had become infinitely more complex. As Hugh explained it to him, Edmund Osborne had married his first cousin, also an Osborne, and several similar matches in succeeding generations meant the Osbornes were not mere usurpers, but had become inextricably enmeshed, truly bound up by blood and fortune to the property and progeny of Cathal Mór O'Flaherty. An ancient and familiar story, Cormac thought, with the length and breadth of Ireland peopled by various waves of invaders, from the Celts themselves to the Norsemen and the Normans, the English, and the Ulster Scots. It was a mistake to imagine the past simply buried underground. There was that element, yes, but it might be more accurate to think of it living, breathing, and walking upon the earth as well. He himself, in every cell of his body, bore the physical essence of his two parents, the blended strands of their DNA, that mysterious continuation of the ancient matter of the universe. He also bore the impressions of everything he had ever learned over the course of his brief life span so far – from his work, from the music, from Gabriel and all the others who had touched his life, Nora and Hugh and the *cailín rua*, each encounter sparking some new pathway, a new divergence in the nexus that bound up body and spirit.

Nora stirred beside him. 'Are you getting warm now?' he asked, inhaling the clean scent of her, enjoying the weight of her hand as it rested lightly upon his chest.

'Mmm,' came her reply. Could it be that she was already drifting off? He deeply envied Nora's genius for sleep, and often lay awake beside her, admiring the seeming ease with which she became steeped in slumber. He wondered whether Hugh Osborne was in his bed at this hour, or still busy in his workshop below. Cormac tried to fathom the fate of the two men who lived in this house, each of whom had returned from a journey to find his future vanished.

Cormac looked down at Nora's peaceful face. He would tell her tomorrow how Hugh planned to request that the remains of the red-haired girl and the infant be returned to him for reburial at Drumcleggan Priory. And how Hugh had asked for his help in convincing the National Museum. He hadn't given an immediate answer, and though he might normally argue against such a course of action, the scientific reasons for preserving the *cailín rua* had to be weighed against the human need to lay the past to rest. Of course, there was no real rest, only the reassuring constant of mutability. Even the strange suspension of time in a bog was only an illusion, a lingering extension of continual, inevitable decay. The opening stanza of an old poem kept circling through his mind:

Cé sin ar mo thuama nó an buachaill den tír tú?
Dá mbeadh barr do dhá lámh agam ní scarfainn leat choíche.
A áilleáin agus a ansacht, ní ham duitse luí liom—
Tá boladh fuar na cré orm, dath na gréine is na gaoithe.

Who is that on my grave? A young man of this place?
Could I touch your two hands I would never let go.
My darling, and sweet one, there is no time to lie here—
I smell of cold earth; I am sun- and wind-coloured.

The image of the red-haired girl intruded upon Cormac's thoughts once more, only this time he did not see her as he had out on the bog, in that terrible, wrenching vision that had plagued him so often in the past few months. This time he saw her features arranged as they might be figured in repose: lips together, brow tranquil, eyes closed. It was hard to conceive how a single act could have such far-reaching effect. Where would he be at this moment, if that tormented, despairing girl had not taken to the roads, and had given up her child without protest? Where would she be? There was only one thing he knew for certain: now that the *cailín rua* was removed from her airless, liquid vault, she had reentered the normal flow of time: her cell walls had begun to break down at an accelerated rate, opening to accept the spread of invading mould and bacteria that would gradually, imperceptibly transform her, as they did all things, living and dead. Cormac felt strangely comforted by the thought. Lulled by the crackling of the fire, the random gusts that buffeted the windows, and Nora's warm breath against his neck, he closed his eyes and let himself be pulled down, rocked, and finally swallowed in the watery darkness of sleep.